THE JACKHAMMER ELEGIES

The Jackhammer Elegies

A NOVEL

Stefan Jaeger

This book is a work of fiction. The settings, situations, events, and characters are all the product of the author's imagination and any resemblance to real counterparts, past or present, is purely coincidental. All real organizations, businesses, and agencies and their operations are used fictitiously, without any intent to describe their actual conduct.

ISBN 978-0-9854055-0-2

Book design by Scheren Communications

In a dark time, the eye begins to see.

—Theodore Roethke

1

At the first explosion, the American News Corp. building shook just slightly, vibrant like a giant tuning fork tapped and then touched for silence. The northwest elevator stopped dead at the twenty-second floor, and Scott Carter stared up at the shining, static "22". "What the hell was that?" he thought.

Carter glanced at the other passengers with a troubled smile, assuming they were all in the news business if they were still here at this hour, and then looked at his watch. It was 7:12 p.m., just three minutes before his meeting with the ANC president, an irritating after-hours appointment that Carter would have just as soon blown off. On that night, all Carter wanted was to get home to his old den couch, his gin and tonic, and a needed break to sort out the biopsy the doctor had sliced from his back at lunchtime.

Carter again glanced at his watch, thinking back to the feel of that vibration. He did not even want to consider a terrorist attack, but Jesus, he thought, the building had shuddered. It would take a lot more than a big blown transformer vault to get this frame to vibrate. A structural engineer, Carter at least knew the ropes about that. His firm had done the engineering for the ANC building, and Carter had designed the twenty-three-story steel-girder skeleton.

The second blast made Carter duck. He felt the shock wave rattle the shaft of the elevator and saw the lights flicker and then go black. A woman trembled with desperation, "Oh my God, what's happened?" Terror had entered the questions that now raced from passenger to passenger, and Carter groped for the emergency phone and pulled out the receiver. "I'll get an answer," he said, straining to keep the fear from his voice.

But as Carter waited for the connection to kick in, he got nothing but silence. He stood in that extended, breathless expectation of the lights coming on, hoping that a comforting hum of activity would again fill the void, that this had just been some gas line blowing in the street.

"We've got to do something to get out," a man said anxiously.

"Right," Carter said, still getting nothing from the phone. "Listen, I designed the frame to this building, so I've got a sense of what it'll take. I'm going to turn on the alarm." Carter felt for the knob and pulled it, then raised his voice above the clang. "Who's got a cell phone that works in this shaft? Tell 911 we're between the twenty-second and twenty-third floors."

Carter sniffed to judge the density of the smoke. It was still just a smell, not a choking, fatal plume, but he knew that an elevator could act like a chimney once the blaze found its path. It wasn't for nothing that the warning signs told you to stay away from elevators in case of a fire.

Anxiously, Carter tried to picture who had gotten into the elevator with him. "Where's the young guy in jeans?" Carter asked.

"Over here," a voice said, reasonably forceful.

A woman was crying and praying in that panicked sing-song of those who have let doom sever their self-control. "We're going to die," she whimpered. "We're all going to die."

"Nobody's going to die," Carter said. But inside he was not so sure. He wished he could give cancer a chance to kill him, if that's what he had, not this goddamn coffin of an elevator.

The young man pushed his way to the front as the others reported they could not get through on their cells.

"What's your name?" Carter asked hurriedly.

"Mark."

Carter's hands palmed the smooth brass of the elevator door. He told everyone to get on both sides, stick their fingers in the crack, and pull on "three."

At the command, everyone strained. The two elevator doors parted just slightly, but just as Carter thought they had got it, their fingers slipped and the doors slid back together.

"All right, let's do it again," Carter said, feeling a flush of new hope. "One, two, *three*!"

Again everyone braced with their full weight and pulled. The door again stuck at one inch, but this time no one gave up. Slowly the slit kept widening, the springs of the door now catching to help. With shouts of encouragement, everybody grunted for one last tug. Suddenly, the door slid all the way open.

"There's a wall here!" the sobbing woman now shrieked. "We can't get out! Oh my god, there's a wall!"

"I know that," Carter said panting.

Excited, Carter now confirmed his memory with the tips of his fingers. The wall in front of him filled their opening. So, Carter thought, they had stopped almost exactly between floors, half their box against the wall above the door on the twenty-second floor and half on the between-floor gap of ventilation shafts. The bottom half, if they could get through it, would let them jump into a hall.

"This wall wasn't built with concrete," Carter said. "It's gypsum, and that's not so hard. Everybody get out whatever you've got for scraping—keys, knives, nail files. With just a little work, I think we can kick through." He didn't say, "if the smoke holds off," and he didn't want to think about it.

Carter fished out his keys, the emergency bell grating on his already tested nerves. Mark began pulling at the emergency phone door to get a sharp corner to hack. One woman complained that her nail file was too flimsy.

"Use a car key," Carter said. "You can get a cab home if it breaks."

"I'd love a cab," the woman said.

The sobbing woman had quieted. "I'm Frances," she said. "I've got a Swiss army knife."

"Well, hell!" Carter said.

Carter reached for the woman. She gave him the knife, then gripped his hand as if to thank him for any small scrap of hope. Carter gave her a squeeze back, even though he had no patience to delay for anything.

Then Carter was back to work. He felt for the tools in the dark and opened the screwdriver to get the sturdiest metal edge. It wasn't perfect. When he started to scrape in both directions, he had to hold it open with the flesh of his finger so the tool would not fold and collapse. Better stay away from the knife blade, Carter thought.

Carter marked off a rectangle wide enough to get a big person through, then gouged it deeper so the others could find it in the dark. By then, Mark and another man had twisted the emergency phone cover free, and Carter put everyone in place.

Carter took off his suit jacket and tie, threw them on the floor, and started scraping, his hand pressed hard against the metal, using all his strength. A new whiff of smoke seeped into the cabin, and that shook him to the core. Carter coughed and scraped even harder.

Suddenly, the alarm bell shut off.

In the new pall of silence, everyone could hear the faint wails of sirens in the muffled distance. Carter reached over to pull at the button but got nothing in return. "The thing was getting on my nerves anyway," he said. Carter returned to the door and switched from the screwdriver to the knife blade. Mark began pounding with the point of the phone cover.

After ten minutes, Carter's finger had turned bloody, and each scrape became a pointed pain. But he did not slow down. Flesh on the fingers would not be of use to a corpse.

And then, for a moment, Carter thought he was going to die. A thick cloud of smoke entered the elevator, and the group gagged in unison. Carter tore his dress shirt from his pants and raised the T-shirt underneath to his mouth, trying to block out the poison. Thoughts of helping the others now dissolved into a panicked focus on himself, helpless in the darkness of a small cell, his heart pounding like a drowning man realizing he might never rise from that depth of air-deprived emptiness. He could see nothing but his own thoughts amid the blackness and stench, his instincts calling to whatever crossed their disintegrating fancy.

And then the cloud lifted and the choking air again became breathable. Carter did not believe it at first, but as his own chest filled, he could hear the others come back to life.

"All right," Carter barked at Mark. "I don't give a damn about losing my fingers to your chop. Pound away like a mad man, and I'm going at it with the knife."

The two worked with a new frenzy, and after another five minutes, they could feel the gypsum board give way at one corner. Drunk with hope, Carter shouted, "OK, let's pull her loose!" He helped Mark push the metal plate through one of the cracks to pry at the weakened square with the full power of their weight. Their fingers smashed into the wall when the first chunk gave way, but the pleasure of that pain made Carter shout in exuberance. The next pieces came more quickly.

"But where's the light!?" Frances shouted.

"It's just paneling after this," Carter said. "That's nothing!"

The final pieces of the board came out, and Carter began kicking through the square hole with the sole of his foot. He could feel the thin panel on the other side bend to each blow. Sweat poured down his face, and winded, he stepped aside. "Mark, you try it," he puffed. "Let's get some fresh muscle."

Mark kicked like a bull, and suddenly his foot crashed through the panel. A few more kicks and tugs of their hands pushed the edges aside, and Carter stuck his head into a dark hallway, the lights of the city shining behind the glass door of the office in front of him, the floor about eight feet below. "Everybody out!" Carter shouted, ducking back in. Mark jumped out first to help everyone through. "Frances, you're next!"

With the last person out, Carter picked up his jacket, left his briefcase behind, and clambered out with Mark guiding his feet. Then they were all running toward the stairs, wondering whether they still had time to make it out alive or whether they would fall in the nightmare collapse that they had once lived on television.

The emergency lights were not working, and the group practically dove into the dark of the stairwell and started leaping their way down. After three floors, they met a pair of firemen coming up with flashlights, a gas mask dangling from each of their necks.

Jesus, Carter thought, those guys still have the balls to come into this place?

A fireman shone a light in their eyes, blinding them like rats in the gutter.

"Where the heck did you come from?" the fireman asked in almost angry surprise. "Time to get outta here!"

"What happened?" Carter said.

"Somebody put some bombs in the basement."

"How bad?"

"Real bad. Down below, the bombs took out one whole side of the building."

Oh man, Carter thought. "What about the chance for collapse?"

"We don't know, but we've been told to get out as soon as we've checked out all the floors."

The fireman gave Carter an extra flashlight, and the group ran down twenty flights of stairs. They did not see anyone else except two other firemen, and Carter realized that everyone must have gotten out while they had been hacking away. At the ground-floor emergency exit, Carter leapt at the door with an unconscious gasp of deliverance, plunging into the cold winter air. The group did not stop until they got to the far side of the street.

Carter felt stunned by the frigid February wind and the flashing lights and the sirens and the television cameras and his own exhaustion. He looked down at his soiled suit jacket, amazed that he was still holding it, and then put it on. The others had all gathered around him and one by one started hugging him. Frances whispered "thank you" into his ear, and then kissed him on the cheek. They all wanted to keep shaking his hand, until the live TV reporters suddenly noticed and rushed over in force. Carter came back to himself and realized he had to get out of there and check the damage. Enough of this, he thought.

The area had not yet been fully sealed off. Some people were still milling around too close for comfort, and when Carter looked up at the buildings next door, he saw figures gawking from the windows. The ANC building could slam right on top of them, he thought, or on top of his own head—neither scenario seemed pleasant.

The TV reporters trained their bright lights and began pulling members of Carter's group aside for live interviews. Frances and Mark pointed at Carter, but before the reporters could grab him, Carter waved good-bye and shouted that he had to inspect the blast area. "Take care!" he said, then dashed to the other side of the building.

Coming around the corner, he could not believe what he saw.

Jackhammer sat alone at the east window of his Rosslyn condominium, the commotion just out of sight, and pondered how long he should hold back with his first public statement. He could see the faint flashing of police car and fire truck lights reflected on the buildings adjacent to the site, and the steady stream of ambulances rushing in for their cargo and then pulling out, their sirens strangely soothing in the cold distance.

He worried about the ring of his code name "Jackhammer." It did not project enough class and seemed to belittle his considerable intellect, but he could not resist the staccato power of its sound, the unswerving, rapacious honesty. Besides, jackhammers would come in handy for another of his projects, and he did not think he had the marketing gifts to come up with anything better. Over time, when everyone got over the first al Qaeda terrorist hysteria, which he was happy to promote to gain some time, the police and the press would catch sight of his powers and absorb his complete image.

Jackhammer rocked the ice in his whiskey, letting it tinkle in the silence of his room, the lights off, wondering if he should take his medicine or just say screw it and let the disease run its course more quickly. From what the doctors had said in their last about-face, he might still have time for his plans either way. Why the hell prolong things?

But as he stared at the commotion flashing off the walls of the distant high-rise glass and the emergency vehicles flitting about like little animals trapped in a cage—all because of his personal destructive genius—he rather liked the idea of more time to squeeze everything out of this world. It would let them feel a little more pain and vengeance, let them bow down to a greater force and pay for their indifference and stupidity, their callous, infantile submission to craven, politically correct, brainwashed propaganda, while the true heroes of the world were shunted aside like rotten meat, instead of honored as the true, proud lions of society.

People don't yet realize how much they owe me, Jackhammer thought, allowing himself a self-satisfied smirk of humility, fingering the hand-held radio detonation device that lay next to him on the table. He set down his drink and picked up the device, no bigger than a walky-talky, stroking it as a symbol of his brazen generosity. He could still feel the cold wind on his face as he had walked the streets, waiting for the right moment, and then deciding, with a soul-satisfied rush of excitement, that the time had come, then reaching into his pocket to set off the first of the explosions. How generous, he thought to himself. The first device had been somewhat symbolic, a big sound to scare off the people, while the next ones would do the real damage. After all, this first project was there only to make a statement of his profound potential, not register the highest body count. That could come later, he thought. Just give him time.

The bastards simply don't realize, he thought with new pride, that he could still bring that building down, not with brute force or luck but with exquisite precision. Just another short stroll and another push of this little red button, and the whole structure would collapse.

And for a moment, he felt tempted. He craved to see that vision of stress-severed steel and shattering glass, the collision of one huge structure against another in the congested streets—but then, briefly, he caught himself for a more elite pleasure. Shouldn't I let them squirm a little, he thought, let them savor what I could have done, what I conceived but through my own charity did not wreak upon them? Shouldn't I let them wonder at my mercy?

Gingerly, his large fingers held the small detonation device—again tempted—motionless in a resonant limbo.

Carter's link to reality drifted skyward with the billowing smoke. The familiar, peaceful, geometrical scene from his everyday drive to work had disintegrated into a chaos of noise and light and shattered surfaces. He measured the scene with eyes that would not quite calibrate what they saw in front of them.

The whole ground-level floor on the block-wide front of the building had been blown out, spewing its rubble onto the sculpted pedestrian plaza. The corner section, where Carter now stood, had been blasted away. He could not tell how badly the structural support columns inside had been damaged, but if they had suffered serious displacement, the load factors would have been shot to hell, effectively narrowing the already slender depth of the building. Focusing more clearly now, Carter knew he had to find out the state of those columns. This was not a question of the top falling in, starting a pancake collapse as in the World Trade Center attack, but of the whole building literally falling over from a lack of support underneath, like a board standing on end dropping flat to its side. He began to jog, heading toward a group of firefighters hosing down the smoke with blistering streams. Looking up, he did not see any list to the building. It appeared straight and stable.

Immediately a policeman grabbed Carter by the shoulder and told him to beat it. The cop outweighed Carter by fifty pounds and began pushing Carter back to the crowd.

"Wait a minute!" Carter shouted, ticked that this guy had fingered him as the one trespasser to kick out. "I've got to inspect the building for safety!"

"We're not lettin' nobody in without an ID."

Carter tried to explain that he was the structural engineer for the building and had just escaped from the top floor, but the policeman did not care about excuses and pushed Carter toward the yellow police tape.

Carter considered kicking the cop, but then thought better of it. Getting arrested would not help his cause. He would just have to find some people from Public Works and get in with them, or sneak in from the other side on his own. There was enough confusion to help him get in under the radar.

Carter raised his hands in surrender and walked the last steps on his own. He ducked under the police tape on the opposite side of the street and blended in with the hundreds of onlookers, intent on circling to the other side of the building.

Carter began simulating the structural frame in his mind, trying to assess a worst-case scenario, but he did not know what had happened underground. The building had a three-floor basement parking garage, and if the bombs had taken out any of the central columns, things could be even worse. My God, Carter thought, the bomber could have parked his explosives anywhere.

"Scott!" a woman called, scampering in high heels at the fringe of the onlookers, a TV crew in pursuit. It was Frances, breathing heavily beneath her brilliant fearfulness. In her late thirties, with long, limp blond hair, she projected a care-filled, homey attractiveness. "I saw the policeman pull you out," she puffed. "You never told us your last name. I've been telling the TV crew everything you did, and we don't even know your name."

"Probably all for the better," Carter said.

"Can I thank you again for what you did for us?" Frances said, taking Carter's hand in both of hers. The light squeeze and pat made Carter wince from pain.

"Oh my goodness," Frances said, "your hand's bleeding."

What does this woman want? Carter thought. She was still holding Carter's hand when a woman reporter took position next to him and the bright lights from the cameraman exploded in his eyes. Reluctantly, Frances let go and stepped aside.

"Can we talk to you?" the reporter asked. "What's your full name?"

"Scott Carter, but I've really gotta go. Sorry." He had only guarded patience for the press, never quite forgiving them for a misquote in the paper after a local hearing on the zoning for a proposed new high-rise. By the creative placement of his words, they had made him sound like a tool for the local developers. He was not going to be painted the stooge in anybody's pocket, and he had written a biting letter to the editor.

"Only a minute," the reporter said.

"Three, two, one," the cameraman said.

"We're still here live at the site of the ANC bombing," the reporter said, her face to the camera, "and have with us one of the true heroes from this scene of destruction. You've already heard the story of the group of five people stuck in an elevator on the twenty-second floor of the American News Corp. building in Rosslyn, Virginia, just across the river from Washington, D.C. You've heard from those who lived through it that Scott Carter, here with me now, took control of the situation and helped them escape from that prison."

Carter was itching to leave, but somehow he could not bring himself to cut the reporter off rudely on live TV. Maybe vanity was getting the better of him.

The reporter now turned to Carter. "So, Mr. Carter, how did you know so much about the building to save those four people?"

"I designed the steel frame," Carter said, skimping on everything to try to cut things short.

"So are you the architect?"

"No, I'm the structural engineer." Jesus, Carter thought. He was tempted to lay into her and let the audience know it was engineers who made these buildings stand up, not the bow-tied architects whose aesthetic penchants would more than likely make them tumble—but now was not the time. "I do apologize," he said. "I have to try to assess the damage."

"Are you saying," the reporter asked, "that the ANC building could collapse?"

"I didn't say that," Carter answered quickly. He could see they were going to leap to sensationalism and worst-case conclusions without any evidence, if they could only find the handle. But hell, Carter thought, he was shitting bricks himself about the danger. "I have no real idea what the damage is, and the odds are the building will stand up just fine." He was unable to resist. "It's a good, solid design."

The reporter smelled pay dirt. "Tell us some more about what you'll be checking."

Carter put his hand on the microphone to push it away. "I have to run," he said. "Sorry." He backed away quickly and could hear the reporter closing down her story with a few boilerplate flourishes.

"Hey!" Frances shouted after him. "How can I get a hold of you? Maybe the whole elevator group could have a reunion."

Man, will these people leave me alone, Carter thought. He reached into his wallet, pulled out his business card, and was ready to just toss it in her direction but then caught himself and stepped forward to hand it to her. The woman's been through a lot, he told himself.

"Thanks," said Frances, allowing a weak, fragile smile. "You need to take care of that hand."

Carter smiled uncomfortably, hoping that giving his address would not come back to haunt him. He had no interest getting involved with her type, even if she did have a good body. He waved good-bye just enough not to be rude and then ran off along the edge of the crowd.

The two streets heading north from the battered ANC building had been blocked off all the way to the Key Bridge, the lanes projecting the eerie feel of a war zone where a few emergency trucks flashed their lights for no audience and the lone survivors staggered lost upon a once-busy thoroughfare. Carter walked a full block away from the blast and then circled back to the main access road. He scanned for police, saw no one looking his way, and slipped under the first outside line of police tape. He began walking quickly back toward the building, acting like someone who belonged there. No one stopped him.

At the northwest corner of the inner security zone, Carter saw a crowd of news teams interviewing Jim Duncan, the board chairman of Arlington County, which counted Rosslyn as one of its jurisdictions. The chairman was young, bright, and artificially articulate, and too cocky for Carter's taste, having put the county board members and county manager in his pocket and priding himself in acting like a big city mayor. Carter had met him numerous times on the county's business and political circuit, especially at political fundraisers where Carter's engineering firm had shown up in force to back its yearly contribution with a personal presence (in a tight race, the firm did the same for the opponent). Carter could see the TV lights reflect on the perfectly coifed head—a remarkable engineering feat, Carter had always thought, each individual hair laid in a perfect, parted parallel, then fused into place with industrial-strength hair spray. He could imagine Duncan's pat phrases and slick scripts of condolence and wondered whether he himself could avoid that nonsense if he ever went into politics.

Duncan looked like Carter's best bet for entry clearance, so Carter parked himself nearby and waited impatiently. He now felt the cold in all its brutality and raised the thin collar of his suit jacket, held the neck closed, and stepped slowly from one foot to the other. He was not optimistic. Duncan loved to hear himself talk.

Suddenly Carter noticed a car approach at high speed. It screeched to a halt, and as the door opened, Carter immediately recognized Samuel Freeport, the Arlington public works director, a tall, balding man who tried to counteract the pitiless plainness of his face with designer clothes. Carter had always stewed that a civil engineering license was not required for Freeport's position, but despite leading a protest through his local engineering society, Carter had not been able to do anything about it. He had guessed the long odds and had been careful not to pan Freeport personally, applauding the man's managerial and financial talents (Carter assumed that the man had them, despite the political-payoff appointment that had gotten Freeport his job). Freeport had not taken the fight personally and, to Carter's surprise, treated Carter with the same cold respect he did anyone who might prove useful to him.

"Scott Carter," Freeport said as he saw Carter approach at a run. Freeport put out his hand but did not bother to smile. "From what I hear on the radio, you're a hero." He seemed obliged to add a gruff compliment. "Good work."

"Don't always believe what you hear in the media," Carter said. "It seems those people are going overboard. But listen—" He had wanted to get on with his business, but Freeport interrupted.

"Let them exaggerate as much as they want," Freeport said. He started to hurry toward Duncan, as Carter and the aide now trailed behind. "Good press is hard to come by. Hell, I was holed up in the sauna at the health club and didn't hear about the bombs until twenty minutes ago. None of the jokers at the club came to tell me! Can you believe it?" His dry distaste neatly allotted blame to others. "What do you know about the damage?"

"I just saw the rough picture, but I need to get closer. That's why I collared you. The police won't let me in."

"You were the structural engineer on this building, weren't you? I guess you've got something to offer."

They needed somebody, Carter thought. The only thing Freeport might contribute was how much money the county might lose financially.

Freeport stopped near Duncan, waiting to get his attention and prove that he had, in fact, shown up. "You look pretty miserable," Freeport said, glancing at Carter. "Aren't you freezing?"

"Can't deny it," Carter said.

Freeport called to his aide to drum up a coat from one of the emergency crews. "I need this man to make inspections."

The aide nodded and trotted off, not quite sure which way to turn, finally spotting someone and making a bee-line across the street. Eventually, he returned with a bright orange parka.

Carter pulled on the coat and felt the warmth jack up his energy and started heading toward the building with Freeport. At the first policeman, Freeport flashed his ID and told everyone that Carter had free run of the outside area, but not inside. "You weren't planning to go into the building, were you?" Freeport asked. "We don't need you killed and then us getting sued."

"Which would bother you more?" Carter asked, a little uncomfortable about cracking a joke, but he needed to do something to keep his head straight.

"Real cute," Freeport said. "Maybe I should just let you kill yourself. Then you'll stop harping on the fact that I'm not a civil engineer. But I don't want you inside, do you understand? You've been enough of a hero for one day, and the FBI and FEMA are going to put a clamp on this any time now. Us county types will just get pushed aside. Anyway, when can I expect a preliminary report? I don't think the county's emergency response engineers have shown up yet."

"Give me twenty minutes, maybe less if I can't get close."

"I'll be waiting, and I'll track down the police chief to make sure they don't give you trouble."

"Thanks," Carter said, never sure whether it was strength of character or careless sloth that kept Freeport from holding a grudge against him.

Carter walked toward the building and smelled the soot and the lingering stink of the explosives. He was glad the building did not contain the old toxic asbestos fireproofing and that the fire now looked under control. There would be no jet-fuel blazes melting the steel here.

Carter began his inspection where the firefighters had stopped kicking up smoke with their hoses. He kept his word to Freeport and did not venture inside, but in the stark glare of the emergency lights, he could already see that a vertical support column had been bowed to the breaking point. That, Carter thought, would not hold a load.

Slowly, Carter moved down the block, seeing more and more columns on the outside row of the structure that had been badly damaged, the glass and cladding of the lower building gone, the broken ribs exposed within the bleeding. Carter tried to guess what might have happened inside. If the bombs had been parked at the edge, the outer columns would have borne the brunt of the force. But from the extent of the damage, the next columns inside might have been displaced as well. That could cut their load-bearing strength up to seventy percent. To his horror, Carter saw the steel columns at the corner of the building nearly blown away.

More worried now, Carter doubled back to check the other corner, then stopped to buttonhole a rescue worker, the man's face gray with soot. Carter asked about the load-bearing columns inside.

"I haven't paid much attention," the man said and pointed him to another crew.

A shout now called the man back to a rubble pile.

Carter hesitated as he watched the crew crowd around a German Shepherd sniffing the jagged debris. The dog barked excitedly each time it stuck its nose into a crack, wagging its tail as though a raccoon would soon bolt from the hideout. Frantic, the crew waved in a small Bobcat bulldozer to raise the concrete slab from the top. Carter knew he should not be watching, but something inside him froze him in place. In jerks, the teeth of the shovel pried under the edge of the slab, then slowly lifted. The men began to shout as they shined their flashlights onto a human body. The leader reached in to feel for a pulse. With an angry hand, he then signaled for the bulldozer to push the slab all the way out. In the stark glare of the flashlight, Carter had seen a woman's head that looked like a concave bowl of tissue, fluid, and cartilage abandoned by a careless dissection lab. The rest of the body lay reasonably intact, the stylish, black business suit merely dusty.

Carter turned away, catching his breath. Jesus Christ, he thought. He now ran to the corner where the worker had pointed, trying hard to scrape the woman from his thoughts. He had not gotten training for that kind of gore on sanitized national TV. He had left that to the emergency crews, and now the reality punched him hard. Carter pushed himself forward and collared a man with a walky-talky.

"Can you get me a visual on the conditions inside?" Carter asked, out of breath.

"Who are you?" the man asked.

Carter told him. The man got a connection, and a static-filled voice barked from the other end: "Most of the columns I've seen are bent just a little, but not as bad as the first row. Except one. I remember a second-row column, right in the middle, that was completely knocked out. Farther in, there doesn't seem to be any damage."

"Thanks," Carter said. He patted the man on the shoulder but wondered whether those teams should be in there at all. Who was making the call on safety for these guys?

Carter swung around, realizing he had to get to a computer fast. He could input the damage to the actual design files and get a read on whether the building might collapse. No one on the county or federal emergency team would have instant access to the electronic design file like he would. The best they could do was thumbnail estimates.

Anxious, Carter turned from the building and saw that the wind had picked up. It was whipping scraps of newspaper in angry somersaults across the street. That scared Carter even more. Given the direction, the wind might just be enough to bend the building at its ankles and ram it all the way over.

Carter began searching for Freeport, cursing himself for not arranging a meeting place, then ran to the street corner where Duncan had been holding court. His hunch paid off. He saw the public works director leaving the cameras, with the Arlington police chief and the county manager at his side.

"Has Nick Handley shown up yet?!" Carter shouted from a distance. Handley was the county's chief engineer.

"We can't find him," Freeport said. "We're trying to reach his deputy."

"Well, have you got somebody on the county construction crew ready to shore up this building? We need supports on the side!"

"We're taking care of it," Freeport said.

Carter felt the wind bite the cold into his face. "What do you know about this weather?"

"I'd heard some strong winds were coming," the police chief said. "They've been predicting a storm since yesterday."

"Heaven help us," Carter said. "We don't need any extra load on this building."

The dark of the living room flickered with the unsteady light from a large flat-screen TV, reflecting from a cocktail glass to the fading luster of Jackhammer's eyes. Jackhammer paced slowly, venturing an acerbic smile at the words of the weatherman, then wandering toward the window to hear the wind blast in gusts through the night.

So, they actually predicted right, Jackhammer thought, allowing himself a moment of closely controlled smugness. He had picked his date in line with the oncoming storm, liking the idea that uncertain fate could mix its force into the fortunes of the city. From his calculations, fifty-mile-an-hour gusts could push the weakened ANC building to the limit, grazing that red zone between damage and complete destruction.

And if the wind did not quite succeed, he always had the last bomb in reserve, hermetically sealed and scrubbed down so no explosive-sniffing dog would find it. He smiled slightly: You just needed a little intellect, and a burst of daring, and the world was at your mercy. In the last analysis, everyone was so small, he thought, all cowards and hypocrites. People made their servile compromises to everything weak and degenerate, and in the end, society had lost the capacity to recognize greatness.

Jackhammer looked at his empty glass, considering a refill of his whiskey. Those damn doctors ordered you not to drink, he scoffed to himself. Why? So you can die a month later than you might otherwise? They've already blown their predictions totally. You should have been dead six months ago. They don't realize that when you have a mission, you can't die. The brute force of your will and your intellect bulldozes the disease until you've reached your goal. Then you can let the sickness kill you. What do you care? You'll have gained the recognition they so slavishly denied you. They'll see their mistake. They didn't know who they were dealing with. God damn, they didn't know—and now they will.

Carter ran the three blocks up Wilson Boulevard to his office, sucking the cold air, still picturing the dead woman. She had been turned in one instant from a vital, conscious being with a full life and perhaps a family into a piece of organic junk buried by inorganic rubble. He realized he could not let that shock overtake his judgment. You can't do design analysis on adrenaline, he thought. Slow down. An extra minute can make all the difference. You've got to keep your head.

Carter kept himself in shape, jogging at lunchtime or riding an exercise bike during the 10:00 o'clock news at night, but when he reached the door to his firm, the uphill sprint had left him winded. He pulled out his Kastle card and swiped the reader. At the click, he swung the door open and ran into a small but elegant foyer, "Blackstone-Waynewright Engineers" inscribed in prominent gold print opposite the entrance. Carter's firm took up five floors of the twelve-story building, but Carter stopped short at the elevators. Do you really want to get into one of these things again? He hesitated only a moment and then pushed the call button. You're not going to get superstitious, Carter told himself. The odds of a terrorist hitting this building too, right at this moment, are about as small as you winning the lottery.

On the eighth-floor landing, Carter punched his security code, entered the BWE area, and walked quickly down the half-lit, empty hall to his office, threw his coat on the conference table and turned on the light. At his desk, he switched on his custom engineering workstation. That was one thing he had not let them take away when he had been kicked upstairs into management—his top-of-the-line hardware. He had still wanted the ability to review and edit designs, but he had to admit, it was more sentiment than necessity. With all his client relations work, he had not had the chance to crank up a design program at work for more than a year, and only a few times in the past two years. Playing around had been left to his home computer.

Carter could hear the wind mounting outside, but the computer did not care. It lagged through its normal boot-up and network log-in. Can't they make these things go faster?! Carter thought. When he finally got the log-in prompt, he typed in his name and password, waited for more screens to appear, and moved to the firm's design modules. There, he called up a structural analysis package and watched the screen fill with a crisp engineering collage. From the file-naming conventions he had helped develop for the firm, Carter still knew what the file name should look like. The network file security system then asked for the area password. Carter typed it and hit enter. He got: *Password not valid.*

"What the hell!"

Carter typed in the password again, this time banging the "enter" key

Password not valid.

Jesus Christ! Carter thought frantically. They've up and changed it! Of course, that's what they're supposed to do.

But why didn't they tell me?! Because you don't do design anymore, and everybody knows it, he told himself. It pained him to think how far he had fallen out of the company design loop. He had never liked anything better—juggling all the options to unite the best combination of elegance and value. And now he was no longer doing it.

Carter called up his personal phone list and found the home number of a design colleague at BWE, an old college buddy from Virginia Tech, and nervously rushed through the dialing. At the first ring, he worried that his friend was still on the street staring at the bomb damage. Then someone answered.

"Todd, is that you? It's Scott."

"Man, good you're OK."

Carter tried to cut him off but Todd started in on the compliments from what he had heard on the news. "I didn't know you were the macho hero type—."

"Shut up," Carter said. "I'm at the office. Do you have the new design login password?"

"Yeah, they changed it last month." Todd spelled it out for him, and Carter jotted it down.

"Need any help?" Todd asked. "We installed the latest release. I don't think you've worked with it yet."

"Great," Carter said worriedly. "You stay put, all right? I may have to call you after all."

"I'm not going anywhere," Todd said. "Jesus, this bombing is something."

"It's something, all right."

Carter hung up and typed in the password. The familiar 3D lines of the ANC frame appeared as a blue grid on a gray background. He tried to rotate the view and, to his relief, noticed that the basic commands and setup looked similar to before. The software developers had probably just added a few bells and whistles that you use once every ten years and yet clog up another fifty megabytes of disk space, Carter thought with resentment, feeling the pressure of what was before him. But that was how competition drove the software treadmill—pile on the features for those few cutting-edge projects so the developer can tout things the competitors lack and then force everyone to learn the new stuff. Right now Carter did not need any surprises.

Carter rotated the ANC building frame to put the main entrance directly in front of him, then saved the file to a new name so as not to change the master. With clicks of the mouse, he began highlighting individual columns at the ground level of the building. For each column, he either removed it entirely or keyed in a greatly reduced load-bearing strength, giving it his best guess from what he had seen during his cursory inspection.

Suddenly, Carter noticed a drop of blood on the keyboard. Damn! he thought, worried that he would short out a key. He grabbed a tissue and wrapped it around the cut on his finger, pressing to stave off the flow.

Carter got back to work, breathing more steadily now, feeling the software push him to a deadline-driven tension. He moved to the second interior row and began weakening the columns there, but not so dramatically. Then he remembered the comment from the interior inspector—one column near the middle had been knocked out completely. Carter could not know which one, so he picked a worst-case scenario—a column at the edge of the entrance rotunda, where a 60-foot void had been spanned by steel arches.

Finally, Carter applied the load of a fully completed building—cladding, floors, windows, piping, HVAC, furniture, office equipment, elevators—and felt his pulse quicken as he clicked for the failure analysis. Silently, the computer ran through the complex calculations, something that a few decades ago might have taken an engineer days with a top-of-the-line mathematical calculator. The results came out ten seconds later, color-coded for localized stress factors. Carter stared in relief. The columns near the damaged area had remained the wished-for green.

Leaning back in his chair, Carter took a deep breath. The green meant that the building would probably not fall, but Carter knew that with all his guess-work assumptions, the frame might be hanging by a thread. Besides, he had one more force to fear—the wind. Carter remembered the sheet of newspaper tearing across the street from a blast of cold—southwest to northeast. Gusts on the eastern and western fronts of the building could bend the structure right over the weakened base. So how the hell do you do a wind load analysis in this new release, Carter thought frantically. Carter scrolled through the menus and finally found the command. Again Carter gave up on precision. He fudged an approximate wind velocity, exaggerating the effect just to be sure.

The computer went through its paces, incredibly fast. Again it painted its results, and this time Carter got a punch in the gut. The damaged frame had turned red exactly where it shouldn't.

Without turning off his computer, Carter ran down the hall to the elevators, slammed the call button, and paced from one side of the foyer to the other. The elevator had returned to the ground, and in the interminable wait, Carter tried to block out the images of slow-bending steel and sky-scraper collisions.

Claudia Reingold and Timothy Beckman lay side by side on the office floor, staring at the bleak, pitted squares of the ceiling tiles, hearts beating in the fear-enhanced darkness. Claudia had come to visit Timothy at 6:30 that evening, when most of her colleagues had left and Timothy's boss had already caught a cab for a flight to Boston. Claudia could hardly contain her excitement. For three days she and Timothy had been sharing lunch and meeting by carefully planned coincidences among the cubicles of mutual colleagues. They still pretended that their interest bordered on careless, shy exploration with offhand invitations to talk about all that they had in common. Yet inside they had begun to tremble just at the sight of each other.

Claudia, fresh out of Oberlin College, had come to Washington with the task of turning an English major into a paying job. She had gotten work as a proofreader with a Rosslyn consulting firm that waylaid the federal government for education- and testing-related contracts. After absorption in the likes of Jane Austin, Charlotte Bronte, and Thomas Hardy, and romantic analysis of depression-era American poets, Claudia now confirmed that proposal headings fit the standard RFP format, that capitalization followed the GPA style book, and that verbs agreed with their antecedents. She had learned soon enough that the bloated text from the company experts need not be intelligible. At 3:00 in the morning before a 10:00 a.m. deadline, there was no time to fix much of it anyway. The text just had to mimic intelligence and sound officially erudite—the contract did not seem to depend on details. When she had first arrived, a particular proposal had sounded like empty jargon strung together for effect, yet it had yielded a sizable two-year research contract. The company had then scrambled to find the people who would actually do the work. The key players on the proposal had been filled in for show.

Claudia had been eager at first, finding the coat-and-tie corporate environment impressive compared with the summer waitress jobs that had helped put her through college.

But after a year, the Rosslyn work had worn thin. She had not found many friends and felt lonely in her cheap Arlington apartment where she could never quite succeed in killing every last roach. Occasionally, she thought about leaving, but she did not know where she would go, except, perhaps, to her parents to lay her head on their shoulders and wait for something she could not define.

Then she had met Timothy in a proposal meeting. She soon discovered that he was also an English major—in his late twenties out of Brown University, with a focus on twentieth century American fiction. He had spent six years in the organization, been promoted to junior management, and as a dubious reward, been given the architectural curiosity of a small window office not much larger than a janitor's closet and of no affront to the higher ups. Claudia had been impressed with his voluble, confident presence in meetings, sometimes flippant but outwardly demanding, knowing all the ropes of the proposal game. Yet sometimes that expertise scared her. She worried that a man who had shown some deeper interests had sold out to a deadening job.

Timothy had not found a woman to prevent such decline. He lived in DC, and the women he stumbled across for dates tended to be journalists or political types, all drawn to Washington by the attraction of power, pecking order, and policy, all saturated with the smell of regulatory and statutory fact. Timothy had countered with a showy cynicism that viewed his work as an expression of command through expediency.

Claudia had reawakened him to the freedom of college studies and the intellectual indulgence of literary conversation. When she came into his office that evening, Timothy put his hands on her cheeks and said, "I really can't stand this anymore. Can I lock the door?"

Claudia had merely nodded, her heart pounding too hard to speak. A long, caressing flush of disbelief in their luck slowly sent the couple to the floor, then out of their clothes.

Claudia held back the fear that someone might pass in the hall, but was then unable to contain herself, and then the first bomb went off. It was far away, and she did not know what had happened, and she held onto Timothy, desperate that he not move away from her, but the silence immediately returned.

The next bomb shook their window, but only in passing. Their eyes opened wide, but the floor still lay silent beneath them; the ceiling still showed faintly in the glow from the city. Timothy stared at Claudia's face. "What the hell happened?" he whispered.

Still breathing heavily, the two got up and looked out the window. Their building stood down the street and cattycorner to the ANC plaza, and they could just make out the edge of the billowing smoke and the panicked racing of people. But the ANC building stood as though undamaged, no hole in the side of its upper floors, no tilt or sag. Sirens emerged from the distance, and soon the night pulsed with the blare of red-flashing fire trucks and the blue-white strobes of police cars.

For a moment, Timothy and Claudia were ready to bolt, but as each second passed, their distance slowly sank into them. Nothing could happen this far away, they thought, and the heart-pounding fear of the blast, the numbing shock, brought their hands unconsciously together, their thoughts telling them that the emergency had isolated them from the world. They had been given a small, enclosed haven with a distant view to a potential tragedy and through that had been handed a strange invincibility. No one would come near them now. Everyone had focused their eyes on that plaza.

Carter had never seen a skyscraper fall like a domino, not on TV and not in a movie. He could still picture the horror of the World Trade Center collapse and the carefully planned demolitions where a building dropped with the surreal harmony of a deflated accordion, disappearing in a cloud of dust. The Tacoma Narrows bridge—one of the century's most spectacular engineering disasters—came closest. It had been captured on film and was shown to most every structural engineer. A large suspension bridge, on par with the Golden Gate, concealed a subtle design flaw. The natural sway of the span matched the rhythm of the valley wind. The random motions did not continually die down, but built up, one wind-shove at a time, like a parent at the playground with his kid, pushing the swing just at the peak of the upward motion, each push sending the kid just a little bit higher. Over time, the deck of the bridge had begun to ripple and roll like a piece of rubber, until ultimately it broke apart, its remnants dangling in defeat above the jaw of the valley. Carter took some hard-nosed pride that the archives of structural engineering disaster films took up a relatively small drawer.

But the ANC building had no design flaw. The blast had been a brutal attack, and as Carter ran down the hill from his office and crossed a side street, he shuddered at the gust of wind that blew through the gap. In the twenty minutes that Carter had spent in his office, the storm front had moved in completely, rattling the street signs and shooting litter in bursts across the pavement.

Carter tried to imagine how the ANC building might react to this stress. Would the start of collapse be gradual, with the steel bending slowly, like a careful bow for applause at the end of a performance? Or would the mismatch of load and support accelerate immediately, the structure finally crashing with 100,000 tons of weight into anything that stood in its path? Either way, Carter knew he did not want that mass coming towards him.

The crowd had not thinned at the new security line, the stubborn, shivering curious in league with those who wanted to volunteer to help. The police had pushed everyone back to a much more distant perimeter, and single-mindedly Carter just fought his way through.

At the barricade, a policeman put out his hand, but when he saw Carter's emergency-crew parka, he let him pass. Don't look at my dress shoes and pants, Carter thought.

Running at full speed, Carter found the police chief, the public works director, the county manager, and board chairman Duncan within two clumps of county officials. The groups had huddled together like cattle trying to ward off the stinging cold through closeness. Carter barged in and collared Freeport with the full charge of his views. "We've got to evacuate a lot more buildings!" he barked, puffing from his run and glancing at the police chief. "Not just the ones next door, but the ones after those. My analysis shows the building could basically fall over with this wind, and you could get one structure pushing into another in a chain reaction. I don't know how the other buildings are built, but we can't take a chance." Nervously, Carter looked over his shoulder at the ANC building, just two blocks away. "And I think everyone except essential personnel ought to move from where we're standing."

Duncan, in the other group, was dictating another public statement to an aide and had not noticed Carter arrive. Freeport took Duncan's arm and introduced Carter. Duncan extended his gloved hand with a well-trained reflex of interest. Man, Carter thought, this is not a cocktail party! Let's get on with it!

"Scott was already on the scene," Freeport said, "so I asked him to run a computer analysis to see if this building might collapse."

Yeah, right, Carter thought, but at the moment he did not care what Freeport said.

"The bottom line is this," said Carter. "With the high wind, it's possible the building could fall and take out some others on the way down. You need a broad evacuation, and I'd again suggest that all you fine people move!"

They all looked at the looming, spot-lighted glare of the building. When the sight sunk in, they did not complain about taking the advice. Carter immediately led them to the sidewalk one block away, then shouted back at the stragglers. Soon they had again gathered into their small herd.

"Just how sure can you be about possible collapse?" Freeport asked Carter.

"As for exact probabilities, no comment," Carter said. "I don't even know the complete extent of the damage. But yes, as I've said a few times already, if we get unlucky, things could be real bad." He looked back at the building and did not yet see any supports in place. His jaw began to tense. He turned to Freeport with a new jolt of urgency. "When are they going to bring in that shoring?!"

"Jane McDonald's working on it," Freeport said. "And we've found Handley. Any minute now."

Carter wanted to ask, "What's taking them?" but he could tell Freeport did not want to discuss it in front of Duncan.

"So let's move on the evacuation!" Duncan told the police chief, taking short, curt satisfaction in making a decision that others would scurry to carry out.

His work done, Carter noticed that even the wind had not defeated Duncan's hair. The gusts merely shifted complete sectors as fluttering, crippled wings.

The police chief, blustery in command, rounded up his forces and fanned them to the buildings in the next perimeter. The bull-horns started shouting that everyone should get out.

At first, Claudia and Timothy heard only the muffled squawk of the bullhorns through their embrace. Later, shouts from the outer hall startled them. "Attention! The county has ordered the evacuation of this building. Do not panic. You are in no immediate danger, but please move immediately to the exits and move north and west."

"What should we do?" Claudia mouthed breathlessly.

Steps came down the hall. "Did you lock the door?" Claudia asked, suddenly terrified that someone would catch them. My god, she thought, what would her co-workers say if they heard what had happened? There would be snickers for weeks.

Timothy held his finger to his mouth and let the footsteps pass. "They said we're in no immediate danger."

"Maybe we should look outside," said Claudia.

Nervously the two got to their feet and walked to the window. The scene had not changed—the flashing lights, the rescue crews, the police cordons. The ANC building could not recreate a new nightmare, they thought. The danger for them seemed to have passed, and now it was just the mopping up, with the police just trying to be careful.

Emergency lights flashed across their eyes and cheeks in the dark. They looked at each other. Claudia raised her hand to Timothy's neck and touched him, pulling him back against the cold glass of the window, the turmoil of the streets an intoxicant to their fantasy of testing fate.

Carter paced the sidewalk, not knowing what he should do with himself. He suddenly felt useless. Response was now the county's job, and most probably FEMA's. The Federal Emergency Management Agency was mobilizing teams right now, including engineers, and bringing them in. Let them do their job, if they could, Carter thought. It's none of your business for the moment. You're just an innocent bystander. Until you get better damage reports, you can't do any more analysis. It's all guesswork until you get better data.

The cold wind swept down the open funnel of the street, and Carter held the fur of his hood tight around his cheeks. The wind had become stronger and more steady, and Carter grew more afraid. Jesus, it wasn't just the danger of being hit by a falling building. Just a single thick sliver of glass, propelled from the collision, would come down from that height with enough force to take off your head.

Carter looked down the street to scan the building opposite the plaza, wondering from the angles where the ANC tower might actually collide, then to the building down the first block, and his eyes suddenly focused. In the distance, he saw a distinct human form, perhaps two people, at a darkened window—a head and some shoulders. The shape turned sideways and then sank away. What the hell . . .

Unconsciously, Carter began trotting toward the building, asking himself how this could have happened: I thought they'd evacuated the place! He looked for a policeman, then saw one walking fast on the opposite side of the street. "Hey!" Carter shouted. "There's still someone in that building!"

"We've been through it," the policeman said. "Everybody should be out."

"But I saw them," Carter said, waving the policeman over. "Look up there."

The policeman looked up for a moment but did not see anything.

"You've got to get up there again!" Carter shouted above the wind.

"Listen, I've got other orders. We don't have enough men. Trust me, we've been through that building."

Before Carter could grab him bodily and maybe shake some sense into him, the policeman had rushed off.

Damn it, Carter thought, irritated that this had fallen into his lap so it could stew in his conscience. This is none of your business. Don't get involved. If those idiots want to stay up there, well it's their goddamn business! He paced briefly, trying to talk himself into turning away, but a gust of wind nearly knocked him off balance. He looked back in fright at the ANC building, and then at the window where he had seen the forms. "Oh hell!" he said out loud and broke into a run for the door.

Carter found the building door open. Ten floors, he told himself as he stood at the elevator, again debating whether to get into one of these death traps. But he was too exhausted to think of the steps.

When the elevator opened at "10," Carter dashed out and tried to get his bearings. He had come in to the left of the people, maybe a few offices over, so he knew where to go. He started down the hall, and it did not take him long to hear them. A woman was moaning, then shouting, then nearly sobbing in her desire. Carter banged on the door. "Time to call it quits! Don't you realize you're in danger!"

The moaning immediately stopped. Carter stared at the door, just barely hearing the wind on the walls outside. "Let's go!" Carter barked. "No more delays. You might want to do this again sometime!"

He still got no answer. OK, they're embarrassed, Carter thought, but I'm not going to risk my neck for somebody else's sex. "Stop screwing around and get a move on! I don't work here and I'm not going to tell anybody. Do you want us all to get killed?!" Carter banged on the door louder, then in frustration, kicked it with his foot.

"OK, we're coming," a man's voice said inside.

"Make it fast!"

Carter did not know why he should wait, but he had already started what he considered damn foolishness, so he was going to see it through. After another interminable two minutes, the door opened and Claudia and Timothy shuffled out. They looked sheepish and hesitant, their clothes ruffled and their hair mussed.

"OK, let's get out of here," Carter said, beginning to trot down the hall, shooing them on, deciding that this time he would take the stairs.

Claudia stumbled toward the stairwell, still tightening her belt, feeling as though the greatest moment of her life had been cut short, never to be recaptured.

"What's happened?" Timothy asked Carter finally.

"Somebody tried to take down the whole ANC building and land it right on your head."

Outside, Carter stood on the street with Freeport, far from the scene, his eyes fixed on the top of the ANC building. The wind buffeted their faces. "What more do you know about the weather?" Carter asked nervously.

"They told me that the wind would soon let up," Freeport said, "that this is the worst of it."

The police and FBI had pushed everyone to a still larger perimeter, and the county officials seemed to have scattered. The police chief, the county manager, and Duncan had each gotten into their private cars to keep warm, and the trucks with the shoring had finally pulled into the plaza. Freeport had followed Duncan to his car but had not been invited in. Duncan either had been carelessly thoughtless or wanted Freeport to stay outside and see his oversight through. Disgruntled, still in shock by the tragedy, Freeport had caught up with Carter and offered his sullen company.

Carter tried to spot some deflection at the top of the ANC building but knew he was too far away to tell. Now it was the repair workers who needed all the luck they could get. Carter had shared his analysis with Handley, and Handley knew that they had to work fast.

A television news crew scurried past, lugging their heavy gear to what they thought must be a better location. Freeport took off his hat and looked their way, but they did not recognized him and did not stop for an interview. Freeport tried to hide his displeasure with an obdurate face, but did not succeed. The thin strands of hair at the side of his bald head fluttered like discarded chick feathers on a rubbish heap. His cold, red nose ran in a stream of defeat. Carter actually felt sorry for him.

"It looks like they're about ready to raise that bracing," Carter said, trying to buck Freeport up. "Your crew's getting the job done."

Freeport nodded and wrapped his arms around his chest. He looked like a general who had lost his command to a subordinate but knew he did not have the battlefield knowledge to reclaim it.

Carter kept trying to gauge the force of the wind. After ten more minutes, he detected a weakening. Was it real? "The gusts seem to be dying," he said.

"My toes are dying," Freeport grumbled.

Carter at least had to give Freeport credit for sticking it out. He could not deny the man's hangdog tenacity to see through what superiors expected of him.

"The wind's dying," Carter repeated, as though repetition might make it come true. Carter pulled down his hood to sense the change more directly. The building, bright in its emergency spotlights, now seemed strangely benign in the quieter air. Carter could feel his heart start to pump in relief. "I think we made it," Carter said louder. "Jesus, I think we made it!" He wanted to give Freeport a smack on the back, but noticed that Freeport was in no mood to celebrate.

Freeport acknowledged Carter with a deadpan voice. "Let's just hope these terrorists don't have another target in line."

2

Carter lived in an antique, corner brownstone in Alexandria, Virginia, three blocks up from the Potomac River. When he and his wife Linda had looked for a new house after years in central Arlington, Linda had lobbied for a townhouse in Northwest DC and Carter for a big lawn and deck out in the Virginia suburbs. They had compromised on this small, but stylish house with its imitation gas-light door lamp and walled-in garden. For open spaces, Carter could walk down to the river and take in the breeze as the planes cruised in for landing at Reagan National and twelve lanes of traffic streamed over the Wilson Bridge in the distance.

Linda had been pleased about all the restaurants that had popped up in Old Town to augment the historical houses and inevitable tourist shops, but cursed each time the gaps in the picturesque redbrick sidewalks took an ugly bite from the leather of her expensive high-heeled shoes. At the start, Carter had kept busy with the house, fixing up wiring, loose bricks, and plumbing, defects that had held the high asking price just within the affordable. Now everything had been hammered into shape, and Carter had felt confident that if house prices ever recovered and he had to sell, he would make some money off the sweat of his handiwork. If the buyers looked inside, the price might go even higher.

There Linda had taken over and made her mark. Before she had died, she had worked professionally as an interior decorator with a passion for American antiques, and as you stepped from the sidewalk through the white, freshly painted front door, you came to an entry hall with elegantly yellowed crystal chandeliers now retrofitted for electricity, Persian runners on original hardwood floors, and on the walls, Virginia landscapes in gold, wood-carved frames. It had always given Carter the feeling that he lived in a museum, not a home.

That night, after the bombing, the silence felt particularly heavy, as though someone had dragged Carter to the Egyptian room of some big-city museum after midnight, his expectations waiting on display in the glass cases. Carter hung up his coat and looked at the small block of Post-Its on the guestbook by the door. It had always given him the client where Linda could be reached.

At first, before their marriage had become strained, Linda had struggled with her one-woman interior decorating business, and one reason Carter had accepted his promotion to upper management was to give Linda the kind of house she had always wanted. Then Linda had struck on the idea of meeting clients at their homes in the evening, when their busy schedules allowed them some time. After that, her business had flourished, and Carter guessed she would soon match his own income. "So much for making a personal gift of your salary hike and this house," he had thought at the time.

Linda had made the same imprint on Carter's office at BWE. After being promoted, Carter had continued the same habits he had followed downstairs—getting so stubbornly involved in his work that his surroundings meant little to him.

The only thing he had ever put on the walls of his old office were project Gantt charts, a message bulletin board, printouts of design drawings, and a travel poster of Monument Valley. When he had moved upstairs into management and done nothing to make the place look better, Blackstone had given up dropping hints and hired Linda to make the tone appropriate for talks with top clients. She had created a stylish space, with a high-tech, chrome-bordered desk; a small, matching conference table; a large bamboo plant in a stainless-steel pot; and chrome-framed 20th century prints from the National Gallery. Carter acknowledged that the place looked good, but he would not have missed it if they had hosed it out the door. What he did like was the view out the window where he could just see a slit of Georgetown out across the Potomac between the Rosslyn buildings. Tired after a long morning, he could look out and think of jogging over the Key Bridge, with the vista west, up the river, to the green cliffs and the lazy water in the sun.

And then Linda had died, six months after they had moved into their house—eight months ago. She had left a note saying she had driven to Leesburg and would not be home before 11:00 that night. On the drive back, tired, she had fumbled briefly with her cell phone and drifted to the median, then lost control.

Carter looked at his watch and saw 11:20 p.m. He hung up his coat and listened to the sound of a car passing on the street outside. At least something still had some energy, he thought. He took a strange comfort in that trace of life filtering into the silence, knowing that on a night like this he could have used someone to talk to.

Only now did Carter realize how emotionally exhausted he was. He walked slowly up the stairs to his bedroom, got undressed, and stepped into the shower, letting his thoughts stream like water down his side. Earlier, he had been so involved in action that he had not had time to digest the shock, but now he felt with full force the anger and sickness from this crime.

He could remember the worst-case scenarios that people had tossed around after 9/11, how an atomic bomb could turn millions into nomads, with no framework in which to achieve anything except the bodily survival of themselves and their loved ones. He did not know how he might react to that violent emptiness. He thought he might do all right. Others had managed throughout the calamities of history, but maybe they had not been so used to comforts for so long. How soon would spoiled suburbanites find the will to rebuild their lives if things really got catastrophically bad?

He could not answer that question, but he knew he wanted vengeance. At least now the country had some better security networks in place, Carter thought. They would get the bastards, eventually. They'd better.

Carter changed into a sweatshirt and sweatpants, leaving his soiled dress clothes on the bed, considering it a good trade—a ruined suit for his life. Downstairs he poured himself a gin and tonic and then dropped himself onto the couch in the den. In a deal with Linda, the den had been the one room Carter had set aside for himself. He had furnished it with garage-sale furniture and Redskins and Virginia Tech paraphernalia—a team photo of the 1992 Superbowl champions, a plaque with a Redskins helmet in relief, and a framed autographed portrait of Frank Beamer at the 2000 Sugar Bowl. Carter could spill his beer on the couch and drip pizza sauce on the rug without fear of desecrating the historical. If Linda had been able to have kids, by necessity more of the house would have looked like this, Carter knew. But with kids, they would have lived out in the suburbs, with a big yard for football, and a basketball goal in the driveway.

Carter stared at the answering machine on the table next to him. He still pictured the site of the explosion, the sirens, and the rescue crews' desperate energy. He saw the red, glowing display telling him he had ten messages. Carter pushed the button and waited as the old tape mechanism whirred to the beginning. He could still feel the darkness of being caught in the elevator and that first smell of smoke. He had thought he was going to die. A little bad luck and everything he had done would have been lynched and left as a memory for others to forget. He would not have a son or a daughter to carry a trace of his interests into the next generation. It seemed so easy. Just substitute smoke for oxygen and from your own point of view, the whole world ends. And, he thought, that same pitiless snuffing-out takes place every minute of every business day all over the place—sometimes with a dramatic bang, sometimes in silence—and the clock just keeps on ticking.

The answering machine clicked to a stranger's voice. It was *The Washington Post*. They wanted an interview about his experiences in the ANC building. Next came Channel 3 News, then Channel 9, then *USA Today*. Some of the same reporters had called back a second time and again left messages, still trying to be polite but letting Carter sense their imminent deadline. Others had also left their requests, but Carter did not want to speak to any of them, at least not now. You're not ready for the talk-show circuit, he thought.

But Carter did not begrudge himself a strange exhilaration. He had faced a heart-pounding, chaotic threat and beat it back. He had risked himself physically and imposed his will on others to get something done. He wondered if that was how a battlefield sergeant felt—with the smell of smoke and death and darkness filling your senses, you dig down and irrationally kick in your rationality, plan your attack on the spur of the moment—and survive. Afterwards, lungs breathing double-time, you experience the vibrancy of an infinite gain, since the loss of everything, in the form of a small, metal bullet, had just missed you by an inch.

Don't aggrandize yourself, Carter thought. You ran around the street and went up a few elevators and did some engineering you were trained to do. There were no bullets in sight.

Carter took a slow drink of his tonic and fingered the TV remote but did not turn on the power, still drawn by the silence. On his back, he could feel the Band-Aid pressed against the pad of the couch. How strangely insignificant the threat of cancer now felt. People had been blown to pieces, and he had this lurking wound. You're just one single person, Carter thought, not the whole city or country. But why did this have to add itself to the mix? Why now?

When Carter turned on the TV, all the major channels carried news of the bombing, and he switched to the station that had collared him for an interview, curious to see if they would offer a replay. The program looked like a late-evening recap, fishing for as much drama as possible. So far, eight people were confirmed dead, with scores injured, but it could have been worse, the news report said. Most offices had already been closed at the time of the bombing. The underground garage had been three-fourths empty, and a first, more minor explosion had sent most people heading for the doors. The tragedy might have reached major proportions just a few hours earlier. So what were those ANC people doing in the elevator so late, Carter wondered. Was the ANC president organizing some after-hours staff party with a business meeting thrown in to multitask? That crazy appointment had almost got you killed.

No one had yet claimed responsibility, but the police had found a bundle of leaflets in a nearby waste can filled with violent, anti-American diatribes—an Islamist call for death to the U.S. government and its ally, the American press. So far, any connection between the bombing and the leaflets was purely speculative, the report emphasized. No one doubted the al Qaeda connection, but there were still the pro forma references to the Oklahoma City missteps, where the early speculation had put egg on everyone's face. Carter figured it had to be a cell of radical Islamists and wondered how the people could get such a screw loose in their head with hate.

The program came to an interview with Nick Handley, who had guided the brace work after the bombing. He stood with floodlights bright on his face, a hard-hat on his head, looking a little startled by the attention. He chose his words like a kid at a science fair explaining his project, working hard so his parents would be proud. He reminded Carter of the early NASA spokesmen, with their Buddy Holly glasses, crew cuts, and unfortunate monotones.

At least a civil engineer is getting some press, Carter thought, and the public's hearing someone who knows what he's talking about technically, not some slick reporter who thinks a load is something stinking up a diaper. But Carter knew the public had no idea whether the TV gets something right technically or not. They just look for the image, and Handley was just not cutting it.

Carter could not deny he held a bias when it came to his profession, and as for speaking out, he had no interest in being passive. If you were going to tell people what was going on, you had to get out there and tell them with some attitude, not fulfill some stereotype of an introspective, geeky number cruncher who had as much desire to interact with people as an opossum. Of course, Carter knew some of those types. You always got all kinds anywhere, but he was out to get the engineer leaders he knew to showcase their public spine. He backed his causes. For one, you had to raise the bar on education to get your engineering license—pack in some more breadth and depth to take care of the future—and he made presentations on a Vision 2025 for the profession, a project that Carter had gotten involved in early on, although sometimes a gadfly among the engineers who had laid the groundwork at a civil engineering summit. In all of it, Carter had tried not to get full of himself. He was convinced it was not about aggrandizing his own ego—that would have made him wince. But what the hell, if he had a little vision, why was he supposed to bury it in the ground like a bone? He just wanted to make sure that people listened to civil engineers so the country could put some teeth into infrastructure renewal and sustainability and not make public policy decisions based on misinformation.

On TV, Handley finally created some news, hinting that the building might have collapsed, and then mentioned Carter by name as the engineer who had run an emergency analysis and shown Handley the danger. The shoring already in place would secure the structure against any future wind storms.

The reporter keyed on Handley's lead-in to retell Carter's story and replay the interviews with Carter's elevator group. Carter had not had much of a chance to take stock of his companions back at the site, and he allowed some satisfaction that he had helped this engaging bunch of people survive. But Carter flinched when Frances came on. Each time she served up a compliment on Carter's heroism, she looked into the camera, as though she were telescoping some kind of come-on right to his couch.

Carter could not remember the last time a woman had made the moves on him, if he did not count the hookers at a downtown strip club some colleagues had organized as a bachelor's birthday party, maybe thinking enough time had passed since the death of his wife and that Carter needed a shot in the crotch. Carter was not immune to a little male vanity, and he focused on Frances a little longer than he would have expected. He did not understand it. He ranked Frances as somewhere between ditsy and flighty and could not imagine spending time with her, except to maybe soak up some more of her compliments. But that sounded pretty depressing. He could not picture putting up with that kind of a relationship just for a night in the sack.

The reporter interrupted her recap with a news flash about the latest victim. The building's rubble had now offered up another body, bringing the total to nine. Carter watched the rescue workers under the floodlights, and images again stabbed his memory—the dead woman's mangled head, the smell of smoke, the cut of sirens disappearing into the distance. Again, the biopsy slipped forward from the back of his mind, and he found it hard to reconcile the immediacy of the bombing with the vacuum uncertainty of his own future, hovering without pain, without substance, on the skin of his back, just waiting for word from the oncologist. Carter did not think he would die, but in the den, with only the TV breaking the silence, he suddenly wondered about the time he still had left, however long or short it might be. He thought of those crazy young lovers he had dragged from the building. Now that he thought about it, they had made him jealous, reminding him of Christine Witherspoon and himself back in his freshman year of engineering school, holed up in a library cubicle after hours and making love on a short, narrow desk, doing their best to keep quiet. He could not believe he had done that, but

Jesus, he would never forget it. Now he wondered whether experiences like that were irretrievably behind him.

But you're not going to die, Carter told himself. The terrorists did not get you, and the blemish on your back is just a blasted teenager pimple. In the end, a glob of Clearasil will take care of that spot, and these terrorists will finally get rooted out, and you'll take a new love to the stacks of a nearby university library, and without further thoughts about all that went wrong with Linda, you'll find some dark corner and see that at thirty-eight years old you can still start fresh.

The sight of Carter turned Jackhammer's stomach. He had recorded the evening news and now rewound to Carter's interview, then to the praise by Carter's elevator group. Jackhammer had no patience for what he considered shallow do-gooders like Scott Carter, and he scoffed angrily at the publicity Carter now milked from the media. You're exactly what's wrong with this country, Jackhammer said, addressing Carter on TV as if he were in the room with him. I've heard you at the conventions trying to get us engineers to sell youngsters on the profession. You're a misguided son of a bitch. We don't need more civil engineers; that just drives down our salaries. We need some more ass-kicking bastards who won't give in to all the weak-willed traitors. I've heard you, Scott Carter. You get on your sick soap box and talk about bringing more women and minorities into the profession, or actually backing the damn tree huggers, just because the brainwashed liberals in the media say so. It's hard to believe you could have stooped so low, because at times you showed a little balls yourself. What happened to your engineer logic? Where the hell's your backbone?

Jackhammer took two deep breaths and tried to calm himself. No reason to raise your blood pressure over a publicity hungry wimp, Jackhammer told himself. He froze the DVR on Carter's face and forced a sour chuckle. Well, Scott, isn't it cute you've got yourself wrapped up in this affair? How should I welcome you—by blowing you away? Or should I just toy with you first?

Jackhammer simpered in satisfaction. He wondered whether the next job would flow as beautifully as this one.

3

A mid-level FBI spokesman offered a blunt lunchtime report in the eighth-floor conference room at Blackstone-Waynewright Engineers: At least three ammonium nitrate, fuel-oil bombs parked in the basement garage in as yet unidentified vehicles had throttled the ANC building. The vehicles had been blown beyond recognition, but lab analysis should soon pinpoint the makes and, if they were lucky, the ID numbers.

Bob Waynewright, co-founder of Carter's firm, had orchestrated the crowded media-fest. He had called in every newspaper, magazine, and TV station that he and his PR director could think of, including a heavy dose of engineering trade publications. *Engineering News Record* and *Civil Engineering* all sent reporters to take notes alongside *Time* and *Newsweek* and vie for space with national network cameramen.

Waynewright had offered the media Scott Carter and the inside story of escape and structural analysis. He had then called the FBI and put his conference room at their disposal, in case any of their people wanted to show up and get a news outlet right next to their fieldwork. They had taken the bait, just to make sure no misinformation got out. In his next call, Waynewright had told his maintenance man to move the sign "Blackstone-Waynewright Engineers" from the side wall to the spot directly behind the podium, low enough to be caught by the cameras.

When Carter had come to work that morning, he had not known what to expect. Following a restless night, he had gotten up at 6:00 a.m., showered, dressed, and then read *The Washington Post* over a bowl of raisin bran and a cup of discount coffee. Since Linda's death, the shiny, chrome-tubed Italian espresso-maker had been left untouched.

Carter's menu and schedule had not changed for the last ten years—except that today Carter read about himself in the newspaper. Below large black headlines about bombs, destruction, and death, and the stark photos of blown-up beams and terrified survivors, Carter had found an article that described what sounded like a collection of semi-heroic acts. Apparently, Carter's elevator group had given the same exaggerated stories to *The Post* as they had given on TV, and somehow the reporters had nabbed Timothy Beckman and Claudia Reingold. The couple had not admitted what they were doing on the floor of their office but had acknowledged that Carter, at apparent personal risk, had come upstairs to warn them to get out. Handley had repeated his TV recital of Carter's additional feat—storming to his office to run his design software and assess the damage.

Carter wanted to know who the hell they were writing about. From the sound of the article, the man they described was some kind of caricature of bravery and saint-like civic duty. Somehow, it all gets twisted when put in the paper, Carter thought. It felt like a movie where the hero comes across as totally under control, having all the right insights and making all the right decisions. Carter knew he had been scared like anyone else. In the bombed elevator, he had acted to save his own skin, and after that he had followed his impulses for the others. The thought of bravery or self-sacrifice had not consciously crossed his mind. He had just acted and could just as soon have ignored the two love birds trying their luck at roulette-wheel fornication.

Later that morning, on his drive up the George Washington Parkway toward Rosslyn, Carter had nevertheless allowed himself some new expectancy. With the deep twilight over the Washington Monument and the shimmering black-turquoise of the Potomac—a sight that accompanied him every clear winter morning—he realized he had entered a new dimension in his work. Unless things got totally twisted, he was certain they would assign him to lead the failure analysis and reconstruction of the ANC building, and with that, he could counteract all that the terrorists stood for and tried to undermine. And if BWE did not ask for his help, he would just barge into Waynewright's office and insist that they do. Who knows, Carter thought, the investigators might even make him a consultant for the technical questions. That would be some good new meat and potatoes, not the *nouveaux cuisine* of client relations and sales that had always left him hungry.

At the office, Carter's secretary could not resist a comment. "Suddenly I work for a hero," she said.

"Yeah, right," Carter replied.

"Well, the phone's been ringing off the hook, and Bob wants to see you in his office ASAP."

"That's just what I need," Carter said, looking at his watch and seeing 7:24 a.m. He had wanted to settle in and get his bearings and find out how his building was standing up. If all the detours in Rosslyn had not slowed him up, he would have gotten to work earlier.

Carter tossed his coat onto the chair in his office and looked at the red light on his multi-line phone. Those, he thought, must be the messages the hordes had left before his secretary had got in that morning. With Waynewright breathing down his neck, there was no time for them now.

Carter walked down the hall toward Waynewright's office, tugging the dress-shirt collar from his throat. He hated ties and wore them only because his position required them. He had been the first to lobby for casual Fridays but had still not convinced the top dogs to relent. "Clients come on Fridays too," they had always told him.

While Carter made his way to Waynewright's office, the few early arrivals tossed polite encouragement and compliments from their desks, still with the numbed inner shock at what had happened. "Hey, way to go" and "You deserve a medal." Carter waved them off and stopped at the desk of Waynewright's assistant. She said hello with the precarious brittleness of caked make-up and assembly-line courtesy, then picked up the phone. "Scott is here to see you," she said precisely.

"Bring him in!" a voice bellowed from behind the door.

Six months ago, Bob Waynewright, the co-owner and co-founder of the Blackstone-Waynewright Engineers, had turned his office into a veritable hunting and fishing memorial, a suspected display of farewell bluster that raised eyebrows across the firm. As Carter stepped in, the decor immediately assaulted him: On the left, pictures of bears and elk were framed in polished oak, and on the right, wood-carved replicas of fish were screwed onto walnut plaques. The rest of the wall showed framed photos of Waynewright posing with various dead game—his foot on the back of an elk, a deer propped up for the camera, a rabbit held up by the ears. Carter did not know much about interior decorating, but he could recognize the taste—egregious. Waynewright beat back any hints of remodeling and growled that he would not "cave in to animal rights fanatics who whined and sniffled about man's God-given right to hunt."

The unstated tack of the firm was to weather Waynewright's recent course and make sure he retired on schedule the following year. The company kept him away from more and more clients and funneled them to Carter. That left Waynewright with internal management, which meant sometimes bullying the staff and other times turning on his good-ol'-boy charm. Gifts for a job well done were always a bottle of Kentucky bourbon, whether the employee liked it or not. That practice had spawned a resale black market in which bourbon drinkers agreed to pay cash, at rock-bottom rates, for the unwanted liquor.

Carter could not quite understand how Blackstone and Waynewright had originally become partners, but maybe Waynewright had been less eccentric in his younger days. Blackstone got the nod for Carter's admiration. The man had a leadership confidence and calm, with a measured assurance in speech that could become eloquent on a public stage. His white hair gave him the look of a landed Virginia patriarch who wore his integrity and professional judgment like a fine tailored suit, with a mind that could cross from design to innovation to risk management to business finances without a hitch. He had been president of the American Society of Civil Engineers and been a prime force in steering Carter to professional activities, but structural happened to come under Waynewright's shop, and that's where Carter was funneled after he joined the firm.

When Carter walked into Waynewright's office, his boss had already gotten up and met him with a brawny slap on the back. "You did our firm proud," he said, practically pushing Carter to the corner couch. "You're suddenly the firm's star."

"This too shall pass," Carter said, again struck by Waynewright's energy. At sixty-nine years old, the man still worked as hard as anyone, but he looked his age. Despite a full head of dyed black hair, sagging cheeks shook when he talked, and a net of fine, red capillaries seemed to support his skin from collapse, flushed from either drink, or high blood pressure, or both. Carter knew as well as anyone that retirement might be Waynewright's best bet, and Carter had stuck with the firm because he wanted to be part of that new direction.

Waynewright lowered his tall, burly frame into the easy chair opposite Carter and cracked his knuckles. "Even if this passes, we're going to milk it for all it's worth. I hope you realize you're going to be center stage at a news conference at noon," he said.

"Oh really?" Carter said, a bit surprised by Waynewright's apparent disregard for the tragedy of the situation. "Is this something you've arranged without telling me?"

"I'm telling you now," Waynewright said gruffly.

Carter had learned through hard knocks that the best way to keep Waynewright at bay was to counterpunch, just tempering the blows a bit. That invited some knockdowns but seemed to defuse the lethal explosions. Today, Waynewright seemed too absorbed in his vision to care.

"At noon you're on stage with some guy from the FBI in the conference room," Waynewright said. "All the press is going to be there and you're going to tell them every detail about what you did."

"So how'd you manage that?"

"I was in early. Earlier than all you young whippersnappers. You don't even know what long hours mean."

Carter decided to swallow that distortion, but he could not shake a guarded respect for the man's bombastic stamina. Waynewright showed his own version of respect by allowing Carter to state his views—and only then bulldozing over them.

Waynewright kept at it. "I've turned our large conference room into a press site, at least for a few days. And I'm going to make you available for the FBI investigation. When I mentioned your background, the FBI did not say 'no.' They're aware you designed the ANC building, so there are all kinds of technical tips you can give. Rolling up your sleeves for the rebuilding effort goes without saying."

"I've got a full plate that's got to be cleared," Carter said, itching to jump headfirst into what Waynewright was offering.

"We'll let the dogs eat your scraps," Waynewright said. "Your first priority now is to promote our firm. With you talking to the press every step of the way, the media will have to mention BWE. And you'll mention us every chance you get. Forget about your clients for now. Hell, are they going to begrudge us letting you work on a national terrorist case that killed nine people and nearly destroyed a whole building? They can watch you on TV instead of in their offices."

Carter could not hold back one more stab: "Doesn't it look a little questionable to make PR the firm's top priority at a time like this? People have suffered here. Are you trying to take advantage of that?"

Waynewright waved his hand dismissively. "If we sit back and whine and don't go full blast on keeping this firm and this economy running, then we've surrendered to the terrorists. Even the president wants us to push on. He's always said that. Hell, it's my responsibility to keep everyone in this firm employed and prosperous, and to do that we've got to get our name out there. I'm not going to let some fanatic terrorist change our way of working. We're going to make money and pay our taxes so we can bomb the bastards to a pulp."

"Sign me on for the technical work," Carter said, "but I'm going soft-pedal being the PR nut."

"Then I'll crack you open so you damn well get nutty. We've never had this kind of opportunity. Think about it, Blackstone-Waynewright Engineers may become a household name. That's a legacy I could retire to, since all you guys apparently want to ship me out."

"Are you accusing me of something?"

"Ah, don't be so slick, Scott. I know your type. On the outside you're all manners, and inside you're ready to send in the vultures to feed off my carcass."

"I've got no time for animals," Carter said. "I stick to my business and leave the office politics to others."

"Well, if you don't play office politics, you'll end up cleaning the toilet."

"Then how did I get promoted? I didn't even want the job."

"Sometimes I don't know when you're serious."

"I'm as serious as I'll ever be."

Carter could not deny Waynewright's role in his own advancement. Waynewright had made Carter the prime client liaison on numerous contracts, ranked above the project manager. He was the first contact to answer questions and the key broker to smooth out trouble. If a project manager got too technical in meetings, Carter would translate, and if Carter saw design alternatives, he would suggest them. Since Carter put results above personalities, he sometimes alienated the PMs, who thought he was trying to override their judgment or usurp their contributions. Carter told them point blank that he was just doing the work the firm had ordered him to do, and that he would not back off suggestions when the pointers made perfect sense. Those who had not gotten to know Carter well suspected arrogance and power-grabbing, where Carter saw it as just being sensible about the firm's interests. Carter could see where the PMs were coming from and tried to patch over the occasional unpleasantness. Just put me back on design, Carter had often said to himself, and get me out of all these pointless turf battles. Now, he thought, maybe the FBI would do just that.

"I really don't care what you're thinking," Waynewright said. "I just want you to repeat 'Blackstone-Waynewright Engineers' on national TV until you're blue in the face."

"I'll be red in the face if I do that," Carter said, "given the circumstances."

Waynewright huffed. "Don't try my patience. I expect you to see the light!"

Carter stood on deck at the side of the conference room and listened as the FBI spokesman ran down a list of preliminary findings, all before a battery of reporters and two rows of TV cameras crammed on risers at the back of the room, the crush of black communications cables looking like the guts of an over-stuffed electrical closet that had finally burst. Carter always felt comfortable in front of an audience, but the hard, unforgiving lenses of national TV made him think twice.

The FBI spokesman said that no, the Bureau had not heard from anyone claiming responsibility for the bombing. No, the anti-American leaflets had not been linked to the crime, but clearly every possibility would be carefully examined. No, they did not yet have any suspects, but the FBI computers were already crunching possible profiles. Yes, they still lacked a motive for this particular target, except that the leaflets—still unsubstantiated in their connection—denounced the press, which fit with the American News Corporation angle.

Waynewright stepped to Carter's side. "Sam Freeport weaseled his way into the press conference ahead of you. Duncan heard you were on tap, so he wanted someone from the county office. I'm surprised Duncan didn't come himself."

Freeport appeared at the door in a Brooks Brothers suit and gold cufflinks, looking like a balding accountant thrust at the last minute into the costume of a stylish CEO but still needing stage lines taped to the inside of his wrist. His face showed the exaggerated confidence of someone unaware of his shortcomings.

When he saw Waynewright and Carter, Freeport approached casually, his manner unwilling to admit he needed anyone's company. He shook hands with both and offered a thin-lipped, bloodless smile that looked more forlorn than friendly. "This is quite a circus you've arranged here Bob. I see you're ready to market Scott like a rock star."

"We market the firm's talent," Waynewright said. "And we've got the best."

"Are you going to argue with that, Scott?" Freeport asked wryly.

"No comment," said Carter.

"No interest in a little fame?"

"Don't know what I'd do with it."

"You can flaunt it with the women."

"Now there's some advice."

The FBI spokesman suddenly waved off the reporters to a few straggler shouts, and the BWE PR director replaced the FBI at the podium. The PR man introduced Arlington Public

Works Director Samuel Freeport, then made a parting comment: "And after Mr. Freeport, you'll hear from Scott Carter of Blackstone-Waynewright Engineers." Carter glanced at Waynewright, wondering whether his boss would keep a running tally of BWE mentions.

Freeport frowned at the double billing, then straightened his back and walked slowly to the podium. He unfolded a prepared statement, cleared his throat, and looked into the cameras. The TV lights reflected off the skin of his bald head as from an apple polished all morning to impress the teacher.

Freeport offered a speech of well-crafted platitudes. He stressed how the county would not rest until the ANC area was completely rebuilt. Work had already begun on repairing the water, electrical, sewage, and gas lines, and county engineers continued their inspection of the ANC building to ensure safety as the owners planned repairs.

Freeport showed an executive talent for confident, measured phrasing that projected composed command of the situation, even when the words, stripped of their official aura, said little. He had ridden that talent up the corporate ladder and now, into the first round of questions, made it clear that for anything he did not know himself, he had the experts lined up at the county government building to get the answers. Only when the questions turned to structural damage to the ANC building did Freeport falter. He worked his way through by repeating the assessments he had heard on TV but eventually realized he would look worse by advertising his technical illiteracy. "I think Scott Carter can best answer those questions. We were out there together last night, and Scott did a magnificent job in sizing up the dangers of the situation."

Freeport scanned the audience for a last question but noticed that everyone had switched their glances to Carter. Freeport folded his prepared speech, said thank you, and extended his hand to Carter in a generous passing-the-baton gesture, slapping him lightly on the shoulder as though Carter were one of his personal brain-trust chums.

Jesus, Carter thought, that man has no shame.

Carter did not make a statement. He shifted the microphone to mouth level and said, "I'm sure you all read the papers and watched the news about what I got involved in last night. The reports were all a bit exaggerated, but the facts were basically there. I don't really want to retell the story unless you force me, so I'll let you just fire away with questions."

The questions made Carter retell everything in even more detail. He even managed a mention of BWE, but he could not bring himself to throw in more artificially. What was Waynewright going to do, Carter thought, substitute someone else as the rock star?

Carter took questions for close to an hour. He felt good about clearing up some misconceptions and even allowed himself a diagrammed, flip-chart description of steel-frame stresses that did not seem to lose the audience.

When Carter came off stage, Freeport again shook his hand and took one last look at the cameras, then quickly left, switching magically to aloof disinterest. Waynewright would not let Carter go that easily.

"Great job," Waynewright said. "But I didn't hear much 'BWE'."

"I think the company logo sticking out of my head was enough," Carter said. "You'd think I was a poster boy."

"Now there's an idea," Waynewright said.

Carter sat in his office and looked at a slice of Georgetown in the cold midday sun. Away from the commotion of the press conference and the violent winds from last night, his office suddenly seemed like a quiet sanctuary of surprising possibilities. Overnight, Carter had returned to substantial work. He did not yet have details, but Waynewright had promised him the ANC building repair and a consulting role in the investigation. Only now did Carter fully realize how much he had missed the nuts and bolts of technical problem-solving, something that actually did real-world good, not just smoothing over egos in his client relations work or guessing which marketing ploy would work best on this or that owner. Carter had always approached his management work as a challenge, and he had become intensely involved, to the point that satisfaction sprang from accomplishment in the same way that exercise lead to fatigue, a physical reaction, but not a substantiated pleasure. And yet now, in the bright sunshine from the window and the media afterglow, the client relations work seemed unusually empty, a way to collect handsomely for selling his blind energy to the firm.

The phone startled Carter from his thoughts. He had told his secretary to block all the press calls—but that left all the others. He picked up and his secretary told him that a Frances had phoned for the second time, someone from the ANC building.

Carter sighed. "If I don't take the call, is she just going to call again?"

"It sounds like it."

Carter gave the OK, held his breath for a moment, then said "Hello" as that line kicked in.

From the sound of Frances's voice, they were long-lost friends now ready for reunion. Carter kept all nuance from his tone. He did not want her taking the slightest encouragement.

"I just saw you on TV," She said. "You were very articulate. Very impressive."

"Thank you."

Frances waited for Carter to say something, but Carter waited for her. She finally came out with it. She still wanted the elevator group to get together at her place for sushi and crabs. She did not want to call the others until she knew the guest of honor could be there.

Who says you'll invite the others, Carter thought. He then gave her a string of uncomfortable excuses about being busy with the investigation and the rebuilding, and at the end of it, he chided himself for not being more direct.

Carter got his opening when his second line lit up—the line reserved only for major clients. "Listen, another important call's just come in. We'll talk some other time, OK?"

"I'm counting on it," Frances said with the vibrant flatness of a mourner not ready to accept a loss.

Carter pressed the other line. "Scott Carter here."

"Mr. Carter," a voice said, "our neighborhood prima donna professional engineer."

"I beg your pardon?" Carter said. The voice sounded electronically altered—low-pitched and flatly vibrant, like a poor-quality voice synthesizer jury-rigged to an old PC.

"I saw you on TV," the voice said. "You and the others sounded so terribly calm, when, in fact, you have no right to be."

"Who are you?" Carter asked, ready to hang up on this crank.

The voice chuckled with a tinny, synthesized echo. "Let me get to the point. I and my comrades in arms set the bombs in the ANC building, but I left an additional calling card that you personally are particularly qualified to receive. Go to the janitor's closet on the fourth floor on the north side of the building. You can take all your FBI friends. The more, the merrier. But I think you're the only one who'll see the true meaning. In fact, for that reason, I think you have to go. If you don't, I'll just get angry and cause a lot more damage. So help your community. Janitor's room, fourth floor, north side—and *you* go."

"Who are you?" Carter asked, his heart pounding. "How did you get this number?"

"You can call me Jackhammer. And you'll find that I've only just begun."

"Begun with what?"

But the line had clicked dead.

Carter burst into the conference room, hoping to find someone from the FBI. He saw the FBI spokesman talking to Waynewright at the podium.

"I need to get in touch with the man leading this investigation," Carter called, breathing hard from his run up the stairs. "I forgot his name."

"You look like a bear's on your tail," Waynewright grunted.

"I've heard one. I got a call from a man who calls himself 'Jackhammer.' He says he planted the bombs and he's left us a 'calling card' on the fourth floor of the ANC building. I don't think we have a choice. We've got to check it out."

The spokesperson stepped away from the podium. "When was this?"

"Just now, on a special phone line the public doesn't know about."

The spokesman pulled out his cell phone. "Could be the usual prank," he said to Carter. He then got a connection and gave the news. Just as fast, the spokesman signed off and turned to Carter. "Frank Gentry heads up the field operation and he's just a block away. He was planning to come this afternoon to interview you. To say the least, he's rearranged his schedule."

"Yeah, I thought he might," said Carter.

Frank Gentry entered the conference room with the stiff but brisk walk of an athlete who has worked out once too often and still tries to hide his soreness. In his early fifties, with a crew cut, a sharp, prominent jaw, and a steadfast stare, he could have also passed for one of his brethren at the Secret Service. He only lacked the microphone wired to his ear. Carter thought: Maybe he kept one tucked in his pocket for his lighter moments.

Gentry extended his hand toward Carter and Waynewright and nodded at the press spokesman. His tight-lipped attempt at a smile quickly foundered on his words. "Is this where you want to talk?" he asked Carter.

"It's as good a place as any," said Carter. "Sit down if you like."

"I don't think we have time to kill," said Gentry. "Shoot with what you heard."

Carter repeated the phone conversation as best he could remember, attempting a word-for-word replay. He regretted he could not vouch for full accuracy. Why hadn't he taken notes right after the call, he asked himself. By now, he could have forgotten a nuance.

Gentry pressed him on the sound of the voice synthesizer. "It couldn't have been a recording, could it?"

"No, there was interaction with me. The man was talking into something."

"It could be a small portable device simply placed over the receiver," Gentry said, "so the masked voice doesn't necessarily mean he called from his home or his base of operations. Did this guy have an accent?"

"Nothing I could hear," Carter said. He thought for a moment. "And the way he talked sounded pretty American. I remember 'the more the merrier.' Would you expect that from a foreigner?"

"But you also heard him say 'comrade in arms.' That sounds a little dated, like someone was learning from a dictionary of Cold War idioms."

"Maybe," Carter said.

Gentry looked from Carter to Waynewright. "Who's in charge of this office?"

"I am," Waynewright said, pushing out his chest just a little.

"I'd like to set up a tracing tap in case this Jackhammer, or one of his comrades, decides to call back. We could then monitor from afar, without cluttering up your offices. It would mean we'd be taping the start of every call Mr. Carter gets."

"Do whatever you gotta do," Waynewright said. "We want to catch these bastards as much as you do. I know Scott agrees."

Gentry turned to Carter, who accepted with a nod. Carter realized he had better start keeping personal dirt out of his phone chatter.

"For some reason this Jackhammer has decided to pick on you," Gentry said. "Maybe because he saw you on TV. Well, you've seen the drill. If he calls again, you try to keep him on the phone as long as you can so we can trace his location. All right?"

"I'll do my best."

"And everyone here keeps our little conversation quiet, understood? Jackhammer will suspect we're bugging him, but there's no reason to advertise it." Gentry got everyone's assent and pulled out his cell phone. "I'm going to call in a bomb squad. This whole thing may be a prank—we get them all the time—but I can't take any chances that this Jackhammer actually left something behind." He looked Carter in the eye. "Are you coming with us into the building?"

"I don't think Jackhammer gave me much choice."

A small stream of adrenaline had started to flow in Carter. He wanted to be part of the FBI team, get in the thick of the hunt and catch this killer, but he was nervous. What was he trying to prove going back to a bomb scene like this?

"I can't force you," Gentry said, "but Jackhammer said that you're the only one who'd understand his secret—whatever that means."

"If that's true, it's probably not explosives, right? If he blows me up, I'd have nothing to report."

"Sure, why not," said Gentry, sufficiently deadpan to offer little comfort. "It sounded like he'd blow us up if you *didn't* come."

"How would this work?" Carter asked.

Gentry held up his hand to make Carter wait for a moment, then put through his phone call. He snapped the request for the bomb squad and with a switch to another call, ordered the ANC building area cleared of all emergency workers. Just as quickly, Gentry slipped the phone back into his inside coat pocket. "You'll just come along for the initial look," he told Carter. "Obviously, if there's something for the bomb squad to tinker with, we'll clear you out immediately."

Carter nodded, not really knowing what he had agreed to.

Waynewright glanced at Carter uneasily. "I don't know if I like the idea of you going out looking for trouble. You're an engineer in the firm, for crying out loud, not an FBI agent."

Carter tried to smile Waynewright away and suppress his own second thoughts. "Right, you could lose your poster boy."

Waynewright frowned but held his tongue.

"So are you coming?" Gentry asked. From his curt impassiveness, clearly he did not want to hear 'no.'

Again Carter nodded.

Out on the street at the ANC building, the two-man bomb squad arrived thirty minutes later. They carried their gear in big nylon duffel bags filled with folded bomb suits and scuffed plastic tool kits, like the carry-on luggage for a mechanics convention. A bomb-sniffing German shepherd trotted on a leash at their side. Carter felt tempted to pet the dog but decided against it and just shook hands with the men. He wondered how someone even got into this line of business. He only had to check his own pulse to know it was probably not up his alley. At least the men were not already donning their bomb-proof suits and making it look intimidating, Carter thought, happy to see that Gentry had come along as well. Maybe Gentry actually believed Carter's theory that there was no real danger.

The ANC building stood abandoned in the cold sun, the north plaza empty and the front ground-level cavern still showing the blackened scar of destruction, the piles of rubble only slightly neater after a half day of cleanup. The steel shoring looked like toothpicks holding up the maw of an angry whale, but Carter knew the building had now been stabilized. It was not going to collapse without some other catastrophic shock.

The bomb team moved along the north side of the building and around the corner to the back entrance. The streets remained clear of people, and the building area itself had now been completely evacuated for the search. In that emptiness, Carter felt the eerie, fear-induced sense of being plucked from the city and placed on a separate planet where the still air became pressurized and where only a madman, out of sight, knew what awaited them.

The back entrance doors opened to a small foyer and a bank of three elevators. The space was only one-fourth the size of the extravagant entrance hall at the main, north entrance, and stepping through the lobby, Carter wondered whether the elevator shafts had been bent. He did not know how much an elevator could deviate from plumb and still work, a curiosity he would someday have to check with the manufacturer. At least the power had been restored to this part of the building, Carter thought.

The four-man, one-dog group turned left to reach the stairwell at the end of the building and then began walking upstairs. Gentry led the way, generally silent, occasionally slicing the emptiness with clipped questions or comments.

"Any idea what this Jackhammer might be wanting to show you?" Gentry asked, talking straight ahead, with Carter behind him.

"I really have no idea."

"Any inkling of who he might be? Maybe he knows you."

"I've wondered myself, but I really can't help you. How many fanatical, cold-blooded killers do I know?"

"Well, we'll talk about that again in a more formal setting."

Carter wondered how much more formal Gentry could get.

When the group reached the third floor, Carter looked to the top of the last flight of stairs, subconsciously measuring the steps that were left him, the confines a volatile mixture of anticipation and nervousness, and Carter realized that even if he wanted to back out, he could not do it because he would look like a coward. Carter had no second thoughts about continuing, but he marveled at the force packed by this social pressure. Carter wondered how many soldiers, or even heroes, had walked to their deaths to avoid simple embarrassment.

Gentry opened the door to the fourth floor hall, and with a slight hesitation, Carter stepped through. He now faced the central corridor, which sliced the building in two. He waited to let the others pass and closed in behind them, their steps no longer the echoing, hard slap on linoleum but quiet thuds on new carpet. The dog had already begun sniffing, and Carter stared at the shaft of the hall with a sudden surreal sense of displacement. His schedule back at the office had originally been packed with high-priority meetings, and yet here he was in an abandoned silence. His whole job rubric had been swept away, as though it had never existed. He no longer had to do what, just yesterday, were unquestioned personal and business necessities. What did that say about their importance, Carter asked himself.

The lingering smell of the fire and explosives had now grown stronger, and Gentry turned to Carter. "All right, you're going to stay here while we check out the janitor's room. I don't think Jackhammer has in-door surveillance of your movements. If he's watching, he probably saw you come in and go upstairs. We'll call you in if we think it's safe. Maybe then you'll find out what he's talking about."

"No problem," Carter said, unconsciously glancing up at the walls to scan for security cameras.

The men moved down the hall, checking the doors against a building plan they had collected earlier. When they found their destination, the bomb squad unpacked its gear and put on its suits. Carter watched from the end of the hall, wishing the men could do all of this faster. He wanted it over with.

After a minute, the team waved Gentry away and opened the door. Gentry began walking toward Carter but stopped halfway down the hall, as though wanting to show that he had to stay closer than the volunteer help. Carter looked at his watch.

He would not have the chance to look again.

Less than two minutes later, the bomb squad leader burst from the door, ripped open his visor, and shouted, "Time to get the hell out of here!" He dashed to Gentry and switched to an anxious summary. "We've got a can full of explosives, sealed off in clear, hard plastic so the earlier dog searches wouldn't have found it. It's got a radio device. This thing can be detonated from a distance."

"Can you disconnect the detonator?" Gentry asked.

"That's what Mike's trying to figure out, but you guys scram. This thing could blow a big hole."

Gentry seemed reluctant to go but then thought better of it. He turned toward Carter and waved him on. "All right, let's go," he said in a tense staccato, as though the need for quick thinking had stolen even more inflection from his speech. He was walking fast now, then switched to a jog. The sight of that urgency scared Carter more than the earlier bomb warning. "What about the other guys?" Carter asked. "How long are they going to stay?"

"As long as it takes. That's their job."

Carter shook his head but kept moving—one bomb blast for the week was enough for him.

Gentry did not slow down until they got to the stairwell. "OK," Gentry said, his feet tapping briskly down the steps, "if Jackhammer's been honest about his threat, he might be watching outside to see that we kept our side of the bargain.

He's got to think that you've been in there and seen his secret. So we're going to show we're afraid. When we hit that back door, we're going to come out running."

"I don't think I'll have to act too hard," Carter said.

"All right, but we're not going to stop until we're a block away, off the plaza. Then we're going to look back at the building to where my men are working. He'll get the point that we found his bomb. I just hope he meant what he said and won't blow everything to hell."

On the ground floor, the two stopped at the stairwell emergency exit. Gentry nodded and then opened the door. The two dashed through, hitting the sidewalk running. Gentry was in good shape and pushed Carter to a fast pace as they rounded the corner. Carter had the urge to look up at the buildings to see if anyone was watching, but he stuck to pumping his legs.

At the plaza, Gentry slowed down to a trot and finally stopped at the far corner. They were both breathing hard as they turned and squinted through the low-angled sun at the reflective glass of the ANC building. Carter focused on the fourth floor and made his best guess for the location of the janitor's room.

"So why did Jackhammer need you to come along just to see there was a bomb?" Gentry puffed. "Why wouldn't the FBI be enough?"

Carter stared at the building. "That's what I'm trying to figure out."

4

Pete Angelino had been traveling for seven days, both driving and hiking, and he now sat at the edge of a forest at dawn and pulled his one-burner portable stove from the top of his soiled backpack, cleared some sticks from the level ground, and set the stove down. He dragged a crushed book of matches from his pocket and lit the propane gas with the same match that lit the cigarette already hanging from his thick, chapped lips. After pouring some water from his canteen into the small tin pot, he stood up, pounded his hands together, and jogged a few disgusted steps in place. "Shit it's cold," he said with a growling New Jersey accent, his breath forming a small plume of vapor in the half-light. "I should've jacked up the fucking price for freezing my ass off."

The fluid curve of the power lines dipped and rose against the deep blue of the twilight, a silent, black geometry that sliced a cleared swath through the forest, farmland, and housing developments of northern Virginia, until the delicate, ribbed towers, their frames now as thin as toothpicks, disappeared over the horizon. A hawk sailed through the twilight calm, and the morning star hung brightly on the turquoise of deep space.

Angelino had no interest in that silence. He rubbed his black, scruffy, three-day beard and paid no attention to the silver sheen of frost on the unmowed grass of the power line right-of-way, or to the gentle sway of the bare twigs at the tops of the trees above him, as though the breeze dared not disturb the pristine calm at ground level. He rolled up his sleeping bag and strapped it to the bottom of his pack. He then crouched to the small pot and put his gloved hands on the heated sides for warmth. When the water boiled, he dumped it into a mug with some instant coffee and drank it black, staring out across the grass at the nearest power line tower.

This is the last one, Angelino thought as he sized up the location. Bushes had grown up near the base of the tower, which would give him cover, and no roads or cultivated fields gave a direct line of sight. You won't have drivers or farmers peeking out their windows at suspicious activity, Angelino thought. Yeah, I think this one'll do just fine.

Before taking a closer look, Angelino pulled out his map and confirmed his location with his hand-held GPS. He had been given a whole collection of marked-up terrain maps showing the power line grid for the area and the location of all the power plants and substations. He had spent his first days staking out three substations that someone had circled on the map, inspecting their lighting and security arrangements, sometimes with binoculars, sometimes from up close in the early dawn, then watching for habits and personnel schedules. He did not know who had prepared the maps and who was paying the money. He did not know what the hell it was all for. But that was all right by him. As long as they delivered the cash—and it had been damn good money so far—he'd do what he was trained to do and not ask any questions. Hell, you start asking questions and the client just gets cold feet, he thought. Shit, I'll take the business.

In his view, all the targets looked like sitting ducks, and this last tower appeared particularly easy. Angelino rolled up the map, stuffed it in the tube inside his backpack, moved the pack farther into the bushes, and began walking out into the cleared ground of the power line alley. The twilight had brightened, and he could now make out the texture of the shrubs and the steel joints in the tower. The tower stood nearly 100 feet high, a ribbed structure designed for nothing else but to stand up in the wind and snow and carry its high-voltage load. Angelino had instructions on how to carry out the work—two charges on one side at ground level, two others strapped higher on the opposite side. When they all blew together, the tower would fall over, like a person cut off at the knees.

Soon Angelino had reached the tower and circled it, noting the thickness of the columns and beams and planning the best way to mask any tampering. He figured he could get to the higher joints and tuck the explosives under the crossbeams and tape the wire down the inside of the column. Among the bushes, the bottom charges would have ready-made camouflage. Somebody would have to get pretty close to see anything unusual, he thought.

He turned to scan possible approaches and check whether someone might see a light when he worked at night. He froze at the sudden sight of an SUV coming over the slope at the next tower. "What the fuck?" Angelino said to himself.

The car slowed down, but then sped up suddenly, as though the driver had seen him. Angelino thought about running but immediately axed that idea. There's no law against taking a walk in the country, he said to himself. You'll just get them suspicious.

Angelino could make out only the vague shape of a company insignia on the vehicle door, and a tall communications antennae—but no roof-top lights. Hell, it's not even the police, Angelino thought. He put his hands on his hips, feigning patience in waiting to say hello. He squeezed off his last trace of tension when the car pulled up and showed its power-company logo. Probably just a bunch of hicks, he thought. He waved at them casually.

Two men sat in the front seats, the driver in his fifties, the other in his thirties. They seemed wary about getting out. The older man rolled down his window.

"What brings you here?" the driver said.

"Just been hiking and camping."

The driver glanced around as though looking for a tent. "You interested in power lines?"

"Not really. But I was over in the trees and thought I might see what they look like up close."

"Well, we don't really like people hangin' around."

"You're here," Angelino said.

The driver grunted, not sure if Angelino was joking or trying to be smart. "We've got our inspections to do. Got an early start so we can finish early."

Angelino smiled and showed his big, crooked teeth. "Party time, huh?"

"Call it what you want," the man said, still wary. "Where're you from?"

"Right now, just about anywhere," Angelino said. "I sleep where I can."

The driver squinted. He supposed the man looked homeless enough.

"Where are you from originally?"

"New York City," Angelino lied.

"Well, we'd appreciate it if you stayed away from the lines."

"I'm leaving now," Angelino said. "You've seen one of these towers, you've seen 'em all."

"Right," the driver said. He offered an uncertain wave and put the car into gear.

Angelino tipped his finger to his head in salute and started walking back to the forest, away from where he had left his pack. He could not tell how suspicious the man had been. A vagrant Arab would have gotten the third degree, but what were they going to do with a homeless WOP camped out in the fields? Report him? They wouldn't find him sleeping there again. He'd have to stake out another tower just to play it safe, and that was a pain in the ass. This one had looked perfect, he grumbled, but if they came back to this tower to snoop, they would have to find it clean. Then they wouldn't go searching the whole line for something they couldn't even expect. Angelino offered a sour, self-satisfied snort, "And that'll be their big mistake."

Carter had not expected the insight quite so fast. Only half an hour ago, at three in the afternoon, he had finally gotten the report from the FBI bomb crew. They had successfully defused the detonator and given Carter an estimate of how many beams that charge might have taken out. The copy of the architectural plans now showed the exact location of the janitor's room in relation to Carter's structural drawings. To confirm, Carter moved his finger up his computer screen and hand-counted the floors of the 3D building frame. He then moved horizontally, just the distance from the edge of the structure to the bomb's location. His finger stopped precisely at the top of the cavernous north entrance hall. That sucked the air right out of him.

Holy shit, Carter thought. But he knew he was just working on instincts. Frantically, he raced to close the original design file and call up the copy he had saved the night of the blast, now updated with the latest reports of damage to the inside beams. The results had shown the building would have held up with no wind, but now he would make one addition. The last, unexploded bomb sat at the peak of an onion-shaped arch Carter had shaped for the architect's sense of the impressive. Zeroing in, Carter simulated the explosion with clicks of his mouse, his heart beating as he removed a particular critical convergence of steel, right below the janitor's room. When Carter then reapplied the full load of the building, the beams from there to the ground all turned red without even the help of a breeze. It was like removing the last supporting piece from the edge of a child's wood-block tower. What had stood before now came tumbling down.

It was all too perfect, Carter thought in shock. Nervously, he ran some more tests, and in a few minutes he had the results: If you put the last bomb more to the right or to the left, the building might still have stood. But right there, in that exact place, it was all over.

Carter had anticipated the overall simulated collapse, but not the terrifying precision he now saw. Jesus, Carter thought, the person who had placed that bomb must have had access to the structural drawings. That was why Jackhammer had wanted you along, Carter thought. Of the FBI bunch, only you would have seen the significance of that placement.

Carter rubbed his face hard in the realization: This madman might be an engineer, or he had the help of one. He knows exactly what he's doing.

Frank Gentry showed up at 4:00 p.m. to meet formally with Carter. He had brought along two others—an FBI technician to finalize the phone tap in Carter's office and Special Agent Michelle Taylor. While still standing, Gentry rushed through the formalities of introduction.

"Michelle's also out of our Washington field office, and she's going to be our prime investigator on the local engineering end. She'll be your main day-to-day contact," Gentry said, talking as though Carter had already been conscripted into the Bureau. Gentry glanced at Taylor. "This is Scott Carter. His firm has agreed to make him fully available as a consultant to our investigation."

"'Fully' might be a bit optimistic," said Carter, "but Bob Waynewright has been pretty generous."

Taylor smiled politely and shook Carter's hand. "It's always nice to see good corporate citizens."

"I guess so," said Carter. He did not mention Waynewright's PR interests. Why ruin a good impression?

Taylor withdrew her hand and waited for Gentry's lead.

Carter guessed Taylor to be in her early thirties and noticed the fresh, fluid beauty that she kept in check with a look of no-nonsense professionalism. Her sandy blond hair had been bound tightly into a French braid in the back, but a few loose strands rebelled into a graceful halo. Carter noticed how her conservative dark gray pants suit hugged the athletic lines of her body like a cloth tarp on the hull of a racing sloop.

"Michelle spent two years in engineering school, and then became a chemist," Gentry said. "We thought she'd fit by speaking your language and picking up quickly on the technical side."

"That's good," said Carter, "because she'll probably have to talk to plenty of engineers. I've found something new. It looks important."

"Then where can we talk?" Gentry asked in an abrupt tone that left as much room for nuance as a drill sergeant's roll call. "I'd like to give our technician free reign on your phone."

"There's a small conference room nearby. We can try that."

Carter opened his office door to let Gentry and Taylor pass and then followed them down the hall. Taylor matched Gentry's straight back, but below she devolved to the graceful determination of a tall gymnast striding the balance beam. Carter glanced at how the lip of her suit jacket curved upward at her behind and how from there the crisp creases of her pants seemed suspended before plunging straight to the ground.

Hold on, Carter thought. Can't you control where you look? She might think you're some kind of jerk. Avoiding that impression suddenly seemed very important to him.

The small eighth-floor conference room stood empty. Carter turned on the lights and ushered Gentry and Taylor to the far side of the long mahogany table. Framed color photos of BWE projects covered the walls, ranging from pre-construction site work to the finished products. No one had told the engineer decorator that photograph wallpaper was perhaps not the best effect. Carter suspected that Waynewright had had something to do with it and that no one had bothered to argue. Of course, you're just reflecting Linda's old views, Carter thought. Without her influence, you'd probably think a crammed collection of engineering projects looked cool.

"Does anyone want some coffee or a soda?" Carter asked.

Gentry and Taylor both said "no thanks."

"But don't mind us if you'd like some," Taylor said. She offered the slightest smile to accompany her courtesy but soon erased it, apparently committed to a serious front. Carter wondered whether she did that as a defense against her good looks, making sure no one would even begin to take any hints. Surprised at himself, Carter was having trouble with his own defenses.

"I'm fine," Carter said and sat down. Forcibly switching gears, he now wanted to share all his thoughts and plunged in with energy. "I analyzed the bomb placements and found something real frightening. This guy seemed to know exactly where to put things. That final unexploded bomb would have brought the whole building down. It had perfect positioning."

"Are you saying the bomber had access to the engineering drawings?" Taylor asked.

"That's my opinion. Especially since he insisted that I go look at the bomb, knowing I might recognize the situation. He knows I'm a structural engineer. I see no other explanation."

"Of course, anyone who saw you on TV knows you're a structural engineer," said Taylor.

"That's true. But I don't think a lay person would have had the same confidence that I'd discover something. I think he wanted us to realize his capabilities."

"What about a demolition expert?" Taylor asked. "Someone like that would know how to set up a placement."

"Sure, but that part of it's engineering too. You've got to consider the loads involved and the geometry, and you'd want the design drawings. It seems that an engineer, someone who knows something about this business, would have a better chance of knowing where to find the plans."

Gentry broke in. "And where's that?"

"Any number of places: In our firm's electronic files, in our hard copy archives, at the architectural firm, or at the county public works office where they once reviewed the drawings—and that's just off the top of my head. It's not classified information. And there's another thing. Jackhammer used the dedicated phone line that I reserve for top clients. It's not like it's a dark secret, but it seems you'd have to know someone who'd been involved with our firm to get a hold of that. It's as if this Jackhammer knows the ropes."

"Are you saying it could be an inside job?" Gentry asked.

The question took Carter aback. "You mean someone at BWE?"

"Yes," said Gentry.

"No," Carter said, backtracking a little. "I can't imagine anyone at our firm who'd be capable of this. That's crazy. And I can't imagine anyone at the architect's office. How would a terrorist recruit someone like that?"

"Maybe you're not the best judge of that," Gentry said. "Obviously there are people besides you at your firm who have access to the drawings."

"Sure, just like people at all the other places I mentioned."

"Well, that's one of the things Michelle is going to check out," said Gentry. "You're going to be a big help in interpreting what we find."

"Well, I'd certainly like to interpret something so we can catch this son of a bitch," Carter said. He immediately glanced at Taylor and said, "Sorry about that." Then just as immediately he wanted to kick himself.

"Why apologize just to me?" Taylor asked with a poker face, content in turning the screw.

Taylor's parry took Carter by surprise. He noticed Gentry shifting in his seat with hard-nosed discomfort, as though a horse fly had bitten him and he wished he could just crush it. Carter decided to clean up his mess. "I apologized just to you because I was brainwashed as a kid," Carter said. "So let me apologize again. You can blame my mother for beating the old-fashioned manners into me. If you want the truth, I prefer being impolite."

Taylor offered the hint of a smile. "I'll try not to hold a grudge against your mother."

"I'll tell her that," Carter said, feeling better that his humor might have helped. Now he wanted to get back to business. "What scares me is the thought of a real engineer turned terrorist—and not some guy who may have studied it in college but then never worked in the field. I'm talking about in-depth, practical knowledge that could open up some real bad scenarios."

"Well, one of our jobs," said Gentry, "is to find out what kind of a character this Jackhammer is. The fact that he contacted you looks strange. Maybe the terrorists are trying to throw us off the track with off-beat behavior. Of course, this guy may be a different animal from what we're used to, or he's somebody the terrorists simply bought—it could range from an actual engineer to simply a voice who can call people up. If he's an engineer, he might like to keep someone like you as his contact. He's already proved he wants some sort of sick publicity. Maybe he'll want more and give us hints of what he's up to, or maybe give away some weakness in his personality. If we're really lucky, we'll trace a call and get to his phone before he splits."

"Well," said Carter, "I got the feeling Jackhammer was trying to toy with me. The voice synthesizer may have distorted it, but I think the guy takes pride in his technical powers and wants to show up the world. He insulted me like he resented me for some reason, maybe because I'm an engineer and could give him competition."

Taylor leaned forward, her hands on the table. She tapped her pen against a small note pad for emphasis. "One thing I'd like to know is why Jackhammer didn't detonate that last bomb. The explosives crew said it was all in working order. A remote control signal from anywhere within a block would have set it off. Is that showing restraint or mercy, or was it a technical failure, or did the guy just get cold feet?"

"He told Scott he'd 'only just begun'," Gentry said. "Maybe he and his comrades like the drama of taking things in stages. This was the appetizer where they get their pleasure in seeing us scurrying around trying to figure out what they're going to do next. For their follow-up, they take down a whole building. Breeding fear can be part of the game."

"It'd be awfully brash to strike twice in the same way," Taylor said. "But it worries me that Jackhammer talked about a 'calling card.' It could imply he's got more cards tucked in his pocket."

Carter looked squarely at Gentry. "There's one thing that gets me a little worried. Jackhammer might just be tempted to come after me. He's singled me out. What's to stop him from a drive-by shooting, or something like that?"

"Not a whole lot," Gentry said. "But I don't know whether a group that's priding itself in mass destruction would take the time to plan an individual murder. The obvious guess is that Islamist terrorists are involved in this. It's possible we have more evidence than just the leaflets. This Jackhammer may be one of the group. Or he may be a psycho they recruited to work for them. Why would terrorists come after you personally?"

"No idea," Carter said.

"Just stick to Michelle," said Gentry. "She packs a gun. If you're out in the field together, she'll give you some protection."

"OK," Carter said, "but in your book, what do you mean 'the field'?"

"Nothing more glamorous than offices," Gentry said.

Carter smiled. "You had me wondering. I thought I might be getting into some real cops and robbers."

Taylor chimed in, "Sometimes the most exciting thing we get into is a file cabinet or a database or a conversation. It may not be glamorous, but I prefer that to getting shot at."

"Maybe we have something in common," Carter said.

Gentry looked at his watch. "Listen, I'm going to let Michelle take over from here. She's going to want all sorts of specifics about your firm and the employees. I've got some other things to take care of right now." Gentry stood up. "If you have a minute, let's check with our technician."

"Sure," Carter said. "But what about public statements? Can I comment about the call I got from Jackhammer, my suspicions about him being an engineer?"

"In this case, I'd recommend it," Gentry said. "The more targeted information like that we make public, the more chance we have of jogging the memory of someone who might have a lead. Michelle will give you the phone number for people to call if they have any evidence. But clear every statement you make with Michelle and me. There might be some sensitive items we'd like to delay making public."

Gentry wasted no more time and led Carter and Taylor out of the conference room and down the hall to Carter's office. Carter noticed the staff glancing out from their doors and felt as though he'd been thrown into the runway spotlight of a designer fashion show. He did not like the attention when he had no control over it.

The FBI technician was sitting in Carter's chair, waiting patiently. He jumped when Gentry entered. "The phone's all set," the technician said. "Let me show Mr. Carter the ropes." He motioned for Carter to sit down and pointed to a small digital clock set next to the phone. The liquid crystal face showed "0:00."

"Whenever you get a call, that timer's going to start counting the seconds," the technician said. "If it's the guy we're interested in, you push this button on top and that helps let us know it's him without having to listen word for word to all your other conversations. It'll probably be a throw-away cell phone, so stretch out the talking. Try to trick him into answering one last question or get him to make one last comment, whatever it takes. When someone hangs up, the timer will reset itself. There you don't need to do anything."

"Pretty neat," Carter said. "How do you get the clock to reset?"

"There's a weak signal as long as one of the phone lines is open. The clock has a sensor that just waits for that to go dead."

"So all I have to do is keep the guy chatting. Is that a pipe dream?"

"The guy's probably too smart to be that stupid," said Gentry, "but you never know."

"*If* he calls back," said Taylor.

The technician had already packed up his tools and now waited for Gentry's cue. Gentry shook Carter's hand and apologized that he would not be available much—the demands of the government-wide anti-terrorist team and the potential work with overseas services would keep him out of commission. He expected daily reports from Taylor on the local engineering front and would keep in touch. He closed the door when he left.

The sudden privacy took Carter off guard. OK, he thought, now you've got to talk to this nice agent. Why should that be more difficult? He asked Taylor to sit down at his personal conference table.

"You've had quite a twenty-four hours," Taylor said as she slid herself into the chair with the smooth grace of a limbo dancer taking the first easy bar.

Carter looked at his watch and took a chair opposite. "Yeah, and it's not over. From here I've gotta go straight to an ASCE Section meeting." He noticed Taylor's questioning look. "The American Society of Civil Engineers. I'm supposed to tell the engineers my story of the bomb blast while they eat rubber chicken. They called me earlier and changed the agenda just like that."

"Something you do often?" Taylor asked. She seemed to have more patience for small talk now that Gentry had left, but her manner implied that these extras were part of their business relationship.

"I've been active with the local section for a while now. Do you want me to get up on my soap box?"

"I think I'll pass," Taylor said and offered one of those sudden cracks in her armor that Carter had noticed earlier—the shimmer of a smile on her delicately determined lips.

Carter felt himself searching for the warmth in her eyes, then immediately checked himself. Jesus, you'd better be careful how you look at her. She might get touchy again.

Taylor must have noticed a hint of discomfort. "Sorry about that jab back there with Frank. I guess that's my soapbox, getting singled out for kid-gloves treatment."

Good, Carter thought. He was hoping to get that monkey off his back. "Hey, I should've known better. I've seen what women engineers have to go through sometimes. I assume it's not a piece of cake in the FBI either."

"No," Taylor said. "They're trying hard, but sometimes it's a little artificial, with the male agents still acting protective and paternalistic."

"You mean Frank?"

"Frank's not bad," Taylor said, leaning her head back as though trying to weigh the appropriateness of what came next, finally voting for informality. "He's as much of a cold stiff with men as with women. Of course, he's relegated me to what he considers the lower priority side of the case. International terrorism packs more glamour."

Carter smiled despite himself. "Well, given that you joined the FBI, I guess you didn't drop out of engineering because you disliked being the minority. What was it, chemical engineering?"

"No, mechanical. But I liked the chemistry classes I took, and I started thinking about getting into forensics. That idea then finally slid over into actually being a field agent." She stopped and unzipped her black shoulder-bag and pulled out a bigger notepad, her signal that she had had enough of preliminaries. "If you've got to get away, I think we'd better start," she said, offering no trace of apology.

Carter liked that she did not sweeten her requests with frills. "Just let me order a sandwich so it has time to get here," Carter said. "That'll be my dinner. Can I order you anything?"

Taylor raised her hand in a quick "no thanks," as an on-duty police officer might refuse a martini. At his desk, Carter pushed the speed dial for the delivery deli and ordered a deluxe Reuben sandwich, then returned to the table.

For half an hour, Taylor politely pumped Carter for the names of the firms and government offices that might have had access to the building design drawings and the people she and Carter might want to meet first. She then returned to Jackhammer—what type of person he might be, whether Carter had possibly met him at some point in his life.

"I don't want to even think about that," Carter said. "The idea that some mainstream civil engineer could be responsible for this . . ." Carter shook his head. "I mean, sure, one criminal engineer doesn't mean the public's going to think we're all bad, but Jesus."

"That's the least of your worries," Taylor said.

She then asked about the types of places Carter met engineers and where someone might learn about his business. Where could someone find out that Carter had a separate telephone number for clients?

Carter spilled out as much as he could—the phone number fact could come from any client, or anyone who had talked to a client, or anyone at BWE. So what good did that do, he wondered, but he played along, admitting that thoroughness could not hurt.

When the sandwich arrived, Taylor started in on the BWE staff. Carter pulled out a company employee list and let Taylor check off all the names that might have had access to the electronic files.

"Of course, if you're talking about hard copy plans," Carter said, "even secretaries and couriers handle that stuff all the time. It's not like we're talking about top-secret documents, although since September 11th we've been a bit more careful about handing out drawings. We've got to know who the requester is."

"I understand," Taylor said, "but we've got to start somewhere."

While Taylor's finger slid down the list of employees, Carter lifted his Reuben and tried to keep the sauerkraut and dressing from oozing into his lap. As always, he had ordered his sandwich with extra kraut, but now, looking at his dripping fingers, he regretted the choice. The deli had given him only two small paper napkins, and Carter knew they would have to last for the whole messy meal. He glanced at Taylor and suddenly worried that he might look like a slob. You'd better keep your mouth closed while you eat, he said to himself.

Taylor stopped at a name. She looked up inquisitively. "Who's this Achmed Andawi?"

"A project manager. A structural engineer."

"Has he been with the firm a long time?"

"More years than I can keep track of."

"Where's he from?"

"He's originally a Palestinian, if I remember correctly. I'm pretty sure he's an American citizen by now."

Taylor pursed her lips casually and made a note on her pad.

Carter frowned. "You don't suspect Achmed, do you? He's one of the nicest guy you'd want to meet."

"I don't suspect him; I don't clear him," she said. "I just have to check out all the angles."

Carter shrugged in protest but let Taylor do her job. Taylor obliged by probing more deeply into the other structural engineers at the firm, wondering out loud whether any might have financial problems that would make them vulnerable to a payoff for lifting some files. Carter dismissed her suspicions as absurd but knew he could not peer into everyone's head and know with certainty there wasn't some fatal flaw hidden away. Wasn't that the basic problem with humanity? You didn't know what they were thinking.

Next Taylor asked for a run-down of Carter's bomb placement analysis and then for a look at the design files. Carter stuffed the last corner of his sandwich into his mouth and dabbed his lips and fingers with the crushed remnants of his napkin. He just barely caught himself from wiping his mouth with the back of his hand.

At the computer, Carter drilled into software that still gave him a thrill. Given Taylor's background, he took time to explain each step of his analysis, playing what-if games with the software like someone trying to impress a friend with a just-bought sports car. The top-of-the-line workstation was Carter's Ferrari.

It was six o'clock when Taylor finally finished all her questions.

"When's your section meeting?" Taylor asked.

"Six-thirty," he said. "I'll make it on time, no problem."

Carter watched Taylor's hand slip her notepad into her briefcase. As she leaned, her jacket fell from her blouse and exposed the tight leather shoulder holster and the handgun tucked beneath her arm. She straightened, swung the briefcase over her shoulder, and held out her hand.

"Thanks for everything," she said. "Tomorrow I can start the interviews of BWE staff."

"Just don't give them too hard a time," Carter said. "They'll think I made you suspicious. Especially Achmed. I mean, you're singling him out just because of his name. Isn't that illegal?"

Taylor shrugged with indifference and put her hand on the doorknob. "I'll treat everyone equally. After all, who says *you* aren't a suspect?"

"I beg your pardon?"

"You know more about the ANC building than anyone else at this firm. And it's only your word that this Jackhammer called."

Carter could not tell whether she was serious. "You're actually saying it could be me?"

Taylor remained unruffled. "It's possible. But I'm betting against it. It means you intentionally put yourself in the building during the explosion. I'm not sure you fit the profile for that."

"Now that's generous," Carter said. "You don't consider me a wacko."

Taylor nodded coolly, then offered a smile to temper the effects of her comment. She swung out the door and said good-bye with the crisp courtesy of a client leaving a scope-of-work meeting.

Carter resisted the temptation to look down the hall at her hips as she walked.

5

Carter drove through the dark on Columbia Pike, the oncoming headlights shining fitfully on his face, as though repeatedly illuminating a chink in his armor. Back at the office, Carter had changed quickly into a sport shirt and slacks, glad to be rid of the suit and tie, but the sudden lull in the car brought not a longed-for relaxation but a prick of unease about his possible cancer. Why the hell did the medical test have to take two days, he asked himself. Doesn't that give the cancer time to advance in the meantime? Don't you want to fight this thing right out of the box? But he knew medical labs did not revolve around his personal wishes, and he knew the doctor had not expressed any concern about a two-day wait. The doctor must know what he's doing, Carter thought. Don't start getting stupid here. Every medical scare you've had in your whole life has been nothing.

Carter shut down the doubts as he pulled into the parking lot of The Gilded Skillet in Arlington and saw Phil Johnson, the ASCE Section president, standing at the door. What's going on here, Carter wondered as he noticed the parking lot jammed with cars. This restaurant was never this busy, certainly not on a Tuesday night. That was one of the reasons the section had picked this place—they would not disturb many people.

So, good old Phil has finally gotten off his duff and done something, Carter thought. Phil must have used the telephone tree and had every section member call everyone in sight. Carter remembered when he was president of this outfit. He had taken the position seriously and busted his butt to round up speakers and organize special events. He had brought the same energy when chairing ASCE committees, but as the workload at his day job grew more demanding, he had turned down calls from his fellow members to run for national office.

So it takes a disaster to bring the Virginia-based meetings back to life, Carter thought ruefully, mildly flattered by the idea that apparently everyone had come to see him.

Johnson's face lit up in relief when he saw Carter approach from the parking lot.

"Man, am I glad to see you," said Johnson, who at 30 was the youngest president in the section's history. Johnson, a wastewater specialist, had been drafted to bring new blood to the office, despite his own vehement arguments that he had no time to do what was needed. Johnson had finally relented to the constant requests and then kept good on his word and done next to nothing. "I wouldn't want to explain to all these folks that you weren't showing up!"

"It looks like you've rounded up quite a crowd."

"We've rented the side banquet room, and we've brought in extra chairs, and people still have to stand along the wall."

"So you must have finally cashed a sponsorship check," Carter quipped.

"Now don't get on that high horse again because I forgot once," Johnson scowled. He did not want anything to spoil the success that had dropped into his lap.

Inside, The Gilded Skillet had never quite made up its mind on decor—a wood gabled, French provincial, Mexican cantina mix that highlighted both impressionist landscapes and framed ceramic tiles. The copper pots and skillets peppering the walls had long ago lost their sheen, and the tiles and paintings seemed to have acquired a dull, transparent patina from years of airborne oils drifting out from the kitchen. Nevertheless, the place maintained a certain careworn respectability. With the lights down low, the glass enclosed candles—centered on each table like dimpled red Coke bottles—did not pack the power to reveal the occasional loose threads and faint, recalcitrant stains on the white tablecloths. The large steaks at reasonable prices helped patrons turn a blind eye.

Carter noticed a few section members standing at the door to the banquet hall, some that he recognized, others that he didn't.

"We've also contacted the press," Johnson said. "One section member apparently called your boss, and he then called me and said I should contact a whole slew of press people."

"When did you have time to do that?"

"I didn't. Your boss volunteered your PR guy to do all the work for me."

Carter shook his head in distaste. "So where's the media?"

"We've already got some newspaper people, but TV hasn't shown up yet—if they're going to show."

"I'll do just fine without them," Carter said.

Carter had now reached the door to the banquet hall, and as he walked through, a few of his colleagues patted him on the back and started to applaud. By the time Carter had walked through the room, everyone at the packed tables had turned around, and soon they were clapping as well. Someone stood up and cheered and someone else whistled and shouted "Way to go, Scott!" and then everyone was on their feet giving him a standing ovation. Carter gave a mock wave of disgust, turning to Johnson. "So what am I supposed to do now?"

"You might as well go up and talk. I think a lot of them have already ordered their dinners."

"Is that what your agenda says?"

"What agenda?"

Carter shook his head and walked straight to the front podium. He tapped the mic to make sure it was on and then let everyone know he did not like formality. People should order their food and feel free to mill around and make sure they asked a lot of questions because he had no real prepared remarks. Before starting, he requested a moment of silence for the victims of the attack, but for him that only brought back images of the dead at the blast, and the moment became very long. When he looked up again, he saw a local TV news crew beginning to drag in their equipment. "Well, now I'm really on the spot," Carter said. "The TV crowd is here to hound me again."

"Give 'em hell, Scott," someone shouted. Another person whooped.

Carter had grown energized that his section actually showed some new life and started right in. "By bad luck, I happened to be in the wrong place at the wrong time and almost became a victim of some lunatic. But I was also lucky enough to have some knowledge that turned out to make a difference. It gives us civil engineers the opportunity to teach the public a thing or two about how their city fits together and also contribute to this investigation and catch these terrorists."

For the first time since the blast, Carter had free reign to report the engineering aspects without stopping to explain basic physical concepts or avoiding technical terms. He could cut right to the chase, and he took the audience step by step through the escape from the elevator to his on-the-fly computer work. He only wished he had some supporting slides and did not have to use destruction for a backdrop.

Carter fielded some pointed technical questions that actually made him think—the uncertainties in the load factors, the lateral displacements from the blast, even the conversion of the old design file to the new software platform. What a change, Carter thought as he finally left the podium after thirty minutes of peppered questioning. Johnson came to pat him on the back, and it was then, with the TV lights on, that Carter actually noticed the big Blackstone-Waynewright Engineers logo hanging on the wall behind the podium.

"Where did that come from?" Carter asked.

"Your boss said he'd donate drinks if we put up that sign. I said, sure why not? You can tell that everyone's real loose with all the booze."

"Well, I'll be damned," Carter said. "So where can *I* get some booze?"

"Just grab a waiter," Johnson said.

Before Carter could do it, the TV and print reporters had collared Carter for interviews, and when he had finished those, he saw the next in line: Frances.

Man, how did she get here? Carter asked himself. He suddenly pitied her and wondered why she couldn't pick up on his hints. He was running out of excuses.

Frances approached him with a fawning smile that she tempered with a blush of shyness. "I guess you're surprised to see me."

"You might say that," Carter said, unable to sound sufficiently indifferent, actually sounding friendly. Why can't you do what you have to do, Carter thought to himself.

"I called your office. They said you were busy, but your secretary admitted that you had an association meeting tonight."

"Well, that was good of her," Carter said.

To Carter's surprise, Frances seemed to sense his reluctance to talk, and her voice took on a hint of embarrassed indecision. Her eyes lost their focus and flicked briefly away from Carter's face. "You gave a wonderful speech," she said to the floor. "I really enjoyed it, although I didn't understand everything." When her eyes risked looking at Carter again, Carter noticed the hurt. "But I'm sure you have a lot of people you need to talk to," she said. "It's probably not the best place for me to butt in."

Carter had not wanted to wound her, but what was he supposed to do? He was groping for some sort of conciliatory remark when a large hand shoved itself forward and a deep voice gruffly pumped out a greeting. "Well, Scott, the hand of fate takes strange turns."

Carter suddenly found himself shaking hands with Edward Babcock—not the person he wanted to spend time with, but also not one he could just brush off. Carter glanced at Frances, confused about using Babcock as an excuse to get away, but before he could come up with anything to soften the blow, Babcock had physically pulled him aside, oblivious of anyone else who might want Carter's attention. The last thing Carter saw was Frances meekly mouthing "Goodbye" and then hurrying for the exit. To hell with infatuations, Carter thought. There was too much pain in the world already. Frances had to quit now and stop tormenting herself.

Babcock, an aging, massive man at six-foot-four and two hundred and sixty pounds, clutched a glass of vodka in one hand and Carter's shoulder in the other, glowering down at Carter both by physical necessity and by his own blunt conception of status. His gray, wavy hair crowned the wide, calculating face of a loan shark coming to pick up a debt.

"Ed, it's been a long time since I saw you at one of our meetings," Carter said, grabbing a waiter and ordering a gin and tonic. He needed one to deal with this guy.

"Well, you know damn well I've had it up to here with your society stuff. You're incapable of going on record with anything."

We won't go on the record with your extremism and Neanderthal ideas, Carter thought. Carter had worked behind the scenes to keep Babcock out of ASCE presidential contention, and that had been good preventative politics. Not long after, Carter had heard that Babcock had been forced into retirement for discriminatory and abusive behavior at work. Carter did not doubt the story and was glad Babcock had made himself scarce.

"So what do you do to keep busy these days?" Carter asked, seeing there was no easy escape.

Babcock took his hand off Carter's shoulder and gulped down some vodka. "Retirement is pure crap," Babcock said, his eyes bright with a disconcerting penetration. "I'm sick of sitting around at home or standing around the golf course. If I wasn't this old, I'd start up a new design-build firm. Of course, with everyone getting so damned politically correct, I probably couldn't get any investors to touch me with a ten-foot pole. Well . . ." He grinned sharply to underscore his eloquence, "they can lick my ass."

Carter shook his head. "You always had a way with words, Ed. But you know, if you tried, I'm sure your firm'd do pretty well." He had to admit, Babcock got things done. An old-hand highway designer, Babcock had come into his own as a hard-driving executive. His conception of management was to bark out orders and fire anyone who didn't obey.

Throughout most of his career, Babcock had succeeded by scaring enough good people into putting up with him. For clients he could project the air of a tough-as-nails general who would do the job right no matter what the odds. And he usually did. Carter had to give him that credit. Fifteen years ago, with less of a hard edge, Babcock had pulled the Arlington Public Works Department into shape after it had fallen into disarray and had worked closely with Carter's firm during the planning of a downtown mall construction project. As a young, inexperienced engineer, Carter remembered being intimidated by Babcock but also impressed by his unwavering, cussing drive. Babcock had then moved on to head a large design-build firm that spearheaded countless facilities projects up and down the east coast. And now Babcock had apparently been put out to pasture.

Babcock again put his arm around Carter's shoulders and held out his drink for gruff emphasis. "You know Scott, I always did like you. Heck, some of your ideas, if I remember right, bordered on pure liberal crap, but you always had some drive and you had a good head on your shoulders. They've got the right engineer to help out with the investigation."

"I never thought I'd hear a compliment from you, Ed."

"And you may never again. But you know . . ." Babcock lowered his head as though whispering a secret just for Carter, "I could be a damned good resource for your FBI friends, from what I heard in your speech. I've got a lot of contacts in this town, and I know a lot of engineers. These Islamist terrorists might have had help from an American traitor. I could help you find these bastards, and it'd give me something to do besides chasing a golf ball."

Carter did not know what to say. He agreed Babcock could be an excellent contact, but he did not know whether he could take him seriously. The guy might just be hunting for publicity and cause more harm than good.

"I really don't know if the FBI needs any more help," Carter said. "From what I hear, they've got hundreds of people on this case."

"Well, I couldn't expect the FBI or anyone else in government to know what they really wanted, even if it came up and sniffed their crotch. If you ask me, they oughta just round up all the Arabs and kick them out of the country. And when they get suspects, they should just beat the information out of them. Do you realize how many lives are lost because we treat scum criminals with kid gloves?"

Carter did not bother to answer.

"So are you going to think about my offer?" Babcock asked.

"I'll mention it to the FBI," Carter said, making no commitments. He could not quite digest the fact that Babcock was asking him for favors. Things had turned cockeyed.

Carter felt a tap on the arm. It was Phil Johnson. "The restaurant says you have a phone call."

That's a bit of luck, Carter thought. "Excuse me," he said to Babcock and followed Johnson out into the restaurant itself. Johnson pointed to the phone at the hostess stand at the entrance. The hostess had long ago abandoned her post, and a light on the active phone line blinked in orange isolation. Carter picked up the receiver. "Hello," he said.

At first there was silence. Then the synthesized hiss turned Carter cold. "This is Jackhammer. I hope your meeting went well. But to help save your restaurant, you have to answer this question. Where do you get a flush that's not in the toilet? Answer that question and you'll find a bomb in The Gilded Skillet that will go off in exactly twenty-five minutes."

Carter lurched for a clarification, but the line had gone dead. He stood for a moment, heart pounding, and then ran to the banquet room door and gathered himself about what to do. He stood where both rooms of the restaurant could hear him. "All right, listen up!" Carter shouted. "Everybody, listen up!" The loud rumble of voices faded to a background flutter. "I want everybody to remain calm. You hear me? Just stay calm." He made sure he had everyone's attention. "I don't know if it's a crank. There are a lot of these scares going around, but somebody just phoned in a bomb threat." A gasp of shock rose from the room, and Carter waved down the commotion. "Listen, the guy said there's plenty of time to get out of here. He's targeting the restaurant, not us. Just everybody stand up and walk quickly to the exit. No running. That's all we have to do and everyone will be all right."

Carter forced himself to manage the exodus like a proctor during fire drills in elementary school. He looked at his watch: 8:51 p.m. He hoped that the twenty-five minute deadline was no lie and started waving the people through at a faster pace. He wanted to get out as well, but he could not bring himself to act spineless, announcing the threat and then skedaddling.

The local TV crew stumbled out with its gear, trying to shoot footage as they moved, stunned that they had fallen right in the middle of a dramatic news story. Babcock lumbered by, grabbed Carter by the arm, and stepped aside for a moment. "Is there a connection to the ANC building?" he asked.

Carter nodded but did not want to say any more.

"We'd better catch these guys!" Babcock barked. "You hear me?"

"Listen," Carter said. "I don't know if the restaurant called 911. Call them and tell the police what happened."

"You got it," Babcock said and turned away.

"Wait," Carter shouted. "Tell them that to find the bomb there's a riddle: 'Where do you get a flush that's not in the toilet?' I don't know what it means, but that's what the caller said."

Babcock nodded, already pondering the question.

Next to Carter, the people filed out, visibly shaken but not losing their heads. The last person stepped out at 8:56 and Carter ran after them, jogging into the far next-door parking lot with the others.

The first police had arrived and now started to close off Columbia Pike in both directions, their lights flashing in a stark repetition of what Carter had experienced only one night before. He suddenly thought of Gentry and Taylor. He dug into his wallet and found their numbers, then pulled out his cell phone. He dialed Taylor first and got an answer after one ring.

"Jackhammer called me at my ASCE Section meeting. He made a bomb threat and according to my watch, it's supposed to go off in about fifteen minutes."

"Are you, is everybody, all right?" Taylor asked, the worry not hidden in her voice.

"We're all outside. But Jackhammer gave a hint about where to find the bomb. He said: 'Where do you get a flush that's not in the toilet?' Maybe you've got some experts who can figure that out."

"I'll make all the calls and I'm on my way. Just give me the address."

Carter told her and hung up, then returned to the crowd. There he found the police pushing people farther away from the restaurant. "Let's go!" they shouted at a few of the reluctant curious. "We don't know how big this'll blow! You wanna get killed?!"

Carter pushed his way to the front of the police line and shouted, "Who's in charge here? I've got some information on this thing."

The policeman pointed to a cluster of cars on the far side of Columbia Pike. Carter began running and immediately noticed Babcock with a high-ranking police officer and a man in civilian clothes. The officer was talking into the mic of his car radio, the elastic cord pulled through the window. Babcock turned around when he heard Carter approach.

"That riddle might be a piece of cake," Babcock said, curtly self-satisfied. "Do you play poker?"

"Sure . . ."

"So, you get a flush. The restaurant manager says the place also has a small banquet room. People could play cards there. I'm laying my money on that."

"Has the bomb squad shown up?" Carter asked.

"They're going to be here any minute."

Carter looked at his watch: 9:03. Thirteen minutes until the 9:16 deadline. Babcock's guess might be a good one, so the bomb squad still had a chance. Carter just worried that the guess might be too obvious. Maybe the riddle had something to do with a red face or with hunting.

Carter paced impatiently in the cold—again he did not have a coat—and soon found himself facing the same TV mic he had talked to inside. Carter offered a few personal emotions but refused to talk about the bomb threat until he had discussed it with the FBI. He did not want to spoil anything for Taylor.

The news crew quickly abandoned him when a police van, its sirens wailing, lurched to a stop. The bomb squad jumped out, a German Shepherd in tow. The officer who had been with Babcock and the restaurant manager ran over to brief the new arrivals. Carter could see the squad members nod their heads, check their watches, and then hurry inside.

The officer approached Carter and asked him to sit tight so he could question him as soon as the bomb threat had cleared. They wanted to know more about the caller.

Waiting, Carter looked over his shoulder, searching for Taylor.

Carter anxiously looked from his watch to the restaurant. It was 9:13. The bomb squad had been inside for seven minutes, and for Carter, the building seemed to vibrate in the surreal prospect of destruction. Jesus, weren't those guys going to get out of there no matter what they found? Don't get yourselves blown up over a lousy restaurant, Carter thought.

The clock moved on. Still nothing. Carter tried to think how long it would take Taylor to drive here. That depended on how many phone calls she had to make first, but he guessed about ten more minutes. When he tried to fine-tune that a little more, he suddenly stopped and faced his own thoughts. How did her arrival time suddenly get so important? What has gotten into you?

Carter shook his head, nervous about his emotions, then felt his heart skip as the front door of The Gilded Skillet swung open. The two-man bomb crew hurried out holding a package and ran straight to their boss, taking no precautions. From a distance, Carter could see them conferring and glancing back at the restaurant. He looked at his watch: 9:16. Carter felt his stomach tighten, but the building returned only silence. OK, give it a little more time. No one said our watches have all been synchronized, or that Jackhammer was completely accurate.

Carter waited, unconsciously taking a few steps backward, but after a few minutes, The Gilded Skillet still stood intact. Maybe the bomb-squad had done it—they had disarmed the device and were just waiting for the deadline to pass in case they had missed something. Carter jumped at the sound of a voice from behind. He turned and saw Taylor approaching from the strip-mall parking lot.

She was wearing the same gray pants suit she had worn earlier in the day, but her hair had now been pulled tight into a long ponytail. Apparently, she had not had time to do anything more complicated than brush it, strap it up, and rush out.

"Have they found the bomb?" Taylor asked, trotting to a stop.

"I think they found something," Carter said, "but I don't know for sure."

"Who's in charge?"

Carter pointed to the group of police cars.

"So let's go," she said. "We'll have to question you about Jackhammer."

The two set off and pushed themselves through the large group of onlookers. As they walked, Carter found it difficult not to look at Taylor. With her chin up, she again showed that mild, yet hard-driving determination that had caught Carter's eye from the beginning. An air of smooth, scented vitality seemed to pervade the athletic flow of her body, now with the girlish touch of a ponytail bobbing behind her.

"Is Frank coming?" Carter asked her.

"He's on his way from the DC office. It's going to take him just a little longer."

"So were you working at home?"

"On the start of a case like this, I don't think Frank would appreciate us spending our evenings watching TV."

Taylor kept walking and flashed her ID to the first police officer who tried to stop her, then walked straight to the leadership. The Arlington County police chief had now arrived and had taken over calling the shots. He recognized Carter. "It looks like you've got a dark cloud over your head," he said with an abrupt, sarcastic growl.

"Certainly not by choice," Carter answered. "This is FBI Special Agent Michelle Taylor. She's working on the ANC bombing case. The same guy who called in responsibility for that bombing called in this one as well, or at least so it sounded."

"I've heard," the police chief said. "It looks like the bomber's moving down in the world, targeting two-bit restaurants."

"So what did you find?" Taylor asked.

Carter watched the seemingly forced squint of her eyes and got the curious sense that her no-nonsense impatience might hide a slight insecurity. Was she just acting the tough-guy? Carter wondered.

"It looks like the bomb threat was a hoax," the police chief said. "We just found a package of anti-American leaflets, no explosives."

"Where are they? Have you left them intact?"

"We're not the Podunk City police force, Ms. Taylor."

Taylor did not bother to react. "We'll need to have them analyzed and see if they match what we found at the ANC site."

"I'm not going to stop you," the police chief said, irritated about ceding jurisdiction in the case.

"Was there any substance to the bomber's riddle?" Taylor asked the man.

"Yeah, one of Mr. Carter's engineer friends gave us his theory that the bomb could be in a private room where groups could play poker, and it turned out to be right." He craned his neck and pointed over at the crowd. Babcock was watching and took it as a cue to approach. Carter introduced him.

"Maybe I got lucky on this one," Babcock said, focusing on Taylor and doing a poor job of pretending humility. "But I told Scott here that I'm retired and have nothing to do with my time except help find the animals responsible for this. I've got contacts with civil engineers up to my ears and could help you track down whatever data or people that might help. Maybe the terrorists got help from Americans. Hell, if they did, I'd like nothing better than to put them in some antique electric chair and watch them fry."

"We appreciate the offer," Taylor said. "I'm sure Scott knows how to reach you if we have any questions."

"I'm sure he does," Babcock said, a gruff twinkle in his eye as he acknowledged Carter's obvious reluctance.

6

The low-slung Washington skyline hunkered flat against the morning cold, as though a child had spread a field of blocks at the edge of a winter pond without an adequate supply to stack the city higher. In the gray half-light, beneath a dark gray blanket of clouds, the lights of the buildings seemed incapable to warm even their own confines. The rippled waves of the Potomac flowed in a black-gray current of awakening to an empty dawn.

On the riverside parkway, Carter lifted a travel mug from the central console of his Chrysler Sebring and tried to ward off the fatigue and uneasiness of another late night of police and FBI questioning and of restless, feckless sleep. A vibrant web of impressions conspired with the bleak morning to breed a new resentment.

How had a terrorist singled him out as a target, as an object to be toyed with? He had not done anything to anyone, and yet he had been chosen as the conduit for messages of mayhem. With the terrorist contacts hanging over him, he did not know if he could ever feel safe.

Yet Carter remained alone in his knowledge of Jackhammer. No one else had heard the voice-synthesized terrorist speak. At the restaurant, the first call apparently had been placed by a man with an Arabic accent. Only when Carter had come to the phone had the caller switched to the old identity. No one on the FBI had said anything, but Carter could not forget Taylor's first insinuation that he himself could have fabricated Jackhammer's existence. And what could counteract that now, except the common sense that he felt sure Taylor possessed?

The thought of Taylor did not make things easier. He could picture her walking, her lips forming the substance of her plans, her eyes questioning him. How had this distraction suddenly hit him? He had not consciously encouraged himself. Since his wife had died, Carter had not entertained other relationships, respecting Linda's memory with a trace of guilt about the strains they had experienced in marriage.

After years of attempts, Linda had discovered she could not have children, and she had blamed herself for denying them a family. In time, she had let worries of self-perceived inadequacies steal the life from her lovemaking, and then she had started meeting with clients each night. After that, Carter and Linda had seen little of each other except on the weekends, and she had started drifting away. Then with her sudden death, Carter had snapped back to the image of their original love, and Carter felt reluctant to acknowledge the more recent memory. He wondered if those reins were now slipping away.

With the latest bomb threat, the FBI ordered tightened security at BWE. The police stationed officers at both the front and back doors and at the parking garage entrance, demanding picture IDs and comparing them to a list of tenants and expected guests. Carter had the uncomfortable knowledge that it was all because he personally worked there.

Upstairs, Waynewright had again left orders for Carter to meet him first thing that morning. Carter hung up his coat and took the time to grab a cup of coffee, but he did not brave email or voicemail before walking down the hall to see Waynewright. Waynewright's assistant immediately showed him in.

Waynewright got up from his desk with a glower. "So what the hell's going on? Why are you getting targeted?" He seemed intent on showing a papa-bear concern but came off more as a grizzly. He motioned for Carter to sit down on the couch and dropped heavily into a chair opposite.

"I have no idea," Carter said. "I won't deny it's scary."

Waynewright shrugged in gruff commiseration. "Yeah. I bet it is. Well, Agent Taylor is poking around the office today. She's going to be interviewing our staff in the conference room outside of here. I don't know what she's after, but it makes me nervous, like we're all suspects."

"She's got to cover every angle. Hey, she may even check me out. It's only my word against the world that I've heard Jackhammer on the phone."

"So she likes to deal in nonsense?"

"I'll pass that along," Carter said.

Waynewright brushed over the jab. "Your job is to tell the media what happened. We've got another press conference scheduled for noon. It's you telling your stories about the restaurant, with the FBI adding a few words." Waynewright could not hold back a tempered satisfaction. "Boy, this has worked better than I ever expected. Last night at your section meeting, the local news flashed our logo when they showed a clip of your speech and then cut to you yelling for everyone to get out of the restaurant. It all looked pretty dramatic."

"You bought off our section president with liquor," Carter said. "Otherwise the ASCE logo would have gotten on TV."

"My heart bleeds for you," Waynewright growled. "You're *our* employee. *We're* paying your salary."

Waynewright leaned forward and picked a large envelope from the table between them. "There's another thing. The first detailed damage reports have come in from the ANC building. I've put copies on your desk. ANC wants us to handle the frame reconstruction, and you're leading the team. Just don't get too caught up in doing it all yourself. You've got Fulton and Green to help."

"Who says I want help?"

Waynewright slapped his thigh like a butcher testing a new side of beef. "*That's* your problem," he barked.

On his way back to his office, Carter thought about checking the conference room and saying hello to Taylor, but he resisted, as if trying to confirm his self-control. Outside his office, his secretary alerted him to a message on his chair. "From Special Agent Taylor," she said.

Carter quickly walked into his office and picked up the slip. The note invited him to lunch after the press conference, with her and an Israel terrorist expert. So what is this all about? Carter wondered. Michelle isn't involved with the international probe.

Impatiently, Carter dispatched his voicemails and emails, printing out some as reminders for later. So much for a paperless office, he thought. He then turned to the ANC damage reports and called up the electronic files for the building. He was determined to get the frame repair on track as soon as possible and give the architectural clean-up free reign. The American News Corporation was counting on the A/E design teams to get the ANC employees back to work, and Carter was not going to let them down.

The latest reports showed more extensive interior column damage than Carter had previously guessed, making the building's earlier survival even more precarious. If Jackhammer had wanted to let the building live, he had cut things too close for comfort and simply lucked out on a higher joint rigidity than Carter would have expected. I guess the design did pretty well, he thought.

Carter put off calling Fulton and Green so he could brainstorm his own solutions just a little bit longer. He wanted to come up with a good sequence for beam replacement and calculate the ongoing stresses so that temporary weaknesses did not sag into further damage. He felt he deserved the solitary challenge after being deprived for so long.

Part of the repair planning would simply be an inventory of the surviving bolts and welds, so it could not match the creativity of a fresh design, where you had the full array of challenges—probing and evaluating the client and the public needs, the research on new technologies or materials that might just work to reach the next level, weighing the sustainability and risk factors, then the logical give and take of possible solutions and the computer experimentation, and finally getting out in front of a public hearing to sell what you think has hit the nail on the head. Carter had always found tremendous satisfaction in arriving at an equilibrium of so many factors. In his speeches to promote engineering, he had searched for comparisons that he assumed might match the feeling—writing a crowd-wowing speech with just the right flair, completing a backbreaking home-improvement project and then seeing it shine, composing a great melody and then hearing it sung on the radio by a famous recording artist.

Only after an hour did he bow to Waynewright's admonition. He called in Fulton and Green to tap their ideas and get them briefed on the details.

It was 11:30 before Fulton and Green left, and noticing the time, Carter tracked down the BWE PR director and asked for a run-down of the press conference agenda. Apparently, the FBI spokesperson would start things off with a general briefing of the events of last night. Carter would follow.

The TV crews had already set up their gear, and reporters milled around talking to colleagues or studying their notes. Carter again felt the anticipation of national TV and wondered how his latest actions would play in the press. He hadn't done much except be the passive victim of a terrorist phone call and order people to get out of a restaurant. Anybody with eardrums and vocal chords could have done that. He wondered how Taylor perceived him, and how he stacked up against her fellow agents.

As the press conference started, Carter saw Taylor come in at the far side of the room. She scanned the area, nodding hello when she met Carter's eyes, and then ducked out.

Thirty seconds later Carter heard a whisper. "Are you OK for lunch?" Taylor asked, having stepped in behind him.

"No problem," Carter said, startled by her closeness. He had turned his head only briefly to acknowledge her presence. Now, as he watched the FBI man at the podium, the thought of Taylor put him on edge. He tried to concentrate on the speaker, yet his focus drove incessantly backward, attempting to verify that Taylor, as the minutes passed, was actually still there. Finally, he glanced around, pretending to look out the door, and saw Taylor not three feet away. OK,

Carter thought, what does that do for you? Jesus, stop acting like a teenager. You're working with this woman.

The FBI man closed with some remarks about the latest Islamist leaflets. The anti-American rhetoric matched the ones found at the ANC bombing site and preliminary tests confirmed a single ink and paper stock. The Gilded Skillet package had also contained a message pieced together from letters cut from magazines, warning about the power that the "comrades in arms" had over a defenseless America.

The spokesman repeated what had already been said at the main Justice Department news conference earlier that day—that the FBI as yet had no confirming evidence that the events were connected to al Qaeda or to any foreign source. Refusing to answer any questions, the spokesman then turned the press conference over to BWE's PR director, who without further delay introduced "Blackstone-Waynewright Engineers' own Scott Carter."

Carter winced at the introduction but felt more at ease striding into the media spotlight than standing at Taylor's side.

Before it was over, Carter had gotten a good twenty minutes on stage by himself, but there was only so much the reporters could pump from such a short restaurant incident. Carter made a point of mentioning the name of his ASCE Section to compensate for the logo Waynewright had swiped at the restaurant. The PR man then closed down shop, and Carter headed for Taylor. She had again woven her hair into a French braid in the back, pulled tighter than Carter could remember. Her hands were folded on a small notebook, and she kept her smile to business-like acknowledgment as Carter reached her.

"Well done," Taylor said. "You always put on a good show." She did not wait for his response. "Hungry?"

"I suppose so," Carter said. "But since when do you have something to do with international terrorist experts? I thought you'd been banished to Northern Virginia and the engineering side of things."

"It's not what it looks like," she said as they turned to head for the elevator. "It's just some glorified babysitting. From what I hear, the Israeli's a terrorism specialist and happened to be in the States for a conference, so they picked his brain and discussed coordinating research on Middle Eastern connections, groups beyond al Qaeda and the like. Frank got his fill and now claims I should get a feel for our foreign resources. It can't be too top secret or we wouldn't be going to a restaurant. I figure Frank owes the guy a free lunch before the man flies home—and Frank's too busy to do it himself."

"So you've got a cynical streak," Carter said.

"Just trying to survive."

An FBI gopher delivered Tuvia Goldblat to the front door of the Hyatt Regency in downtown Rosslyn. In his late thirties, Goldblat had that Israeli look of barely tolerant impatience checked by a focused friendliness, with a slight paunch of a desk job blemishing a tanned, athletic build. He seemed to demand proof that Carter deserved his respect, but his eyes sparkled for Taylor, advertising that his lunch company had turned out better than expected.

Carter had entertained countless clients to two-martini lunches in the hotel's upstairs restaurant, classic all-American cuisine dressed up in lean elegance with a glass-walled overlook of the city. Carter led everyone to the elevator and then took the lead in securing a table off to the side by the window above the streets far below. Following Taylor's lead, they all piled their winter coats on the empty fourth chair and sat down.

"So, Ms. Taylor," Goldblat said in good but heavily accented English, "you must let me know what I can do for you. Your boss only briefed me in general."

"I don't know if I can do much better," Taylor said. "Scott here feels it took an engineer to plant the unexploded ANC bomb in just the right location. I'm assigned to explore some of the engineering connections. If the question comes up, what can you find out about potential terrorists or terrorist sympathizers who have a civil engineering background—and if we have to narrow it down, maybe a focus on structural?"

Goldblat nodded, squinting slightly, projecting a smug, calculating command of his subject. Carter noticed and did not like the hint of condescension. "We have databases that track a great deal," Goldblat said. "If you have a name or other identifying source, we can crosscheck our records, as a secondary to what your own government already has on file. We can also search for those with engineering course work and cross-check with U.S. records on who entered your country. We can't share everything, but I am told to cooperate. After all, if Islamist terrorists are responsible, we don't want to leave them free to strike Israel."

"Have there been any further conclusions about the foreign connection, from what Frank told you?" Taylor asked.

"Not any more than I have heard on CNN. But this latest package of papers at the restaurant gives me trouble. It seems like just a game, and terrorists usually stay with serious targets. It does not fit the profile." He leaned back in his chair. "But it did get publicity for them."

A waiter interrupted to take their drink orders, and everyone took the break to study the menus. With quick decisions on rib-eye steak and grilled wild salmon, they ordered their main course as well. Taylor then immediately turned to Goldblat, intent on keeping the meeting focused on business and not playing the babysitter she knew that she was. "If I give you the name of an engineer, can you look into that person's past and into connections the family might have?"

"I can do my best."

Taylor tore a sheet from her notebook, wrote down Achmed Andawi and an address, and slid the slip to Goldblat. "He's not a suspect," she said, "but he's a Palestinian by origin and an employee of Scott's firm. I'd like to know more about him and about his family, just to see if there's something in his past that we don't know about."

Carter had seen the name as she wrote it and looked at Taylor in disappointment. "There's no way this guy could be involved. Didn't you interview him today?"

"I did," Taylor said, "but I'd be irresponsible not checking it out."

"Did he have access to the engineering drawings that Scott feels were essential for placing the bombs?" Goldblat inquired.

"He did," Taylor said, turning to Carter. "I haven't had a chance to brief you yet, but your systems administrator showed me your firm's file management system and the check-in and check-out log for the design files. It gave me a history of who accessed those electronic files in the last few years."

Carter waited for more but did not get anything. His eye's questioned Taylor's.

"I'll give you a run-down," Taylor said, "but if you'll excuse me, I'd prefer not to do it here in the open."

Carter nodded but was taken aback that she had gone into the BWE file management log without him at her side. He had thought they were partners.

Goldblat broke in to wipe out the lull. "The frightening part is that you do not need to be a technical expert to do great damage. You can just be a simple man like Timothy McVeigh and half a building, and the people in it, are gone." Goldblat shook his head at the prospects. "The United States is still very, very vulnerable. I notice all the parking garages under the buildings here in Rosslyn, and like other cities, some are clearly marked for public parking. Anyone can drive in with a bomb. They can leave the car and keep the parking ticket as a memory. No need to be a suicide martyr."

"No question," Carter said, "and if you add the technical knowledge, that scares the daylights out of me."

Goldblat smiled. "Nothing worse than an insane engineer."

When the food arrived, no one could dredge up any more topics that resembled serious business, and the conversation slipped to official small talk. Soon enough, Goldblat had to leave for the airport, and Taylor used her cell phone to call for a cab.

When Goldblat had finally been packed away in his taxi to catch his flight, Carter and Taylor returned to their table. Carter immediately asked Taylor for more on the file management log. He was still annoyed that she had left him out of it. "So what did you find in our access records?"

Taylor shrugged. "I don't really know. You and Andawi both show up. Your own dates, besides the initial design, come after the bombing, which fits your story. Andawi says he looked at the files for reference on another project. Does that sound plausible to you?"

"Completely. So am *I* at least in the clear now?"

Taylor smiled. "As the original designer, maybe you wouldn't need the drawings to know where to place those bombs."

The good-humored warmth beneath Taylor's professional front always cut deep into Carter, as though she had opened the window from a neat, carefully furnished parlor to the sun and grass of an unkept spring garden.

"You are tenacious, aren't you?" Carter said, unable to hold back a smile of his own.

"Do you really think I'd have you assist me if I thought you were a serious suspect? You do realize that the FBI checked you out before they OK'd your partnership."

"It doesn't look like I've been much assistance. You went into those file records without me. How come?"

Unruffled, Taylor said, "It was never our plan to pass everything by you. I interviewed your systems man and we went right to it. You're a busy man too. Do you want me tracking you down every time I have a request someone else can fill?

"I guess not," Carter lied.

"What I'd like you to do now is go through that log yourself and see if there's any access that looks unusual, somebody who wouldn't have a natural need for the information. My only worry is that anyone with the smarts to pull off this job would know he'd leave electronic footprints."

Taylor waved to the waiter for the check. "Let's get back to business. What do you think of Mr. Babcock's offer for help? Would he be able to open some doors for us?"

Carter had no choice but to step back into line. "I suppose so," he said, "but with a battering ram. Personally, I'd prefer to have nothing to do with the guy. But if he can pull some strings on his connections, I suppose I shouldn't let personalities get in the way."

"I thought he had a certain cold, calculating charm. He makes you think he can get things done."

"The latter I won't argue with," Carter said.

Taylor looked at her watch, then rose to gather her coat as the waiter delivered the bill. Taylor gave him her credit card and said they would wait at the door to sign. She turned to Carter. "Suddenly I'm in a hurry. I have to run an errand before I get back to your firm for more interviews."

As Taylor put one arm into her coat, Carter lifted the other side, careful not to touch her. She turned her head in a quick thank you, and Carter saw the smooth slope of her throat as though, for an instant, she had offered it for a kiss.

"So you'll look into that log?" Taylor asked as she signed the receipt at the hostess station.

"I will," Carter said

Down on the street Carter raised his collar against the cold. He could see his breath in a gray-white plume and glanced for a moment through that personal mist as Taylor waved good-bye and walked down the street to the Metro.

Back at his office, Carter wanted to move right to the electronic log and then to the ANC repair project but felt compelled to get rid of the red message light. He picked up the phone, dialed in his password, and heard the computerized voice announce that his mailbox had four unheard messages.

At the second message, Carter paused. Dr. Blake had called. Carter should stop by that afternoon for the results of his biopsy.

At 3:15 p.m. Carter walked fast through the cold to reach his appointment, trying to analyze the tone of the doctor's message—but there had been no nuance, just the uninflected words. Why hadn't the doctor given him some concrete news,

Carter asked himself in irritation. If everything was all right, the doctor could have just said so immediately, right there in the message. "Mr. Carter, everything looks good" was all he had to spit out. It wouldn't have taken any more time, no matter how busy the guy's schedule. But obviously the doctor had not said that. He had just asked him to come, and Carter had to admit that it made perfect sense—you don't give bad news through voicemail. Not even Dr. Blake would be that callous, Carter thought, even though the man was not known to be a charmer. Or could the guy just be forgetful? Carter could imagine Dr. Blake shuffling through his calls and forgetting that it was not just routine news to the receiver. Yeah, he could imagine that. The doctor would drone through his call-backs and not personalize anything.

But as Carter entered the Rosslyn building where Dr. Blake had run his practice for the past ten years, Carter thought, "Don't kid yourself. The first scenario looks a hell of a lot more likely."

Carter ducked into the stairwell and climbed fast to the second floor.

The door to the doctor's office opened to the antiseptic smell of alcohol and disinfectant, and to the sudden sense that such a white, clinical environment, with its uncomfortable aroma and awkward memories, had become the key to Carter's future.

Carter signed himself in and sat down next to a table littered with old magazines. He felt too impatient to read, but sitting in a chair doing nothing became increasingly unpleasant. Finally, he reached for a *Sports Illustrated* and leafed to the first mention of the Washington Redskins to see what the national press was saying about the local team. He had gotten through ten minutes of that when the nurse called him in. Of course, Carter knew what that meant. He was merely transferred to a private examination room to wait even more. And then he sat, looking at the four walls and the black throne of an examination table protected by a fresh white sheet of paper that unrolled for unending sickness. He could not really bring himself to read and stared out the window at an office across the street. A man sat at a desk working diligently, apparently absorbed in what he was doing. Carter envied the man.

The sound of the door surprised him. Dr. Blake walked in quickly, shook Carter's hand, and sat down in the swivel chair in front of the corner desk. The *Sports Illustrated* lay in a tight tube at Carter's side.

Dr. Blake showed no emotion, offering his welcoming small talk with the cool pace of someone who has seen too much messy suffering to acknowledge any more of it, indifferent that the sick expected an immediate hint of their future. The manner had never bothered Carter. He had picked this doctor because of some good professional recommendations and the convenient proximity to work, ignoring his own secretary's complaint that Blake lacked warmth.

When the doctor got to the real point, his routine delivery seemed strangely incongruous.

"I'm afraid the results were not what we wanted to see, Mr. Carter. The biopsy found malignant melanoma. That's a serious skin cancer. The treatment and danger depends on how deep the tumor has grown. I've taken the liberty to make an appointment with Dr. Stern, a dermatologist and skin cancer specialist. He's right in this building, and we've checked that he'll take your insurance."

Everything had moved too quickly. Carter sensed that Blake was ready to close the consultation and defer everything to Dr. Stern. Carter wanted some facts. "What are we talking about here? I've obviously heard of melanoma, but I don't know the prognosis."

"I'd really prefer that Dr. Stern give you an examination and have him explain the options."

"That's fine, but before I get there, I'd like to know what I'm dealing with. I assume melanoma can kill me."

Dr. Blake shrugged, as though he had no choice but to give in to Carter's wishes. "It can be fatal, but that depends on how far the tumor has progressed. If it's still in the epidermis, the outer layer of the skin, recovery rates are very high."

"How high?"

"Maybe ninety percent."

"And if it's gotten below the epidermis?"

"Then there's a greater danger of metastasis, of the cancer cells migrating through the lymph system to other parts of the neighboring skin or to other parts of the body."

"And a new cancer can then start in some other place?"

"Yes it can," said Dr. Blake.

"And what if it's a minor case and you treat it. What are the chances of recurrence?"

"I don't remember the exact figures. You'll have to ask Dr. Stern about that. But for someone who has had one tumor, the chances of having another later are always much higher."

Carter took a deep breath to force back the sudden weight on his chest. For a moment he had found refuge in the technical facts and statistical details, but he again faced a void as Dr. Blake stood up to leave.

"Is this Stern a good doctor?" Carter asked.

"I rate him very highly. You can ask others and they'll tell you the same. He's on the third floor. You'll be in good hands."

Carter did not appreciate the short shrift Dr. Blake made of the news, but what did he want, Carter asked himself, for

Dr. Blake to hold his hand? He did not need a shrink to get him through this, and Dr. Stern could answer the essential questions.

Dr. Blake shook Carter's hand with a tight squeeze—apparently his sign for encouragement—and left for his next patient. Carter stopped at the front desk, settled his insurance co-payment, and asked for the suite number of Dr. Stern. The receptionist told him 375.

The corridor outside Dr. Blake's office, familiar from such a short time ago, now seemed narrower and the surroundings more confined. A space that Carter had entered with the hope for complete absolution had now been transformed by the insertion of fact, closing off the one wished-for outcome and cloaking all the rest in a vibrant uncertainty. From now on, not a single scenario allowed a complete, unchecked escape—ever—for the rest of his life.

This time Carter waited for the elevator, expectant about the next confrontation with news. Standing in that silence, he thought about the many times in his life he had imagined a brutal brush with death, often after reading newspaper accounts of a car-jacking, or a mugging, or a burglary in someone's home. He had always liked to think he would stand firm in such circumstances, overcome his fear, and stare down the risk with some toughness and a little dignity. He did not want to cheapen his last moments with whimpering, and he had taken pride in his reactions during the ANC bombing. But somehow that had all been easier—the outward, threatening environment offered options for a personal strike-back, allowed his own ingenuity to combat the enemy. Now he stood powerless, unable to perceive the danger in his own body, feeling no less healthy than he had one hour ago, realizing that he had no way of laying hands on the force that now worked inside him. He would be dependent on others' treatment and others' advice. It was like being a kid again, his life no longer wholly his own to protect. He resented that hollowness.

Upstairs, Dr. Stern did not make Carter wait long. A tall, thin man, he entered the examination room with a bony smile and threw out a few get-to-know-you questions. Carter politely laid down the law as a way to buttress his own self-respect.

"I appreciate your taking me on such short notice," Carter said, "and since we don't know each other, I just wanted to request how I'd like us to deal with this. I don't want any sugar-coating. I like to work with facts, and I want to know the real prospects, no matter how pessimistic. I know doctors don't like to say negative things when the possibility for the positive still exists. That's all well and good, but for me that looks like a lie that denies me the chance for real judgment. Can we agree on that?"

Dr. Stern accepted the speech with equanimity. "You call the shots," he said, "but I won't go out of my way to alarm you. There are too many variables."

"I just want to know all the variables," Carter said. "I know there's never one right answer."

"So let's take a look at you," Dr. Stern said. "Please take off your shirt and lie face down on the examination table."

Carter obeyed, and Dr. Stern laid his long fingers on Carter's back and began pressing lightly around Carter's tumor, then on top of it. To Carter, the fingers felt cool and aggressive, but after two quick rounds, the doctor was done.

"You can sit up," Dr. Stern said.

Carter raised himself, the paper crumpling and crackling beneath him, and sat facing the doctor.

"I'm reasonably confident the melanoma is still in the epidermis," Dr. Stern said, "but it's a borderline case. There's a chance it has already descended to the dermis. Are you familiar with those terms?"

"Dr. Blake explained them. He said that if it's reached the dermis, there's a bigger chance that I'm toast—if you'll pardon my translation."

Dr. Stern smiled. "That's right, if you want to put it that way. The cancer cells have a much greater chance of migrating."

Carter nodded.

"So here's what we're going to do," Dr. Stern said. "Dr. Blake has already arranged through me to have minor surgery done at Alexandria Hospital on the day after tomorrow. A Dr. Samson will do the honors, a very fine and experienced cancer as well as plastic surgeon. I'll be there, and we'll try it with local anesthesia, but if we need to make you more comfortable, we'll put you out. What we'll do is examine the cancer under the knife to make a more precise determination of how deep it's gone and how it might be spreading. The more shallow the tumor, the less we'll have to cut out. If the removal goes beyond a certain point, we'll take some skin from the inside of your leg to help plug the hole. If it's warranted, we may also inject some radioactive dye and scan to see which lymph node would be the first to get a migrating cancer cell. We might then do a biopsy on that lymph node. Odds are we'll have you out of there in a jiffy, the same day."

"And then what?"

"If things have spread, there are various options—radiation, chemotherapy, or biological therapy—but to be honest, I don't see your cancer having progressed to the point where the potential, unknown benefits are worth the hard physical side effects of the treatment."

"Would radiation reduce the risk of the cancer spreading?"

"Not necessarily. And it wouldn't be that appropriate in your case. It's usually used when cancer cells have reached the liver or the brain."

"What's the biological treatment?"

"That's where we give you drugs to help your own immune system fight the cancer cells. But you can have flu-like symptoms, headaches, nausea. Again, we usually restrict clinical trials to those whose cancers have reached into the dermis and there's evidence the cells might spread."

"I guess the side-effects of chemotherapy are what you read about in the newspaper."

"They can be quite devastating, depending on the dose. Chemotherapy also kills healthy cells, so it's not a treatment you take lightly. In my book, you need a greater mortality risk to use it in an unproved fashion."

Carter weighed the options. The basic outline of the situation seemed to make sense—just remove the sick flesh.

"So let's go ahead with the knife," Carter said. "We'll have to do that one way or the other. After that procedure, what are the survival rates?"

"Overall, about eighty percent of those who are diagnosed with malignant melanoma survive the disease."

"So twenty percent die," said Carter.

"If you care to put it like that. But we're talking about all cases, serious and minor. In that context, the five-year survival rate is about seventy-two percent, but if the cancer is localized, as I would hope your case is, that jumps to ninety percent. Of course, the thickness of the cancer becomes very important in all this. For thin melanomas, the probability of a recurrence within ten years is less than ten percent."

"So there's always a chance a tumor will come back, no matter what."

"That's right. In all this, we never really talk about the cancer being cured. We talk in terms of remission."

"How soon might I know whether the cancer has spread?"

"That's impossible to say," Dr. Stern said. "It can be years."

"I was thinking about a lower limit. How soon after the operation might I know that I've got a more serious problem?"

"The soonest from my experience?"

"I suppose that'll do."

"OK. Within a few weeks."

For a while, Carter found asylum in the hard-nosed goal of getting back to work. He walked to his office, slapping shut his emotional shutters so that the news merely vibrated at the edges, while at the center, he grit his teeth and plowed ahead with what others expected of him. An unconscious voice kept telling him that feeling sorry for himself was the sign of a loser.

At the office, Carter did not say anything to anyone. The idea of telling his colleagues looked too distasteful. It would be like fishing for sympathy, then having to stand there and acknowledge the awkward, embarrassed condolences while they debated how they could finally escape without looking callous, while he coaxed them inwardly that yes, they were allowed to run away, immediately, that they could not do anything for him anyway.

Carter told his secretary to hold all calls, then closed the door to his office. On the computer, he pulled up the electronic file management log, stumbling here and there where he did not remember the commands, but finally getting a clear picture. Since completion of the ANC project, only four people had accessed the structural files—Carter, Andawi,

Thompson, and Jacobs. That did not look unusual. All had worked on similar building projects and had probably looked at the plans for reference. That's exactly what Andawi had told Taylor.

Carter made notes and entered them into a short written report for Taylor, telling her that she was the one who should raise the issue with Thompson and Jacobs—he himself would have a hard time probing without bias. Carter also knew that the BWE electronic logs were probably a dead end. The hard-copy drawings could have been copied at any number of places.

As Carter slipped the notes into an envelope and sealed it, he looked out the window at a sliver of sunset knifing the late afternoon gray, gilding a window on the high bank of the Potomac in Georgetown. The light glowed for a moment, as though the glass had melted into a liquid flame, then faded as the wind-borne clouds closed all gaps to the outer world. Carter felt a sudden draw to be out in that brilliance, jogging across the Key Bridge, his eyes squinting to the light and his legs and arms pumping. And suddenly Carter could no longer keep his emotional shutters completely down. He decided to go home, hoping that some new surroundings would straighten him out.

Carter shut down his computer, grabbed his coat from the rack, and opened his office door. He knew his pace looked too fast, and he forced himself to slow down as he handed the log report to his secretary, asking her to deliver it to Taylor. "I've got to run," he said. "If Bob calls, tell him I'll be in touch later today. At least I'll try."

Carter did not wait for questions and started down the hall, but as he came to the exit, he thought of Andawi on the other side of that floor. Would a visit be interpreted as meddling in the investigation? Carter did not think it would, and at the moment he did not really care. He entered that wing and found Andawi at his desk, a small, dark-skinned man about Carter's age with a high-pitched laugh and a quick, quiet smile. Andawi looked up from his computer screen in pained surprise.

"Is the FBI treating you OK?" Carter asked.

Andawi shrugged. "What can I say?"

"They're just doing their job," said Carter. "You've got nothing to worry about. I've been speaking up for you."

"I appreciate it," he said.

"It's a knee-jerk reaction because of where you're from. They don't know you, so they're digging around."

"Unfortunately, that's often how it works."

Carter nodded.

"Are you heading out?" Andawi asked.

"Yeah. I've got some things I've gotta do."

"Take care," said Andawi.

Carter did not know what else to say. He ducked out before having to explain himself.

In the winter, it was always dark before Carter drove home along the Potomac, the illuminated monuments and the city lights a guide for his self-contained capsule, smooth jazz on a CD and thoughts from work losing some of their intensity. But today, the gray afternoon light consigned him to a barren openness, with the silence from the radio and a glance in the rearview mirror poised to catch him off guard.

At home, Carter walked to his bedroom, changed into a sweat shirt and sweat pants, and sat down at the phone by his bed. He did not want to, but he had to call Waynewright. He would be missing a day of work for the minor surgery, and Waynewright had to know. Carter stamped out his reluctance and dialed. The assistant picked up, and Carter waited for the familiar voice.

"Scott, where're you hiding?" Waynewright asked, making it sound like a question from a game show.

"I went home," Carter said.

"What's up? Your office computer break down?"

"No, I got some news from my doctor and I'm going to be out at least a full day on the day after tomorrow. I've apparently got some skin cancer. No big deal, but they're going to cut."

Waynewright's voice had suddenly slipped to half its normal volume. "I'm sorry to hear it," he said, finding it hard to squeeze bluster into compassion. "Well . . ." He groped for words that might show a trace of concern. "Don't worry about anything here. I assume we'll manage. We don't really have a new angle for a news conference anyway."

Carter had actually looked forward to another shot at the public. He liked sorting out things for the average person to understand, and despite his protests to Waynewright, he had been drawn by the charge of a big audience. He wondered whether his fifteen minutes of fame had now passed.

"When did you say you'd be back?" Waynewright asked.

"I'll be there tomorrow; then I'll be gone the next day. Do me one favor, OK?"

"Shoot."

"Don't spread this news to anybody. I don't want things getting sappy. We can tell people as we need to."

"All right. I'll try to gum up the rumor mill. Now, you get some rest and then I expect you to beat this thing. Ya hear?"

"I hear," Carter said.

Carter hung up, glad he had gotten that behind him but not sure what to do with himself. He walked downstairs to the kitchen and there stepped out the back door into the small, walled-in garden and the gathering darkness. A large oak tree rose black to a small section of cloud-covered sky, the trunk encircled by an antique wrought-iron bench. Narrow flagstone paths created a miniature walkway amid the brown-green grass, the empty flower beds, and the leafless vines climbing the high brick walls bordering the back alley and the street. Carter had always kidded Linda that she had created an exquisite miniature prison yard for convicts to walk off some pent-up energy—except the prisoners would not get this nice bench for tea and cakes. Linda had never failed to remind him that the prisoners, unlike Carter, could not walk out the gate to the street.

Carter took in his own contribution—a landscaped, tiled drainage grid that kept the water from collecting near the house, sending it neatly into the back-alley gutter. He remembered the kid-like thrill of the first rain after completion, watching the quick streams of water shunt as directed, like an electric train track hurtling a small locomotive through tunnels under a Christmas tree. He remembered what an old coot of a professor had once told him back in college—civil engineering all came down to one thing: drainage.

But the idea of design work now only pained him. So that was how it worked, Carter thought. Just when you thought you were breaking out, when your work suddenly takes a turn toward design, when the boss himself has reassigned you and plotted to redirect your duties, when you meet a woman that takes your breath away; when all that happens, the doctor calls and cuts you down to size and says you might not be able to look forward to anything. Jesus, how does fate have a right to do that?

Carter found himself looking at the ground, breathing the fresh air through his nose, his teeth pressed together. So that was it. His life had become a crapshoot of statistics, points on a mathematical curve. He could be that one impersonal data-point that fits low on the probability scale and dies after a few months, or that slightly better bet of living until old age cuts him down like the rest of the human race. Or he could be somewhere in-between. So what good did these statistics do? He could argue as hard as he wanted that he fit into the ninety percent that did not have a recurrence—if his tumor fit the bill on thickness—but he could never discard the other tenth of the equation. It was always out there, a Cheshire cat smiling in the tree, shining probabilities with its sharp, thin teeth, telling him with its cut-throat eyes that he just may be the one that the cat swallows today. What good were the facts and the numbers when it was all an unknown? What the hell good were they?

Carter lifted his head and walked back into the house.

7

Michelle Taylor looked at her watch. It was nearly 10:00 p.m. and she could think of no more excuses not to call Colin. He had left messages at carefully spaced intervals—7:00, 8:00, and 9:00 p.m.—demanding to know why he could not see her this weekend, insisting that even a high-profile FBI investigation left a person a few hours of private life. He wanted to know what was going on.

Taylor had realized for weeks that it would get to this point, and now with the bombing and the profound commitment to the investigation, she would have to make herself and Colin face facts. She could no longer continue the dead end path of lessening her interactions with polite excuses.

That night, she had listened to the answering machine for each of his calls, wondering what she could possibly say if she picked up. For a while she could have told the truth—she was doing investigative homework and did not want to be interrupted, but now she was too tired to scan any more dossiers and reports, and she fully expected Colin, in his irritatingly regular fashion, to call again at 10:00.

Taylor knew what she finally had tell him: They should

not see each other for a while; she needed a break. But he would demand explanations, and that was what she dreaded. Taylor stood up, walked to a dining room cabinet, and pulled out a wine glass and an open bottle of cabernet. She poured the glass full and returned to the couch in the living room, her loose flannel pajamas swaying comfortably across her limbs, her fur-lined moccasins warm on her feet. Taylor had splurged on a few pieces of furniture—a black leather couch with matching easy-chair and a glass coffee table on a flat black, Z-shaped metal frame—but the rest of her townhouse showed a more practical elegance, with a lot of white and black assemble-yourself items from IKEA and some modern finds from local second-hand sales. She kept her townhouse neat, but not compulsively spotless, and whenever she cleaned, she kept a few things tossed randomly on the tables to make sure she felt at home. Now, during her work, papers surrounded the couch like a brim-full moat.

It was high time to let Colin go, she thought. He had lost that irresistible glow of their first six months together, when what had captured her was the brash sensuality of his loose hair blowing in the breeze from his BMW convertible. A good lawyer with a top salary, he had flaunted his good looks and classic clothes with relaxed confidence and drawn Taylor with a winning smile, squash-court body, and brisk conversation. But what had once been his playful chuckle about her down-to-earth work habits and crime-fighting dedication had now taken on the air of superiority. He had grown used to her presence at his condominium and grown testy when she now wanted more time for herself, as though he unconsciously perceived her as a property that his charm and money had bought on installment and had now paid off. Taylor began to see more subsurface, pedantic quirks that undermined her image of a rich spirit fully in control. She saw more instances of petty habits and self-centered viewpoints. This was not the first time this had happened to her.

At 9:55 Taylor decided to take charge and call Colin herself.

As soon as he heard her voice, he broke in. "Michelle, I've been trying to reach you. Have you actually been out working all night?"

"I've been here working. I just couldn't be interrupted."

Colin grew silent on the other end, as though holding back his irritation. His words came out flat and quiet. "So basically you've been avoiding my calls."

"I delayed getting back to you," Taylor said firmly, determined not to make this an emotional scene.

"Can I see you tomorrow night?"

"Colin . . ." Taylor took a deep breath. "Let's be honest. Here it is straight. I don't think we should see each other anymore. At least not for a while." There, she had said it.

He paused. "What are you talking about?"

"I'm just not sure if things are working out, and I can't have a relationship half-way."

Colin became incredulous, like a trial lawyer playing to the jury with a recalcitrant witness. "What are you confused about? Things have been great between us. Where are you suddenly digging this up?"

"I really don't want to talk about it. Things have happened."

"What, have you met someone else?"

"Don't be ridiculous."

"You've met someone else, haven't you?" A pain had entered his voice, this time not as a play for the jury but from within himself. "Who is it? I at least have a right to know that."

Taylor bit her lip and would not let herself be swayed. "Colin, there are no rights in these things."

"So you admit it."

"I told you it's nonsense."

"I love you Michelle. I'm going to come over there right now so we can talk this out. I can't stop seeing you while you feed me these mysteries. I have to know what's happening."

Taylor did not doubt he would come and did not doubt he would continue to pursue her. He would never admit someone could reject him. "All right," Taylor said, faltering somewhat, "I'll lay it on the table, but only on the condition that you don't come back with all sorts of arguments and protests. I just don't want to discuss it."

"OK."

"Do I have your word?"

"Didn't I already give it?" The irritation had again found its way into his voice but he quickly repressed it. "Yes, you have my word."

"All right," Taylor said, breathing in deeply. "I just don't feel I have your respect anymore. I think you look down on me, and for that matter, our sex life simply hasn't worked for a while."

"What?"

"Are you asking me to repeat it?"

"I just don't understand."

"There's nothing to understand. It's not logical. It's not analyzable. It's just how I feel and it's too powerful a feeling to ignore. I'm sorry."

"You've hit me with a baseball bat. What am I supposed to do?"

"Just say you'll respect my wishes."

"I want to see you, Michelle."

"I know you Colin. You'll do just fine without me. Trust me."

"I don't think so."

"Just give it some time. I'm sorry. I have to go now. I didn't want this to happen. Good-bye."

When Taylor hung up, she could tell from the shock in Colin's voice that she had headed off a relentless pursuit. She felt bad about being so curt, but she knew nothing else would have worked. He thought too much of himself to believe another could be sincere in anything that went against him. He would always suspect an ulterior motive.

Taylor now had the task of putting her own emotional house in order and deciding where to go from here. Just stay away from all the nice, clamoring men and stick to the investigation, she told herself firmly.

For an hour now, Jack Bleeker had cruised the streets and highways in his brown Econoline van looking for road repair and utility crews, and he was getting ticked that he could not call it quits. In the winter, he would not find many maintenance sites on the road, and when he did find them, they were not sufficiently isolated.

"You'd think I could've gotten some dope on where these guys are working," Bleeker said to himself. "I'm burnin' gas when I could've just bought the fuckin' signs on the Internet."

But Bleeker made money by doing what he was told, and the command last fall—when he had made his first round of heists—had been "no purchase records" and "low-risk theft." Now he had gotten an anonymous call that had outlined where he could find the down-payment for a follow-up. Full payment came when he delivered the goods. He did not know who had hired him, and he got paid for not asking questions. It sounded nuts not buying from a simple supply shop, he thought. Somehow this client must be paranoid.

"Who the hell wants road repair signs," he cursed to himself, tossing a cigarette out the window, spitting after it. The order had been for a full set of gear, including signs and flags. His orders had said one theft maximum from any crew, to make the crew think it was all a college prank for some catchy dorm-room decorations.

Bleeker now turned from the I-295 bypass around Richmond, Virginia, and merged onto Route 301 heading south, looking for one last "Road Narrows" diamond on its aluminum tripod. He preferred a high-speed road so that the warning signs stood far from the actual work. He would then simply pull over, lift the sign into the back of the van, and drive on. He had splattered his license plate with mud just in case somebody spotted him.

Bleeker hoped for a major pipe repair that left its equipment standing overnight, but now in the dark, he wanted to get off the road to a bar and was ready to try the next crew he could find. It was just a matter of driving up and down every road around town and hoping to run into something. At least they were paying him good money, he thought. They just should have made up their minds for the whole heist in the fall when the crews were still out in force, or hell, knock out a water main themselves. Why go through this nonsense now?

It was dark before Bleeker finally came across a cherry picker parked near a utility pole with a big orange diamond blocking off half of the far-right lane. A man worked intently at the top of the pole, facing away from the sign, and as Bleeker drove by slowly, he saw the second man sitting inside the truck away from the cold, nursing a thermos of coffee. "Bingo," Bleeker thought. Bleeker pulled left at the next street and circled around to re-enter the road four blocks away.

There, he waited at the curb for a large break in traffic. It took only five minutes to materialize. Bleeker looked at the repair men—nothing had changed in their position—and pulled his van down the street. He coasted closer, keeping his motor noise low, and stopped right in front of the sign. Now he just had to act naturally, swinging out his door as though he was just going to enter the strip mall off to his right.

Bleeker took one last glance at the workmen, then opened the back doors of the van, stepped over to the sign, and lifted it in. Coolly, he pressed the doors closed, careful not to slam, and got back into the driver's seat. As he made a sharp U-turn away from the workers, he heard a shout. "Hey, what the heck're you doing?!"

Damn! Bleeker thought. The guy in the truck must have seen him in his rearview mirror. Bleeker gunned the van and turned at the first side street. He knew there was no way the cherry picker could chase him, but he wanted to get out of there fast in case the guy called the cops. That was all he needed, he thought. Instead of a bar, he now had to hit the back roads and return to DC in the dead of night. He did not think the police would post an APB for someone stealing a goddamn sign—hell, the repair crew might not even call it in—but he was not going to take any chances.

Just make the delivery, he told himself. He couldn't care less what the client was going to do with the stuff.

He probably would not have believed it if they had told him.

Jackhammer sat in bed and glared at the TV. His head had been aching for hours and nothing he had taken had done any good. He could barely tolerate the sound of CNN, but he needed something to fill the night void.

A news item finally caught his attention. An editor hurt in the ANC blast had died of his injuries, bringing the death toll to twelve. Well, good for him, Jackhammer thought. The guy's got no more headaches, and he isn't polluting the world with his blasted liberal pen. That's the kind of bonus I'll take any day—immorality and weakness purged from society.

Jackhammer pressed the fingers of his right hand to his forehead and turned down the sound with his left. The constant pain had pushed his thoughts toward victimized impatience, and only his sense of purpose maintained a satisfaction.

Over the past months, Jackhammer had learned to sidetrack the disgust of his imminent death with a calculated urge to tear something down. So many years of his engineer life had been geared toward building—moving and molding earth, concrete, and steel. And what recognition had it gotten him? Nothing. All he ever heard was weak-kneed whiners. Well, destruction was going to get their attention—and not just mindless blasts, but carefully planned scenarios that would showcase the power of design and modern society's iron-grip dependence on the gifts of people like him.

National Engineers Week was just around the corner, and Jackhammer grunted in contempt at the thought of student bridge-building contests and misguided engineers going into schools to talk up technology and their profession, as if that would do any good with those school-kid degenerates. He had devised something better to get the world's attention—his brainchild with electric power. He knew it was not original. He had read the bestsellers and seen the made-for-TV movies that spooned up similar plots, but those stories were all fiction and media speculation. His genius, he thought, was in bringing that to life. Taking the idea and making it reality. His only regret was being lumped with that Islamist terrorist slime, but he had not found an alternative. Get some cover after the first creation to push ahead with the second. He was willing, if reluctantly, to pay that price.

Everything was in place, and once he gave the go-ahead, he would make his announcement: Rosslyn had been turned upside down courtesy of Jackhammer. He'd dispense with the Islamist smoke screen—if they hadn't figured it out already—and start letting them search for the real mastermind.

Oh, he could take all comers. By the time they had something to chew on, the third and final phase of his trilogy would be buried and waiting. He could set it off at will, and even if they caught him, there was nothing they could do. He sneered at their impotence. He was indestructible, because he was already dead. They were dealing with absolute power, absolute death. Nothing could scare him because he had been stripped of life and risen to a new plain of grandeur.

It must have been preordained, he thought. Why else would he have been blessed with such a rich wife who had politely died and left him her fortune? Oh, it had taken discipline not to go out and spend it on the outward glitz of wealth. He had invested wisely and then bought a whole network of anonymous help. Large bundles of cash made things so easy for a man who could think things out and harness others in the construction of his own advantage. Negotiations had been simple, since a fair price did not matter. He could not take the money with him.

Even the little sidelights seemed like gifts from a greater force. How else could he explain the spectacle of Scott Carter suddenly getting mixed up in everything up to his eyeballs, and providing such keen diversions of manipulation, as though Jackhammer had returned to his childhood and been given a nice grasshopper to poke, prod, and dismember, and then finally squash.

The next day at the office, Carter sat down at his desk and looked out the window. Every day the office had provided an automatic activity switch. No matter how routine the day's tasks might have been—or mildly distasteful, given his sales work—he found himself getting fully involved, moving from one item to the next, or devoting the whole day to a major initiative, the time flowing quickly until the day had disappeared. He took pride in his productivity and never dreaded coming to work. If anything, he thought the time passed too quickly and left him coming up short on what he hoped to accomplish. Work had become an automatic pilot that Carter called dedication and that his superiors rewarded with promotions.

That morning, the switch had not turned on. For a moment, the uncertainty of his cancer shimmered within the everyday view of his life, as though a slight, nearly undetectable quake shook the earth that he had always considered so stable. He could not quite focus on what he saw out the window.

The silence caught him off guard and left him questioning what he was supposed to do. Why had the doctors even given him this day of limbo before the operation? What if the cancer had not yet spread and yet exactly that day, a first malignant cell had pulled lose and begun its slow journey to other parts of his body? He would have been killed by scheduling. But the doctors must know what they're doing, he repeated to himself. They can't be totally irresponsible.

One question pushed the others aside. What if tomorrow the surgeon found a deep, dangerous cancer? Why be conscientious at work today? How could he justify focusing on the office when he might just have to regroup his whole outlook?

Each question stretched his uncertainty until finally he just told himself: Get off this garbage. He was letting a chicken-livered weakness knock him out of his habits. He turned on the computer and let it crank through the boot-up. An email from Taylor brought Carter fully back. She wanted to see him at 8:30 that morning. Carter glanced at his watch—it said 8:02. Suddenly, those twenty-eight minutes looked like a very long time.

Taylor's natural, unpretentious beauty hit Carter particularly hard that day. The image of her striding into the room in her pants suit dispelled any last denials of where he had fallen. Her radiant vitality made his first moments of concentration difficult. She looked like a better alternative to dying.

"We've got a breakthrough on the bombs," Taylor said, "but maybe not what we'd hoped for. Forensics got ID numbers on two of the three vans used in the bombing. They found most of the bits and could put them together. Both vans were stolen and repainted, so we suspect the third was stolen as well. What it means is that we don't have a rental that's going to give us an identification like in the original World Trade Center bombing."

"I guess nobody's going to be that stupid again."

"A shame, isn't it?"

"So what does the FBI do now?"

"We've got a whole group of agents checking out the thefts, seeing if there were any witnesses, checking where the vans were stolen from, where they might have been painted." Taylor shook her head and looked at Carter with a troubled questioning. "If our bomber's an engineer, is he also a professional car thief?"

"Probably not."

"Right, so we've got hired hands, or a group of like-minded people. We probably don't have just a lone, mad bomber."

"Or we've got al Qaeda."

"That's not our scope of work."

"OK," Carter said, "let's stick to domestic involvement. Is this wider network of helpers good or bad for us?"

"Both. It's bad because it gives the guy more options and power. It's good because we've got more people to track down, more people who can make mistakes and then lead us to the others, more people to talk."

Taylor's rapid-fire involvement kept Carter off balance. With so many sideshows to his morning, he was grateful she was dragging him along, as though in her slipstream.

"So what theory's winning out?" Carter asked. "Islamist terrorists, domestic terrorists, or some madman with resources?"

"Everybody's obviously leaning toward the al Qaeda angle, but we've turned up nothing except the leaflets. No group has called in responsibility except Jackhammer, and all the monitoring we've put into al Qaeda gave no hints that this was going to happen. That doesn't necessarily mean anything, but people are starting to look my way and wonder whether I may be at the heart of the investigation."

"I can't say I have a preference on the killers. I just want to find them."

Taylor nodded. "But one thing I can't figure out is why this Jackhammer latched on to you, why he would bother, and how he would know your whereabouts. Not too many people are going to know about an ASCE Section meeting."

"I suppose you're right there."

"Somebody either got a hold of your schedule or knew from the start that you're involved with that group."

"My secretary might have told someone. I don't keep that schedule a secret."

"I questioned her. She doesn't remember telling anyone except some woman about it."

Carter shrugged. "Well, you already know that the section phone tree contacted nearly every member. They started in the morning. It would have given anyone time to go plant a package of papers."

"It's a crazy question, but do you know anyone in your section capable of doing something like this?"

"I don't know anyone anywhere capable of this," he said.

"The problem is, you can't always recognize it. These psychos don't always show signs. I saw all kinds of case studies in my training, and the outside image isn't always going to reveal the inside, not like in the movies where they like to show the crazy gleam in the madman's eyes."

"The other fact is that it obviously doesn't have to be a section member," Carter said. "The initial newspaper accounts said I was active in ASCE. Whoever read that could just call the national office right up the road in Reston. Hell, the meeting location was posted on the web."

"But why would the man go to the trouble? He knows he can go after you right outside your office every day. Of course, there are more cops prowling here."

Carter looked at the insistent purpose in her eyes. "Doesn't it ever discourage you that you don't really know where to look? You're focusing on the DC area, and this man could be in California, watching the news and deciding he wants to pick on me, and then hiring one of his people to go out and do the dirty work."

Taylor nodded, but without letting herself get down. "It's more depressing than discouraging," she said. "If you're discouraged, you're ready to give up. I hope I don't ever get there. I'm not an old-timer, but I've already learned you take it one little step at a time and look under every little stone. You know that most of your work comes to nothing, but you also know that eventually, after enough stones, you're going to turn up the right one. In most cases, you, or one of your colleagues, eventually gets there."

"It's not the kind of work I'm used to," Carter said. "I may have occasionally gone down a blind design alley if I was trying to be creative, testing a new twist, but I always knew how I got there and had a strong sense of where I might go next and my chances for success. I'd hate to be so dependent on luck."

"There's luck," Taylor admitted, "but if you do good work, you increase your chances of hitting the jackpot." Taylor then squinted, but still keeping her good humor. "Aren't we getting a little off track here?"

Carter smiled. "Yeah, I think I've been a little distracted this morning."

"I don't doubt it," Taylor said. "This Jackhammer would make anyone nervous."

"Right," Carter said. He felt the urge to just throw caution overboard and fish for her sympathy with a curt report on his melanoma and then tell her that—in the meantime—he was crazy about her. Yeah, right, he thought. You do just that. "So what's the agenda?" Carter asked, keeping things strictly business.

"As you suggested, I've made appointments at the Arlington Public Works Department and the construction managers for the ANC building. What was their name?"

"Porter and McGee."

"Right," Taylor said. "We'll see what insights they have on who had access to the design drawings. We've just got to cover all the bases. Are you ready to go?"

"I'm game," said Carter.

The two took Taylor's red Mitsubishi Eclipse to the Arlington Public Works office in the county's government office building. On the way, Carter watched Taylor push through the gears of the five-speed stick with curt authority, but always staying close to the posted speed limit. Carter had expected more low-keyed practicality in a car, and he wondered whether her choice revealed a new side to her character.

Taylor had made individual appointments with Chief Engineer Handley and his two primary subordinates. All three had been with the department for only two years, when the chief engineer had resigned after being passed over for public works director in favor of Freeport. It meant none of the new engineers had been around when planning and approvals for the ANC building had started.

Handley met Taylor and Carter in his large but spare eighth-floor office. It was furnished with government hand-me-downs from the 1980s, and Taylor and Carter sat in chrome-pipe chairs opposite Handley's battleship desk. As was her habit, Taylor cut off the small talk. She asked Handley about the steps of the design and construction approval process and how many offices and people would get their hands on the plans. Disturbingly, the process was as open as Carter had described it earlier—the signed plans had never been considered top-secret materials.

Carter asked if any building inspector had made an unusual or out-of-sequence request for the plans after construction. Someone could have paid off an inspector to provide information.

Handley protested the implication but said he would look into any unusual requests. When Taylor asked him whether any disgruntled employees had worked for the department,

Handley shook his head. As far as he knew, he could vouch for all his staff's integrity—certainly when it came to violent crime. Whether some bad apple beat his wife or shoplifted on the side, he couldn't guarantee.

At Taylor's request, Handley took them on a tour of the document archives, a large room of flat-files that reached halfway to the ceiling. Handley said the department was planning to make all the new storage electronic. They would have preferred the original electronic design files, but they realized engineering software upgrades would eventually make the data obsolete. After all, he said, who can still call up a WordPerfect 1.0 document with all the formatting intact? And WordPerfect 1.0 was not that long ago. That left scanning of paper and PDFs, but the budget was never big enough to get their arms around it. The completely Mylar-free office still looked like a pipe dream.

As they left, Taylor noted that the document room's door-lock could have been opened by any professional thief, and that the drawer holding the ANC plans had no safeguard at all.

Back in the chief engineer's office, Taylor again asked Handley to research his records for any other unusual access and to put a complete list together as soon as he could. When Handley looked to Carter for some reprieve for what he thought was a dead end search, Carter shrugged that he was powerless to intervene.

The meetings with the next two engineers took similar turns. Taylor had hoped for some facts from the trenches, but Taylor got nothing new. According to the engineers, interviewed separately, the permits for water and electrical hook-ups had all followed their usual course. Carter asked if a heavy workload in the transition to the Freeport administration had forced them to hire any private contractors to help in plan review and approval, but both engineers verified that the work had been done in-house. Besides, they did not think county policy would even allow such contracting out.

When Carter and Taylor had finally said their thanks and got back in the car, Taylor gunned the motor in a brief show of frustration.

"So, to your professional ear did it all sound legit?" Taylor asked, pointing them west on Wilson Boulevard on their way to Porter & McGee in Clifton, Virginia.

"It's pretty much what I expected," Carter said.

"Well, we'll need to get more than this if we expect to get anywhere."

On the drive to Clifton, Carter briefed Taylor on how a construction manager fit into the ANC building project. Once ANC had chosen a design firm and then a construction contractor, the company wanted someone to keep everyone in line when it came to schedules, change orders, materials, and the various building trades. Sometimes it could be like holding the reins on a wild chariot, with individual horses taking their turn getting sick or lying down altogether, or bolting off in some side direction. It also gave the owner one-stop-shopping for tantrums if things started to go sour. The CM then had the privilege of passing those tantrums along.

"So that means the CM has access to all the building plans as well?" Taylor asked wearily.

"That's right, and the architectural firm."

Taylor shook her head and looked at Carter with an uncharacteristic sigh.

For Carter, Taylor's candor seemed like a subtle seduction that put a new crack in his defenses. "It's a tough job, no doubt about it," Carter said. "How'd you get into this line of work anyway? Taking the plunge from chemistry and forensics to actually being a field agent is no small dive. Isn't that a little scary?"

"It's not a decision you make in a minute." Taylor hesitated with the next. "In a way, I pushed myself after what happened to my Dad."

Carter did not say anything. He was not ready to pry into something that looked personal, but Taylor went on without prompting.

"My Dad was kidnapped when I was in college, a crazy mistaken identity. We saw what the FBI does and how they can help and how they're awfully good at what they do. In our case, they found the kidnappers but not before the hoodlums had gotten so mad about not getting a big ransom that they killed him." Taylor stared straight at the road. "My older brother was ready to join the Marines, but after what happened, he applied to the FBI. He's now a special agent working in LA." The thought of her brother brought a muted satisfaction to her face. "There's always been something of a competition between us. He said I'd make a good agent too, and hearing his stories, I got attracted, maybe a little to that hint of danger, and he finally convinced me. I told him that eventually, I'd be better than him."

"I'm sorry about your father," Carter said. "Are you happy with your choice? I mean, being an agent?"

Taylor tipped her head back and shrugged. "I'm pretty sure, but there are always days when you wonder which way you might have gone. This bombing case is obviously a turning point. My brother is watching this one real close."

"Why, are you ready to win the family competition?"

Taylor shook her head and smiled, not wanting to take the question seriously. "Not yet," she said. "But hey, if I make a name for myself, I'm ready for a lot more responsibility. I hate to put the pressure on, but it may be a make-or-break kind of thing between an average career and a really good one. Because I'm a woman, I'm sure Gentry is looking extra hard at how I might screw up, despite what the law and the regulations say about equal treatment."

Carter knew he had to come out with the next, and now seemed the best time as any. "Well, I'm not going to deny the pressures, but I'm afraid I've got to duck out on you for the next day or two—some unexpected business." He hated the idea of lying about his operation.

"Oh? Where are you going?"

"Richmond," he said, hoping to keep the lie to one word.

"Well, I'm sure I can handle the architectural firm on my own. But you could have helped with the construction contractor."

Carter smirked. "So you have different takes on those guys?"

"Well, the architects are going to have more accommodating flair, aren't they? They'll be less intimidated by a woman."

Carter could see the sparkle in her eyes. "Are you going to include engineers in your stereotyping?"

"Sure," she said. "But I've got the feeling you can handle it."

On the surface, the meetings at the construction manager turned up nothing. Taylor probed whether the relevant employees might possibly be involved with domestic hate groups or—in a real stretch—have Islamist network ties, and whether any of their engineers had been absent the day of the bombing. Records in human resources revealed that one person had taken that day off as annual leave, but a subsequent interview pointed not to a bombing but to a son's birthday party. Taylor gathered up her new list of names and returned to the office to run checks in the Bureau database, dropping Carter at BWE on the way.

Carter had expected his FBI work to take up most of the day, but now it was only 3:00 p.m., and he felt strangely lost about what to do. His mind drifted to Taylor and to the thought of his operation in the morning, but on checking email, he saw that Waynewright had other ideas on how to kill his afternoon. Waynewright told him to call four reporters as soon as he had the chance—from *The Washington Post, Engineering News Record, Time,* and *Civil Engineering*. Waynewright had promised each of them 20 minutes and reminded Carter to talk up BWE. The email finished with Waynewright wishing Carter well under the knife. "Let's hope they don't slip up and skin you alive," Waynewright added with boundless affection.

Waynewright's second email—with another bright-red high-priority icon—asked Carter to contact a potential client. Fairfax County was looking for some new wastewater capacity and was now hinting at a low-bid approach to pick its engineering firm. Waynewright wanted Carter to talk some sense into them. "I need you because you know the players," Waynewright wrote. "Besides, you've got the best touch for kicking ass without insulting them."

So much for being taken off client relations and marketing work, Carter thought, but he shared Waynewright's impatience with low-bid owners. What were they thinking? Engineering design was a professional service, not some defined product from the hardware shelf at Walmart. How many times had he spit out the logic to local government bureaucrats and private owners who knew nothing about what they were doing? Sure, they could take the low price and feel good about it for a second and moon to the voters that they were fiscally responsible, and then find out that what they got was not exactly what they needed, or would last only half as long and actually cost more for the full life-cycle, or would involve countless, costly change orders once the inadequacies of the low-bid design finally surfaced, or would simply be a piece of crap because they picked an unqualified firm in the first place. Carter remembered one questionable firm that had low-balled a parking garage project and done it by getting rid of the central expansion joint despite the rigid sheer walls outside. The garage was perfectly safe but had no capacity to give to stresses, so the garage just kept developing cracks and the owner had to keep fixing them. Carter wondered if the firm had supplied a crack repair manual as their going away present. Jesus, Carter thought, it was like getting medical services. Do you want the cheaper, Band-Aid procedure that will let you live two years or the slightly more expensive one that might let you live ten? If the doctor knows the up-front price is the only factor, he'll bid the two-year deal and forget about mentioning what would actually do more good. Carter just had to think of his own situation and shake his head. BWE constantly got low-bid requests, putting them on notice to propose the minimum-priced design or lose the contract—in other words, skimp on everything possible and forget about suggesting what might be the best deal for the public.

Carter dialed the Fairfax County official and tried to work up a sales enthusiasm that he did not actually feel. By the time the man answered, Carter had pushed himself, if not to enthusiasm, then to a forced persuasiveness that mixed old-boy casualness with cool insistence. He did not know whether he had changed the man's mind, but as he hung up, he felt as though he were removing a mask and laying the grinning jester back in his drawer.

Carter hesitated about calling the reporters, but he did not feel like blowing off Waynewright's request or dragging out the task until tomorrow. In the end, the interviews offered a passable distraction, with the added benefit of stroking his ego. A lot of people wanted to hear about his ongoing role in a major news event. That was nothing to sneeze at.

It was 6:00 p.m. by the time Carter finished with the last reporter. Out his office window, the view had turned black, reflecting Carter's image against the few Rosslyn lights that could penetrate the interior glare. Carter could imagine the cold of the street and the bitter breeze, and the thought of an empty house after work suddenly left him dispirited.

Carter stared through his reflection and could not escape Michelle, her image moving through his thoughts with insistent slow motion. He saw her legs plant and her arms sway, her smile hinting of something beyond him. He could see the shape of her hips molded by her clothes, and feel the ache of her clothes falling away.

His mood did not rest in expectation but in a sense of futility whose exact source he could not pin down. The bombing had delivered a quick uppercut of shock and uncertainty—doubts about whether he could ever return to a basic happiness. He lived as a random pendulum that did not know which blow had knocked it which way. At the moment, Carter's pushback was a tough-minded pessimism. Why not go after the loud, smoke-filled sleaziness of a downtown strip club where his friends had once dragged him, even though he knew the anticipation sank to the sewer when it was all over. He could still picture the tall, beefy woman who had sat down beside him the one time he had been there. She had laid her hand on his thigh while his friends had whooped, and even in the darkness, Carter had seen the thick layer of make-up filling the first lines of her middle-aged face like silt in the dried streambed of a desert. Now, without his friends to mock him with their drunken grins, Carter did not think he could face it, and as he walked through the cold of the office parking garage, he realized that this time it had not been the picture of an aging hooker that had kept him away, but Michelle Taylor.

8

Carter checked into Alexandria Hospital at 9:00 a.m. the next morning. After a visit with Dr. Samson, a nurse led Carter down the hall to the operating ward, and on the way, Carter watched the jaded, joking staff stream by with thick-skinned acceptance of the patients on their gurneys, the white sheets covering defective flesh. Carter saw an old man being carted to recovery, an I-V pouch above him like a transparent piece of meat emptying its juices, the man's skin pale and his mouth open. Carter wondered whether they would soon be pulling the sheet all the way up.

The nurse deposited Carter in a small room and handed him a smock. Dr. Stern, the dermatologist, stopped by to say hello, and then left Carter to his stripping. In the end, Carter stood with the white smock hanging loose along his naked body, tied in the back by little strings. He felt chilled and foolish, unable to sit down without exposing himself, wondering what he was supposed to do now.

Finally, another nurse took him to the operating room.

Carter received local anesthesia on his back and lay down on his stomach as the surgical team got to work. He did not notice any pain, but after a while Dr. Stern said that they wanted to dig around a little deeper and that they were going to put him under.

"No big deal," Dr. Stern said. "Just like at the dentist if you were getting an implant. We'll have you out of here in no time."

The next thing Carter knew, he had awoken in recovery. He did not remember at first what had happened but then saw a young female nurse at his side. Carter closed his eyes for a moment, the effects of the anesthesia still draining slowly. He tried to put the sequence of events back into place, shutting his eyes again, and the next time he opened them, he could tell from the hard light through the window that he had returned for good.

Carter offered a tired smile to the nurse, feeling a bandage and a slight sensitivity in his back, but he felt no real pain. He looked at the empty bed at the far side of the room. "So I get a private room for the price of a double?"

"It looks that way," the nurse said. "Let me take your temperature." She put a gun to his ear and fired a puff of air. "By the way," the nurse said, "you've gotten a few calls while you were asleep but no messages that I know of."

After fifteen minutes, Dr. Stern stepped through the door. "May I come in?" he asked stiffly, approaching the bed without waiting for an answer. "So how are you doing?"

"You tell me," Carter said. "I feel fine, just like before."

"Well, you told me that you always liked things straight, so here it is: The melanoma has reached into the dermis.

That's not good, but it does mean that we have to be thankful that we caught it now. Things can still be fine."

"But the odds are a lot lower," Carter said.

"That's right. Of course, it doesn't change the fact that we simply have to wait and monitor you closely. We did do a lymph node scan to see a possible route for any cancer, and the biopsy on the first lymph node came up negative, so that's good. But we'll want to run some additional tests while we already have you here."

"So there was no need for a skin graft?" Carter asked.

"No. We had no visual evidence of the melanoma spreading to the adjacent tissue. That's good."

Carter straightened himself in bed unconvinced. He felt as though he had been convicted of murder—but with the ultimate sentence, either life in prison or death, sealed in an envelope until some crude future day of revelation.

Sitting up in bed, Carter spooned down the last of his dessert from lunch—a grainy chocolate pudding—when the telephone rang. He pushed his tray aside and lifted the receiver. "Hello," he said.

"Mr. Carter, are you resting well?"

The voice-synthesized speech made Carter sit up straight.

"I have the sneaking suspicion," the voice went on, "that the FBI has not bugged your hospital room phone, so we can actually share the pleasure of a slightly longer conversation."

"How did you know I was here?" Carter asked, pushing the emergency call button clamped to the bed frame.

The voice continued. "One of my friends happened to see you go in. The operator was kind enough to forward my call."

"Am I supposed to thank her?" Carter asked.

Jackhammer did not respond but continued talking. Carter waved to the responding nurse, who came in worried. Carter held the phone with his shoulder and acted out writing. "Your pen," he mouthed, grabbing his wallet. The nurse handed him the pen, and Carter dug for Taylor's phone number.

Carter wrote: "Call FBI agent Taylor. Tell her I'm on phone with J. Emergency." He handed her the paper and mouthed "Go!"

"Are you giving me your undivided attention?" Jackhammer asked.

"Sure. Just tell me who this friend is that followed me."

"Why do I get the sneaking suspicion you're trying some monkey business with the phone?" Jackhammer said. "Of course, it's not going to do you any good."

"I'm just a little surprised by the call," Carter said, wondering if Taylor could actually rig some sort of trace so fast. It did not seem likely. "What is it you want with me anyway?"

"Just to see you squirm. I somehow find that strangely invigorating—Mr. Goody Two-Shoes suddenly frightened about who might be lurking in the shadows."

Carter was tempted to say "Screw you" but instead said, "What does this have to do with Islamist terrorist demands?"

Jackhammer chuckled. "That's not for you to worry about."

"How do I know you're Jackhammer and not some practical joker who read about me in the papers? Anybody can rig up a voice synthesizer."

"Not a nice portable model that fits inconspicuously on any phone. You need some decent engineering for that. And that's why tracing this call is such a waste of your time. The FBI will just get an empty receiver."

Carter looked at the door, hoping for word from the nurse. "Prove that you're Jackhammer," Carter said.

Jackhammer grunted at having to stoop to this level, but he obliged. "Where do you get a flush that's not in the toilet?"

Carter tried to think whether that had been part of the news reports. "You could have read about that in the paper."

"I don't think I like this interrogation," Jackhammer said. "Frankly, your attempts at self-righteousness make me sick. That's why your life needs to be made a little more uncomfortable, maybe cut short."

Carter took a breath. "Do you know me from before the bombing?"

"What got you into the hospital anyway?" Jackhammer asked, ignoring Carter's question.

"That's none of your business," Carter said.

"And your question is none of yours."

The nurse came through the door holding up the business card, shaking her head. Carter realized there was no more hope.

"What sort of engineer are you?" Carter asked.

"I really think we've had enough," Jackhammer said. "Maybe the next time we can have a more pleasant chat."

"I'd be happy to talk some more now," Carter said.

Jackhammer hung up. Carter looked at the receiver and then slowly laid it down, as though he had not yet digested what he had heard.

"So that was Jackhammer from the bombing?" the nurse asked anxiously.

Carter nodded. "There's nothing like a murder threat to get your mind off dying from cancer."

Carter dialed Taylor again to leave a message, telling her what had happened and where she could find him. He realized that meant eating his lie about going to Richmond, but he had no choice. The idea that he had not been honest now cut deep. He wondered whether Taylor would lose her trust in him.

During the afternoon, the doctors took some more blood for their tests and ran some scans that would let them compare his present state against a possible future cancer growth. Carter watched TV, read the newspaper, chatted with the occasional visiting nurse, and wondered why he could not just go home right away.

At 4:00 p.m., Carter picked up the ringing phone. It was Taylor.

"I'm downstairs," Taylor said. "Do you mind if I come up?"

"I guess I can't stop you," Carter tried to joke, but it came up lame.

"That's a fine invitation."

"Don't mind me."

Soon enough Taylor leaned through the open door and knocked, then strode in with a nod of polite, even gracious, concern. "I'll have to tell you, it was quite a surprise to hear you were in the hospital. I don't want to pry, but I hope everything's all right."

"For the time being," Carter said. "But I apologize that I lied about going to Richmond. The bottom line is that this morning I had some malignant melanoma removed from my back, along with a little exploratory surgery in the area. I didn't want to bother you with it, you know, forcing you to pretend concern and all that."

Taylor glanced at Carter worriedly. His phone message had been vague. "I'm sorry," she said quietly. "Do the doctors say they've got everything out?"

"For now. Recurrence is all just a crap shoot." He smiled. "But take heart. I'd definitely be batting low on the odds if I didn't live long enough to get through the ANC investigation. No worries for you there."

Taylor was not sure where to go with this quip. "If that means you want to talk business, I'll do it."

"Absolutely," Carter said. "First of all, this Jackhammer is not foreign-born—at least not the guy I talked to. He's a native speaker. Forget the synthesizer; it's clear from just the way he puts his sentences together. And I can tell he's playing games. He's got some sick resentment for me, God knows from where. No Islamist terrorist is going to act like that."

"I've believed that from the beginning," Taylor said, pulling a pocket tape recorder from her purse. "But start from the top. Tell me everything you remember."

Carter spelled out the conversation from memory, and when he was done, Taylor paced slowly in front of him, thinking about what Carter had told her. "When you asked Jackhammer whether he knew you from before, he didn't deny it, did he?"

"No, but logically that doesn't mean anything."

"True," Taylor said. "But it's possible that if Jackhammer hadn't known you, he might have just denied it outright, maybe even laughed at you, claiming that was ridiculous."

"Possible," Carter said. "But anything's possible."

Taylor stood still. "Would he have laughed at your question if it were patently false, or would he have just ignored it, like he did?"

"He's obviously taking pleasure in this," Carter said, "but he strikes me as being too smart to give anything away, even if it's just off hand. By not telling me anything, he maximizes the doubt."

Taylor bit her lower lip in thought. "So, do you still think this guy's a civil engineer?"

"I'm obviously not proud of having a psycho as part of the profession, but there's been nothing that would change my mind."

"Well, with his direct threat against your life, I think we should get someone to keep an eye on you, at least when I'm not around. If Jackhammer, or some hired hand, tries to make a move, we want to be there to stop him."

"Maybe him bumping me off would be your big break," Carter said.

Taylor frowned. "So how could Jackhammer have found out you were in the hospital? Do you think you were followed?"

"He seems to imply it, but I haven't been paying attention whether there's somebody behind me."

"Who else knew that you were here?"

"The only person I told was Bob, my boss. I didn't even tell my secretary. I gave her the same lie I gave you. I just didn't feel like gathering condolences."

"Here's something really out there," Taylor said, "but just for completeness. Is it possible Bob is Jackhammer?"

Carter practically laughed. "That's nuts. Sure, the guy's about as courteous as a tank, but I always thought he was decent. He's always treated me pretty well."

"Does he hold political grudges? Has he got some kind of ax to grind that could turn violent? Maybe he hates the press, and that's the building that was bombed."

"Boy, you're really stretching things. If Bob had some beef with me, I'd know it firsthand. No need for a cover named Jackhammer."

"I know it doesn't add up, but I've got to check the angles. A priority now is to find out where Bob was during all the Jackhammer calls. We've got pretty accurate times for all the contacts. Let me see what his alibis are."

"He's going to love that conversation."

"He's not my boss, so he can bluster all he wants," Taylor said. She looked at her watch. "In the meantime I'm going to order some protection for you. You'll have someone parked outside your room pretty soon."

"Nothing like feeling important," Carter said.

In the late afternoon, a young, clean-cut FBI agent introduced himself to Carter, took his post outside Carter's room, and later, when Carter left the hospital, followed him home to Old Town. The agent parked himself at the street corner of Carter's house, where he could see both the front door and the entrance to the narrow back alley. Carter pitied the guy. The man had to sit out in his car for hours waiting for something that was not likely to happen. At one point Carter came outside and invited him in, but the agent said his orders had placed him on the street.

That night, Carter did not sleep well. His back had grown more sensitive, and when he turned from side to side, the incision smarted. Before dawn, he woke from a dream and felt sweat on his forehead. He had been back in the ANC building, just after the bombing, with the smoke pouring into the elevator, and this time the smoke did not stop and he was ready to choke and then die when Jackhammer's synthesized voice came in over the intercom. The voice filled Carter's lungs until they nearly burst, and then he woke to the dark of his bedroom, his heart beating.

Goddamn, Carter thought. Don't let this guy get to you. But that did not come easily. Carter found himself lying awake for an hour poring over Jackhammer's threat and the relentless chain of events that had turned his life upside down.

At 3:00 a.m., Jackhammer stood in the kitchen doubled over in pain. He clenched his teeth, head down, and steadied himself on the counter. He tried not to move as he braced himself for the next violent stab, the background pain already excruciating. When the big one came, he gasped and hissed through his teeth, cussing so as not to scream, the pain like a red-hot knife hitting the full length of a nerve. Shit! he blurted, struggling to the cabinet that held some painkillers. He could hardly straighten to open the cabinet door, and he just got his hand on the canister when he bent double again. He fumbled with the child-proof top and then dumped some pills onto the counter, scooping up two and limping to the sink where he popped them in his mouth and held his lips under the faucet, the water running down his cheek like from an open sore. He almost choked as the next bolt shot through his stomach. Coughing, he lurched to a bar stool and sat hunched, his hand kneading his abdomen, wondering whether the pills would even have a chance to kick in.

It had not been this bad for a long time, and Jackhammer glared at the floor, eyes bloodshot from no sleep, and wondered whether this was a sign of the end. He could not let that happen, especially now when this attack of neuralgia might have been triggered by the blast of news he had received earlier that evening. That double-crosser! he snarled in outrage. He could not let this new jolt cause his death. He would not give the man that pleasure, this two-bit vermin asking for double the money to complete the next job, when he had already been paid his advance. The guy was ready to back out at the last minute! That bastard! Oh, the guy knew what he was doing. He knew there was no time to get a substitute. It was all in place, and now it would all go to hell unless he gave in to this blackmail. Jackhammer shook in rage, wanting to take a knife and flay that man's stomach so he knew what agony meant, twist that blade, slice while the guy stayed alive to watch. Oh, that would be a pleasure, but he knew it was no use. The pleasure of his master plan was so much greater. He had to look at his larger legacy and not let a greedy louse cloud his priorities. He would have to cough up the cash. He saw no other way. It was too late for contingencies, but when it was all over, he would track the guy down and blow his brains out. That would show him what the extra money was worth.

Jackhammer considered what bank accounts he could tap to get that kind of money, gasping as the pain shot through him. He might have to skim from five different sources and then package it up for a drop in Rock Creek Park, if he could live to do it. He braced himself for the next jolt, but it came dialed down just a little. So were the pills beginning to work? Jackhammer straightened himself, still holding his stomach, and looked at a point beyond the floor. He would have to survive until the end of everything. The plan was just too beautiful to trash when he could already taste it. If he died now, who would know what he had done? Who would know? Maybe he should write up his exploits for the papers in the event he suddenly, without warning, keeled over. Yes, he would have to do that. He could put it in his safe deposit box. His executor could then make the glorified discovery and reveal it to the world.

Jackhammer kept pressing his abdomen, but the pain seemed to have dimmed. Was it possible? Yes, it was what fate required. Jackhammer sat up a little straighter, pumping his will with a new confidence that he took for an omen. Yes, he would make it. He would see it through despite this new setback! He would give in to this one blackmail and then make everyone pay.

It was Saturday and Carter's day off for recovery, and with nothing pressing scheduled, he cooked up a massive breakfast, piling butter and syrup onto a stack of hot pancakes and filling a side plate with smoked country sausage. The liquid fat glazed the ceramic with a shiny pool. Why worry about cholesterol when I might get murdered tomorrow, Carter thought. He then sat down in the den for a third cup of coffee and *The Washington Post*, and his hard-nosed resignation took a new blow. On page 3 of the Metro section stood an article that boiled down to this: The engineer who had saved four people during the ANC bombing and then received contacts from the bomber himself, had just been operated on for malignant melanoma at Alexandria Hospital. Carter could not believe it. Who the hell had called *The Post* about that?! Would Bob do such a stupid thing, just to get more publicity for BWE? Waynewright knows I want my privacy, Carter thought. Now the whole city gets the scoop!

Carter dialed Waynewright at the office and got his assistant. Apparently everyone was working that Saturday.

"Bob just got done with Special Agent Taylor," the secretary said, "and from what I can tell, he might not be in the mood to talk."

"I'll take my chances," Carter said.

Carter waited and finally heard the second line break in.

"What is it?" Waynewright barked.

"This is Scott. Did you see the 'Metro' section of *The Post* today?"

"No I didn't," Waynewright said. "What of it?"

"*The Post* wrote a short article that said I was in the hospital being operated on. How did they find that out?"

"How should I know?"

"Did you tell our PR guy?"

"Why would I do that?"

"I don't know. I'm just asking whether you told him or whether it slipped out when you talked to some reporter."

"Now listen here, Scott. I didn't tell a damn soul."

"OK, just looking for the facts."

"Well, you can stuff the facts. First that FBI agent comes in here and starts asking where I was when Jackhammer called you, and now you start with this stuff. I'll have you all sued for libel!"

"Listen, Bob. Michelle is not out to get you or anybody else. Second, I'm not accusing you of anything. I'd just like to know who invaded my privacy and gave *The Post* this information. I'd be a fool if I didn't check with you first."

"All I can say is that with the FBI starting to act like it's on a witch hunt, I'm liable to jerk you off the case. And I'd do it in a minute if I didn't think the firm could still milk this for some points. You better make the PR your first priority or you'll be back in your office letting Michelle do her dirty work herself."

"You do what you want, Bob. I'm not asking you for anything."

"That's good," Waynewright said, "because I'm not givin'."

Carter heard the click of Waynewright's phone. Quietly, Carter hung up the receiver. I guess I believe him, Carter thought, but with that, it suddenly dawned on him. He reached for the phone and punched in the numbers for Waynewright's assistant.

"Blackstone-Waynewright Engineers," the lady said.

"This is Scott again. Could you check if Michelle Taylor's left the building. If she's there and you can interrupt her, have her call my cell. I'll wait on the line from my home phone."

"Sure, Scott. I'll put you on hold."

Carter paced the kitchen with the phone to his ear, wondering if his suspicions could possibly be right. It seemed like a long time before the assistant picked up, and then his cell phone rang. He answered it fast.

"Hi. It's Scott. Did you see the 'Metro' section of *The Post* today?"

"Haven't had time," Taylor said.

"Well, they wrote a short article about me being in the hospital. I didn't tell anyone, and I just got off the phone with Bob, and he said he didn't tell anyone either. You didn't leak this, right?"

"Of course not. But I'm surprised Bob even talked to you. He was flying off the handle."

"That's Bob. Do you actually suspect him?"

"I just have to check out his statements."

"Well, the guy can be a loose cannon when he's angry, but I never knew him to lie to me. So if he's not the leak, who does that leave for telling *The Post*? Jackhammer. He found out I was in the hospital and could have called a reporter. Any reporter worth his salt could have then found out why I was there."

"You've got a point. But it could also have been the nurses and doctors or just some reception staff."

"Sure, maybe, but I'd say you find that reporter and see how he got his information. He might be a witness to another Jackhammer contact."

"Are you telling me how to do my job?" Taylor asked.

For a moment Carter did not know if she was serious. "No."

Taylor laughed. "Hey, just giving you a hard time."

"So you'll check it out?"

"You bet. Thanks."

The bad night had caught up with Carter, and he decided to kill time with a nap. Upstairs, he set his coffee mug and newspaper on the antique nightstand, got undressed, and sat down on the four-post bed in his pajamas. He thought he would read a little first but instead looked up at the black, bare branches of the tree outside the window and the gray sky behind it. He thought of Waynewright's threat to put him back on full-time sales work, and how advancing the case just now had been such a shot in the arm. The stark contrast of this investigation with his former work troubled him more than he wanted to admit, as though a large, mangy blackbird had flown in and perched beside his bed, daring him with its glassy eyes to guess its meaning. He wondered, somewhat against his will, what had happened to the lofty view of engineering he had held on leaving high school, setting off to study at Virginia Tech and then, after a Master's, matching his wits against large-scale structural design. The nostalgia gave no pleasure. He knew it would not be long before he got back to the hours of client relations, the tedious proposal administration, and the care and feeding of unapologetic egos. He produced no tangible product, but merely a marketing context for the creations of others. Where had it all gone? Had he gotten too old for all his earlier ideals?

Isolated in the bedroom, the gray winter sky out the window, he felt his loss as a hollow, physical presence. For the first time he could not just shake off the regret as an acceptable inevitability with its accompanying financial perks and upper-management status—but he did not feel comfortable questioning his career like this. Why should this scrape with death, or his wife's accident before that, undermine the basic satisfaction he found in his days? What difference should it make if he had two years left to live or twenty when it came to counting the time well spent? Without Linda's death or the recent shocks, he would have inevitably gone climbing the corporate ladder feeling generally, if blindly, good about it. So why should that work suddenly feel cheap? Was twenty years of a corporate climb all right to waste but not two years, if that's all that was left him now?

Carter picked up the newspaper, sat back in bed, and tried to read, but when he had gotten through the first long article, he realized he had not remembered a single word. He folded the paper, pushed away the extra pillow, and pulled up the blanket.

Eventually, he fell asleep.

Carter woke up at lunchtime. He had no more patience to just sit around, and after a shower and getting dressed, he pulled his briefcase onto the bed and took out his iPhone. He pushed for appointments—meetings he had entered long before the current crisis—to see what he might be missing. The 3:00 p.m. MATHCOUNTS practice at an Arlington middle school jumped from the list. It had slipped his mind. Through the recommendation of a colleague, Carter had volunteered as one of the coaches for a seventh- and eighth-grade math team that was now training for the upcoming state championships. The special weekend practice was the one thing that actually looked worthwhile among the week's list of now outdated meetings. Why should he miss that, he thought. And hey, his coaching partner used to work at Arlington Public Works. That was another chance for some questions about the office operations.

Carter walked through the abandoned parking lot of the Arlington middle school, the FBI bodyguard a polite distance behind him. Carter had picked a MATHCOUNTS school near his work so that a late lunch break would handle the after-school practices and still get him back to the office for the end of the day. The school's side entrance led past the gym, and Carter could see the girls' basketball team running a drill and the boys working a scrimmage on the opposite side.

The sight always tended to sting. He knew that if he had had children of his own, he would have tossed them a basketball and taken them out to the driveway for some hoops. Heck, he thought, he would have coached in a suburban league and seen if he could bring the pip-squeaks to a semblance of play-making discipline. But without his own children as part of the mix, he had opted for MATHCOUNTS to get his weekly fix with the youngsters. He also brought his competitive streak and tried to push the team to respectability.

Carter was determined to keep today's session as normal as possible, despite the recent events. He had asked the FBI bodyguard to remain inconspicuous, and he had told himself to put on his regular game face. That meant coming into the room with his keep-on-truckin' stride and high-fives for everyone.

At the door to the classroom, Carter leaned backwards—hands splayed, his torso rocking from side to side—put on a goofy smile, and strode into the room like one of the cartoon zanies from the sixties that Carter had been fed by a wacky uncle as a kid, offering one polite wink for the teacher. The kids knew no Zap Comix history and gave no mercy. As soon as Carter got through the door, Jason Kim, the team star, waved his hand in bored disgust. "Mr. Carter, you look like a dork!"

"I *am* a dork!" Carter said, moving from desk to desk to get a lazy high-five from each of the team members. They had spread themselves around the room to finish some practice problems assigned at the previous meeting. Carter stopped in front of Eric Butler, a fat kid with a big grin. Donut crumbs covered his desk. "You're not going to do anything until you clean up that mess, Mr. Butler."

"Do you want a donut?" Eric asked.

"Don't try to bribe me," Carter said.

Carter moved to April Goldman. She looked up for a moment to offer a whispered, sheepish hello, then buried her head in her practice sheet. Carter tried his now traditional ritual to get her out of her shell. "OK, put 'em up," Carter said, raising his fists and starting to dance and weave like a boxer. "I'm waiting."

April blushed, smiled, and raised her hand for protection, but would not give in to Carter's antics.

"Hey, where's the team spirit?" Carter said. "I want a little fire!"

"Hey, Mr. Carter, I saw you on TV!" Tim Johnson shouted. "Pretty cool."

"Well, the whole thing's not so cool," Carter said. "But we're working hard on finding that bomber."

"So are you part of the police?" Tim asked.

"I'm sort of working with the FBI," Carter said. "I don't do a whole lot."

Jason shouted at Carter. "Hey, you and me are going head to head in a countdown round today. Remember?"

Carter had not remembered but figured he finally had to give Jason a chance to embarrass his mentor.

"With all this going on, I haven't practiced," Carter said.

"Ah, man, that's just excuses," Jason groused.

George Bender, the second coach for the team, had now arrived. A civil engineer in his late fifties, he had spent years with the Arlington County government and now worked for a local engineering firm on traffic systems. "Sorry I'm late," Bender said, waving cordially to Carter. "I didn't think you'd be here."

"Maybe I shouldn't be," Carter said, guessing that Bender had not read today's Metro section. "Jason says I promised him a head-to-head countdown round. That's what frightens me."

"I think Jason's right," Bender said with his slowpoke speech and reserved friendliness. He looked like a man who could sit in front of a fireplace with a pipe and be content to stare and blow smoke for hours. "You've got to put up or shut up."

Carter knew it was all a game, but he did not want this skinny little kid beating him too badly. Hey, winning wouldn't be so bad either, Carter thought. It would build respect for the coach.

The team members slipped two desks to the front of the room where their math teacher sat grading papers. The teacher always came as the required school chaperone but left the coaching to the engineers. Carter assumed she'd had enough of the kids after a full day of their mischief.

Carter squeezed himself into a little desk and looked at his tiny competitor. Jason twisted and turned in his chair with his wire-rim glasses, waiting for the first problem like a little league batter staring down a pitch with the winning run on second. Carter could tell the kid would just love to destroy him. Bender pulled out a packet of problems and asked whether each competitor had their paper and pencils ready.

"Shoot," Jason said.

"OK," said Bender, "you pound the desk with your fist when you know the answer. I'm the final judge on who pounded first. First person to get ten right answers wins. Ready?"

"Ready," both Jason and Carter said.

Bender read slowly: "Soldiers take 85 steps per minute when marching, and they take 115 steps per minute when quick-marching. How many steps would each member of a platoon take in 3 hours if half of the time is spent quick-marching?"

Carter started scribbling on paper. Jason did the problem in his head. Carter's fist went up but Jason's had already come down.

"18,000," Jason shouted.

"Right," Bender said.

Jason bounced up and down in his chair as though he had won a prize at a toddler's birthday party. He glanced at Carter and smirked.

"Good going," Carter said. "Do that in the state championships."

Bender read the next question: "Compute 29 squared, minus 58 times 9, plus 9 squared."

This time Jason was not so fast. Carter had time to scribble, trying to confirm his answer before blurting out the wrong one and giving Jason a leisurely thirty seconds to follow up.

Jason pounded. "400."

"Right again," Bender said.

The teammates cheered, and Jason pumped his fist in the air, twisting in his chair. "Yes!" he whispered under his breath, grinning at Carter.

All right, Carter said to himself. Don't embarrass yourself. You used to be good at this.

Bender had gotten only halfway through the next question when Jason shouted the answer.

"Wrong," Bender said. "Scott, you now have thirty seconds."

Carter casually solved the problem and got it right.

"Don't get overconfident," Carter told Jason. "It can come back to bite you."

Jason blew Carter away on the next question and took a 3-1 lead. Carter realized he would have to stop writing things down. Risk it and do it all in your head, he told himself, or Jason'll get too confident and stop pushing himself. Carter felt like a brute-force oaf compared to his nimble competitor, but he figured raw power still had a chance to win.

Bender took his time and drawled the next question. Carter had a flash of insight and rattled the figures through his brain. "Twenty-nine!" he said, surprised by his volume. He did not want the kids to think he took this too seriously. That would just triple their glee when he lost.

The answer was right. "Just getting warmed up," Carter said, trying to act cool. Jason frowned in his direction, leaning forward, poised to pounce.

On the next question, Jason blurted the wrong answer, and Carter followed up with the right one. With the score 3-3, Carter could see Jason had become rattled. "Keep calm in these situations," Carter told him. "When you're in a competition, if you get frustrated you're just going to open the door for the other guy. Forget what's come before. It's a new question. You're fresh. You're cool. You understand?"

Jason nodded, but he had not understood. He played it too safe on the next question and Carter snuck in the answer. Jason's lips moved in a silent pep-talk, as though he were praying, and he clenched both fists. More focused now, Jason won the next two points, but Carter launched a lucky spurt and swept three in a row. The team booed Carter and shouted for Jason to pull it out. Visibly nervous, Jason still kept his wits and traded answers until they were tied at 9-9. The team whooped. Bender's voice actually showed a trace of interest, and Carter felt himself tense.

"A ladder that is 3.4 meters long is leaning against a wall. Its base is 1.6 meters from the wall," Bender read. "How many meters up the wall does the ladder reach?"

Carter had it but did not pound fast enough. Jason practically screamed, "Nine!"

Bender shook his head in consolation. "I'm sorry," he said.

Carter did not bother to wait and quietly offered his response. "Three."

"That's right," Bender said.

Jason slammed his fist on the desk. "Man!" he groaned. "I was robbed! I knew that answer. It was Mickey Mouse!"

"Hey, calm down," Carter said. "That's not how you're going to act at the state finals."

"I had you beat!" He was still hitting the desk over his stupid mistake.

"You'd have beaten me if you hadn't gotten nervous." Carter said. "It was just plain carelessness. But you did great. I thought I was done for. In fact, that's the last time I'll play you because I won't have a prayer the next time!"

"No fair!" Jason protested. "I want a rematch!"

"I need some self-respect!" Carter said. "So I'm ducking you from now on!"

"Sore winner!"

"Right!" Carter said.

Carter pulled himself out of the little chair and felt his back smart. He straightened himself slowly and then went to his briefcase to pull out another practice sheet. He turned to the team. "These are sample questions from a MATHCOUNTS written test. Take a shot at 1 through 10 and then we'll talk about some tricks about getting the answers faster."

Carter passed out the sheets and sat down at the side of the room with Bender.

"I'm glad *you* were the sacrificial lamb," Bender said with a smile. "I would have been killed."

"I lucked out," Carter said. "Man, I can't believe Jason made such a stupid mistake."

"He'll shape up. But let's get to a real topic. What have you found out about the bombing? Are you really part of the investigation?"

"I tag along with an FBI agent," Carter said, "and give my two bits whenever I can." Carter told him about all the interviews with the engineers at BWE and the visit to the Arlington Public Works Department. He mentioned his frustration with all the dead ends and the multiple possibilities on access to the engineering drawings. Security had looked pretty lax at the county's design archives, Carter said, so anyone could have gotten hold of the things. "Has it always been like that?" Carter asked.

"No question," Bender said nonchalantly. "I'd often come down and find drawings left out on the tables. Everyone was supposed to clean up after themselves, but there was an unwritten understanding that if they didn't do it, an admin assistant would."

"Was there ever anything suspicious?"

"Suspicious about the engineers being messy?"

"No, I guess not . . . But did you ever see anybody in there that shouldn't have been?"

Bender looked up at the ceiling as though contemplating a smoke ring he hoped to create. He shrugged. "There was a time when I made a little stink about putting things away, and nobody fessed up that they'd done anything. Usually everybody was happy to claim credit for being a slob, so that was a little odd."

"When was that?"

Bender blew wind through his lips so they rattled. "Heck if I know. What, two years ago maybe. Something like that."

"Do you happen to remember what had been left on the tables?"

"Jesus, you really have turned into a detective," Bender said. He thought for a moment. "I just remember it was a bunch of plans, maybe more than normal, all laid out pretty neatly. I obviously wasn't going to pin it on a break-in. Are you telling me I should have been suspicious?"

Carter kept pressing. "Do you remember what kind of plans they were?"

"Let's see…if I go by the odds, they were Rosslyn building and street plans. But you're asking too much if you want specifics."

"Could the ANC building have been one of them?"

Bender shrugged. "I have no idea."

"Why would a thief leave them lying out on the tables and call attention to himself?"

Bender said, "It was pretty late in the evening. If it was a thief, maybe he heard me coming and took off."

"Is there another way out of that room?"

"Yeah, there's a side door."

"When was this exactly?"

Bender rolled his eyes. "You've got to be kidding. You think I kept a diary? Maybe it was winter two years ago. I sure couldn't say the month."

Carter thought for a moment. "The ANC plans had obviously been in the county's hands by that time. The department would have had them. Is there any reason our bomber couldn't have started this whole scheme two years ago? His access didn't have to be recent."

"I suppose so," Bender said. "But it sounds like you're pushing it."

"Maybe," Carter said. "Who else knows about this?"

Bender thought for a moment. "Debbie Baker comes to mind."

"Is she still with the department?"

"As far as I know."

"So she could tell me which drawings had been left on the tables."

"Scott, are you smoking something? She'd have to have a pretty sharp memory, or have some reason to remember it."

"Well, who says she doesn't?" Carter said.

"Wishful thinking," said Bender.

"I'll take it. Do you realize what you've done, George? We might, for the first time, have an actual, honest-to-goodness, goddamn lead."

9

Working late, Taylor sat in her DC office poring over database record checks and Gentry's daily investigation progress reports. The telephone rang, and she picked up and heard Colin.

"Michelle," he said, surprisingly quiet and contrite. "I'm willing to make things up to you. We've got to stop this silence between us."

Taylor kept her voice down, self-conscious about speaking loudly in her open cubicle. "Please, Colin, I can't really talk here. I've got a lot of work to do. We've been through everything."

"Please, don't hang up. You don't have to talk, just listen. I've been doing a lot of thinking. I've come to realize that living without you is not going to work. Maybe I did take you for granted and didn't let you know how much you meant to me, but that just came out of ignorance. I'm thankful that you gave me this chance to learn what was important, and I'm going to prove it to you. Michelle . . . we should really think about getting married."

Taylor took a deep breath. She had not expected this declaration and now felt a pang of pity for Colin. He suddenly sounded defeated, groping for any straw to hang on to—and that lowered him even more in her esteem. Suddenly she was also questioning herself. How had she reached age 33 without a long, stable relationship to show for it? Now another one lay in ruins at her feet. Since turning 30, she had often thought about marriage and wondered how, for whatever reason, the real opportunity had never presented itself. There were excuses, of course. Years before, she had remained steadfast in not tying herself down while her career took root—the FBI could have stationed her anywhere—and later she had felt determined not to succumb to a relationship that she did not consider perfect. She knew she was good looking, so couldn't she afford to wait? Now Colin's half-proposal hit her hard as another proclamation of failure. "Colin, you flatter me, and I'm touched, but this is hardly the time to bring something like that up. We can't change what's happened with words. It's impossible. I'm sorry."

"Michelle, I know I can't expect some miraculous turnaround tonight. Just say you'll think about it. Things can't be as final as you paint them. Give yourself a chance."

Taylor had never heard Colin so defenseless, and she found it difficult to just brush him off, even if that was the only right thing to do. "Colin, I don't want to hurt you . . ."

"Then just think about it. Don't say any more."

Taylor was shaking her head. "It's not going to help," she said quietly. Another side of her said: I wish it would.

"We'll talk again," Colin said.

"Good night," said Taylor.

Taylor found it hard to concentrate on the tail-end of her work, and on the drive home her mind sped from one thought to another, unable to shake off the pressure from so many sides. The investigation had started to wear her down, not just because of the usual dead ends, but from the simple fact of not getting enough sleep. She wished she could lie in someone's arms and just talk off all the strains she had burdened herself with, and she knew that Colin would be happy to oblige. Had she really needed to be so harsh in cutting him off? He still had his appeal.

Then there was the FBI—she was trying to impress them. She wondered if success was important enough to block out every other facet of her life. Right now, that was what she was doing. She could feel it, driving herself at every turn to get the maximum result, as she had done in high school and in college, and as she had done with her brother at every competitive game they had ever played.

The thought of Scott Carter dampened her perspective. How would all this look if you had just been diagnosed with cancer, she wondered. It might be tough to give things the same importance. She again saw Carter in his hospital bed, stripped of his daily wardrobe and routine, and she remembered how she had been shaken. In the image she held, the man had practically been a hero during the ANC bombing. Since Taylor had met him, he had projected a sturdy determination. She had looked forward to that daily foil of support and the simple pleasure of his good-looking presence. But now, with the added burden of Jackhammer breathing down his neck, Carter had suddenly had stability pulled out from under him. In that hospital bed he had lost his armor. She felt sorry and knew that there was not a thing she could do about it. Just act like nothing has happened and carry on, she told herself. Yet that felt inadequate and callous. The swift, potentially dangerous nature of his situation had left her hollow.

At home, Taylor dropped her briefcase by the door, tossed her coat on the couch, and walked to the message machine. She found two messages and hit "play."

"Michelle, this is Colin. I just wanted to follow up from our phone call and give you a goodnight kiss from afar. Excuse the romanticism, but you're all I can think about. What I said was not just a spur of the moment ploy. Please don't consider it in those terms. Think about us when you go to bed."

Then Carter's voice came on. "Hello, Michelle. I was talking to a colleague this afternoon and I found out that someone might—and it's a big might—have been rummaging around the county's engineering drawing files about two years ago. I didn't call you right away because I wanted to see if I could track down who's available to talk to. I've set up a tentative appointment with the county engineers for tomorrow. We can touch base in the morning about whether that's all right. This might be a good lead—at least the first tangible one I've seen. I guess we shouldn't get our hopes up too much. Talk to you later."

After taking down the gist in a note, Taylor pressed the delete. At least that was a straightforward message, she thought. It's all so much easier when someone isn't trying to climb into your mind and into your bed. She wondered how Carter was taking the medical uncertainties. She wondered if Colin had really meant what he had said.

Taylor took Carter's lead, and that Monday the two met at BWE and drove in the bright sunshine to the county offices. Taylor felt self-conscious about how Carter had lied to keep his cancer a secret. He was probably still embarrassed he had done it, she thought, but she finally decided she could not simply ignore the fact. "So how's your back?" she asked.

"Not much there except some cuts," Carter said.

"Any further news from the doctor?"

"It's just wait and see," Carter said. "I appreciate your asking, but the best thing to do is just forget it."

"I'm sure that's not always so easy."

"I suppose not," Carter said and smiled. He did not like talking openly to Taylor about his health—the mere mention would brand him as an undesirable. He knew that this woman had no romantic interest in him, and he also knew he had now placed a big neon sign on his forehead that said: "Don't even think about falling for this guy; he may drop dead."

At the county government building, Taylor could not find a parking space on the adjacent courthouse lot and settled for a curbside space four blocks away. The temperature had climbed just above freezing, and the two walked the short distance without buttoning their coats, as though unconsciously trying to impress the other with their hardiness. Taylor had pulled her hair into a wide, flat bun in the back and stabbed it with a big wood pin. Light, individual strands of hair escaped at the fringes and glowed in the sunlight, hitting Carter hard as he roamed from there to her neck and the soft line of her cheek.

The two walked through the glass doors of the county building and into the long, wide lobby. It felt pleasantly warm inside, and the two took the elevator at the far end to the eighth floor and Handley's office. The secretary looked up when she saw them enter.

"Oh, the meeting has been moved to Director Freeport's office. That's down on the seventh floor. Do you need me to show you the way?"

"Thanks, I know where it is," said Carter. At the elevator he turned to Taylor. "I suppose Sam Freeport is trying to grab some political points."

"Sounds like you're fond of the guy."

"Nothing personal. I just don't think a non-civil engineer should be public works director."

"For him, that's probably as personal as you can get."

"I suppose so," said Carter.

Freeport's administrative assistant showed Carter and Taylor into the director's large office. Handley and Baker were already there, waiting on a leather couch in the corner. Everyone stood up to shake hands when Taylor and Carter came in.

Freeport looked sharp in a dark gray pinstriped suit, his back unnaturally straight as he strode forward to greet them. His pedestrian face seemed more confident in the protective confines of his office.

Carter scanned the décor and got the sense of a Wall Street law firm. Carter wondered if the taxpayers knew what kind of money Freeport had spent on his furnishings. At least Carter did not have to worry about that detail—he paid taxes in Alexandria.

"So what can we do for you?" Freeport asked, motioning for Carter and Taylor to sit down across from Handley and Baker. "I'm here to offer you the complete resources of our department, anything to further the investigation."

"That's very good of you," Taylor said. "For now we simply want to question Ms. Baker about what she remembers of a possible irregularity reported by George Bender, who used to work for your department. You could help us by getting the word out that we'd like to talk to anyone who knows anything about the supposed incident, both current and former employees."

"No problem," Freeport said. He pulled his iPhone from his inside jacket pocket and made a note.

Carter wondered about Freeport's motives. Did he hope to get his name mentioned in the same breath as the investigation to give a boost to some future run for office?

Taylor moved her attention to Baker, a young, dynamic civil engineer in her early thirties. "Two years ago your superior, Mr. Bender, said he came into the document archive room and found a number of drawings on the table, after hours, when the plans should have been put away. He said that was pretty common, but what was unusual this time, when he complained the next day, nobody admitted doing it. Usually everybody seemed to like to confess, like it was something of a running joke."

"That sounds right," Baker said.

"So you know what I'm talking about?" Taylor asked.

"I've been searching my memory after I heard about it, and I think yes."

"So what did you see?"

"Early the next morning, George had left me a note asking me to refile them. That was the part that made it stand out. I was a little ticked. The admin was sick that day and I got someone else's clean-up. George also asked me to find who'd done it, and I was happy to do that part."

"So Mr. Bender had not suspected the possibility of a break-in?"

"No, and neither had I. Why, do you really think there was one?"

"That's what we're trying to find out. So no one admitted anything?"

"No, not as far as I can remember."

"Did you press everyone?"

Baker shrugged. "Maybe. Who can remember if it was everyone? I guess I'm usually pretty thorough."

"So how many drawings were there?"

Baker inhaled with doubt but did fix on something. "I do remember that there were a lot of drawings, maybe two tables full. I was going around the office complaining about the volume."

"Were the drawings for the ANC building among them?"

"I don't remember that one in particular, but I do remember checking out what kind of drawings they were, you know, for curiosity on what somebody's dragging out, and I noticed a building design. I remember taking interest in that, since I was relatively new. When Mr. Carter called me yesterday and told me the situation, I looked back at the records and the only major building that fits in that category at that time was the ANC."

"You're sure of that?" Taylor asked.

"Yes."

"What about the other drawings. What types were they?"

"I've just got vague recollections there. I remember they were from all areas, but I couldn't give you an exact list. You know, they might have been county sewer grids, utility lines, bridges and overpasses, water distribution grids, building permit locations—those types of things. I remember the variety because I put them back in all sorts of drawers, not just one place for one project."

"Would somebody have to know where to find those drawings to get that kind of a collection together? Would they have to be familiar with the filing system?"

"I suppose so," Baker said, "but maybe not real intimate knowledge. The drawers have labels, and once you start poking around, you can get the idea. Of course, the other option is they were just random pulls."

"Do you think they could have been random?"

"Probably not. Not from the way they were laid out."

"How was that?"

"Neatly, around the edge of the two tables. There was nothing in the middle."

"Is that a procedure of your department?" Taylor asked.

"Not that I know of," Baker said. "And it's a bit unusual to grab so many kinds of plans."

Freeport broke in with an air of professional helpfulness. "Is there a chance somebody was making a year-end review of our maintenance progress?"

"Plans for maintenance operations are kept in a different archive," Baker said.

Carter tried to hold back a smile. Freeport sat back, lips pressed together, and acknowledged the answer with a curt nod of his head.

"Can we see the archives again?" Taylor asked Baker. "I'd like to see the exact location."

"Certainly," Freeport said, cutting Baker off. He seemed determined to play the indispensable host.

The whole group trouped down to the document archive for another tour, and Taylor asked Baker for more details on security procedures. Baker was the only one of the group who had worked there at the time of the incident, and Taylor asked her to pull several plans and place them on the table to recreate the events, and then to show her all the exits and where they led. When they were done, Taylor seemed pleased, focusing her eyes back on the drawers and the tables and tapping her pen on her note pad in thought. Then she suddenly seemed to wake up, noticed the people around her, and thanked them with energy. "It's been very helpful," she said, "very. I think I've got all I need."

"So what do you think?" Carter asked Taylor as they stepped out into the cold sunshine of the street.

"Let's talk over coffee," Taylor said. "I haven't had any breakfast and I'm famished."

Taylor remembered a small diner not far from where she had parked her car and led Carter to a narrow glass front that showed a counter and stools and a single row of booths moving straight back from the street. Inside it was warm, and they sat down in the farthest booth. Taylor told Carter to let her sit facing the door. "I'm supposedly on duty as your bodyguard, you know. I better see who happens to walk in."

"Not the most pleasant feeling," Carter said.

"It's probably all a bluff."

The waitress came to the table, and Taylor ordered two glazed donuts. She cajoled Carter to order one for himself. "I need company to take in all these calories."

"I can't imagine you worrying about calories," Carter said.

"Is that supposed to be a compliment?" Taylor asked.

"Why not," Carter said, but he preferred to change the subject. "So what do you think about Debbie's story?"

Taylor smiled but then spoke quietly to make sure no one could hear. "Here's what I think. The plans were laid out around the edge of the table so a person could make photos. You just have to walk around, lean over, and snap."

Carter was impressed. "That sounds plausible.

"If this incident has something to do with the ANC bombing, which is still a big if, I'm also wondering whether Debbie's scenario requires it to be an inside job, somebody from the department who knew how things were filed."

"It would make it go faster," Carter said, "but like Harry said, if somebody knows how to recognize an engineering plan, they could start pulling out drawers and look at the labeled subject categories and start seeing pretty fast what's going on."

"I think you're right. Things did have comprehensible labels."

"Which opens it up to the whole world again."

"I don't even want to think about that," Taylor said. "But what scares me even more is the variety of plans. If this actually is the bomber we're talking about, does that mean he's got other targets lined up?"

"From the sound of the collection," Carter said, "the guy could blow up the county's whole infrastructure."

"I'd hate to think that's what he has in mind."

"The guy, or his network, would need to have some pretty big resources, but we know that's not so farfetched. What else have your FBI friends found out?"

"We've tracked down the owners of the stolen bomb vans and are trying to link the MO to any known rings, in case it's a job for hire. But connections to the people we have in our files are pretty tenuous."

"Even if you found the car thief, would he necessarily know who hired him?"

"Not necessarily," Taylor said grimly. She sat in thought for a moment. "What about that Babcock?" Taylor asked. "Didn't you say he was the public works director at one time? Maybe we should take him up on his offer to help. He might know some people who could drum up some unexpected things. I mean, look at you. You tapped George Bender at a middle-school math team practice. Who's to say Babcock couldn't hit the jackpot?"

"I can't tell you not to."

"Who should contact him initially, you or me?"

Carter shook his head with a smirk. "I'll let you do the honors. I want Ed off my back as much as possible."

Taylor emptied her coffee with a tilt of the head and polished off the last bite of her donut. Carter noticed Taylor lick the sugar from the tip of her finger. She raised the same moist finger to flag down the waitress for a refill. She turned back to Carter. "I need more caffeine," she said.

"Not getting enough sleep?"

"Just too busy and restless," she said. "It's been a tough few days. You wake up thinking about this and that angle." She shrugged. "And now I might even have Frank eyeing my territory. With the foreign terrorist angle still coming up dry, suddenly I'm more central to the investigation. He didn't intend that. He saw me as some sort of fringe player, covering a far corner in the mandate for thoroughness."

"Is he planning to give someone else your responsibilities?"

"He wouldn't dare. But if I slip up, he'll have his excuse. So I don't plan to slip up."

Carter looked at Taylor's face and suddenly wanted to throw down the business façade. To hell with Gentry and Baker and Babcock, he thought. This investigation can't be everything. "So, what do you do to escape the pressure, in your free time?"

"It's been a while since I've had free time," Taylor said. "But I like to eat out, go dancing, things like that."

"What kind of dancing?"

"Salsa. I've got a weakness there."

"Good for you," Carter said. The thought stirred him. Without thinking he said, "I'd like to try that sometime." Carter immediately regretted his comment. Did she think he was asking her out?

Taylor spared him the worry. "So what kind of dancing does an engineer do?"

Carter pretended a scowl. "Are you trying to generalize again?"

"Never," Taylor said slyly.

"Well, I'll take your old classic rock—Zeppelin, Cream, Dooby Brothers. I had an uncle who introduced me to all those bands, but I'll admit, if you're talking about dancing, I've also got a streak that likes a Harry Connick Jr. .... But I *don't* speak for the engineering profession."

Taylor winked. "I thought that you did."

10

Carter looked out the window of his office at the snow falling through the February gray. It was a week later, the beginning of National Engineers Week, and Carter had taken a day off from the ANC investigation to talk to kids about engineering at a local elementary school and to help judge an egg-drop contest at George Mason University. The morning snowflakes fell straight in the windless silence, a soft curtain that turned the far banks of Georgetown into a faint shadow. The first layer of snow had been packed and soiled by the traffic on the street below, but Carter could see a layer of build-up on top of a delivery van in front of BWE.

The weather report had predicted at most one inch of accumulation, but Carter could picture the Washington area entering its usual panic, with schools closing and the federal government offering liberal leave, all for a snowfall that anywhere north would be laughed off as a dusting. Carter's secretary had already asked about the possibility of leaving early, and now Carter wondered whether his date with the elementary school might be called off.

Carter sat down at his desk and searched for the school's

phone number. He found it tucked inside his Engineers Week volunteer kit. The ring of the phone interrupted him.

"Scott Carter, BWE," he answered.

The familiar mechanical voice spoke quickly but calmly. "Happy Engineers Week. In three minutes our profession will again make its mark. An engineer will show the world what he can do. For all my FBI friends tracing this call, those Islamist leaflets were just a joke. No more fronts from now on. And you, Mr. Carter, you should look out the window to get the best view before judgment day." Jackhammer hung up.

Carter froze. The tracing timer showed 12 seconds. He realized frantically that he did not need to contact the FBI—he had hit the alert switch as soon as he had heard Jackhammer's voice. Supposedly they had not only taped, but listened. Carter looked toward the window. A sniper? He moved to the side and put his back against the wall. That made him feel foolish, but the race of his heart let him know that he had no choice. What was he supposed to watch for, he asked himself, a new bomb, a rocket-propelled grenade? Then suddenly the answer shot through his chest. The van. Carter looked down to the street and pulled his head back. The van was still there. Where was the delivery guy? Oklahoma City flashed through his head, and he realized he could not just wait and figure this thing out. He looked at his watch and ran through the door.

"We've got a possible emergency!" Carter shouted to the secretary. "Go down the back steps! I'm gonna pull the fire alarm. Tell everybody to go down the back. Not the front, the back!"

Carter ran to the elevators, jerked down the fire alarm, and felt the deafening blare drill into his head. He ducked into the stairwell and ran to the next floor up. "Go down the back stairs!" Carter shouted. "Tell everyone! Only the back!"

Carter ran up another floor and shouted the same thing. After that, people had already started going down just from the alarm, and Carter yelled his instructions, then got someone to play traffic cop so everyone went out the back.

Carter then called 911, told them about a possible bomb in a van, then ran into the front stairwell and looked down the central gap. He could see people descending, chatting leisurely as they would in a fire drill. He again shouted his orders, each second feeling the crushing imminence of a blast, then bounded down the steps, swinging himself around by the rail at each landing. His voice carried in the shaft of the stairwell, and he could see people returning inside.

At each floor, Carter waved people back through the doors and desperately asked everyone to spread the word. By the time he got to the first floor, the people seemed to have gotten the message. Carter looked at his watch but could not remember when he had started. He ran into the building, past the elevators, and into the offices of the first-floor management consulting firm. He followed the last stragglers, pushing them to move faster, and finally, heart still racing, got himself into the rear stairwell when the lights suddenly blacked out. Carter ducked, his hands over his head in the darkness. When he dared to look up, everything was silent, the emergency exit lights shining feebly below, the people next to him wondering what he was doing hunkered against the wall.

At the Chapman Power Station in Langley, Virginia, Stu Hopkins stood in the main control room and stared at the power distribution console. It showed a flashing red warning light that pinpointed a major failure in the Chapman power feed. He had heard the far boom of an explosion outside and now tapped a pencil nervously on the edge of the console.

"What have you heard?" he shouted again to his young assistant, John Holbrook. "We've got zero power on the feeder line. Nothing's leaving this place." Hopkins remembered the cold he had felt on coming to work that morning and shook his head in frustration. The public is not going to like this power loss, he thought.

The Chapman Power Station, a twenty-year-old oil-fired combustion turbine, generated 250 megawatts of power for 100,000 Arlington users, including all of Rosslyn. Hopkins, in his mid-forties, had been the chief control room operator for one month, after being recruited from a small, 95 megawatt plant in upstate New York. He had beaten out several more experienced operators and was itching to prove that management had not made a mistake.

Hopkins eyed the status read-out and kept tapping his pencil. He wanted to confirm the extent of the local problem before allowing the computer to reroute the power through some outlying grids. Ever since the massive Northeast blackouts of 1965 and 2003, coordination of interlinked power grids had become increasingly sophisticated. If lightning, or ice, or mechanical failure took out a major line, the computer could find a new route and plot end-runs around the failure, keeping track that the new paths did not overstep the maximum loads. Hopkins already knew what the first-order reroute would be—he had made a point of memorizing every detail, not wanting the computer to outshine him on a breakdown in his own plant. Now he just wanted to know whether the plant could get back on line quickly or whether he should tap the alternate paths.

Then Holbrook put down the phone at the far side of the control room and came running. "Somebody's bombed us! They tell me the feeder lines are gone, wiped out. They don't know about injuries, but we'll get nothing out of here. Jesus, what the hell's going on?"

"Find out about injuries," Hopkins ordered and turned to the console. "Oh my God," he said under his breath. He could not help the people outside—the emergency crews would have to take care of that. He had to stick to getting power back to the city. "Has someone called 911?!"

"I'm doing it again!" Holbrook said. When he hung up, he was pale. "What if they bomb this office?"

Hopkins had not really thought about that and now swallowed hard. "I'm betting against that, but you go! Get out of here!"

Quickly, Hopkins keyed in the pre-programmed commands so that a pair of regional plants could pick up the slack. With the cold outside, heating demands would be high, but daylight meant lighting demands would not be at maximum. The regional plants that served as first-order back-up would be able to pick up the loss at least until late afternoon. Hopkins activated the command sequence and watched the reroute program trace out the green of a spider-web grid on his large-console monitor. A flashing "X" above Dumfries, Virginia, told him the reroute was not going to work.

"What the hell?!" Hopkins said out loud.

Carter straightened up in the stairwell, still expecting an explosion, but nothing came, only the mumbling complaints from the straggler tenants who now continued out through the back door of the building.

"Who scheduled a fire drill during a blackout," somebody asked.

"Waynewright," somebody answered.

Carter looked up into the darkened shaft of the stairwell, the emergency lights glowing like dying candles in the niche of a catacomb. He did not know what to think or expect and followed the last person out the door into the street. There the daylight and the fitful morning traffic insisted on normalcy, but when Carter scanned the office buildings of the street, he saw no lights and no computer screens—just people standing by the windows wondering when the power would come back.

Carter walked fast to the corner and looked down the avenue. All the storefront signs had gone out, and as far as he could see, the office buildings stood mute within the gray of the falling snow, as though the living soul had died within the rigid city carapace.

Is this what Jackhammer was talking about? Carter asked himself, still breathless from his exertion and fear. A blackout of the city? This can't be a coincidence. The timing was perfect.

Carter heard the fire truck sirens approach in the distance. They grew louder and more insistent, until Carter heard them plow to a halt in front of the building, the flashing lights reflecting off the windows across the street opposite Carter. Office workers stared from behind the glass, the reflected red and white bursts repeatedly drowning their faces.

Carter thought of the van. Could it still be possible? He ran to the front of the building and shot a glance around the corner. The fire trucks, angled into the street, had seized the whole front sidewalk, and firefighters clamored from their trucks.

The van was gone.

Carter saw his FBI bodyguard trotting toward him. The man had parked across the street to stand watch on BWE.

"What's with the fire alarm?" the bodyguard asked.

"I got a call from Jackhammer warning about something big. I saw a delivery van parked in front of the building and thought I needed to evacuate everybody. I guess I jumped the gun."

"I don't think so," the bodyguard said. "As soon as I saw the driver trying to go in with that van unattended, I was suspicious and ran over and asked to take a look."

"So what was he carrying?"

"Potted plants."

"I guess that's better than ammonium nitrate fertilizer."

"They did have the little fertilizer bags tied to the stems."

Carter shook his head, almost ready to smile. "I appreciate you looking after these things."

Carter approached the fire trucks and looked for someone in charge. He found a man in a fireman's coat and helmet barking some orders. Carter told him about the false alarm—they did not have to search the building for fire. The man did not want to hear any stories and kept things in motion. Carter called over the FBI bodyguard and had him flash his Bureau ID to corroborate. Carter said, "I know you have your procedures, but you're going to have enough work on your hands with this blackout."

The fireman looked around at the darkened buildings. A fine layer of snow clung to the top of his visor. "Let's hope the lights come on soon."

"I've got a feeling it might not be so quick," Carter said.

Carter apologized for the trouble, jogged to the back of the building where the tenants and BWE colleagues stood in the cold, and told them it was a false alarm. When he turned around, he saw that the fire department still intended to inspect the building before letting anyone in. Well, I could be the arsonist, Carter thought. Why trust me and some fake ID?

At a loss, Carter just paced, watching the tenants standing around in the street, an occasional colleague kidding him about all the excitement, Carter, in his own world, wondering what else Jackhammer had up his sleeve. Many of his colleagues had picked up their winter coats on the way out and now returned reasonably comfortable. Carter again found himself shivering with only a sports jacket to ward off the cold. When are you going to learn, he asked himself.

In his black Mercedes, Jackhammer passed the southwest corner of the Lincoln Memorial and swung north along the Potomac, the Rosslyn skyline visible to his left out the window. At the time of the blackout, Jackhammer had stood on the western steps of the Lincoln Memorial and, checking his watch, had stared across the gray, snow-veiled water toward the dominant twin towers of the former *USA Today* buildings, the rest of the Rosslyn skyline stepping down from that summit. The skyscraper lights winked through the snow, huddling around the lone dark shape of the crippled ANC building.

Jackhammer could feel the massive white marble beneath his feet, the tons of stone piled as a base to an overpowering temple. He liked to think that the columns, a dead weight fluted toward the sky, rose from his own body, as though his backbone had been multiplied into a ribbed monolith of power. Jackhammer counted down the seconds, and in the slight delay from the preordained time, he felt his guts tense in an unbearable limbo. Then suddenly, silently, the far skyline went instantly black, as though a mischievous child had unplugged the Christmas tree. A rush of raw joy surged through him. He had controlled the destiny of a whole city, with his own financing and design. Ever since the miscreants had stripped him of his right to practice engineering, he had waited for these moments, showing that their license meant nothing when it came to taming his powers. As the adrenaline pumped through his veins, he would let the misguided souls know where they stood.

Rosslyn disappeared from sight as Jackhammer turned east and headed across town toward Northeast DC. He still breathed heavily in the pleasure of anticipation and spent the fifteen-minute drive in thought. He had staked out a street the day before and found a light post where, relatively unobserved, he could place his message. Jackhammer parked his car two blocks away, around a corner, and walked back to the site, watching for people but finding the street empty.

Unobtrusively, Jackhammer stopped near the light pole at the corner, pretending to wait for the traffic light, and pulled a small metal box from his pocket. He had machined the box himself, attaching a curved magnet to fit the shape of the pole, painting it a weathered green to match like a chameleon. A passerby would think the box had been in place for years, containing nothing more than some old-time wiring.

Jackhammer then returned to his car and took out a disposable cell phone. Checking for pedestrians, he placed his compact voice synthesizer onto the mouthpiece, letting the thin power cord lead through the front gap of his coat to a battery pack tucked in his shirt pocket. He dialed the number of David Renfroe, a Channel 3 Northern-Virginia beat reporter. Renfroe answered on the fourth ring.

"This is Jackhammer, the engineer responsible for the ANC building blast and the current blackout in Rosslyn. If you want a lead for your story, come to the light pole near the northwest corner of 14th and Rhode Island Avenue and remove the small box attached by magnet about three feet up from the base. You'll find the reading enlightening."

"Who are you?" the reporter asked.

Jackhammer hung up, removed the voice synthesizer, and tossed the phone into an empty box on the floor. He had enjoyed the startled sound of the reporter's voice, but now, as he drove to the downtown Willard Hotel to escape the power loss at his own Rosslyn condominium, he mildly regretted he had not triggered his blackout at night. The spectacle from the Lincoln Memorial would have been so much more dramatic, but then he would not have caught so many people at work. He had wanted that grating inconvenience, that staggering loss of revenue. He had also wanted it all on the 6:00 o'clock news. Take the damage as you can get it, Jackhammer thought. Save the aesthetics for later.

When Stu Hopkins ran the next scan to reroute the Rosslyn power, he had again come up empty. Stymied, heart pounding, he had given up for a minute and charged outside to check the damage to his power plant. Now he was back and trying hard to regain his composure. He had heard the screams of a man within the rubble and the flashing lights of an ambulance, and now that injured man's agony haunted him as he stood before his control room console wondering how he could get some juice back into Rosslyn. He had never heard the sound of real suffering, just from everyday pain or reenactments in the movies, and his mind kept flashing to a man whose bowels may have been torn from his body or whose severed limb may be pumping out blood. Hopkins' stomach had turned, and he still breathed hard.

OK, he thought, pull yourself together and get back to your job. You can't do anything to help the victim. It's done. It's not your responsibility. The medical people will do what they can. Goddamn it, I hope they can save him.

Hopkins took another deep breath and stared at the computer screen. He could not understand the rerouting failure at Dumfries. The major power line had just recently been inspected and no high winds or storms had struck since that time. The break meant the first backup plants could not complete the loop to the Arlington area.

Nervous, Hopkins told the computer to map out the next alternative. The routes swung farther afield and painted their green web on a larger-scale map so the whole could still fit on the monitor. This time Hopkins got no instantaneous warnings, but he knew that this particular view did not provide real-time feedback on breakdowns. He would have to make a few calls.

He first dialed the power plant in Mineral, Virginia, and asked if they could spare some extra capacity.

"No dice," the head operator said. "We could have sent up some juice, but we're dealing with a substation outage in one of our own areas. Preliminary reports say someone actually attacked the place."

"What?" Hopkins said in disbelief. "We've had a bomb at our own plant. We've got no more feeder lines. We've got serious injuries."

"Are you kidding me?" the operator said.

"I wish I were."

"OK, why don't you try Mountain Grove. We can take care of ourselves, but they've added some capacity for new industry slated for the area. The factories are behind schedule, so they're sitting there waiting to deliver."

"Yeah, I know about that," Hopkins said. "It's worth a shot. Thanks."

Hopkins looked up the phone number in the plant database and was ready to call when his boss walked up behind him, agitated and impatient.

"We've got a real mess out there," the director said. "One of our guys is hurt bad. They've taken him to the hospital." He shook his head in contempt for the situation. "So have you got us rerouted yet? If not, we're going to have some mighty cold customers."

Hopkins chafed that he could not show results for his work. He thought: So this was the first impression he made when an emergency struck. "Not yet. It looks like there were other attacks. I've already hit two dead ends."

"What are you talking about?" the director said. "We've got all sorts of contingency plans. They can't all be down. Get me that power. The switchboard's already lit up like a Christmas tree."

"This isn't just natural causes," Hopkins said, trying to show he was still in command. "Terrorists have attacked the power system. But the next reroute's gotta work. Just let me make that contact."

"You make it," the director said.

Hopkins fired off the call, but no one answered. He redialed to make sure he had not dialed the wrong number. This time, after six rings, someone picked up.

"Chesterfield Power Station," a voice said. "Make it quick."

"Stu Hopkins here, at Chapman. We've taken a terrorist attack and need some back-up. Can you step things up and give us some extra?"

"What line do you propose we use?"

"Through Charlottesville."

"Sorry, we're showing that one down. Don't have details yet. As soon as I hear more reports about what caused it, we can give you an estimate on repair time. Why don't you try North Anna?"

"Already have," Hopkins said. "Listen, give me a call when you get a repair estimate. You may still be the fastest fix for us. You know, this is getting scary."

"Are you saying our line might have been taken down deliberately?"

"It's possible. It's very possible."

"OK, I'll call you back when I know something new."

Hopkins hung up and stared at his monitor. With the main grid lines down, the computer offered no more options in Virginia, so he branched out to Maryland and BGE. There he got the same kind of reports. At a loss, he sent his map to the printer. "Man oh man," he said to himself as the printer eased its sheet into the bin like a deli slicer laying out a thin piece of ham. "This can't be happening."

Hopkins took his printout to the corner table and switched on the light. From memory, he began marking all the downed lines, X-ing the breaks with a red felt-tip pen. Anxiously, he searched for a way through the grid that could end up in Rosslyn. Every alternative he traced stopped at an X, as though a phantom general had declared war on the city. When a line from a plant did stand open, the available power fell far below needs.

Hopkins heard footsteps behind him and glanced up. The director bore down.

"So what's the deal?" the director asked impatiently, visibly shaken himself.

"Well, you look at this map of the damage in Northern Virginia and Maryland," Hopkins said, raising his tone to bolster his own sinking confidence. "There isn't a single line open to us. They're all blown."

After climbing eight flights of steps in the dark, Carter now sat at his office desk in the gray light from the window.

The phone and voicemail still worked, and Taylor had left him a message. Carter dialed her cell phone.

"Are you all right?" Taylor asked when she picked up. Her voice echoed in the hiss of traffic. "I heard from the monitoring team about Jackhammer's call."

"I'm fine. What do you know about the blackout so far?"

"Nothing except Jackhammer's warning and reports there's been an attack at the main power plant supplying Rosslyn."

"So Jackhammer planned this blackout," Carter said.

"It looks like it. That's where I'm headed."

"Do you need any help?"

"For now, there's nothing you can do," Taylor said. "I'm going to be one of a whole hive of agents swarming over the place. I suppose you don't have any special expertise in electric power distribution?"

"No," Carter said. His breath caught at the import. "Where'd the bastard call from?"

"A cell phone somewhere in DC, but he didn't leave us a calling card."

"One of these days the guy's going to make a mistake."

"I hope so," Taylor said. "I'll talk to you later when I hear more."

"All right," Carter said.

Carter set down the phone and stared out the window. All he could think about was what Taylor had said: He had no special expertise in electric power distribution. So, was he now out of the loop, second fiddle to some new expert? Beneath his anger at this new attack, he could feel the faint jealousy of someone else supplanting him at Taylor's side. At least Jackhammer was still calling him, Carter thought. As long as that threat came his way, Taylor and the FBI would stay interested.

Then Carter caught himself. So that's what it's come to, he thought, watching the snow fall like ash from a far-away explosion. While you pray that no one gets hurt in a blast, you redeem a madman's threats for the chance to still see the woman you love.

David Renfroe arrived at the corner of 14th and Rhode Island out of breath from the run. In his mid-thirties, he had covered the Northern-Virginia beat for five years and the ANC bombing had been his first big story, smothering his whole portfolio of drug busts, car-jackings, and city hall shenanigans. Hell, he thought, he must have really put his imprint on the Jackhammer coverage if the madman behind the news had picked him for a tip. This latest lead might be the clincher, and he had nearly missed it. If the call had come two minutes later, he would have been out on the street on his way to the Rosslyn blackout. Now he had asked his boss for a back-up to start on the power plant story while he checked out this lead. He had not told his boss exactly what he was after. He liked dramatics and surprise.

When Renfroe saw the small metal box exactly as Jackhammer had described it, he suddenly hesitated. What if this was a booby trap? For a moment Renfroe chided himself for being afraid—he just wanted the quick scoop—but he also realized that he was dealing with a bomber and that it would not do him much good if the box blew his head off. He pulled out his cell phone and dialed a contact in the DC police department.

"Lieutenant Brown here," a man answered.

"Jarret, it's Dave Renfroe. I need your help. I got a call from some guy who said I should look at a box he's put on a lamp post here in DC. He says it's got a message for me inside. It sounded like a hoax, some jerk having fun putting a reporter on a wild goose chase. But it was nearby, so I checked it out. Jarret, there *is* something there. It looks pretty harmless, but now I'm wondering whether it couldn't be some kind of bomb. You wouldn't want to leave something like that out there for a kid to play with, would you? I think you ought to send a bomb squad to take a look."

"Where do you get the idea this thing is dangerous?"

"I can't be sure. But do I want to risk blowing myself up for some practical joker? Do you want some kid doing the experiment?"

"Man, I can't send a bomb squad out on any little shit."

"So you're just going to leave it there, for some kid?"

"Right," Brown growled. "And if some kid gets hurt, guess who you're going to blame on the 6:00 o'clock news?"

"I wouldn't think of it," Renfroe said.

"Right," Brown grumbled. "OK, you wait there and I'll send down a team. But we're gonna make this fast."

"I appreciate it."

"Yeah, right."

Self-satisfied, Renfroe hung up the phone and walked back to the corner. He made sure no one stopped by to inspect his box. He regretted having lied to his friend, but he did not want the police stealing the note inside, if that's what it was. He figured that as soon as Lt. Brown confirmed there were no explosives involved, Brown would let him keep his booty with a few curses and a slap on the wrist. After all, they were not going to investigate an anonymous crackpot who attached notes to light poles. There was no law against that.

A two-man bomb squad arrived half an hour later with Lt. Brown tagging along.

"Why do I get the feeling you've set us up for nothing?" Brown asked.

"I hope I have," Renfroe said. "And you hope I have too. So don't kid yourself."

"Stop being a wise-ass," Brown said. "We want outta here."

Wearing protective suits, the bomb squad cordoned off the site with yellow police tape and let their bomb-sniffing dog take a whiff of the box. The dog found no interest. Additional tests also came up negative. Finally, one member removed the box from the pole and placed it into a protective barrel where he could pry at the cover with mechanical hooks.

When Renfroe saw the thumbs up, he rushed through the tape to make sure they did not inspect things any closer.

"Did your caller say this might be an explosive?" Lt. Brown asked, following behind.

"Not exactly. I was just being cautious."

"So I guess there's nothing we could charge this guy with, even if we did track him down," Brown said with disgust.

"I can't argue with that. So, can I have the box for my scrapbook of cranks?"

"You oughta put yourself in that scrap book," Brown said angrily. He turned to his team. "Let him have the trash and let's get outta here. I don't even want a record of this on the books." Brown pointed a fat finger at Renfroe. "*You've* now used up about every last chit you've ever had."

The bomb squad tossed the box to Renfroe, who grabbed it from the air with the same greed of a fan grabbing a home run from the bat of an all-star.

As the police packed up their gear, a new hesitation dimmed Renfroe's euphoria. He wondered how long he could wait before contacting the FBI and not be charged with obstructing justice.

The blackout was two hours old, and despite its good double-pane windows, Carter's office was beginning to get cold. Carter had tracked down some batteries for his office clock radio and now listened to Arlington Board Chairman Duncan denounce the "despicable and cowardly terrorist attack" against the county's power supply. Utility workers were working non-stop to correct the situation, Duncan said, but attacks here and in other parts of Northern Virginia and Maryland made a quick restoration of power unlikely. The county manager had encouraged businesses to send their workers home and private citizens to spend time with friends outside of Rosslyn until the situation cleared up. Duncan said he would spare no effort to end the emergency.

I think the utility workers will sense the urgency without you, Carter thought wearily, but he knew any politician was forced to say that kind of stuff.

Carter looked at his watch, then made some phone calls. He found out that his presentation at the local elementary school had been canceled because of the snow, but George Mason University was open and the egg-drop contest was still on. Carter put on his coat, phoned his bodyguard, and began the long walk down the stairs to the parking garage. At least this time, he thought, he did not have to run.

The snow let up during his drive out I-66 toward Fairfax, Virginia, and Carter suddenly felt abandoned in the new openness of clear air. He thought about all the feverish activity around the latest bombing and how he, by contrast, was out in the mid-day quiet of the Virginia suburbs ready to judge contraptions that would protect an egg from breaking in a 30-foot fall. He had always enjoyed the raucous enthusiasm of the engineering students, but today he would find it difficult to get hooked. News of the bombings would no doubt cloud the students as well.

Carter put on a good face for the participants, but the students' occasional whoops at a success and failure made Carter feel like an old man among kids. When the slime of a broken egg was pulled from the framed capsule of one of the losers, Carter wondered if that was how his life would turn out as he tried to juggle Michelle, Jackhammer, and cancer. He found it difficult to believe he had once been one of these kids himself, ready to get out and bulldoze anything that got in his way—of course, back then he had been ignorant that there was anything that tough to tackle.

Renfroe did not wait for the 6:00 o'clock news. In the small metal box, he had found a neatly typed manifesto, and after reading it, he realized he risked big trouble if he delayed calling the FBI. He made himself a copy and was careful to handle the box only with gloves. On the phone, he told the FBI he had thought his caller had been some crank pretending to be the Rosslyn bomber. Maybe the guy actually was a crank, Renfroe stressed, but he wanted to hand over what he had found and get back to his reporting.

Then Renfroe's hands almost shook when he began to compare the note with the corroborating evidence—the damage Jackhammer had claimed credit for matched the news reports exactly. No one except the perpetrator could have known those details so early. Big-eyed, Renfroe went live on a 3:00 p.m. special report, "Engineer Bomber Goes Public."

Standing in the cold outside the crippled power plant to the north of Rosslyn, Renfroe looked into the camera, a copy of Jackhammer's manifesto prominently in hand, relishing the hype.

"In an exclusive for Channel 3 News, the bomber of the American News Corp. building and now the Chapman Power Station, has bared his twisted vision to the public in what he calls an Engineers Week manifesto, provided exclusively to our newsroom. Even more dramatic, there is no more reference to Islamist terrorists, but to the apparent act of an American, unless, of course, this is just a trick to cover up for the true perpetrators." Renfroe took a breath and continued. "Still calling himself Jackhammer, the bomber outlines a series of six pinpoint bomb attacks throughout Northern Virginia and Maryland, to power lines and electric power substations. These attacks—and this has been confirmed with the utilities involved—have blocked off any chance for an immediate restoration of power to Rosslyn, which has now been in the dark for five hours."

Renfroe related Jackhammer's "great pride in the careful planning of his attacks," noting the road blocks to every possible detour in rerouting the power lines.

"On the surface, Jackhammer is trying to put to rest any speculation that the ANC bombing was carried out by a foreign terrorist group. Whether that turns out to be true is yet to be seen. Jackhammer also mentions no links to domestic hate groups, although references of what would be characterized as right-wing extremism can be found in his statement."

For dramatic effect, Renfroe held up his copy of Jackhammer's words and glanced at it knowingly. "What is most striking in Jackhammer's manifesto, and what might be considered a bizarre twist for such a terrorist act, is that Jackhammer timed his power plant attack to coincide with what is called

National Engineers Week. Apparently, engineering associations and corporations fund activities that promote recognition of engineer contributions to society and teach school kids how an engineering career will help them shape the future.

"Curiously, the two-page, wordprocessed manifesto shows a strange love-hate relationship with the engineering profession, of which Jackhammer claims to be a member. He attacks engineers, who he says should be, and I quote, 'the rational backbone of this country,' unquote, but instead have sold out to, and again I quote, 'the politically correct liberals who have undercut national security and a strong defense, ravaged moral values, and corrupted citizen integrity through surrender to fringe-group blackmail.' But beyond these types of blasts, Jackhammer goes into a lengthy litany of everything that 'geniuses' like him have given to this country. Jackhammer says that for proof, the public only has to look at his acts to see how much an engineer like him controls their safety and livelihoods. For example, he writes that the bombing of the ANC building showed perfect placement of explosives that, and I quote, 'by careful planning and mercy, left the building standing by a thread.' He says people can now see that the steel frame that holds them up each day in their offices comes from a power they take completely for granted. As I've mentioned, Jackhammer makes the same sort of claim with the Rosslyn power outage. I quote, 'Just as brains and creativity can build the essentials we so deeply depend on, that talent can also destroy, as the Great Almighty both builds and destroys'."

The camera now zoomed away as a woman stepped into the picture. Renfroe turned to her and said, "I have with me Dr. Janice Sheldon, a clinical psychologist at Georgetown University, who agreed to analyze Jackhammer's manifesto and speak to us about her interpretation. Dr. Sheldon, first in a general sense, what type of person would write and do something like this?"

Carter had come home and flipped the remote to watch the Channel 3 News for the latest on the bombings, and after seeing the psychiatrist come on, he now hit the mute in protest. Jesus Christ, he muttered. He could not stand the sound of psychological double-talk and cursed that Jackhammer had not only killed innocent people but now twisted the image of engineers into a Georgetown shrink analyzing the crazed writing of a wacko murderer.

Carter got up and circled the den, pained that an American might be committing these crimes and angered by the bad name engineers were getting. He recalled how a website after September 11 had implied structural engineers had been asleep at the switch in designing a skyscraper that could collapse like the World Trade Center. Carter had bristled at the insinuation. This was the same World Trade Center that had been hailed for its strength after the 1993 bombing had failed to take it down, the same buildings that on September 11 had stood up long enough to save thousands of lives. How were engineers back in the 70s expected to anticipate a fully fueled airplane of the future making a deliberate impact and melting the steel in the inferno? Well, what if several cruise missiles had been aimed at the place? Was it supposed to be designed to withstand those too? Carter would not deny that structural engineers had learned important lessons. They had pored over the studies and adopted design alternatives for the future. But this was a new world, with a new set of realistic possibilities, and like everyone else, engineers would have to consider new "what ifs" in everything they did. But that was how the press operated, Carter thought, or at least that web columnist. Look for the sensational and the negative to beef up your readership.

Carter picked up the phone and dialed Bob Waynewright at home.

"Bob, Scott here. Can you get me a press conference tomorrow? Jackhammer contacted me again, so I assume there'll be interest."

"Now you're talking," Waynewright said. "I never liked a reluctant superstar."

"Knock it off Bob. I just have to slam some of this Jackhammer BS."

"We'll have to find a new place. Your Jackhammer has kindly knocked out the power in our office too. Do you realize the money that's costing us?"

"You don't have to tell me, Bob."

"Well, I know the manager of the Alexandria Holiday Inn. Maybe I can get a meeting room cheap. Hell, maybe he'll give it free for the publicity."

"Who could resist that," Carter said, trying to project his quip over the phone.

Waynewright scowled, suppressing a smile of his own. "If you don't watch it, I'll make you the gopher who carts the BWE logo down to the hotel. One way or another, it's gonna hang behind your head!"

11

When Carter woke the next morning, he got up quietly, walked down to the kitchen, and with two tired flicks, turned on both the radio and his old, stained coffee maker. As the water slowly built to a boil, the all-news radio station spoke of the Rosslyn blackout. The governor of Virginia had called out the National Guard to help protect the state's power lines and substations, and the Arlington County manager had set up shelters to harbor the elderly and the infirm who had now faced nearly a full day of subfreezing temperatures and no electric heat. The president of the United States had condemned the power grid attack and promised an all-out effort to bring the perpetrators to justice.

In the streets of Rosslyn, frozen foods began appearing on the city's windowsills, sidewalks, and parking lots as apartments and restaurants fought to preserve the perishables in their freezers, while many pharmacies transported their refrigerated drugs to other sites. Local medical clinics without back-up generators had been crippled, and during the night, the prospect of crime in the darkened streets forced the county manager to bring out the police in force.

Nearly every store and business depended on computers to push their paper, and they all told their workers to stay home. If they had not done it voluntarily, the county manager would have ordered it. With metro stations dark and traffic lights out, a load of commuters would have turned the Rosslyn streets into gridlock. Arlington County had not yet estimated the total financial cost, be it the extra cops and work crews on the street or private sector work flushed down the toilet.

Permeating the reports of loss were psychological analyses of the "engineer bomber," and the more Carter heard, the more he hoped to counteract the damaging publicity. But he did not even know if Waynewright could make the arrangements.

Carter poured himself a half cup of coffee and lifted his mug to down it in two short swallows. He then headed for the shower and when finished, put his pajamas back on and sat down in front of his computer with a donut and more coffee.

Carter had brought home some work for the ANC rebuilding project, but he found the concentration hard going. His mind continually wandered to Jackhammer and how the man toyed with everyone involved, how the investigation seemed to be getting nowhere, and how he personally wanted to nail that son of a bitch. And when Carter thought of the investigation, he thought of Michelle, and that brought a blunt nervousness. The investigation had turned to electric utilities, and again he thought about how that could mean losing his FBI tie-in. Maybe he just had to break down and ask Michelle out on a date, give a clear hint that he was interested, and see what happened. He had no idea what her feelings might be and how she might react.

Carter did not like this vulnerability. It nipped at his hard-nosed self-respect and the sense that he had control of his emotions. How often had he taken pride in the rational substrate to his actions, feeling superior to so many people's petty hysteria?

And now that self-mastery seemed to be going to hell.

At 3:00 p.m. Carter stepped before the TV lights in a cramped conference room full of reporters at the Old Town Alexandria Holiday Inn. Waynewright had kept the PR wheels turning and stood in the wings like a self-satisfied ruffian who had bullied everything into place, including the big BWE logo directly behind the podium.

The van-mounted satellite dishes outside and the concentration of cameras inside again pushed the adrenaline through Carter's veins. He looked out at the glinting lenses with a new sense of presence. He supposed this was what the politicians lived for, and he could not deny the temporary rush. People would now listen to his views and probably find it important enough to broadcast and write about. The main thing was not to let it get to your head, Carter thought. You're basically an average Joe who happened to get caught up in things. That's where the politicians fell down, he told himself—they were full of themselves.

As Carter unfolded his notes, he quickly scanned the entrances and suddenly noticed Michelle Taylor just inside the door. He had told her the schedule but had not known whether she could make it. The sight shifted his determination one gear higher.

"Before I take your questions, let me say a few words about Jackhammer," Carter began. "I don't doubt that this sick bomber has a civil engineering background. I've suspected that from the beginning, but let me just remind the public that this man has absolutely no right to say anything in terms of engineers or National Engineers Week. Look, I've spent a lot of my career talking up what engineers do to improve people's lives with the hope of attracting young people from all backgrounds to the profession. And now we have this psycho trying to play up engineers in his twisted way and he's getting more airtime than all of us engineers put together over the last decade. I guess that's an irony we have to live with. The bad news always gets the airtime. Well, all I can do is ask everyone to simply ignore this criminal. Flush him away. Don't listen to him. He's killed and maimed people and now caused untold more suffering, when the commitment of any real professional engineer is to protect the public. OK, that's enough of my soapbox. Let me just emphasize that I and my firm Blackstone-Waynewright Engineers continue to pledge our time and resources to bringing this Jackhammer to justice."

When he finished, Carter realized how much he had gotten caught up in the moment and now wondered whether his direct attack would put him right back in Jackhammer's crosshairs, maybe even push him to pull the trigger. Well, it was too late to do anything about that, he thought. "OK, any questions?"

The reporters' hands shot up and Carter pointed to one at random. He was not the president of the United States and had no idea who was who.

"Could you speculate on Jackhammer's motivations and personality. What do you think makes him tick?"

"I'm sorry, but I can't analyze the mental make-up of a madman. You know, when you're an engineer, you like to think you approach things with a level head and make sound decisions for what's good for the owner of a project and for society. This Jackhammer has some screws loose—I don't know, like some crazy villain from a Batman comic book. I'm no comic book writer, so I can't begin to speculate."

Another reporter asked, "How are you dealing with the threats you've personally received?"

"I didn't know I'd talked about that publically."

"I've got my sources," the reporter said.

"OK. I can't say it's too pleasant. Who wants to be constantly checking his back? It can wear a person down. But I'll tell you, what I'm looking forward to is seeing this Jackhammer behind bars. That would let me sleep well."

Other questions bored into Jackhammer's latest phone call to Carter and the Engineers Week manifesto, and Carter did his best to discount everything Jackhammer had said and turn it into positives. At times it was like trying to extract the good from a Hitler pet project.

Finally a reporter asked, "Could this Jackhammer be someone you know?"

Carter shook his head, somewhat wearily. "It would mean I'm pretty blind to what's inside a person." He glanced at Michelle as if to confirm she was still there, and then glanced quickly away, his eyes back on the reporter. "But I guess that kind of blindness isn't all that impossible. How are we supposed to tell what's going on inside a person's head? I've read enough news stories about the friendly enough neighbor turning out to be a serial killer. I've met a lot of people in my career. Bottom line: Very doubtful, but I have no idea."

Taylor watched Carter fold his notes and slip them into his suit pocket as he left the podium. She did not know why he had bothered to bring the notes, since he had not referred to them once. As she followed his movements, she was glad she had gotten away to see his performance. She wanted to track what the public was hearing, and she liked Carter's determined style. Face it, she thought, after the U.S. president had again commented about apprehending Jackhammer, Gentry had started posturing himself as the new day-to-day shot-caller, and she found Carter's down-to-earth smarts a refreshing contrast. She felt she had nothing to prove in his presence and did not have to expect any ego trips or put-ons in return. At times she wondered whether that comfort level could border on affection. He was nice to have around, especially without the pretense of a relationship.

At the side of the room, Carter accepted a whack on the back from Waynewright.

"Home run!" Waynewright barked. "The way you worked BWE into your statement made us look like a bunch of saints!"

"I thought you might like it," Carter said. "Of course, it was just my ploy to keep myself on the investigation. I want to nab this guy, and now you definitely can't pull me off the case. That would be a PR disaster."

"Don't advertise you're that devious. Of course, as long as you keep plugging the firm, you don't need to cook up any schemes. The FBI can steal you all they want—within reason."

"What does that mean…that I can use the evenings to make up the regular work hours?"

Waynewright grunted and waved him off. Carter then turned to look for Taylor. He found her waiting in the hotel lobby.

"Glad you could make it," Carter said. "I hope I didn't spout too many clichés."

"Don't act so modest," Taylor chided good-naturedly. "Of course, there's always the danger of being a little melodramatic when you start touting the honor of the engineering profession, but I thought it was just fine."

"Now that's a compliment. When you wince, you'll let me know."

Taylor smiled. "I promise."

Carter asked if she had time to give him the latest about any new evidence, maybe over a coffee.

"Sorry, no time to sit down, but you can walk me to my car and I'll give you what I can."

Taylor wasted no time and swung her handbag over her shoulder like a scout master setting off to lead a pack through the mountains. Carter fell in beside her.

Outside, the temperature had climbed to 45 degrees, and the white-washed spire of the colonial Alexandria Town Hall stood bright in the light of the afternoon sun. The broad pool of the fountain lay drained and empty in the square, with a few patches of ice still left in the puddles. At Taylor's side, Carter felt an aching flush of spring in the afternoon thaw.

"Can you keep something under your hat?" Taylor asked, her pace brisk across the red brick of the square.

"Sure," Carter said. "I don't assume somebody will torture me for information."

"Well, the lab has confirmed that Jackhammer's manifesto was printed on a low-end HP printer, with an HP-brand toner cartridge. Apparently no toner refills involved."

"How's that possibly going to do you any good?"

"Probably won't. The list of area purchasers is in the thousands and thousands."

"And the guy might not even live in the area."

"Well, if we spot some interesting suspect, I'll flag him for you. But I'll have to admit, I'm not as independent as before."

Carter could sense a trace of regret in her voice.

"The foreign connection is now even weaker," Taylor went on, "and the president has promised a full-court press, so Frank's getting on his high horse and muscling in. For the domestic engineering side, I'm now just part of a much bigger team. I've got less authority to call the shots for what I do every day."

"Is Frank finally showing his prejudice against you as a woman?"

"No. The way things have turned out, Frank would have done the same thing one way or the other. He's got the experience, and that's what you need when the president calls, and he's out for glory as much as the rest of us."

"So the chance to boost your career has taken a blow?"

Taylor lifted her chin with a warm flair of defiance. "I'm not ashamed to admit it. Yeah, besides catching the guy, I wanted to make my mark. Before I was a shark prowling around for a target. Maybe I was a small one, but still a shark. The way it looks now, I'm just one of the minnows."

Wendel Smith, chairman of the Virginia engineering licensure board, clutched his chin in nervous disbelief and reread the anonymous letter, hoping he had misunderstood the contents. But as his old, puffy eyes peered through his thick-framed reading glasses, he mumbled a "gosh darn" and then a "what the heck?" before finally letting the letter drop to the table and rubbing his hand hard across his fleshy face.

Smith did not want commotion. He had retired from active work in his engineering consulting firm in Richmond, Virginia, and was now rounding out a final year as head of the board that oversaw the state's design professionals, regulating competency standards and handling cases of illegal and unethical practice, much like a state bar association or a state medical board. Smith had won the chairmanship two years ago through an "aw-shucks" collection of political chits and a folksy willingness to put in the hours of what was basically volunteer work. His leadership had been marked by a nervous obsession not to raise controversy and a friendly befuddlement in establishing priorities. His performance had left some of his board colleagues looking forward to the day when he would finally step down.

The letter, unsigned but closing with "a licensed civil engineer colleague," stated in knowledgeable terms that Scott Carter had been involved in plan stamping on a project to expand an Arlington County office building two years ago. The charge meant that design plans had been drawn up by unlicensed engineers and that Carter had then signed and sealed the plans as the P.E. in responsible charge, yet without direct involvement or oversight. If true, that constituted a violation of the state engineering practice act. The letter emphasized that the engineering profession was not well served when the individual combating recent terrorist acts and suddenly acting as the profession's chief spokesman had acted unethically. The writer also stated, or threatened, that if the board did not at least hold a hearing on these charges, the writer would go to the press and let them know that the licensure board chairman was sweeping this serious issue under the rug. The press would enjoy speculating why the chairman was trying to protect Scott Carter against legitimate charges.

The letter acknowledged that Smith might feel uncomfortable about pursuing an anonymous tip, so the writer offered a source and a phone number. John Franklin, once an Arlington County Public Works engineer and now with Burnside Consulting in Rockville, Maryland, could confirm the gist of these charges. The writer gave the chairman one day to set the wheels in motion before he contacted the press.

Smith felt an anxious frustration shred his earlier peace. At first, his thoughts stuttered in outrage at the threats. Who does this guy think he is? Smith blustered to himself. I'm not going to call exploratory hearings on something out of the blue like this. But as he fingered the letter, his posturing soon gave way to a fumbling fear. What if the press came to his door and started badgering him about why he didn't explore these charges? Scott Carter was all over the news these days, and it would look like some kind of favoritism or even weakness on the chairman's part. He dreaded that kind of publicity. He dreaded publicity, period. Wouldn't it be best to at least look into it? Who was this guy John Franklin, anyway? Smith didn't know him. Maybe a phone call would not do any harm. Right, he thought. Just check it out, one step at a time. You can't act like nothing's happened. That would be sweeping things under the rug. That would be unprofessional, wouldn't it? Wouldn't it?

Smith felt his hands tremble as he stared at the phone.

John Franklin had been unable to sleep the previous night. He now sat in his office cubicle and stared at plans for an industrial environmental cleanup project, unable to concentrate, knowing that he risked losing his career and even facing jail time.

The night before, he had received a call from a man with an electronically altered voice. The voice had reminded him of his theft two years ago, when he had worked with the Arlington County government. At the time, Franklin had taken a loan to play a sure-thing stock tip from a broker friend and saw the exuberance of gambling turn into disaster. He faced losing his house and could not imagine telling his wife. He suspected his wife would take his recklessness as an excuse to divorce him.

Franklin had received a letter offering some quick money for off-hours engineering work. A few others in the county government had received the same proposal, but the offer had been vague and no one had bothered to follow up. Anxious for anything, Franklin had made the call. That led to several exploratory phone interviews with a Thomas Miller, and a discussion of how much money Franklin might need. Then the talk suddenly shifted from engineering design. Franklin received a registered-mail envelope with a $5,000 cash down payment and a letter describing the required work: photographing a series of design plans from the county archives, including the ANC building. According to the letter, a design firm was chasing some upgrade work and wanted a better overview of the county infrastructure so it could make the lowest bids on upcoming contracts. Franklin knew that such RFPs were coming up, so the letter's request seemed credible, if illegal.

Faced with the truth, Franklin had agonized about whether to accept the work, but the shame of admitting financial failure and the fear of losing his wife had won out. What harm would it do, he had asked himself. The design drawings held nothing truly confidential, and it was just going to affect a few bucks here or there in a bunch of rotten business deals. Nobody was going to get hurt, and the job would not be that risky. Besides, Franklin could not ignore the $20,000 in cash promised on delivery of the photos. In the end, he shut down his doubts and worked with an anonymous contact to set up a system of drops. He got a specialized camera and instructions and later picked up the payment. He met no one in person.

Now, two years later, an electronic voice told Franklin that the stolen designs had been used in the ANC bombing and that Franklin was now an accomplice in a plot to commit murder. The voice chuckled that Franklin could protest the innocence of his motives, but that it would be his word against the bomber's. The voice emphasized he would be happy to contact the FBI and claim that discussions for the theft of the drawings had explicitly mentioned the terrorist bombing, and that for that reason Franklin had required the high sum of $25,000 for what would otherwise have been a negligible misdemeanor and a much cheaper job. To avoid the damning connection, Franklin merely had to do one favor—acknowledge to the Virginia engineering licensure board that design drawings for a county office building extension, sealed by Scott Carter, had the mark of plan stamping, given the short deadline involved and the things Franklin had heard. There was no need to eventually prove the charges, just to get it a hearing. That was a simple request, the voice claimed, given the alternative.

Two years earlier, Franklin had realized that his act might come back to haunt him, but when nothing had happened, he had thought he had made the right decision, bailing himself out of debt and moving ahead with his career. Now he realized he had no way out. If he refused the request, he would expose his original theft. Even if the authorities could not make the murder conspiracy stick, he did not think he could lie himself out of the rest. The FBI would find the $25,000 in his bank accounts matching the dates from his accuser. They would wonder why he had gotten so much money for such a simple assignment. At the very least, he would lose his engineering license, and with that his job and his career. What was he going to do, start selling life insurance? Who would hire him with a criminal record and all the publicity that would follow this high-profile case? Franklin saw his life collapsing around him.

Later the telephone rang.

"Hello, is this John Franklin?" a man said.

"Yes," Franklin answered. He did not recognize the voice. Was the FBI already onto him?

"This is Wendel Smith, chairman of the Virginia licensure board. How're you today?"

Smith's voice sounded cheery, if perhaps forced, and Franklin mustered a "just fine," realizing he would have no more time to put off a decision.

"I'm sorry to disturb you," Smith said, "but I received some information about alleged plan stamping on a project you were apparently aware of within the Arlington County government. It involves Scott Carter of Blackstone-Waynewright Engineers—you've certainly heard about Scott with the recent terrorist bombings. Well anyway, I don't put a whole lotta stock in it, since it comes from an anonymous source, but the source did give your name as possibly having some information, so I just wanted to hear out what you might have to say."

Franklin's nervousness squeezed down his breathing. What would happen if he admitted suspicions about Carter? There would be a hearing, but the blackmailer had said he did not have to prove anything. This would all just be a major inconvenience, an embarrassment, but no real harm. And if you don't do it, your life is down the tubes. Are you going to be noble just so Scott Carter doesn't get ruffled a bit?

"I did have suspicions," Franklin said cautiously.

"Oh, you did?" Smith had hoped it would all come to nothing. "Is this something you'd be willing to bring up at a hearing?"

Franklin swallowed hard. "I don't know how much concrete proof I can give you, but I can state what I know."

"OK," Smith said, "why don't you give me a run-down so I know what to expect."

The blackmailer had given Franklin details to augment his own experiences, and he now sketched them for Smith. When he finished, Smith did not sound happy. "Heck, I might just have to look into this." Smith paused, as if to accentuate his regret. "It's not what I wanted to hear. If it's true, it's a black eye for Scott." Smith found himself fumbling in the surprise of having to act. "Well, I may have to schedule this fast so it's cleared up and over with. Are you going to be available in the next few days?"

"I suppose so," Franklin said.

"Well, I may be in touch."

Wendel Smith looked for a way to lessen the sting and immediately contacted Carter, whom he knew through past ASCE committee work. It's the least I can do, Smith said to himself. Scott will appreciate the heads up.

Smith knew he would not find Carter in his blacked-out Rosslyn office, so he called the licensure board to get the home number. It was 5:00 p.m. on the Friday afternoon of the latest press conference. Carter picked up the phone.

"Is this Scott?" Smith asked.

"Yes it is," Carter said with a slight delay, fearing a reporter or a salesperson.

"Well, hello. I could'a sworn that was your voice. This is Wendel Smith, chairman of the Virginia engineering licensure board."

"Hello. How are you doing Wendel?"

"Can't complain. And you?"

"All right, I guess, given the circumstances. I didn't see you at ASCE committee week. What've you been up to?"

"Oh," Smith said, "I gave up my committee slots; you know, let the younger guys have a chance. Pretty soon I'll be retiring from the state board too. I'm ready to go out to pasture."

"I'm sure there's a committee that can find you some work."

"Yeah, Scott, you always were the active one. But I'm getting tired. I'll stick to badgering my grandkids."

"I can't argue with that. So what can I do for you?"

Smith cleared his throat and stuttered briefly. "Well, uh, I find this all a little . . . a little distasteful and unfortunate, and I don't really think there's that much to it, but you know, I don't think I have much choice in the matter."

"What's that, Wendel?"

"Well, uh, you see, we've gotten information that there might'a been some irregularities on your part in that Arlington County office building expansion two years ago. We've gotten a tip that says you may have been involved in plan stamping on the project. Now, before you start to protest, let me tell you that I don't believe a word of it. I know you, Scott, and I can't imagine you doing something like this, but my hands may be tied in the matter."

"What do you mean, a tip?"

"Well, I got this letter that appears to be very knowledgeable about the whole affair."

"From whom?"

"The writer didn't say, but—"

Carter would not let him go any farther. "Are you telling me you're going to pursue something on an anonymous tip? Isn't that against board regulations?"

"Well, it's not totally anonymous. The writer gave John Franklin as a source, a former Arlington County engineer who apparently heard something about the situation." Smith paused and took a breath. "And he says there may be something to it."

Carter's exasperation spilled into his voice. "Man oh man, Wendel. You know this is all a bunch of bull. I know we did that project fast, and I had a lot of engineers involved, but I spent every night of that week, and the weekends, going over those plans before I put my seal on them. You talk to anyone at my firm and they'll tell you the same thing."

"I don't doubt it," Smith said. "And that's why I need to have a hearing, to get it all out on the table."

"A hearing? Wendel, you want to question my reputation in public? Just calling the hearing is going to do that, no matter what happens afterwards."

"I won't even make it a full-blown hearing, just something quiet to get things examined."

"Why are you rushing into this?" Carter asked. "What was in that letter anyway?"

"Well, I'll be honest with you. The guy who wrote the letter is playing hardball. He says he's going to the press with the story if I don't hold a hearing. So if I don't, then the press'll come knocking, wondering why I didn't follow up. They'll notice that we know each other, and they'll notice you've gotten a lot of publicity, and they'll immediately jump to the conclusion that the Virginia engineering board is in the business of protecting its own. I don't want that kind of publicity."

"Jesus, Wendel, you can just give the press the facts and not have a hearing. You can't give in to this blackmailer. He may be some jerk who's jealous of me getting publicity."

Smith let self-righteousness suppress his qualms. "I know where you're coming from, Scott, and I have great respect for that, but I've decided to hold at least a preliminary hearing. I'm doing it real fast, in the next few days, and we'll have this thing aired in the proper fashion and your name will be cleared."

"I can't believe you're doing this Wendel. You really have to reconsider. I mean, this is nuts."

"I'm sorry, Scott," said Smith, defending himself with the tone of a preacher. "I've got to protect the board and its reputation, not just yours."

And your own rear end, Carter thought. But he did not say it.

That night, Carter read in *The Washington Post* about a man from the Chapman power plant who had been unconscious since the blast and had now died of his injuries. Carter laid down the paper and stared at the silence of his living room and then felt it happen again. With all the continued threats, he would suddenly look up from the newspaper or a book, or open his eyes to the predawn darkness in bed, and feel that everything he might have wanted had been taken away. It was as though he had suddenly slipped into a prison in which the cell shrank at unexpected moments.

Carter had no true picture of death. Sometimes the anticipation of dying made the view in front of him race like a film reel jacked up to high speed, the background uncertainty spinning recklessly while the picture itself moved in the sluggish normalcy of existence, hundreds of frames per second whirring beneath the slowness of a repetitive day.

At times, he found himself downplaying everyday risks. Why, when he was parking his car, should he bother to lock the door if he might get shot anyway? Why worry about a presentation to a client? He himself might not even be around when the project was built.

And now, in the silence of that Friday night, Carter suddenly felt one of those cracks and saw himself mortgaged to what looked like an empty landscape. Every day he came home to this elegant museum, with nobody home, with no kids running to the door and dragging him in to play games, with no woman at his side, with no sound but his own footsteps and the click of the radio as he turned on the news, reheating his dinner to the hum of the microwave. It pained him to think of his last years with Linda and her visits to psychiatrists that never came to anything. How tragically ironic that he had secured this house and its collection of antiques for Linda by accepting the move into management just so they would have the money for a little more luxury. He had been lured by the status and by the pull to make Linda happy—but she had not been happy and then she had died, having already earned enough to make Carter's original sacrifice pointless. The extra money had piled up at the feet of their financial manager. The house had turned into a finely appointed coffin.

From within those walls, Carter could see Michelle walking fast across the square in Alexandria, the afternoon sun lighting the vitality of her face. It was as though she were running away from him, anxious to get to her next appointment, perhaps never coming back. Just today, in that hint of winter warmth, Carter had imagined inviting her to the beach at Assateague Island in the early spring and pitching a tent at the corner of the campgrounds, then jogging on the hard sand by the water while the sun set across the grass at the top of the dunes. Michelle would take down her hair, and the sea salt and perspiration would mingle when they finally touched. After a T-bone steak on an open fire in the night, they would walk by the shore, the moon just coming up, and he would feel that he had made something of his life, even if it all might end in the next instant.

Carter stood up to shake himself free from these thoughts. He had to distract himself and walked to his computer and logged on to the ASCE on-line mentoring forum, hoping to do something useful while he killed some time. Carter was one of the few who logged in regularly to see what questions his young engineers had posted, and even when Carter did not have the time, he felt guilty about staying away.

Carter scrolled through the questions and came to an engineer in Ohio. The young man asked about the pros and cons of the technical and management tracks. For a moment, Carter wanted to charge in and tell the kid to stick with whatever gave him the most pleasure. Do technical design work all your life if that's what your passion is. Forget about all the temptations of money and rank and the accepted formula for advancement. Carter thought of the young man still at the beginning of his career, and then of his own college goal to design a New York City skyscraper. Jesus, how you threw yourself into structural engineering puzzlers, Carter thought. You could spend a whole night programming solutions. And where was that now?

But as Carter pulled up the response screen and thought of the wide potential audience, he could not bring himself to bare his thoughts. He retreated to a canned answer that laid out some of the attractions of either track, then posted it with a lingering distaste for his surrender. Are you always going to be so stingy about saying what you feel, Carter wondered. What if you knew for certain you had only six months to live? What about that? Would you just go on with your job as is? Would you just stay silent with Michelle, waiting for her to get out of your life without saying a word? Would you really do that? No, you wouldn't. But why is six months any different from anything else? Because you'd have nothing to lose? Because you'd be dead and gone and any embarrassment or failure would mean nothing anyway? You've asked yourself this before and you haven't answered it—why should six months be any different from thirty years? Don't you pride yourself in being logical? You're going to be dead and gone no matter what, so is it OK to discard everything that's important just because you have thirty years to digest it? And what makes the first six months of those next thirty years any less important than six months all on their own? Is time really that cheap to trash?

Carter stared at the computer and knew he could not just sit back and let everything be shot to hell. He had to ask Michelle out and find out where he stood.

12

Michelle Taylor turned on a CD of Cuban salsa and nursed her second glass of Cabernet, her legs stretched on her black leather couch, a *Newsweek* open on her lap. It was Friday night, and after a long push at the office, she had been to the health club late for some aerobic weights, come home and showered, then slipped nude into a sweatshirt and sweat pants, and now sat with the languid, sensual fatigue of honed limbs and a smooth heartbeat.

The pointed backbeat of the music began to work into her blood, and her hips moved imperceptibly against the cool surface of the leather. She had bought the magazine on her way home from the gym, wanting to see what *Newsweek* had to say about the FBI investigation compared to *Time*, her mailed subscription. It had been 10:30 when she had started, and when she finally laid down the magazine at 11:15, she suddenly wondered what had become of her Friday night, and what would become of her Saturday night as well. She had been so used to having her evenings scheduled for Colin that it now seemed strange to think of finding a date.

She leafed through the TV listings for a movie classic, but

coming up empty, leaned back on the couch and stared at her wine glass on the coffee table, again aware that for the first time in a long time she had no one.

With the music, she thought of an old boyfriend from the Dominican Republic who had introduced her to salsa. Ever since that fling, the beat of this music had become an antidote to the pressures of her work. But now she hesitated about going to a nightclub by herself. Suddenly, she would be back in the singles bar scene, a pretty face on the rack just asking to be picked up. But so what, she asked herself. A nightlife without commitments still played to her sense of adventure. It gave her a shot of her late twenties when she had tried sky diving and bungee jumping and taken on the challenge of the FBI. But somehow the weekend search for men now looked distasteful, as though she were back to playing teenage dating games.

Taylor downplayed the thought that she was getting "old," but she knew fertility got no kickback from her health club membership. She did not want to be a forty-year-old mom with a newborn, or a woman who finds out too late that complications have shut the door on childbearing. She did want children, but now with Colin on the sidelines, she shrank at the subconscious pressure of finding someone who was supposed to be right forever—and that on a date. Insidiously, each steady boyfriend, if another failure, would steal another increment from her ticking clock.

Hell, she thought, why not just stick to the Jackhammer investigation for your fix of frustrations? But what about after that? Would you still want to sacrifice so much of your personal life to an FBI career? Or is the work really just a competition with your brother that continued kids' games that you should have put behind you long ago?

The music still pulsed on the stereo, and suddenly determined, Taylor got up, walked to her bedroom, and began pushing through the hangers in her closet to see what she could wear for a night out. She frowned at the old skimpy blouses and tight pants and knew she had to be more conservative if she did not want too many jackals putting on the moves. She picked out a black silk blouse and black creased slacks and put on a dash of make-up. Fastening some long, Inca-motif silver earrings, she looked at herself in the bathroom mirror with a questioning curiosity. She did not really know what she was after, but she knew she would look good doing it.

In the living room, Taylor turned off the music and called for a cab. The dispatcher said they would be there in ten minutes, and Taylor, mildly intimidated by the silence, turned on the music again and stepped lightly to the beat, moving her hips with a sexual twist that she knew she would not dare in public.

Finally, she heard the honk of a car horn and looked out the window, spotting an old blue-and-white taxi waiting patiently under the street light. It was as though a run-down Dodge had replaced a Cinderella carriage. Taylor clasped her purse, took a breath, and walked out the door.

Tío Fuego in Georgetown lay one and a half blocks off the main M Street drag, near the tail end of a crowded collection of restaurants, cafés, boutiques, and shops. Georgetown students and Washingtonians shared M Street as reluctant partners with the tourists.

The club offered live Latin music on the first floor of a large, redbrick office building, and Taylor went often, depending on her boyfriends' tolerance for Latin beats.

She tipped her Pakistani driver, walked up the brick steps to the entrance, and checked her coat inside the club. She felt mildly self-conscious about coming alone, but the flood of electric piano and drums quickly cut off her doubts. By the time she sat down at the bar, with a view across the dark tables and the dance floor to a nine-man salsa band, she was glad that the sheer volume of the beat could drive any doubts from her thoughts and the workday from her system.

One of the bartenders, a young Puerto Rican with a big smile and a tough-guy manner, recognized Taylor and came to take her order with a sly wink and a pointing finger, his thumb cocked like a gun.

"Hey, *bonita*," he said, "what'll it be?"

Taylor smiled back. "A Cabernet. And don't leave the glass half empty."

"Full up for the lady," he said, raising his brows and grinning, again pointing his finger.

Taylor had seen this bartender before. A tight T-shirt showed off biceps and a gym-honed chest, and she wondered what it would be like going home with a guy like that. With the music, Taylor felt restlessly sensual and then thought about Colin. Could she invite him back just for one night? No, she couldn't imagine dealing with those complications.

Taylor accepted her wine, the glass two-thirds full, and with a smile of thanks to the bartender, turned to the band and watched them belt out their tune, their hips rocking, and the Spanish hurled from their lips with a throaty hunger. Taylor let her butt shift to the beat, self-consciously holding the motion inside her, waiting for the chance to break out.

Into the second song, a short, stocky Latino with a black, wide-lapelled sports jacket, pointy shoes, and a shirt unbuttoned to mid-chest asked Taylor to dance. She said OK and followed him to the dance floor without conversation. The man put on a good show with his hips and shoulders, twitching to the beat, one hand firmly around Taylor's waist, the other lifting her arm in a pulsing confidence. When he saw his gringo partner match the rhythm with an insider's flair, he smiled at the luck of his catch and introduced himself as Javier.

Don't get any ideas, Taylor thought to herself. I'm just going to dance with you. In fact, I'm dancing with myself.

Taylor stayed four songs with Javier and worked up a pleasurable perspiration, letting the music crowd out the shortcomings of her partner. She had to smile when Javier dipped and swayed his shoulders with the suave insinuation that he was a man to show her what it meant to be a stud. Finally, Taylor fanned her face, said thanks, and told Javier she needed a breather. She walked straight back to her bar stool and sat down.

Taylor did not want to advertise a lie, so she turned from possible partners and put on a show that she was resting. Her eyes drifted to the bartender, and she followed his weightlifter's chest and abdomen. Suddenly, he caught her eye and stopped by to chat.

"You know you're a hell of a dancer. Where'd you learn?"

"Right here," Taylor said, amused at herself for even entertaining a chat with this man. She pursed her lips in good-natured mockery. "What were you doing, spying on me?"

"Man, I'd look at you all night if I didn't have to work." He offered his broad, sharp-edged smile and pulled a glass from the overhead rack to shine it. Taylor saw his forearms flex with each wipe of the towel.

"Hold the flattery," Taylor said.

The bartender pointed his finger with a laugh. *"Mi corazón es tuyo."*

"Watch it buddy," she said with her own laugh. "I understand some Spanish. I'll tell your boss you're harassing the customers."

"My pleasure," the bartender said, tipping his finger to his forehead in a salute. He hung up the glasses and turned to another customer.

Taylor switched from wine to margaritas and turned her eyes back to the dance floor. She was on her first glass when a lanky young man in his thirties stopped at her stool. "Would you like to dance?" he asked, brushing an unruly lock of blond hair from his forehead, smiling nervously.

"OK," Taylor said, wanting to get back to the rhythm.

The man turned out to be a U.S. foreign service officer who had served in Latin America and had now been banished to a desk job in Foggy Bottom. He said the music took him back to his earlier years abroad, and Taylor soon realized that she now had to listen to a tiresome nostalgia about all the countries and cities where he had worked, with great detail on the "exquisite" restaurants and the "dynamic" clubs. Apparently, none of the South American flair had rubbed off on his awkward limbs, and he jerked and shuffled like a kid who was always picked last in gym and twenty years later still tried desperately to shed the stigma. The band was throwing him balls that kept hitting him in the chest and face.

After two songs, Taylor excused herself politely and wound back through the crowd to the bar. The man looked after her with the blinking, hang-dog disbelief of someone who still cannot accept the continuing onslaught of rejection.

Taylor finished her drink and ordered another. The music still worked in her blood, but she had grown discouraged about finding a partner. You'd forgotten how tough this job is, she thought to herself. And when you do find one, how do you know he's not a psycho? But the subtle, insistent thoughts of a lover would not die, and she wondered who would minimize the risk for a one-night stand. She thought of Scott Carter and pictured him in bed, but then immediately scolded herself. My God, the guy practically works as your partner. Much too complicated.

She tried to repress the next thought, but she had felt it coming, and now, with a full charge of tequila in her system, she let the bartender slip to the surface. She glanced his way and saw him lift a new keg of beer into its cabinet, his fingers clipping the hoses with quick experience. He happened to look to his side and saw Taylor watching. Taylor glanced away in surprise but knew it would be tough to wiggle out of this one.

At first, Taylor did not notice the man who had stopped beside her and asked her to dance. When his voice had finally penetrated the racket and she had turned to look at him, she knew immediately from his preposterously coifed hair and pretentious smile that this was not a good idea, but she could not sit still with the idea of the bartender sizing her up.

"All right," Taylor said.

Taylor stepped through the songs with practiced indifference, her thoughts still on the bartender. Hadn't she told herself to break out of her rut and live? But this was crazy, wasn't it? Maybe, she thought. Maybe not. Her imagination had already undressed the bartender and slipped her lips to the full slyness of his smile. She could make conditions to protect herself. That was in her power.

When Taylor finally excused herself from the dance floor and walked back to the bar, the bartender had already moved to her place and now watched her sit down. With the tequila working double time, Taylor did not look away. She slipped onto her stool with a smooth, sleek determination, her eyes answering his.

The bartender leaned forward. "Hey, *bonita*," he whispered, "do I feel a little chemistry here?"

"Hard to tell," Taylor said. She took a swallow of her drink, looking over the rim at the bartender's sculpted face, her eyes telling him all he needed to know.

He smiled. "You doing something after I get off work?"

Taylor put down her glass. She held off her answer as long as her good sense would let her. "I'm free," she said.

On Saturday morning, Carter sat in his old den recliner, reading *The Washington Post* about partially restored power in Rosslyn and drinking coffee from a Washington Redskins mug. Outside, the sun was shining through the trees of the garden, and the stereo played Earth, Wind, & Fire. When Carter had finally gotten to sleep the night before, he had slept deeply and now felt as though the day held a precarious hope.

That sentiment exploded when he came to a small, one-column article on the second page of the Metro section: "Bombing Hero Implicated in Practice Violations."

What the hell? Carter thought. In three short paragraphs the article told how the Virginia licensing board would hold a preliminary hearing to examine allegations that Scott Carter had been involved in violations of the engineering practice act by engaging in "plan stamping."

"That bastard," Carter said aloud, "he's leaked this to the press!"

Carter wondered if he had Wendel Smith's home phone number, realized he didn't, and in frustration looked online at the White Pages for Richmond, Virginia, afraid about searching for a name like Smith.

Luckily for Carter, there were only two Wendels, and Carter got the board chairman on the first try of his coin-toss guess.

"Wendel," Carter said. "Scott Carter here. We've got a problem."

"Scott, how are you?"

"Not too good, Wendel. *The Washington Post* ran an article about my upcoming hearing. It was short, and buried, but they had all the details. Did you leak this?"

Smith sounded flustered. "Those reporters! I told them not to cover it."

"Wendel, what were you doing talking to the press? You said you'd keep it quiet."

"I didn't call the press," Smith said. "They called me. Out of the blue last night. The reporter said he'd gotten a tip and he just wanted to confirm the information. What am I going to do, lie to him?"

"You could have said something vague, Wendel."

Wendel slipped into a front of self-righteous rationalization. "The reporter caught me by surprise. It would have sounded like I was trying some kind of cover-up."

Carter could picture Wendel's jowls shake with each bob of the head. "So don't lie," Carter said. "Just tell them it's all a bunch of baloney that you're looking into as a formality. That's the truth and you know it. This article made it sound like a serious charge, like it was all on the level."

"What are you saying, Scott? I can't tell the press I've made up my mind before I've even held the hearing. What would that look like?"

"So what do I get? You think I like having my reputation stained like this? It doesn't matter what happens now, this is going to stick in people's heads."

"I'm not going to defend the evils of the press, Scott."

"Did the reporter say who gave him the information?"

"We didn't get into that."

"Well, I sure want to find out."

"You do that Scott. I like this as little as you do."

Carter hung up with only the coldest good-bye. He felt Wendel had sold him down the river, and now Carter had to clean up the mess.

So what are you going to do as damage control, Carter asked himself. Get out and call a press conference and contradict this? That'll just draw more attention. How about finding that engineer John Franklin and punching him in the mouth. Yeah, that'd do you a lot of good.

Carter realized he had better just swallow it, hope nobody he knew read the third page of the Metro section, have the board clear his name, and after that was official, get back to the press. He wondered if Waynewright had seen this.

Carter walked to the kitchen to get his cell phone and dialed Waynewright at home. He waited impatiently for someone to pick up. Finally, a voice said "Hello." Waynewright did not sound happy.

"Bob, it's Scott here. Sorry to bother you at home. I was wondering if you'd read *The Post* today."

"Yeah, I was ready to call you. Where did that story come from?"

"So it wasn't as buried as I'd hoped."

"My wife pointed it out. What the hell's going on?"

"Some jerk's accusing me of plan stamping on the Arlington County office building expansion. They're saying I didn't oversee the work I sealed."

"That's ridiculous."

"I know it is. And Wendel Smith, the board chairman, knows it is, but he's been threatened with bad publicity if he doesn't hold a hearing on this."

"Threatened by who?"

"Nobody knows."

"Well, we'll support you as much as it takes. I mean, your good name is not something the firm wants to lose. Get the details to Jerry, and we'll all go down to Richmond and tell them where they can stick it."

"Giving them the facts will be good enough," Carter said.

"Yeah, we'll tell them where to stick the facts too."

"Thanks, Bob. I appreciate it."

"Don't worry about a thing."

Carter began to feel better about the hearing, but he started to wonder who was behind this setup. The person who had written the anonymous letter could have had only one motive—to make him look bad. But who would go to such trouble for no good reason? Nothing would come of this but a big hassle. What was there to gain? There was no money involved. It would all just blow over, right?

Carter thought of his press conference the day before. He had blasted Jackhammer, and he began to wonder if Jackhammer had done the dirty work. Jackhammer had already had his fun with his phone calls, so maybe this was just an extension. If the guy had resources to blow up an electric power grid, he had resources for small-time mischief. If that were true, it meant Jackhammer, or someone working for him, had contacted *The Post*. Carter knew it sounded far-fetched, but he realized he had better call Michelle.

Carter guessed he would find Michelle at home and dialed her. After a few rings he was ready to hang up, when a sleepy voice suddenly answered.

"Did I wake you?" Carter asked apologetically.

"Who is this, Scott?"

"That's right. I'm sorry. I didn't know it was that early."

After a pause, Taylor said, "It's not that early. I just had a late night, and I treated myself to sleeping in." Her voice had slowly gathered itself and no longer showed the muffled disorientation.

"I suppose you haven't read today's paper."

"Not yet."

"Somebody's set me up with the state engineering licensure board. They produced a bogus witness who's going to testify against me. You know what I think? I think Jackhammer's behind this."

"Do you have any proof of that?"

"No, but somebody leaked it to the press, and it made today's Metro section. Do you want to meet me for lunch and talk about it?"

"Yeah, sure. I'll probably have some updates for you as well."

Carter had to catch up on some work at BWE, and with the power restored at the office, they agreed on Rosslyn. "And make it casual," Carter added.

When he hung up, he thought back to his resolve from last night. I'll just lay things on the line and ask her out, Carter thought. No more hemming and hawing. No more cave-ins.

At the office, Carter did his best to concentrate on the ANC rebuilding plans. Fulton and Greene had done their work according to his instructions, and now Carter had to review the plans before passing them to the contractor. Carter double-checked the I-beam and weld specifications and began to confirm the shoring's load-bearing setup for the transition to permanent beams. The blackout had thrown him behind schedule, and he knew he would have to come in during the afternoon as well.

At noon Carter got the call from Taylor. He logged out of his computer, put on his coat, and headed downstairs. Taylor was standing on the sidewalk, her red Eclipse parked on the other side of the street.

"It's nice to have some life back in Rosslyn," Taylor said with a smile.

"You bet," said Carter. "How about if we just walk up the street to the strip mall. There's a little French-Italian restaurant there." He thought that sounded classier than the nearby barbecue pit.

"Fine with me," said Taylor.

The two walked uphill in the sunny cold and offered chitchat about the blackout and the story of the old lady they had both read about in the papers. The lady had refused to leave her apartment and had bundled herself up into a ball of blankets and lived off the cans and crackers she had left in her cupboard. When a social worker tipped off the press, she became a symbol of a crazy grittiness that drew one interview after another. Carter wondered how many other characters were locked up in this concrete stack of buildings, anonymous until some disaster rooted them out. Looking around, he wished he could have offered Michelle more than these non-descript high-rises and cluttered, mom-and-pop store fronts. A strip mall was not exactly brownstone Georgetown, and he mentioned to Taylor how nice it would be to jog across the Potomac in today's brisk sun.

A block farther up, the two crossed the street and entered the Village Bistro, a casual attempt at European dining, with spare tables and a schizophrenic French-Italian menu. The place was relatively empty without the staple weekday business crowd, and Taylor picked a table by the window, as far away from the four other customers as possible. When Taylor took off her coat and sat down, the tight blue jeans and the gray designer sweatshirt hit Carter hard. It was the first time he had ever seen her in truly casual clothes. For Carter, the relaxed get-up made her look even more beautiful, as though she had dropped her inhibitions and would accept Carter as a friend. He felt almost overdressed in his khaki slacks and dark green shirt.

"I guess we're just a bunch of workaholics working Saturday again," Carter said.

Taylor smiled, then sighed with a shake of her head. "Yeah, I sometimes wonder about that. You end up slaving away, throwing your whole life to your job. Who says that's the best way of spending your time?"

"You have to hope that you at least like your work."

"You know," she said, pausing to accept a menu from the waitress, "I sometimes tell myself to just back off the work, but then I wonder, what's so important about reading a book or watching TV or going shopping? I might as well be plotting to put a criminal behind bars."

"Sure," Carter said. "And speaking of arrests, do your big shots at the FBI still have any more use for me, now that you're off into the electric power field?"

"What do you think, we're going to push you aside? I've told Frank we'll keep you as long as your boss says it's OK. You seem to have a knack for getting to the bottom of things, and that's what we need, not this or that technical specialty."

"Glad to hear it," Carter said. He wondered whether her recommendation meant she liked having him around or whether she realized he was the best bait for Jackhammer.

The two looked over their menus and got their orders in quickly—for Carter a Veal Scaloppini Saltimboca and for Taylor a caper and lemon sauce salmon, along with two glasses of Orvieto Classico. "Now, tell me what's going on with the engineering board," Taylor said.

Carter gave Taylor the details and his hunch that Jackhammer was paying him back for the previous press conference. "I just don't believe anybody besides Jackhammer would be crazy enough to pull this kind of stunt out of the blue, with anonymous letters and mystery witnesses, and for what, just to dirty my name?"

"It means I've got to see this John Franklin and find out what suddenly made him want to talk," Taylor said. "And like you told me, I've got to talk to *The Washington Post*." Taylor looked satisfied and raised her water in a toast. "You've given some interesting leads. Maybe we can make some progress like the other teams. I heard this morning they've tested all the explosives from the various power grid sites, and most of it comes from the same batch. So we're talking a single source. Also, two power line inspectors recall seeing a man early one morning out by a tower close to the one that was blown up last week. They've got a pretty good description and the Bureau's working hard to track somebody down."

"Not bad."

"Well, I'm personally going after anything I can, no matter how farfetched. I called up your Ed Babcock since he's got a background in county government and I asked him what county design drawings a person might want to steal, taking it from any angle—terrorism, business, some kind of revenge. He seemed a little skeptical that a contractor or engineering firm would do something illegal just for a competitive edge. They risked losing their whole business. And he didn't know about any personal grudges that could have turned violent."

"I'd have to agree."

"He said he was going to ask around about other possibilities. He worries about the wrong kind of knowledge getting into a terrorist's hands."

"He's not too original there," Carter said.

The waitress dropped off the two glasses of wine, and with business so slow, it did not take long for the entrées to come.

The two then drifted to a blow-by-blow rehash of the ANC investigation. They both wondered whether they had overlooked some angle or some less than obvious detail. Carter did his best to concentrate but became drunk with Taylor's relaxed, college-girl prettiness, as though he were again a young buck back at Virginia Tech cruising around Blacksburg to stalk a coed at a local pizza joint. After 10 years of married life, it felt strange pursuing Taylor, but he told himself, What do you care if you make a fool of yourself? You might be a dead fool soon enough.

Taylor finally changed subjects with a wicked smile. "Do you remember that Mr. Goldblat? Well, he was back in the States and called to ask if I needed any more help. I told him I wasn't involved in the international side, and that the Islamist terrorist theory was getting cold." She shook her head in amusement. "Well, he didn't want to back off, and when he realized he couldn't get a business meeting, he started looking for other excuses. I think the guy actually wanted to go out on a date."

"So did you accept?" Carter asked. Her comment had punched him hard. Was this how she was going to treat him too—just poking fun because a man happens to like her? He wondered if she realized that.

"Not on your life. I told him I was busy."

The Goldblat story suddenly put a damper on Carter's plans, closing off the spigot that just a minute ago was ready to pour out all his hopes. Carter suddenly saw the lunch deteriorate into ordinary small talk, ready to drift out of sight without him risking anything. That woke him up, and when they had finished their meal and Taylor declined coffee, ready to get back to the office, Carter finally knocked himself into shape.

"You know," Carter said, his voice with a casual, it-means-nothing nuance, "I was wondering. We have all these business meetings, but just talking about anything under the sun can be a nice change. So let me imitate your Mr. Goldblat and take the consequences. How about going out to dinner with me sometime?"

Taylor blinked in surprise. She was not sure she had understood. "You mean socially?"

"Yeah, I guess you could call it that."

Taylor appeared flattered but could not hide her unease. "I appreciate your asking," she said, "but we still have to work together. Wouldn't that maybe interfere?"

"So what are you saying? You'd consider going out if I got off the case?"

Taylor smiled in embarrassment. "I didn't mean it that way."

"So how do you mean it?" he asked quietly, but insistently. He was not going to back down now, although he could already feel the weight of defeat pressing hard.

Taylor had to think fast. "I just feel it'd be awkward," she apologized. "People might think I was keeping you on the case for social reasons." She hoped her attempt at logic would fill in for her personal doubts. He had caught her off guard.

Carter felt he was digging an even deeper hole, but for the moment, that was just tough. He tried some weak humor. "Hey, I know all sorts of restaurants outside of town where nobody would see us. We could even talk business." He immediately regretted the comment.

"I'm honored," Taylor said, inwardly startled that she had just put Colin behind her only to have these new complications surface without even the chance for a break. "I really am." She lowered her eyes. "But I'm afraid I'll have to say no. I've had a lot of things going on, and I just don't think it'd be practical."

Carter heard the excuses and realized she was beating around the bush like any woman trying to brush off a date without being overly rude. Carter lifted his hand to show it was fine. "I'm sorry I brought it up," he said, forcing a smile. "It was a mistake. Let's just forget it happened, OK? I'm here for the professional side of things, and we'll keep it at that. No hard feelings, all right?"

"I don't hold it against you," Taylor said, trying to project some warmth. She felt terrible about hurting him.

Carter waved for the check and hoped the waitress would hurry up and settle the bill and get him out of there fast before what had happened really sank in.

13

On a one-way residential street on the west side of Rosslyn, Victor Brogasi set up a large "Men at Work" sign to shift the traffic around his jackhammer power unit, an aging backhoe, and a truckload of cold-mix asphalt. He and his three men had received the equipment from an anonymous source, driven it down from New York City on a mud-caked flatbed trailer, and now took up their stations like an ordinary Arlington County work crew, in their orange reflective jackets and their hard hats. The instructions had required Saturday to avoid workday traffic and complaints from commuters, but the one thing Brogasi feared most was an Arlington Public Works employee driving by and recognizing that this dig was not on the schedule.

At least the odds had been doctored in their favor, Brogasi thought. Someone had done their homework and confirmed that this location would not fall on a downtown commute of a Public Works manager. Brogasi had demanded every possible edge to accept such a risky job, and his gut now told him why. As the men turned on the blast of the backhoe motor and primed the jackhammer, the operation felt like running an unarmed bank heist out in the open, asking for loot with a bullhorn. Brogasi had demanded $60,000 on top of expenses, half of it up front, to even consider risking this kind of jail time for somebody he did not even know—some kind of brilliant eccentric with good connections, he had been told; somebody set on a practical joke to get back at an enemy. He had been assured this was no foreign plot but a solid, all-American revenge, and that helped quiet the faintest shred of conscience Brogasi had left in him. When the money came through without even a question, Brogasi knew this guy liked to have serious fun.

Brogasi double-checked the utility blueprints, squinting with nervous energy, knowing that the last thing he needed was to hit an underground power line and have the county breathing down his neck for causing a blackout. The site had been picked to be free of other lines, but he worried that some junior jerk had forgotten to include one on the master plan. Hell, he thought to himself, he remembered back in his days in New York City when he had turned up a whole spaghetti of cable and pipe that wasn't even hinted at on the plans. Who said these drawings were up to date, anyway, he thought, sucking in a wad of saliva and then spitting to the ground in disgust. He mumbled, "I'm gonna kill somebody if this shit is wrong."

Brogasi glared down the street at the passing cars, the wrinkles in his hollowed cheeks like putty-molded slits on a young actor playing a geezer. He didn't want to see police cars, but he knew there'd be one sooner or later. He just hoped that the cop would not try to be friendly and stop to shoot the breeze. If it happened, Brogasi would tell him he was just doing a spot-check on cracks in the water main after a warning from the pipe manufacturer. If a cop came toward the end of the job, Brogasi would say he was installing sensors to monitor downtown water pressure. Brogasi spat again, as if trying to hurl out his last wad of fear.

Brogasi referenced the street corner and the nearest manhole and confirmed that the chalk-marked rectangle he had outlined next to the curb lay just above the cast-iron water main. His crew cranked up the jackhammer compression motor and began slicing the blacktop, like putting a crude butter knife through brittle taffy. Brogasi's head ached without earplugs, and he wondered how his jackpot had been tied to the old dusty grind of road repair work. At sixty, he had been out of the construction and road crew business for ten years, turning connections with the Mob into some small-time racketeering work. Now he was in the dirt and the noise again, knowing that if he just got through this job clean, he could make the down payment on that beach house in Florida with no assholes on his back and no assholes looking to double-cross him.

The initial jackhammer cut went fast. Then the steel teeth of the backhoe dropped into the end-slice of the asphalt, prying backward until thick slabs broke free. The backhoe lurched at each pull, its engine grating at the strain, the side stabilizer braces digging into the road like an automaton doing push-ups on its last angry power. Soon, the whole rectangle had been stripped to the underlying dirt and gravel, and the backhoe turned to lifting the loose slabs gently into the waiting pick-up truck. The pieces thundered to the metal bed.

Brogasi called off the backhoe before digging farther. He wanted a first probe with hand shovels to check on unexpected utility lines. He ordered his crew spaced across the area and had them dig three-foot-deep holes with the care of gravediggers exhuming a skeleton. Everyone scooped lightly but made steady progress. By the time they had worked up a good sweat in the cold of the morning, they were done with the probes, awaiting their next order.

Brogasi nodded in churlish satisfaction and motioned the backhoe into action. It would take out the rest of the dirt to the three-foot level and pile it on the road next to the dig. With that done, it was back to the hand shovels to scout the terrain.

At six feet down, the crew reached the cast-iron hulk of the water main. Brogasi grabbed a hand shovel and cleared away a three-foot circle along the arc of the pipe, then wiped it clean with a wet, wadded towel. Now for the challenge, Brogasi thought. If someone stopped him at this point, he would have some explaining to do.

The crew pulled a large wooden crate from the cab of the truck, pried off the top with a crowbar, and cleared out the thick braces and padding. The box was heavy, and Brogasi had the men set it down at the edge of the hole before they pulled out the contents. The finely machined device looked like a top hat made of steel, with a wide, curved brim and four stiff ribbons projecting from the rim edge in a rigid, extended cross. Brogasi lowered himself and the device into the hole and puffing, placed it on the cleared top of the water main. The curve of the brim and the metal cross fit the curve of the pipe perfectly. Somebody had done some heads-up design work, Brogasi thought. Relieved, he returned to the truck and picked up some quick-drying caulk. He cut off the application tip, popped the tube into a caulking gun, and started for the hole when he saw the police car. It was just two blocks away, heading towards him, and Brogasi knew he just had to stick to his work. He continued toward the hole and jumped inside, squatting, facing away from the street. He had kept his team in the dark about what, exactly, they were doing and let them stand around with the same inactive lethargy of a normal work crew. But he did not want the policeman to see his face. Brogasi could only guess about the ultimate goal of the job, but he knew that for the money he was being paid, this was no child's play.

Brogasi tried to block off the policeman's sight line to the device, denying the cop anything unusual to remember. Brogasi's machinery was turned off, and in the relative quiet, he could hear the police car approach, gradually getting louder, in no hurry, apparently patrolling the neighborhood rather than rushing to the scene of a crime.

OK, you bastard, Brogasi thought, don't try to act friendly and ask us how the work's going. You just keep right on going, like a good little boy.

The car seemed to slow down, and Brogasi sucked in some air, wondering if this was it—thrown in the slammer for the rest of his life, with no more beach house and no more women to screw in the sand. He spat and pretended to examine the device in his mildly shaking hands, and then the sound of the police car passed and began to fade. Jesus Christ! Brogasi cursed to himself, angry that he had been so terrified. Jesus, you're getting soft!

With the picture of his arrest still pulsing, Brogasi wanted no more delays. He turned the device on its side and began pumping a neat bead of caulk onto a circular groove on the bottom of the hat brim. With the help of the crew, he lowered the heavy device onto the curve of the pipe and felt it fit snugly against the rough metal surface, the caulking making a soft, solid seal. "OK, guys, time for some welding," Brogasi said.

The crew handed down the pressurized gas canister and the welding mask, and Brogasi fired up the torch to a lean blue flame. He was anxious to finish, but he was not going to blow the job by skimping on welds. He had been told that if he messed up the seal, the device could pop loose while he was still nearby and call down the cops with a jet stream of water. With an unbroken weld, this thing was not going to budge, no matter how much pressure came from inside.

The welds were all fusing cleanly, and after an hour, Brogasi pulled the final instructions from the inside of his jacket. He had tried to memorize the steps, but now worried about getting it right. He did not want to lose the second half of the payoff.

Brogasi glanced from the paper to the device and examined the connection to the built-in drill bit. It looked like a short broomstick stuck through the top of a hat. He called for the generator and latched on the drill motor, knowing that once he turned on the juice, the diamond teeth would start boring through the water main's cast-iron shell. When he hit the switch, Brogasi winced at the loud whine and scrape.

It took twenty minutes of racket before the drill finally broke through and water surged into the top-hat chamber. Brogasi disconnected the motor, pulled the sealed bit to full extension, slammed closed a door to shut off the spray of the temporary leak, and then, with a final glance at his instructions, pulled out a thin antenna. Anxious to be done, Brogasi waved to his men to get their shovels flying, and within fifteen minutes the crew had hidden the device in a mound of dirt. The backhoe scooped in the rest, and the crew topped off the soil with a compacted layer of gravel. The dump truck then unloaded its pile of asphalt, and the rakes and shovels spread it flat.

The crew had already refitted the jackhammer with a compacting mallet and now pummeled the black surface. Brogasi wished they had brought a steamroller to make the job look more professional, but he knew the small compactor would have to do. He supervised closely and made sure the crew left a hard, stable surface that would not draw attention with immediate cracks.

When Brogasi stood back to examine the work, he did not have any complaints.

Now get the hell out of here, he thought, before it's too late.

On that same Sunday morning, Carter delivered the ANC building plans to the general contractor and discussed the repair implementation on site. Work had continued around the clock, and the ANC grounds had now been cleared of all rubble and prepared for new limbs.

Carter put on his hard hat and walked among the bare steel shoring, trading pointers with the building chief, amazed by the sanitized remains of what had once been a smoke- and dust-filled death trap. The sunshine poured through the columns, as though the darkness and flashing ambulance lights of three weeks ago had been an unfathomable nightmare from which Carter had finally woken.

Yet when he finished his work, Carter did not feel the freedom of that sun. His last encounter with Michelle had darkened his view, and he tried to dodge that bad memory by taking a long detour back to the office. You've put her on guard, Carter thought. It's just a matter of time before she avoids you altogether. Time to flush it down the toilet.

Carter approached the Key Bridge and watched as a stream of students and young professionals walked and biked across the Potomac, enjoying the 50-degree weather as though it were suddenly spring and the classes at Georgetown had just let out. Carter could not imagine going home. He did not want to face himself in the solitude of that house and have his whole infatuation back up from the drainage of his soul. He searched for some distraction, something different so he could tamp down his pursuit of Michelle and get back to some sanity. He wondered if Todd Kirkland was up for a drive to the country for a beer.

Carter had always gotten a kick out of Kirkland's unabashed low-life interests and biting tongue, a relationship Carter might have outgrown if not for the rough-edged college bond from before Carter was old enough to worry about respectable company. Todd's just the ticket to kill your sentimentality, Carter thought. He walked back to the office and rang him up.

"Well, if it isn't the media star," Kirkland said. "I thought you were too good for us punks in the trenches."

"Lay off it, Todd. I've been busy, and you know it."

"No problemo. So why are you interrupting my basketball game?"

"I thought you might want to drive out to Front Royal for a beer. It's great weather."

"There's a bar down the street. I don't need Front Royal."

"The weather's too nice for that."

"Are you buying?"

"If you force me."

"Well, if you want me to put up with your drive, you're going to have to pay."

"I'm at the office. I'll be at your place in twenty minutes."

"At the office? Is BWE still squeezing you dry?"

"Well, some of us still have a sense of responsibility."

"Horse shit," Kirkland said.

Carter already felt better.

Carter and Kirkland drove west on I-66, past Bull Run and the Manassas Civil War battlefields, then into the rolling farmland at the foot of the Shenandoah Mountains an hour outside of Washington, D.C. At the rise of each successive hill, the mountains had turned from a distant pale blue silhouette into the closer brown-gray austerity of bare trees and leaf-covered ground, the highway following the shifting slope of the land, giving Carter a smooth sense of terrain, as though he might still gun it to the top of the next hill-crest and find only clear air to the end of his days.

The slopes and valleys grew higher, and near Front Royal, Carter remembered all the weekend trips to the mountains he had taken with Linda, and with regret, the trips she had refused. Carter always wanted to go camping on Skyline Drive and wake up to the morning silence and look down on the Shenandoah River winding through the far forest and farms. He had only managed to convince Linda once to give camping a shot, but for her the bugs and morning cold represented just another form of torture, and after that Carter saw the years pass with his outdoor hankerings slowly locked away. Carter could not imagine Michelle being bothered by bears and bugs—but enough of that, he thought.

In Front Royal, Carter pulled into the backside parking lot of a country tavern, and the two got out and walked inside and found the place nearly empty.

Todd Kirkland stood six-foot three, with lanky limbs, hard, wrangler hips, and the face of an aging teenage prankster who, with time, had mixed disgust into his wry humor. His old jeans had faded to nearly white, and one of his dirty tennis shoes had split at the toe. Carter led him to a dim table in the corner and called for two bottles of Michelob and some peanuts.

"This place looks like a real winner," Kirkland groused as he scanned the empty tables.

"Afternoon isn't exactly drinking time," said Carter.

"Maybe in your book."

A tired old man gathered up the beers from behind the bar and then dropped them on the table with the peanuts.

"So what are you doing after work these days?" Carter asked.

"I play around with my computer."

"Any new equipment?"

"My cable internet wasn't cutting it so I switched to a fiber optics deal."

"Nothing like bringing up the porn faster."

Kirkland scowled as though a fly fresh from manure had landed on his cheek. He swatted it away. "Speed's not always what it's cut out to be. I remember the good old days of dial-up. Man, that's when the porn photos banded in slow. You got a little suspense about what you were going to see. If the thing hung up, you'd be stuck at the top of a woman's neck."

Carter shook his head. "Don't you get tired of that stuff?"

"Don't act so superior," Kirkland said. "Back at Tech you borrowed my porn mags like everybody else."

"Maybe I did."

"Shit, you probably brought me out to Front Royal because you were too embarrassed to be seen with me in town."

"No logic to that," Carter said. "I can always pretend we're talking BWE design issues. My reputation stays clean."

"Fuck you," Kirkland said.

Carter took a long swallow of beer, content to soak in Kirkland's belligerent nostalgia. "So what else are you doing online these days? Last time we talked, you had me worried about some of the things you were up to. You're probably a professional hacker by now."

Kirkland took a swig from his bottle, his Adam's apple bouncing on his wiry neck. He then wiped his lips with the back of his hand. "Hell, I don't do anything illegal. I just play around, see how far I can push the envelope."

"Like what?"

"Well, I was trying to see if I could break into BWE's design network."

"But you can already get in there legally."

Kirkland shrugged. "That's just the point. I can't steal anything, so no harm done."

"How can you be so sure? Can't you still screw something up for us?"

"Nah," Kirkland droned, unfazed. "I know what I'm doing."

"I've known what I was doing a lot of times and screwed things up anyway."

"That's you, not me."

"All right." Carter said, but he eyed him curiously. "So did you get in?"

"Yeah," Kirkland said, not sounding too impressed with himself.

"Maybe you better tell IT that we're vulnerable."

"Are you kidding? They'd blow their tops. They've already given me a warning about playing around on our network."

"At least they did one thing right," Carter said. "Maybe I'll drop them an anonymous tip."

"Can't hurt," Kirkland said.

"So is this the kind of thing you do all night these days?"

"Pretty much. That or TV."

Carter wished his own life were that easy.

"And what about you?" Kirkland asked. "You still hanging out with that FBI broad?"

"From time to time."

"So are you getting the hots real bad?"

Carter smiled. "What are you, a mind reader?"

Kirkland frowned. "What the hell does that mean?"

Carter had not really wanted to bring up Michelle. Talking about her with Kirkland was like discussing the Venus de Milo with a pervert armed with a sledgehammer. But he had already let the cat out of the bag. "So, you want the best joke of the world? I've actually fallen for that agent. There you have it."

Kirkland stared for a moment, then burst out laughing. "When the hell are you going to stop asking for trouble?!"

"I didn't ask for it. It just happened."

"Shit happens."

"I won't argue with that."

"So, is this lady as hot as she looks?"

"I refuse to stoop to your level," Carter said. "She's very nice. Too nice."

"And she's married, right?"

"No, but I asked her out, and she didn't exactly jump at the chance."

"Get yourself a hooker. It's a lot easier. You don't have to dance around like some jungle bird trying to look snappy."

"I don't think a hooker would cut it in the long run."

"Just switch around, get some variety."

"Sometimes I wonder whether you're really serious," Carter said.

"You get too serious and all you get is shit."

"I think you've already said that in one form or another."

"Don't keep count of how many times I say things. I had enough of that from my ex-wife."

"Excuse *me*."

"Listen, don't set yourself up for another marriage. I've never been better off since I got divorced. I should've done it a lot earlier."

"I'm sure you weren't exactly an easy load for your wife."

Kirkland scoffed. "Hell, she did it all to herself, her and her freaking ideas. I'd leave some clothes or a few dishes lying around, and she'd blow her top. Then at other times, she'd corner me and want to talk, and hell, I didn't know what she was after. I don't know why she married me in the first place. I make no bones about it. I had no interest in all her sentimental junk. If I want to watch a football game with a beer and burp and scratch my belly, I don't want some dame giving me a hard time."

"I'm no woman, and I wouldn't want to live with a pig either."

"So now you're taking her side?"

"Totally impartial. I just remember what your room looked like in college. Jesus, when you ran out of clean clothes, you'd recycle the dirty laundry."

"Then why are you here with me? You're just jealous. Even at Tech you were jealous, always the reasonably respectable guy, smooth talker, when deep down you just wanted to be a grunge like the rest of us."

"Ah, don't start your generalizations. If all engineers were like you, I'd disown the profession."

"So how's your wonderful profession treating you these days? You talk about all the stress, so what the hell good is it?"

"You like to put me on the spot, don't you?" Carter looked at the old bartender staring at the sunlight through a porthole in the entrance door. "I'm not too wild about the work I got myself into. All this sales and customer relations stuff wasn't real engineering. I was trying to convince people that BWE was better than anybody else on the planet by talking up a supposedly intelligent storm when, face it, there are other perfectly good firms around. I'm just brown-nosing and playing off one personality against another, trying to bite my tongue when I hit the losers. Is that what I got a civil engineering degree for?"

"I'd say you're finally talking sense," Kirkland said. "Of course, what you were doing is what anybody in any private business does. You try to beat the competition. What's the big revelation?"

"I'm seriously thinking about getting back into design work."

"It's not going to be any better. You just crank out the gusset plate connections or the cookbook frame for a strip mall and punch your time clock."

Carter shook his head. "Why do you come to work if that's how you feel?"

"For a paycheck," Kirkland said. "I'm not like you, and thank God. You always got caught up in your grand ideas. Don't ask me to follow."

"Giving a damn can make your life a little more interesting."

Kirkland took another gulp of his beer. "That's your theory. But where does it get you? You put in sixty-hour weeks and don't get a dime extra for it."

"Some people get their kicks out of completing a job, getting over the hump of a deadline. If I've made a commitment, I'll meet it, even it means a lot of hours."

"That's just what BWE wants. Squeeze every billable hour out of you for the minimum cost."

"They'll show you some loyalty and let you advance."

"Horse shit again. As soon as the contracts dry up and they have to downsize, they'll throw you out like yesterday's garbage. Don't talk to me about loyalty. You're just kidding yourself to make yourself feel better about all the time you're wasting on them. Nine to five is what I'll give them. If they don't like it, they can kiss my ass."

Carter smiled. "That's one thing I like about you, Todd. You don't take any crap."

Kirkland lifted his bottle. "Maybe it's time you did the same."

14

Jackhammer walked in the first twilight that Monday morning, the light an ice turquoise above the trees on the south side of Rosslyn, above him the sky still black behind an isolated street light. The temperature had dropped from yesterday's warmth and now hovered just below freezing, and the wind had calmed to the faintest trace of a breeze.

Jackhammer had not yet seen Brogasi's roadwork, and as he neared the dark rectangle of freshly repaired pavement, the empty stillness and the dawning light filled Jackhammer with the grand image of a godly messenger of justice, the destroyer of the meek, the giant who roams the streets before daybreak and determines the city's fate with personally forged power.

Buried beneath that asphalt lay a device of his own making, an instrument that to him ranked in neat sophistication to a robotic rover, awaiting commands in the immobile inner space of a Rosslyn roadbed. Jackhammer fingered the remote-control in his pocket, thinking back with pleasure to how it had felt in setting off the bombs in the ANC basement. But that had all been primitive hardware, accessible to any terrorist hack. This device reached a new level of achievement. He wished he could have heard the built-in drill bit pierce the iron of the water main while still locking in the water pressure, or even the hum of the two remote-controlled injection canisters inside. With a quick signal from his pocket, one of the two battery-powered probes would descend like the slow-motion leg of an insect into the pipe and release the contents of a pressurized, battery-heated canister—the contents: *giardia lamblia,* a one-celled protozoan. Then the living microbes would begin to move slowly down that subterranean thoroughfare as taps off the residential and office feeder lines pulled water from that source. The crafted, interlocking harmony of his design produced a sharp bodily thrill of achievement.

Jackhammer had now reached the burial spot and without slowing down, he inspected Brogasi's asphalt patchwork. He judged the job acceptable—it should not cause suspicion—and gratified, his finger gently grazed the left remote-control button with a burst of anticipation. Now! he told himself.

Not looking back, he continued on like a proud old man taking his morning stroll, picturing in his thoughts the *giardia* hanging weightless in a slow diffusion, poised for the morning pull of showers and baths that would drag that nectar up into the water lines and into people's homes and businesses.

And that was not all, Jackhammer thought with riveting anticipation. Just wait for the second canister. It's not just microbes, and it takes the same small wireless command.

Maria Lockwood lay awake in her chronic insomnia, watching the twilight brighten through the dusty window, hearing the groan and rattle of the old pipes as her early-to-rise neighbors one by one turned on the water for their showers and flushed their toilets. She pictured their movements and wished she herself had somewhere to go like they did, but at seventy-six years old and weakened by a bad back and a bad knee and lack of sleep, she knew she would spend the day sitting in her old redbrick apartment house reading the newspaper, watching TV, and looking out the window at the children playing on the trampled grass of the apartment grounds.

Slowly, Lockwood forced herself to sit up on the edge of the bed and grasp the battered cane leaning against the night-stand. She pushed her feet into her furry slippers and groaned quietly as she rose. The short walk from the bedroom to the kitchenette on the far side of the living room already caused her pain, and she stopped to glance at the dirty window and wondered when she would ever find the energy to clean it.

At the kitchen sink, Lockwood turned on the water and let it run, following the advice she had once read in the paper that a long-lasting stream in the morning would flush the dissolved lead from the aging pipes. In this old building, she could imagine the pipes decaying as fast as she was, but the place was all she could afford on Social Security and a tiny pension.

Today that extra steam of water brought the *giardia lamblia* up from the feeder pipes and into the glass Lockwood now held under the faucet with a trembling, age-stained hand. Thirsty, she drank half the contents before putting the glass down, then filled her coffee pot, set it on the gas stove, and lit the burner. The *giardia* protozoa now entered her stomach, and then, as the slow morning progressed and Lockwood settled into another uneventful day, the *giardia* moved to her intestine and attached themselves by suction to the tissue of the inner wall and began to replicate.

In another week, Lockwood's life would become the first spark of a firestorm.

Carter looked at his iPhone and saw his doctor's appointment set for the next morning. Well, he could take some more bad news if needed—he was practically getting used to it. For today, his schedule showed the trip to Richmond and the hearing before the engineering licensure board. Carter would have cursed the nuisance, but he knew that Michelle would be there to interrogate John Franklin, and that changed the whole picture. Franklin had refused to speak with Taylor before the hearing, calling any connection to the anonymous letter to Smith totally absurd, and Taylor did not have enough hard evidence to force the issue legally. She maintained a polite badgering mixed with veiled threats, and finally Franklin had agreed to an interview if Taylor took the trouble to track him down in Richmond, when he would not have to miss more work or come up with another excuse for his wife. Taylor immediately arranged for a meeting room with the state licensing board—Wendel Smith had strained to be cooperative—but she worried about what she could pull out of her suspect. Fishing on hunches did not give her much leverage.

For the trip to Richmond, Jerry Donahue, the BWE general counsel, had rented a minivan, and at 8:30 in the morning, Waynewright, Carter, and three BWE design engineers piled in for the two-hour drive. Waynewright had pulled out all the stops to slam dunk the defense and clear Carter's name, but as the van reached I-95, Waynewright started looking at his staff and thinking about all the billable hours the firm would lose that day and got sick in his stomach. "That board chair's a chicken-livered joker pulling a stunt like this," Waynewright growled. "He gets some harebrained letter and takes it at face value! And he actually believes some scum who's making all sorts of ignorant, wild guesses about what happened."

Waynewright turned to Donahue. "Are you going to do some good character assassination at this hearing? It would serve them right."

Donahue smiled. "Given the fact that you want a positive outcome, I assume you'd—."

"Stuff the legal speak, Jerry," Waynewright interrupted, enjoying himself with the bluster. "Can't you say 'win' like a decent human being?"

"It's not a case to win," Donahue said, never knowing exactly when to take Waynewright seriously. "It's just an exploratory hearing."

"It doesn't matter what it is. This Smith is doing exactly what you'd do as a lawyer—ignore what's right and sue everybody. Shoot, if you didn't work for us, I bet you'd track down some minor contractor mistake and get a sick pleasure out of citing everyone involved in a project, meaning BWE as well, even if we had nothing to do with the case. While we build things, you guys just latch on to the work and squeeze out your ransom, hoping we'll settle to save us the badgering. It's like Mafiosos extorting protection money."

Donahue had heard the speech before and just smiled. "You seem to forget I'm the one who defends *you*."

"Yeah, and I've got to pay you a fortune to keep your partners in crime from driving us and all other design firms out of business. I've got to pay to keep leeches on staff."

Carter turned to Donahue with a smirk. "Take heart, we don't all consider you a leech."

"Aw, give up," Waynewright said. "You're always trying to paint yourself as the stand-up guy."

"I *am* the stand-up guy," Carter cracked, "and that's why I always get shot at. Next time I'll be as corrupt as the next guy, and my bad luck will probably stop."

The licensure board had its offices in a nondescript suburban Richmond office building, about ten miles from the white-columned nineteenth century state house designed by Thomas Jefferson. Waynewright had settled down, and as the BWE team stepped into Wendel Smith's borrowed office to announce their arrival, Waynewright had put on his public face of gruff accommodation.

Smith tried hard to project a proper impartiality but pressed the flesh with such profusion that he practically advertised where he stood and how he wanted this whole affair behind him as quickly as possible. The spectacle only increased Waynewright's irritation—it confirmed that this trip was a complete waste of time.

Smith invited them to wait in the hearing room and said the board would be there on time for the 11:00 o'clock start. Everyone shuffled in, and the BWE team took their seats around a U-shaped array of tables used for the various state regulatory boards that oversaw everything from barbers to opticians. Carter noticed what looked like a single reporter in the back of the room. So, Carter thought, it did not appear to be a media extravaganza.

The governor-appointed, thirteen-member board consisted of three professional engineers, three architects, three land surveyors, two landscape architects, and two interior designers. One by one, ten of them filtered into the room a little before 11:00, and when everyone had sat down, Smith called the meeting to order with theatrical gravity. John Franklin had now taken his seat at the second witness table, and Carter studied his face to try to assess the man's motivation. Despite an inclination to punch him out, Carter could not pinpoint anything malicious in Franklin's eyes. Scanning the room, Carter now noticed that Michelle had taken a seat at the back.

Smith got started and thanked all the attendees for their presence on such short notice. He explained that given the anonymous and unorthodox nature of the accusation, this session was only exploratory in nature—the board would consider what it heard and decide whether the issue required a more formal proceeding. Smith then outlined the charge that Scott Carter, P.E., duly licensed in the Commonwealth of Virginia to practice engineering, had put his seal to numerous design plans for the Womack Building in Arlington, Virginia, without exercising due oversight over the unlicensed engineers who had done some of the work. Smith then noted that the anonymous letter that had made the accusations had offered John Franklin as a corroborating witness. Smith invited Franklin to relate what he knew about the issue.

Franklin appeared nervous. He avoided looking anywhere but straight ahead, as though he were ashamed to show his face to the BWE team. He spoke so softly that Smith repeatedly asked him to raise his voice. Everyone remained quiet just to hear.

"I was working with the Arlington County government at the time," Franklin said, "and I knew that Sue Walton was the engineer of record for the project, and I'd heard that she'd been in an auto accident and had to be in the hospital and away from work for an extended period. A week later I saw all the plans for this project come in with Scott Carter's seal. It looked a little fishy to me, that's all."

"What do you exactly mean by 'fishy'," Smith asked with a spiced dash of theatrical skepticism.

"I didn't think Mr. Carter could have had the time to really know what he was sealing."

"Do you have any idea how much time Mr. Carter spent on reviewing the plans?" Smith asked.

"No, sir."

"Don't you feel that's a mighty important piece of information in a charge like this?"

Franklin leaned back in his chair and raised his hands defensively. "I didn't send that letter. I'm not making any charges. I was just asked here to say what I thought at the time. I'm not saying I know everything that went on. I just made the observation, did not pursue it, but somebody obviously heard something about it and is now passing it along. I've got no beef against anybody."

"Well, maybe we should hear some of those missing facts," Smith said.

"By all means," said Franklin.

Carter, seated at his own table, made sure his tone and words stayed even keeled and did not hint what he thought—that this hearing was a joke. He related that he had dropped all his work after Walton's accident and devoted himself full-time during the day, evenings, and weekends to tie up the loose ends while reviewing the project and to seal the drawings. Moreover, he had already been involved since the preliminary design stage, so he had not come in cold. Not only that, to keep costs down, the building had been based on an earlier BWE job for the same owner, and he had been personally involved in that project as well, so this was eighty-percent familiar. He took full responsibility that the designs would protect the public.

Carter then sat back and hoped the blatantly obvious ethics of his actions had hit the board between the eyes like a hatchet. Waynewright then spelled out the firm's ethics and practice standards and said nothing was ever let out the door without following proper procedures. It sounded more like grandstanding than convincing fact, but when two unlicensed engineers from the project then testified about Carter's intimate involvement and how he had raised numerous detailed questions about specifics in the plans, it became clear that Carter had done enough to constitute oversight and responsible charge.

The hearing took only forty minutes, and at the conclusion, Smith asked for the room to be cleared so that the board could consider its course. Carter knew things had gone well, and on his way out, thanked Waynewright for carting down all those guns to defend him.

"What a farce," Waynewright said. "The way this thing turned out, you could have come down by yourself and snowed them. This Franklin character didn't have a thing to say!"

"Let's just be happy we got it behind us."

"That's about the only thing we can be happy about."

In the hall, Carter saw Taylor waiting on the opposite side of the corridor, but the lone reporter stepped into his path.

"Excuse me, I'm from *The Washington Post*, and I was wondering if you could comment on the significance this hearing holds for your career."

"I'd say it has no significance," Carter said tersely, "since it was a mistake in the first place. I respect the board's responsibility to pursue such accusations, but in this case I knew I'd done nothing wrong, so I clearly would have preferred that this whole thing had not come up in the first place."

The reporter showed little interest in Carter's canned answer, and Carter felt mildly embarrassed about giving it. He wondered whether he was beginning to sound like a politician.

"Do you have any idea who might have sent the anonymous letter?" the reporter asked.

Carter noticed Taylor approach with a slight shake of her head. "No," Carter said, "I don't want to speculate."

"Could it have something to do with the recent bombings and Jackhammer's connection to you?"

"That sounds like the same question," Carter said with a smile.

"Does that mean you have a hunch but don't want to say?"

"I don't want to speculate."

"What about John Franklin?" the reporter asked. "What do you know about his motivations?"

"I have no idea," Carter said. "You'll have to ask him."

Taylor had stayed in the background, not wanting to draw the reporter to herself, and Wendel Smith provided the next diversion. He emerged from the hearing room and approached Carter with the expected news—the board did not feel the evidence merited additional exploration; nothing pointed to improper actions. Smith shook Carter's hand, and Carter thanked him for moving quickly to clear things up.

The reporter now collared Smith with the fading energy of someone trying to squeeze a drop of life from a non-story. Carter turned to Taylor, who put on a playful smile. "Your colleagues sure put up the noble fight to protect your honor," Taylor said.

"Yeah, like I expected, it turned out to be a pointless piece of cake."

Carter was taken by Taylor's surprising friendliness but felt uncomfortable by the inherent awkwardness of the situation. He knew that Taylor knew he wanted to go out with her, and now they both had to dance around that issue as though nothing had happened, each one taking pains to judge the secret code of the other's actions with a put-on lightheartedness that tried to hide the obvious falseness of what they were doing. Carter looked to his colleagues, then flung out a question laced with business formality. "Would you like to join us BWE guys for lunch?"

"I appreciate it," Taylor said, "but I've got to interview John Franklin." After a moment, she felt compelled to add, "I would have preferred to have you in the interview and get your read on any engineering-related things, but I don't think Mr. Franklin would feel at ease with you around." She apologized with her eyes, but Carter could not tell whether it was politeness or sincerity. The doubt stung.

"Well, good luck," said Carter, nodding a makeshift good-bye before heading back to his colleagues.

Taylor watched Franklin try unsuccessfully to avoid the reporter. Clearly ill at ease, Franklin refused to answer any questions, and Taylor waited until the reporter had finally given up. When Taylor approached to introduce herself, she flashed her FBI ID, and Franklin's eyes opened wide. Taylor liked the look of it—this man was no pro at whatever dissimulation he had up his sleeves—and for the first time she thought a mild dose of intimidation might actually work. If she blew it, or if Franklin had nothing to offer, she and the investigation would be no worse for the wear.

Smith had arranged for a small conference room down the hall from the licensing board office, and Taylor led the way, stepping aside at the entrance to let Franklin through first. She had him sit at the broad side of the long walnut-veneer table and walked to the opposite side. There she tossed down her bag, leaned on the table with two straight arms, and looked Franklin squarely in the face.

"Mr. Franklin, you've done your best to delay this conversation until now, but that's past and it's time for hard answers. How is it that the anonymous letter received by Wendel Smith cited you as a person who would testify about Scott Carter?"

"I have no idea," Franklin said. He swallowed, and his Adam's apple bobbed perceptibly.

"Somebody at some point in the past heard you express suspicions about Carter's alleged plan stamping. I want to hear the name of every person you told that story to."

Franklin looked at her in disbelief. "I can't remember that. I probably mentioned it to a lot of people around the office, just as conversation."

"But you didn't report it officially?"

"I didn't think that much of it. BWE is a reputable firm. I figured everything was just fine even if they did stretch the law."

"And you talked to no one recently about this accusation?"

"No," Franklin said. Again his Adam's apple bobbed, and his eyes blinked.

Taylor noticed the growing discomfort, how he rubbed the top of his thumb with his forefinger and how he took an extra breath before he spoke. Franklin did not seem to be even a passable liar, and Taylor felt certain he was hiding something important. She began to feel the adrenaline flow in stalking bigger game than she had expected. She stood up and paced back and forth, not saying anything, ostensibly letting Franklin squirm a little but inwardly gearing up to sound tough, like an actor ready to step slightly out of character but enjoying the prospect of the transformation. Taylor looked up at the ceiling for effect. "Why is it I don't believe a word you're saying?" she said calmly, then placed both hands back on the table, again leaning over Franklin, raising her voice only slightly, hardening the tone to an accusation. "Do you know that the letter sent to Wendel Smith came from the same laser printer that sent Jackhammer's terrorist notes?" She left out the fact that she knew nothing of the kind, but what did Franklin know about forensic possibilities? She continued as hard-nosed as before. "Do you know that if I give the word, the full force of the FBI is going to come down on your head and turn you and your family inside out looking for a connection? We'll dig into every one of your bank records and your contacts and talk to your employer. And the next time Jackhammer calls Scott Carter, we'll make sure Scott asks about you. Jackhammer is always a fun-loving guy on the phone, happy to screw everybody over, and I know he'll throw you to the dogs just for the fun of it. Now, if that all comes out after the fact, everybody's going to be pissed off and is going to go after your throat to the full extent of the law. And since that could go as high as conspiracy to commit murder, we're not talking kid's stuff." Taylor stood up and put her hands on her hips. "So maybe you ought to just reconsider because somehow I get the feeling you're probably a decent engineer trying to do his job who somehow got mixed up in this without really knowing what he was doing. And that's why I don't care about you. I have no interest righting your wrongs. Jackhammer's the only thing I care about, and the only thing the FBI administrator cares about, and when it comes to this investigation, the only thing the president of the United States cares about. So if you tell me what you know about Jackhammer, I'm not going to go after you."

"You can't talk to me like that," Franklin said nervously.

"I just did," said Taylor.

"If you're talking like that, I need to have a lawyer."

"That's probably a good idea, but a lawyer's not going to stop an FBI investigation of your affairs, and if I don't get answers now, here on the spot, that investigation is coming, so you'll have the pleasure of weathering that storm while you hold a lawyer's leaky umbrella."

Frightened, Franklin thought about his bank records and knew they would damn him. He had received his $25,000 in cash payments and had deposited them gradually, but the fact remained that this unexpected money stream had turned up without a clear source, money he had not reported on his tax return. He did not see how he could lie his way out of it, and facing that prospect, his hope and his will began to crumble. He did not want to go to jail.

"What did you mean when you said you wouldn't go after me?" Franklin asked.

"It meant that every day we don't catch Jackhammer, there's a chance of him killing more people. So I'm going to turn a blind eye to whatever you may have done and hope for any small clue."

"How do I know I can trust you?"

Taylor sensed she had beaten him, but a slight pity mixed with her surging satisfaction. Franklin looked more awkward than criminal and seemed to be cowering out of his element. Taylor did not take pleasure in humiliating him. "You don't know you can trust me," she said, "but right now you don't have a choice. Stay silent and a lot worse happens than me breaking my word. Besides that, I'd say you *can* trust me."

Franklin looked at Taylor anxiously. Since the beginning, the pressure had oppressed him, and now he gave in almost thankfully. "I want your word of honor that you or any of your FBI friends won't investigate me."

Taylor sat down in front of him and spoke quietly. "I have no problem with that, and unless you talk to somebody else, I think we can contain things."

"You're sure?"

"You can never be completely sure, but the odds are good."

Franklin accepted her sliver of doubt as honesty and took a breath. "OK, here's the deal. A guy with a disguised voice called me on the phone and threatened me that I had to corroborate the plan-stamping story."

"When was this?"

"About a week ago, or a little more."

"Was the plan-stamping story a lie?"

"No, it was the truth. You see, I didn't even come down here to lie. I didn't have to prove anything against Scott Carter. I just had to say what I knew, talk about my doubts. You can't hold that against me."

"Did this man identify himself as Jackhammer?"

"Not by name."

"But?"

"He said he was responsible for the bombings."

"Why didn't you come forward and tell the FBI?"

"Because the guy threatened me."

"How?" Taylor asked, trying to be supportive.

Franklin pulled at his ear. He did not want to speak, but he knew it was too late to retreat. "The man said he'd tell the FBI that I'd photographed the plans to help him carry out his attack on the ANC building."

"And did you?"

"No! I mean, yes, I photographed some plans. But that was two years ago, and I had no idea what they were for. I was told it was for an engineering firm to get one leg up on submitting the lowest bids." Franklin became desperate that she believe him. "Jesus, I never did anything really illegal. I just took some pictures of building and county plans while I worked for the Arlington Public Works Department. As far as I know, the plans were pretty much all in the public record, so it wasn't really theft. I needed money bad, and this stranger was offering it. I thought it was commercial espionage, something to make somebody a buck, not to physically hurt anyone."

"All right," Taylor said, her heart pumping from this new information. From the sparse and sporadic trails she had pursued so far, this one seemed like a wide, flowing river. "How did Jackhammer contact you two years ago?"

"First it was all through anonymous letters. I never knew who sent them."

"How could you trust this contact to pay up?"

"He gave me a $5,000 advance, just like that, along with a special camera. We had drop points at various places around the city."

"All right, we'll get to those later. Do you have any of the correspondence?"

"No, I burned them. I was afraid of keeping any evidence."

"Too bad, but I guess I would have done the same thing. Do you remember any postmarks on the letters?"

"Yeah, I actually did look at that, since there was no return address. It was different each time, but always from the Washington area. Arlington once. Also Bethesda and DC."

"This is good," Taylor said. "Now tell me about the photographs. Which plans did Jackhammer want?"

"All kinds of stuff. The ANC building, the county government building, an Arlington mall, the court house, the county's electric power grid, the area bridges, the underground water and utility lines, the sewers. That's what I remember."

"That's quite a collection."

"It all seemed like random stuff to me. I didn't think much of it." He lowered his head. "I mean, hell, I had no idea this guy could be a terrorist. How should I know that? I was desperate for money, and I just didn't think beyond what the guy told me."

"Did the utility plans cover the whole county, or just one part?"

"I don't remember. I'm sorry. I wasn't that familiar with all the plans, and I didn't take time to look where they started and where they left off."

"Do you remember Rosslyn being included? Jackhammer seemed to have singled it out for the blackout."

"I remember Rosslyn, but there was probably more than that. I was nervous and rushing through things."

"Well, I'd be nervous too," Taylor said, projecting commiseration, trying to keep Franklin on her side. "How did Jackhammer spell out what he wanted? Did he seem to know how the department kept things organized?"

Franklin looked down at the table for a moment, thinking. "I don't know if he showed any kind of knowledge of the actual filing system, but he did speak like a civil engineer in spelling out what he needed. I mean, that's why his business explanations seemed so believable. It was like talking shop. Of course, we already know he's an engineer, don't we?"

"Yeah, we know. So what about the drops? Did you ever make contact with a person?"

"Never. That's when he started using phone calls, with the same kind of disguised voice that he called me with a week ago. He told me where I could pick up the first payment and the camera, and the second time, where I should stash the camera with the photos I'd taken."

"Did you make any copies?"

"No."

"So the letters and the camera, they're all gone?"

"Yes."

"Where did he have the drops?"

"One was at Fort Washington on the Potomac. The other was in Manassas Battlefield Park."

"Did you ever see anyone nearby?"

"Never anyone that looked suspicious. There were a few visitors in the parks, so I had to wait for them to pass by."

"Families, individuals?"

"I wasn't checking them out. I was trying not to act suspicious. It looked like random people. There were a couple of families, as far as I remember."

"Do you still have any of the actual cash?"

"No. It all went into the bank, or was spent."

Taylor wanted to lay into him for being so stupid and irresponsible in putting people at risk with his actions, but to keep him as a source, Taylor held her tongue and just listened to answers.

"Did anyone else assist you in all this? Or did anyone else know about it?" Taylor asked.

"No. I was completely on my own."

"Your wife?"

Franklin implored Taylor with his eyes. "No, and we have to keep it like that. That's why you have to keep your word. I've got a family, and don't want it destroyed. I know I did the wrong thing, but I had no idea what it would lead to. I thought I'd rebuilt my life, and now this." He again bowed his head. "Jesus."

"I can't help you with your life," Taylor said, "but I need you as a source and to sign a statement. I may have some more questions. I expect your cooperation."

Franklin nodded.

"All right," Taylor said. "You go home and stay quiet about all this and I'm going to get back to chasing Jackhammer. You've been a very big help. It's the one thing you can do to make amends."

Franklin shook his head. "I've screwed up too much to fix anything."

Taylor stood up and stretched her arm across the table to shake hands. She felt sorry for the man for being a greedy jerk who had risked his career and his family and helped get people killed, but she knew such sympathy had no place in her dealings. The next time she might have to bash him around and not feel the slightest compunction. "We'll be in touch," Taylor said. "And thanks again."

Flush in her success, Taylor turned onto I-95 north across downtown Richmond and pushed the gas to the floor. She had reached seventy miles per hour of satisfaction before she eased off reluctantly, while the skyline of Richmond disappeared behind her and a vibrant flicker of excitement shimmered into pride. One thing was clear—Jackhammer had already been active in the Washington area two years ago. The postmarks on the anonymous letters confirmed that. So he probably lived there. Even a terrorist liked his comforts and would probably not fly into a strange city over two full years to hatch a plan, especially with that connection to the Arlington Public Works Department, which looked strong. Jackhammer may not have worked there himself, but he certainly had contacts, or he would never have heard Franklin's story about Scott's alleged plan stamping. Somewhere, somebody at Public Works had spoken to Jackhammer and probably not known it.

Finally, the document theft was no longer speculation, but fact. And she had been right about the photography. She felt smug about her lucky guess and smiled at the highway stretching out in front of her. Maybe you've got talent for this game, after all, she said to herself. Maybe you shouldn't think about giving it up.

But why would Jackhammer take risks to set up Scott like this? Did Jackhammer get morbid fun out of things that had nothing to do with his terrorist purpose? Why had he exposed himself to Franklin's evidence? Jackhammer must have known they would question the man. It was as though Jackhammer did it for fun, brandishing his arrogant confidence that he would leave no tracks no matter how rashly he operated.

The thought sobered Taylor. Despite her glow, she realized she had gotten no closer to pinpointing a suspect. The evidence only fenced in the search a little, cleared a few doubts, but left the potential pool nearly as broad as before.

She wondered how she would tell Gentry without compromising Franklin. She could hear Gentry now in his sergeant's bark: "You can't offer suspects immunity! Who do you think you are, a federal prosecutor?!" She knew he was right, but the results showed the risk had been worth it. What are you going to say about that, Frank, she asked in her thoughts.

The broad, rolling hills of northern Virginia now opened before her, and Taylor scanned the bare trees in the distance, anxious to get back to Washington and sort out all the leads. The moment she had left the interrogation and walked down the hall alone, she had wanted to share her exhilaration, and the person she really wanted to tell was Scott. He seemed like the one contact who would take interest beyond pure business and might actually encourage her. She had to admit, when she looked for conviction in work, he was no slouch. His backbone did not seem artificially forced in the same way she sometimes considered her own.

Soon, at the edges of her thoughts, she allowed images of Scott to flicker as a tease, but she did not want to take them seriously. For God's sake, she repeated to herself, Scott's fighting cancer. The latter thought stung quietly and confused her. She could never tell where pity merged with affection.

But my God, she thought, you're not going to repeat crazy nights like the one with that bartender. That experience had cleansed her. The bartender had been a spectacular, empty thrill, an embarrassing excess that she realized she did not want to resurrect.

It did not take long for Taylor to start scolding herself for getting bogged down in these thoughts. She had more important things to worry about than who would be her next dinner date. Jackhammer seemed to have a cache of design plans to attack about anything in Arlington County. How are you, or anyone else, going to deal with that?

15

The moment came when Scott Carter did not recognize himself. He was sitting in his Rosslyn office, the door closed and the window blinds open, when the reasonable, purposeful order that had carried him throughout his career turned into a backlash of emotions. The tasteful office decor that had become part of his everyday chemistry now stood as a strange, unchanging shell for an unfamiliar tenant. Everything seemed to have been stripped of its past, silently bare and unforgiving, indifferently awaiting his reaction.

The morning had started well enough. Taylor had called and told him about her success with Franklin. She had shown a new, if still reserved, enthusiasm, a willingness to lift her professional veneer and share a thrill on a personal level. Carter had felt himself drink from the clear spring of her stories. He had thrown compliments her way with the same hope of a fan tossing roses onto the stage for a favorite actress. She had warned about the range of targets Jackhammer might have put up his sleeve, but the threat of that merely scratched at the edge of Carter's intoxication.

Carter had told Taylor he was off to the doctor, and when he had arrived in the waiting room and looked at the four white antiseptic walls, all he could think about was the doctor making pronouncements that would undercut any potential future with Michelle. He leafed through magazines in which he had no interest.

The call from the nurse had gotten his attention, and after the blood pressure and the temperature checks, Carter had again waited, the distaste re-strung and stretched, now within the inner limbo of the patient rooms.

Soon Dr. Stern had entered and checked Carter's incision with a laconic efficiency that seemed like indifference. He pronounced it perfect and, as if in an afterthought, ran his fingers over the rest of Carter's back. At one point, his finger stopped and Carter could feel him bend low to take a closer look. Without speaking, Dr. Stern then pulled a magnifying glass from a desk drawer, rolled up a chair, and carefully examined a blemish on Carter's lower back. Carter wanted to ask what he had found but remained silent.

"I'd like you to lie on your stomach," Dr. Stern said. "I want to take a quick sample of some skin."

"What do you see?" Carter asked.

"I don't know yet. That's why we need to do a biopsy."

Carter paused, then didn't hold back. "With all due respect, Dr. Stern, you know I want real answers."

"And I don't like causing undue alarm. I've found the first beginnings of a spot that, in another patient, I would probably think nothing of, but since you have a history of melanoma, I'm going to be cautious and do a biopsy."

Back in his office that morning, Carter had sat down and looked at his desk. He had extracted an admission that a second occurrence of malignant melanoma, if that's what it was, could point to a higher mortality rate, but the doctor would not let himself be pinned down. Carter now sat with Michelle's voice still in his memory, while the doctor's prognosis beat that down into silence. Carter wanted to plow into his work, but the pressure had built there as well. Waynewright had slipped Carter more customer relations tasks, forgetting his earlier promises and pushing Carter's workdays later and later into the evening. Today, Carter could not even get started.

Carter was ready to get up and leave, take a walk around the block and try to recover some every-day focus, then return to a clear, uncomplicated dependability and find his old self. A buzz from his secretary stopped him.

"A Mr. Edward Babcock is here to see you. He says he doesn't have an appointment, but he says he won't trouble you more than a few minutes. Would you be able to see him?"

Babcock, Carter thought. What the hell does he want? "Sure, send him in," Carter said without conviction.

Carter got up and opened the door and found Babcock standing before him, smiling broadly, as though trying to lessen the intimidation of his big frame and tough reputation. His handshake held nothing back and made Carter squeeze in return to protect his knuckles.

"Good to see you again," Babcock said.

"Come on in," said Carter, still not focused but now almost grateful for distraction. "What can I do for you?"

"Well, I was passing by and I had some things to discuss with that Agent Taylor, and I said hell, why talk with her when I've got an engineer I can talk to."

"Have a seat," Carter said coolly, not liking Babcock's tone.

Babcock tossed his coat onto Carter's conference table and dropped into a chair, gruffly satisfied to rest his bulk. He swung one leg over the other and leaned back. "I've been fishing around, Scott, and I don't like what I see."

"Oh, really?"

"Well, ever since Miss. Taylor contacted me for help, I've been calling everyone in sight, especially all the guys at the Public Works Department, old guys, new guys. I don't suppose I've rooted out anything you haven't already found, but it got me to worrying." He glowered for effect, having fun with the drama.

"Why's that?" Carter said, dutifully offering the cue like a parent for a kid's knock-knock joke.

"This Jackhammer may have gotten his hands on all sorts of county design plans."

"How do you know that?" Carter could not imagine that Taylor had told him about Franklin.

"I heard that story about the possible break-in. I heard there were plans out on a table and no one fessing up that they had done it."

"Who told you that?"

"The same guy who probably told you, but I promised him I wouldn't blab."

Carter realized it must have been Bender. It didn't matter. There was nothing confidential here.

"It's possible," Babcock went on, "with all the sheets that were in those drawers, that this Jackhammer has the design plans for all kinds of things—county buildings, electric power lines, bridges, drinking water grids, natural gas networks. When you think of the possibilities, it's enough to make your head spin."

"Did you find out which plans specifically?"

"Nah, not that good, but I was wondering if you already made the connection to the danger we're talking about?"

"I think we have."

"So have you ever thought what could happen if this guy attacked all those areas?" Babcock asked, not hiding the relish he might feel in watching a disaster movie. "He could blow up a bridge during rush hour. He could blow up natural gas lines all over the county. Hell, he's already blown up a whole electric power grid and a large building! Are you guys going to put this other stuff past him?"

"No," Carter said, but strangely, the same warning had not registered as powerfully before. When Taylor had mentioned it, his mind had been elsewhere.

"So what are you and your lady friend going to do about it?"

"The investigation's going on as intensely as always."

"Well thank god your Miss. Taylor has someone to help her out. I'd hate to think the county's safety rested on a woman who doesn't know a gas line from a water main."

That did it for Carter. He spoke quietly and coldly. "You know, Ed, why are you coming in here just to throw insults? Do you have any final point to make?"

Babcock raised his eyebrows unfazed, suppressing a smile. "Well, Scott, getting a little testy for your FBI friend? I guess you always were the gallant one."

"Maybe this conversation has ended," Carter said, standing up. "I've got no expertise in gas lines or water mains either, so you might as well say the same thing about me."

"Yeah, but I know you've got some common sense." Babcock got up from his chair. "I wasn't lying about being a minute. I'm on my way."

Carter nodded goodbye, but Babcock stopped and pointed at Carter. "If this leads to anything, you can tell everybody I warned them. I've got a feeling I know the way this Jackhammer thinks."

"Are you suspicious of someone?"

Babcock laughed. "No, I'm not that good a detective. Just remember that when the reporters come round wondering what happened, you think of me. Tell 'em I saw it coming."

"Maybe not," Carter said. "Michelle has already had the exact same suspicions you did." He wondered if that would let the air out of Babcock's inflated chest.

"You don't say," Babcock replied, striding like an old-time robber baron toward the door. "What's she found out?"

"You'd have to ask her."

Babcock grinned slyly. "All hush-hush, huh? You must be in real deep with the FBI."

"Very deep," said Carter.

"Well, let's wish us all luck. I'd hate to be on the wrong end of Jackhammer's gun sights."

Carter closed the door to his office and hated the idea of Babcock being right. What if Jackhammer did take things in turn and attacked one type of target after another? Which one would be next? A bridge? But certainly the police could patrol that. There weren't that many bridges in DC. How about the gas lines? That could be devastating, but at least the explosions would be localized, wouldn't they? The water system sent chills through Carter, but he assumed the treatment plant could detect anything dumped into the reservoir stream. They test that stuff every day, don't they?

However distastefully, Carter had to agree with Babcock. Maybe the county had to put itself on even higher alert. He could ask Taylor to arrange a meeting with Board Chairman Duncan, and at least they could lay out the possibilities. That was best for the county, wasn't it? Sure it was, Carter thought. But he did not know what pushed him more at the moment, the new speculation or another excuse to get near Michelle.

"Guess who just stopped by?" Carter asked, trying to sound lighthearted in a phone call to Taylor.

"You tell me."

"The grand Edward Babcock. He's taken you more seriously than maybe you even intended. He acts like he's part of the investigation. He's been calling everybody in sight, and now he's got worries for the county."

"Legitimate ones?"

"As legitimate as ours, especially after what you found out from Franklin about the design plans involved. Babcock repeated something you already hinted at. What if Jackhammer goes after these targets one by one? We need to brief the county that these plans have been compromised."

"So let's set up a meeting," Taylor said. "If we get them to pay more attention, we might get lucky like we did yesterday. We made a photo ID of the guy the electric utility workers spotted at one of the bombing sights, and we tracked him down. He's got Mob connections, but he hasn't given us anything. Jackhammer seems to stay out of all this personally. Guys get paid but no one can put their finger on where the money comes from. This latest guy seemed to have heard rumors that we're talking about some rich Lone Ranger. So what it comes down to is we're going to put somebody in jail but we're not any closer to the big fish. We need another minnow."

Before Taylor hung up, Carter asked her to invite Handley, the county engineer, to the meeting to make sure it was not just Freeport from Public Works. Carter then left his office and walked to the firm's reference shelf. He wanted to bone up on the basics of drinking water systems—he had not considered that subject since college, and he did not want to look totally ignorant.

Carter found the book he was looking for and read the water purification steps. He did not know how the plant that served Arlington configured things, but the process would probably match what he found in front of him. Pipes brought the water from a natural source—a lake, a reservoir, or a river—into a basin and then sent it through screens to take out the fish, plants, and any other floating trash. The water was then pumped to a higher level, where the plant then added alum along with chemicals such as chlorine and stirred it all together in large mixing basins, then passed it to settling basins, where bacteria, silt, and other impurities clung to the alum and sank to the bottom. The resulting water was then sent to trickle through sand and gravel filters to take out the remaining impurities. Finally, the water got another shot of chlorine before it was pumped to the public. Carter supposed that any one of those steps offered the chance for insider sabotage, but there was always that final quality test that would supposedly monitor what got sent to the city. Carter had to doubt that with all the ID checks some outsider could get into that closed environment and do some dangerous sabotage, unless some employee had been bought off and turned criminal. But what were the odds of that? Carter did not know.

Taylor painted a sufficiently dangerous picture and arranged for a meeting with Duncan at 5:30 that afternoon. Because of commitments, Taylor could not pick Carter up, and they arranged to meet in the lobby of the county government building.

On his drive over, Carter told himself to continue the act that nothing had happened between them. Today was strictly business—no invitations, no soul-baring, no long looks. He had to let things cool down and just show Michelle he was a regular guy who did not threaten her with any kind of baggage. Of course, he knew that in reality he had no idea what was best for the situation. He hoped he could do better for the county than he could for himself.

Carter parked his car in the lot by the county offices and unconsciously looked around to see if Taylor might be passing nearby. Carter's new bodyguard parked next to him and walked with Carter the few blocks to the entrance, then waited inside the door. Carter wondered what purpose the bodyguard served when snipers could have picked him off any time they wanted.

Taylor had not yet arrived, and Carter paced back and forth by a rack of Arlington County public service brochures. With the end of the workday, a stream of government workers were pouring through the lobby as though fleeing Carter's destination. Taylor arrived five minutes later, her shin-length winter coat bouncing as she came through the door in a hurry. She was brimming with energy.

"Well," she said in a lively apology, "you almost caught me being late." She looked at her watch. "Have you been here long?"

"Just a few minutes," Carter said, startled by her seeming exuberance. Did she think the investigation was going that well? "What's the game plan?" he asked.

"We let them make all the policy decisions. We just do our duty and tell them what they might be facing. After all, we don't have a shred of evidence that anything else is going to happen."

"Except that Jackhammer is a dangerous psycho."

"Except that," she said.

Outside Board Chairman Duncan's office, Carter and Taylor waited fifteen minutes for Duncan to clear his desk. Chief Engineer Handley and the county manager joined the wait, but Public Works Director Freeport apparently received a personal page. He arrived only after Duncan had opened his door to invite everyone in.

Duncan's office felt large and airy, with several expansive windows that showed the city lights and the gathering darkness outside. In contrast to Freeport's law-office gloom, Duncan had opted for an authoritative sportiness that mixed a classic oak desk with light brown carpet and sleek, modern oak shelves.

Carter could still not stand the plastic, unnatural perfection of Duncan's face, as though the man had his own private make-up artist continually on call to create that polyurethane look. The effect might have been appropriate for TV, Carter thought, but in person Carter could never be sure when the artificial packaging hijacked Duncan's words as well. As always, not a hair on Duncan's head had budged out of place, combed from left to right in a shimmering, chemical part.

The county manager, Duncan, and Freeport took the three separate chairs, while Handley, Carter, and Taylor sat down on the couches. Duncan offered everyone coffee, but with no takers, turned his eyes to Taylor. "All right, since we all want to keep this meeting short, describe the kind of threats we may be facing. If there's something the county can do, we'll want to do it."

"We can only speculate about motives," Taylor said, "but we've now confirmed the types of county design plans that Jackhammer got hold of. In addition to buildings and electric power distribution, we're talking bridges, natural gas lines, and drinking water."

"May I ask how you confirmed that?" Freeport asked. He was suffering from a cold, and his raw, red nose made his peevish face appear especially forlorn. "Our own interviews have not brought that to closure."

"I'm not at liberty to say," Taylor said.

Freeport straightened in his chair and glanced at Duncan. "I find that a little disturbing," he said. "If it's someone in my office, I need to know about it."

"Sorry, can't do it," Taylor said. "But I can tell you this: The person doesn't work for you."

"Well, let's get back to the issue," Duncan said, uninterested in Freeport's attempt at self-righteousness. "Do we have any ideas on what the next target might be, if there is one?"

"I'm afraid not," said Taylor. "We just know that there's no reason Jackhammer would necessarily stop now. He seems to be enjoying himself."

Duncan looked to Handley. "So which area presents the greatest danger?"

"I haven't had much time to think it through," Handley said, always hesitant to pass judgment without exact data, "but hitting the bridges looks questionable to me. A bomb attack might have more impact on the cars than the bridge. Scott's our structural engineer. What do you think, Scott?"

"I agree," said Carter. "It'd take some awfully big explosives to actually bring down one of the Potomac bridges. You'd have to have them strategically placed, and you'd have to do it all out in the open. There aren't any parking garages you can just drive in under cover. I'd say some extra police patrols, especially at night, would go a long way there. The only thing left would be driving a surface level bomb into traffic, but that wouldn't be much different from an attack on any street in the county when it comes to taking lives."

"Could a big enough van on the span bring down a bridge?" Duncan asked.

"Hard to say exactly without looking into it, but you'd probably just put a big hole in the deck and the underlying framework. Given the multiple arches and pylon spans we've got on the Potomac, you might take out one whole section of the bridge. That would of course close it down, but I don't think you could breach the whole structural integrity for complete end-to-end collapse. Unless, of course, you're talking about a military-size bomb that could wipe things out totally."

"What about multiple vans?" Duncan asked.

"Well, sure," Carter said, "if you get that kind of sophistication and coordination. But as for loss of life, you could probably do the same or more parking multiple vans downtown in rush hour."

"Natural gas lines are worrisome," Handley said, "but the person would have to dig or go through man-holes to get to them. Setting one of those off could rock a whole street. But if Jackhammer's trying to kill a lot of people, that might not be the best way, since the ground itself is going to absorb some of the force of the explosion."

"How accessible are those pipes?" Duncan asked.

"Like I said, manholes will get you there, if you know which ones."

"Can we provide any security?"

"I suppose you could cruise all the streets that have those manholes, especially at night."

"And drinking water?" the board chairman asked.

"You've got the water treatment plant where the county buys its water," Handley said. "If Jackhammer bought off some inside employee, I suppose you could do some damage, but the water's tested every day, and there's not just one person involved. If something got through, it would probably be short-term—it would be noticed pretty soon."

"What are the chances of somebody breaching security over there?"

"From my tours of the place, it'd be pretty tough. There are ID checks, and everybody knows everybody else, so I can't see some stranger just walking in doing something. I also can't imagine an employee trying to poison the county."

"I'd hope not," Duncan said, "but if you've got a lot of money involved, you're never sure of anything."

"Should we be making any of these concerns public?" Freeport asked. "It would put the whole county on guard. People might spot suspicious activity."

"I'd prefer not," Taylor said. "Everybody's completely on edge about terrorism anyway, and everybody's read all the dredged up scenarios in the paper. If we go public with the same kind of unfocused list and Jackhammer knows we're watching him in these areas, he might just adjust his plans to slip by in some other way. Surprise gives us a better chance of catching his operatives red-handed."

"It makes me nervous not to get the public involved," Duncan said. He hesitated. "But maybe I agree. I don't want to create any more panic than we've got. If we make what we know about Jackhammer public—that everything might be a serious target—it's like Michelle said, we'll just be bombarded with more questions about all the worst-case scenarios. Reassuring everyone when you're talking about every piece of our infrastructure is going to be tough."

"One thing's for sure," Carter added, "it would probably make Jackhammer happy if we did give him the publicity. I think he relishes the power he has in causing chaos."

"I think," Duncan said, "we need a general reminder for the public to be vigilant for suspicious activities in general, with no reference to a Jackhammer hit list. With the respective county officials and employees, we'll be more specific. We'll have them really raise their antennas and tighten their security. Then there are some other basic precautions we can take. I'll order extra surveillance of the bridges and the streets that have access to the natural gas lines. Sam, you and Nick need to meet with the police commissioner to work that out. I'll also want some plain-clothes policemen at the water treatment plant, round the clock. Everybody who has a piece of county services needs to be aware of a possible threat in their area."

"I'll see whether the FBI can contribute to that effort," Taylor said.

"That would be much appreciated," Duncan said.

"You might want to increase the water testing frequency," Handley added.

"That sounds good," said Duncan, wanting to wrap things up. "Any final suggestions?"

Everyone shook their heads.

Duncan stood up and extended his hand to Taylor. "Then thank you very much. The county appreciates your cooperation."

"Any time," Taylor said.

Outside the office, Carter again found himself alone with Taylor, but the ring of the elevator saved him from another comment. At the next floor going down, other people stepped in, and Carter did not feel compelled to talk. In the lobby, Carter and Taylor exchanged a few remarks about the extra police patrols and potential FBI security involvement and passed through the doors to the plaza outside.

Carter found an inconsequential good-bye very difficult, but he offered one anyway, not daring to even shake Taylor's hand.

16

Maria Lockwood could not pull herself out of bed. For a day she had suffered from diarrhea, nausea, and flatulence, and now a profound weakness had overpowered her decrepit body. In the morning, she lay flat and did not know how she could get up to go to the bathroom. She pressed her hands against the mattress to raise her back, but the nausea flooded her chest and shoved her down again. Lockwood lay motionless, breathing hard, her mouth open like a corpse that had not yet gone cold.

Above her, the morning movements of her neighbors seemed to emanate from a strange, external world of which she was no longer a part. Am I going to die, she asked herself. Is this the first way station to the afterlife? But why should that journey feel so horrible?

At times, she was too weak to care, but then occasionally she would turn her head and see the phone at her bedside and think that somehow that could help ease the sickness, or at least speed her departure from this earth. But whom should she call? She did not know anyone, and she was embarrassed to dial 911, imagining a noisy, flashing ambulance and all the neighbors gawking.

But as she lay another hour and felt herself grow weaker, her embarrassment turned to exhausted indifference, and she slid her wrinkled hand sideways to the phone and made a feeble lurch for the receiver. The clumsy thrust knocked the receiver from its perch, and she thought she had lost it. But there had not been a final thud, and she realized the receiver had remained on the nightstand. She turned her head to see where it lay and then groping, clutched it with a willed sigh of strength. She had gained more confidence with her success and now held the receiver with less insecurity, feebly punching out the three emergency numbers.

"I can't get up," she said with a whisper. "Can somebody take me to the hospital?"

The 911 dispatcher called for an ambulance, then asked whether the paramedics could get into her apartment.

"It's locked right now."

"Can you open it?"

"I don't think so. They can go to the apartment manager and get the key. That would be best."

"All right. We'll be right there. Can you—"

"Thank you," Lockwood said, dropping the receiver to the nightstand, too weak to actually hang up. No one needs to call you, she thought. It's too late for any of that.

At the emergency room, the ER doctor suspected a stomach virus or a bacterial attack, but not being sure, ordered a battery of tests. The doctor then admitted Lockwood, but initial treatments only mitigated the symptoms, without restoring her strength. The doctors then brought in a specialist.

When he took his first look, he realized they had better get those tests fast or Maria Lockwood might soon be gone.

Dr. Stern had accepted Carter's request to give him biopsy results over the phone, and the next day, in the late afternoon, he gave Carter a call. The new blemish was malignant, the doctor said. He stressed that this did not necessarily change Carter's prognosis for the worse. It did not necessarily mean that the cancer had spread. Since the two tumors developed at nearly the same time, it might merely be a double manifestation of an inherent skin sensitivity, perhaps to ultraviolet rays from the sun.

"I suppose that's possible," Carter said, "but couldn't it also mean that melanoma is going to start popping up everywhere and that the cancer is going to spread internally as well?"

"In a worst-case scenario."

"Right," Carter said.

"We'll want to take our exploratory look again," said Dr. Stern. "I guess you know the drill."

"Yes, I guess I do."

Melissa Campbell sat down in the bedroom of her four-year-old daughter, just beneath a large Winnie the Pooh poster, and let her face fall into her hands, kneading the fatigue from her forehead, too drained to cry. Her daughter, Judy, lay on her back in bed, her head propped on a pillow, breathing haltingly in her sleep, as though a demon from her dreams played hide and seek in a game to smother her. Campbell did not understand it. The doctors had told her that Judy's recovery from a kidney infection was nearly complete.

Then, in the afternoon, the babysitter had called Campbell at work and told her to come home early. Judy was suffering from stomach pains and diarrhea and needed her mother.

Campbell had not hesitated leaving the office, but the stress of that exit still rocked within her. She worked as a secretary for Sylar Integration, a computer software company in downtown Rosslyn, and for the past week and a half, SI had been putting together a proposal for a large networking contract. Campbell's role was to feed the analysts' text and spreadsheets into the final wordprocessed package and present each part for review as it became available, then, on an assembly-line basis, input the corrections. About a week ago, despite her hesitations, she had been forced to come in on a Saturday. Her daughter was not yet completely well, but the babysitter did not work on the weekend, and Campbell had convinced herself that Judy's sitting in a spare cubical with some coloring books would be no worse than doing the same at home.

Campbell knew her life depended on this job. Six months ago, her auto-mechanic husband had gotten fed up with his work, fed up with his wife, and without warning had quit his job, saying he was leaving for Montana to start fresh. He had told Campbell that she could keep the run-down, two-bedroom house in Manassas, at least till they got around to settling a divorce. Campbell had bid the man good riddance, but now the pressure of only one income and only one parent to get Judy through the worst of her illness had become overwhelming.

Campbell moved her chair closer to the side of the bed and gently lifted Judy's hand into hers. "Pumpkin, you'll be fine," Campbell whispered. "You're all I've got, and I'm going to look after you. You hear me? No, I guess you shouldn't hear me. Just sleep and get your strength back. I don't know what the babysitter fed you, but you'll get that out of your system, and things'll be fine in the morning. And if they're not, I'll just take you to the doctor, and SI will just have to wait."

Campbell knew she was right in her priorities, but she agonized over her precarious job security. She could tell that all the programmers at work looked down on her, addressing her as though she would never quite understand what they handed her. Sure, she did not know their complicated code and could not always decipher what they wrote. When the pressure rose, so did their impatience with her questions.

My god, Campbell thought to herself, what will you do if you lose your job? The company is depending on this new contract. If they don't get it, then they'll start laying people off, and then what? Already a large bite of her paycheck went to a babysitter, and another bite to the family health insurance premiums. But that health insurance was her lifesaver. If she lost her job, those premiums would triple. And how would she pay that with no income? Campbell could feel herself trembling inside, her usual determination faltering on despair. So much had fallen on her shoulders. Judy had been born with one kidney and had had numerous infection scares, and Campbell had been poised to donate one of her own. Maybe with Judy's health deteriorating, Campbell would finally have to do it. But who's going to pay for that if you lose your job, she asked herself. My god, what will become of you?

Campbell took a deep breath and tried to compose herself. For strength, she looked at the pale face of her daughter and the few strands of blond hair that had slipped onto the girl's cheek. Quietly, Campbell reached out and lifted the hair to the side, and then grazed the side of Judy's cheek with the back of her hand. She took strength from the soft feel of Judy's skin and from the face that Campbell knew was the cutest in the world.

Campbell intoned to herself that no matter what happened with her work, there would be a hospital for Judy; there would be food on the table. Campbell did not know whether it would come from welfare or from a surprise gift from her no-good husband, but something would have to materialize, no matter how dark things looked.

Campbell tried to convince herself with a kiss on her daughter's hand, but before she could plant it, Judy had woken with a moan. "Oh my tummy," Judy groaned. Her eyes opened and closed, her hands on her abdomen, and when she fully came to, she whimpered, "I have to go to the bathroom."

Campbell jumped from her chair, pulled the blanket aside, lifted her daughter onto her chest, and then ran. She helped Judy onto the toilet, and when she was sure Judy had woken enough to hold herself up, she stood aside. "You let it all out," Campbell commanded. "Just get out the bad stuff, and you'll be all right."

But the evening did not work that way. The diarrhea would not stop and Judy grew increasingly weak. Exhausted from worry, Campbell bundled her daughter up and drove at full speed to the hospital emergency room. On the surface she tried to project an image of strength, but inside she was falling apart.

Carter sat in the Alexandria Hospital lobby awaiting his brief outpatient surgery and thought with intolerant distaste about this new joke of a blow. For all he knew, this could be just one more sinkhole in a blatant series of impersonal, inconsiderate downfalls, his cellular machinery taking it upon itself to go haywire and eventually do him in. He wished he could just get this procedure over with now, immediately, and not have to deal with all these onlookers. Around him were a constantly replenished supply of families awaiting reports of their loved ones—killing time with magazines, forcing trivial small talk, taking trips to the vending machines. Carter's sense of isolation grew increasingly uncomfortable, as though hit by a cramp in his leg that came on unexpectedly and required a fast reverse stretch. What the heck was he fighting for in this ultimate recovery? He figured he was strong enough to accept whatever shot of bitter news the doctors might give him and then set his jaw and beat the thing. And then what? What good was his health if he could not share it with anyone? He would just go home alone to his house and find nothing better to do than continue his office work. Wasn't there a point to the comment "get a life"?

The call from the front desk interrupted his thoughts. He was glad to break things off and finally get one more move in this medical game behind him. He followed the nurse down the hall to a dressing room and went through the mildly degrading prep of stripping down to the loose-hanging cotton smock that would now be his only armor against fate.

In the procedure room, Dr. Samson told him that the actual surgery would take only minutes—they were talking about a very small tumor, caught in the very early stages—but that some additional probes and tests would prolong things a little. With a trace of sympathy, he asked if Carter had any questions. Carter shook his head. By this time, there were no more questions to ask.

On the operating table, the local anesthetic did little good for Carter's other wound. He thought only of Michelle.

In the days following Carter's trip to the hospital, Rosslyn doctors began reporting one case of diarrhea and nausea after another. When the health department finally got a handle on the news, they realized they had the makings of a local epidemic, and test results, at first unclear, now pointed to the culprit: *giardia lamblia*, a virulent protozoan. The broad range of victims had not eaten at the same restaurant nor worked for the same employer nor gone on the same field trip. But they had drunk the same tap water. When the county health commissioner, Dorothy Connel, heard the report, she phoned Duncan and the county manager and asked them to tell Rosslyn citizens to boil their water until further notice. The county had to find the source of the contamination and then clean it up.

"We've had one person die already," the health commissioner said. "Looking back at the records, an elderly woman who was already frail appears to have been the first victim."

"Jesus," Duncan said, "is this an intentional or a natural contamination?" He did not want more bad news under his watch.

"It's not a first in the U.S.," Connel said. "I've done a little research, and in 1985 Scranton, Pennsylvania, had a big *giardia* problem. About 300,000 people were told to boil their water and not wash clothes. That's what you need to tell the citizens of Arlington."

"Is it everywhere in the county?"

"As of now, most of the cases come from Rosslyn, although we've had a few people in other areas of the county. We're trying to confirm that. I'd guess anyone who has the same drinking water source should be included. That includes you, Mr. Chairman."

"Well, how long can this last?"

"You'll have to ask your water people about that. All I can address is the health end, and we're talking about prescribing strong antibiotics for a good number of people. If you don't treat this in the worst cases, symptoms can last for months or years. The downside is that these antibiotics can have side effects, potential liver dysfunction and perhaps cancer. Not a good situation."

"I'll say," Duncan said. "It'll look like we can't keep a watch over things even during the highest alert."

"They can't blame you," said Connel.

"They sure as hell can, especially if this is a deliberate attack."

"I'd look for natural causes first," Connel said. "How do you manage to get by security for something like this? And why *giardia lamblia*? It's not really a killer. A terrorist could have done a lot worse."

"We sure as hell better find out what's behind it."

Duncan hung up and called his PR chief to contact all the local media to get out the emergency message. He wanted it on every radio station and running as a banner across every TV set, and he wanted a truck driving the streets with a bull-horn telling people about what precautions to take. He then barked at his administrative assistant to track down Special Agent Taylor and get her on the line. If he couldn't prevent the bad news, he at least was going to look like someone who reacts with energy. Elections were only a year away and any opponent would look for a hole in his armor and start stabbing away.

Duncan then dialed Freeport. "Sam, do you realize we've got contaminated drinking water. The health commissioner just called me. We've got what looks like an epidemic in Rosslyn."

"From what?"

"Something like *garda lamilo* or whatever. I don't remember. That's your job. You call over to your water treatment people ASAP and find out where that contamination came from. I don't want any stone unturned, do you understand?"

"Sure. I'll get right on it."

"As soon as you find out what they can do, and how fast, you tell me."

"Absolutely."

Duncan hung up and rose to pace his office, thinking about what else he could do—when the phone rang. He jumped back to his desk. "Yes?"

"I've got Special Agent Taylor on the line," his assistant said.

"Great. You put her on."

"Chairman Duncan?" Taylor said.

"Yes, Michelle, how are you? Have you heard the news?"

"I'm not sure what news you're talking about."

"We've got contaminated drinking water in Rosslyn. People are starting to get sick from a protozoan. It could be getting out of hand. Has somebody taken responsibility?"

"We haven't heard anything. We'd know from Scott if Jackhammer had called him. Couldn't it be a natural contamination?"

"Sure, but after our meeting, doesn't this look a little ominous?"

"I won't deny it," Taylor said. "We'll obviously tell you the instant we hear something."

"Everybody in Arlington's got to boil their water. It's a mess."

"My request for FBI security help is still pending. This new development should push things through in a jiffy."

"Thanks very much."

"We'll get this guy," Taylor said. "We'll get there."

Duncan could not sit still and called his assistant to contact an action team—his press secretary, the county manager, his chief policy assistant, Freeport, the water treatment plant director, and the health commissioner. He ordered them to come to a meeting as soon as they had put their own emergency response in place. Duncan wanted to go over the complete set of facts and nail down a plan.

Something snapped in Melissa Campbell the afternoon Judy died. For days she had quietly inured herself for calamity. She had prepared herself to lose her job and her house, even take another blow from her ex-husband. But she had never admitted the possibility that Judy might leave her. That scenario had simply not existed.

And yet at the hospital, Judy had never recovered her strength. The weakness from the kidney infection had already sapped Judy's immune system, and now the virulent growth of the *giardia lamblia* had taken command of her intestines. Campbell had been desperate to donate a kidney, but the doctors had said the kidney, although again in trouble, was no longer the central problem.

Through it all, Campbell would not leave her daughter's hospital bedside. Her employer called in a temp to finish the proposal job and assured Campbell they would manage without her. They even sent Judy a stuffed toy and Campbell some flowers, but Campbell had moved beyond a capacity for comfort. Her daughter deteriorated each day, and when Judy finally used her last strength to blink a statement of love, Campbell buried her face in her daughter's hand and sobbed inconsolably, unable to imagine how she herself could go on living.

Later, when Campbell heard the first report that her daughter's death had been caused by an impurity in Rosslyn's drinking water and that the danger might still exist, she could no longer contain herself. What was Arlington County going to do to atone for this negligence? If terrorists were responsible, the county should have set up measures to stop them.

The county was supposedly on high alert after all that had happened. And if this was a breakdown in the water system, the fault was even more inexcusable. What was the county going to do to make this right?

At 5:10 p.m., Duncan's action team converged on the chairman's office and took their seats at his personal conference table. The arrangement gave everyone a place to spread their material and Duncan a surface to pound if he did not get straight answers.

Duncan's team settled in nervously, concerned about their incomplete knowledge of how the emergency had started. They also did not know how much Duncan and the county manager would find them accountable. The only exception was James McCracken, director of the water treatment plant that supplied Arlington County. A civil engineer specializing in drinking water, McCracken had moved up to the director's post four years ago, after eighteen years with the plant. Beneath a bulbous bald head, he wore a bow tie and suspenders, and over the years, he had cultivated his unorthodoxy by remaining maddeningly unruffled. His manner said: Fire me if you want, but what you get from me now is all you're going to get. Duncan had not dealt with McCracken before and had made a point of checking his first name just before the meeting.

"Okay, Jim," Duncan said. "You're on the front lines here. Where's this protozoan coming from?"

McCracken stayed true to his reputation. "We have no idea," he said.

Duncan had expected some sort of hedging that he could needle, even ridicule, but the directness caught him off guard. "What does that mean?"

"Preliminary tests from inside the plant haven't shown anything, and we haven't had time to get final results on additional daily samples. You see, we don't regularly test for protozoa. They're very hard to detect, and we've got filtration and disinfection in place to greatly reduce any potential threat."

Duncan leaned forward in disbelief. "So what are you telling me? The bug that's getting everybody sick and has already killed an old lady—you don't usually test for? That's going to sound great on the news!"

McCracken did not take offense. He indulged ignorance with facts. "We don't do anything differently from any other top-notch water treatment plant anywhere in the country. You can tell that to the public."

"So why are the tests taking so long?" Duncan asked.

"First of all, we had to track down what to test first—which particular days from our daily samples. In humans, the symptoms from *giardia* can take anywhere from a week to several weeks to show up, so we don't exactly know the date *giardia* might have come through the plant. Second, the simplest, fastest test looks for coliforms, which are what we call 'indicator bacteria.' If you find them, the bad stuff might be present as well. We're still running that indicator test on all the various stored samples to narrow down the time frame. That first round gave us no positive indications, so we've got to dig deeper, and those tests take time."

"How long?"

"Another day or two."

"You better make it a day, and not two," Duncan said.

"We're doing whatever's possible," McCracken said. "We don't like poisoning our customers any more than you do."

Duncan was losing his patience with what he considered McCracken's impertinence, but there was no one else to deal with and he held his tongue. "Now, you obviously realize that this contamination could have been intentional. In talking with the FBI, the same lunatic who blew up the ANC building and the power plants may have his dirty fingers in this. That means I want all your investigators to keep that in the back of their minds. Ask yourselves: How could a terrorist have gotten into the water system?"

McCracken spoke up. "I'd certainly like to pinpoint exactly where the people who got sick drank their water. Maybe it's a localized contamination in one of the Rosslyn buildings or in one of the pipes. It's obviously not just where they live, but also where they work." He turned to the health commissioner. "What are the prospects there?"

"We're trying to interview everyone outside the Rosslyn area who came down with symptoms to see if they might have been in the area around the critical time," Connel said. "We have about forty such cases on record so far, out of the total of about two hundred sick. But it takes time to track them down."

"You'll get police support on that," Duncan said. "I'll have the police commissioner contact you, and you tell him exactly what you need. And I want the work continuing as long as there's a victim awake to accept our interview calls."

"That will help," Connel said. "I appreciate it."

Duncan's assistant came into the room without knocking. "Sorry for interrupting," she said, "but there's a special report on TV."

Duncan grabbed the remote and turned on the TV that sat in the corner of his office. A local news reporter was standing outside an emergency care clinic in Rosslyn, detailing the contamination story in dramatic terms. The reporter ran taped clips of interviews with a doctor and two patients and then switched to a colleague at another clinic. With each new image of someone sick and the ultimate origin of the *giardia* still a mystery, the news began to paint a picture of crisis. At the same time, a warning banner about the need to boil county water was moving across the bottom of the screen. A check of all the other local stations showed the identical banner moving silently from right to left.

"OK," Duncan said with mildly distasteful fatalism, "it's all out in the open. As soon as the media finds out you're all sitting in here, they're going to grab every one of you. I want a consistent story, so here's how I see it. We're working as fast as we can on all angles. There's the slight chance this was a terrorist attack, but there's no evidence of that yet. We have the FBI involved. The Arlington police department is bolstering the health side of the investigation, and we hope to pinpoint geographical boundaries of those affected. Anyone who's sick who lives outside of the Rosslyn area should come forward and tell where they might have drunk public water in the last few weeks. The water plant lab is working around the clock to explore the extent and timing of the contamination. Did I leave anything out?"

"Sounds good to me," Freeport said. "I—"

Freeport could not continue. The door to the chairman's office had burst open, and a woman stormed in, Duncan's assistant right behind her. "You can't go in there!" the assistant shouted. The woman paid no attention and approached the conference table with frightening, sobbing determination. She stared at them through her tears as though the group epitomized her desolation. "So here you all are," she said, her voice cracking. "You're now planning what to do! All after the fact. But my daughter's dead because she drank your water. My Judy's dead! I'm going to bury her!" Her voice suddenly dropped as she put her hand to her mouth in a shaking hopelessness. "Well, I can't change that. It's the will of the Lord, but I can make sure you don't sleep until you do something to make it right."

The conference table had gone silent. McCracken knew the woman was not being fair, but her despairing, pitiful face stopped him from trying to offer an explanation. He could not answer a daughter's death with a balanced, logical look at the unknowns of the case.

Duncan spoke up. "Ma'am, we want to help. Please, tell us your name."

"Melissa Campbell," she sobbed, "and don't ma'am me!"

"Ms. Campbell," Duncan said, "we're doing everything—."

Campbell raised her hand and knifed her tear-filled eyes into Duncan. She could not bear hearing anything. "Please! Nothing you say is going to matter at this point." Her voice was trembling. "Do something. Fix your water. Anything. Oh my God—" Her eyes searched the group and, seeing nothing to help her, she turned and walked out, her hand to her mouth, her shoulders shaking.

Duncan's assistant sought forgiveness from her boss before hurrying after Campbell. "I tried to stop her. She just pushed her way through!"

Duncan told her not to worry, his thoughts still processing what Campbell had told him. He turned to the group. "OK, folks, you can see what we're up against. Show a little compassion when you speak. Get past the scientific details and let the county know you feel for them. It will play better for all of us, and for the county."

McCracken snorted under his breath: If you have to plan your compassion, Mr. Chairman, it's really not worth a damn.

17

Every day since injecting the *giardia,* Jackhammer had lowered himself into the large, leather easy chair in the corner of his living room to watch the 4:00 p.m. local news, expectant about when the big story might break. He had hated this delay between cause and effect, the *giardia* taking weeks to show its full power, but he had wanted a less-than-lethal appetizer to his ultimate plan, something to get the county and its officials stirred up for his final coup de grace. Everything had a price.

With the TV still off, his condominium in silence, Jackhammer picked up his whiskey and held the Waterford crystal up against the light from the balcony door. The brown-gold liquid winked with each movement of his hand. "Doctor's orders," Jackhammer grumbled. The weeks' wait for news had gripped him more than he had expected. As before, he had flouted his health, but now he had grown restless about how much time he still had left to live. There had been additional days when fatigue had undermined his iron confidence, hitting him with spikes of fear that his work would remain undone. Yet with a reasonable night's sleep, he had always rebounded to the full, chimeral strength of his memories, tinged with an edge of fatalistic recklessness. Repeatedly, as he waited for the days to pass, the last months of his life seemed to hold little value unless stretched to a new, brazen limit—danger and manipulation as the path to redemption.

Jackhammer turned on the TV and immediately his chest tightened. He saw the warning banner running slowly across the screen. He set down his glass and stared with a seminal smile. Here it finally was, an eerie, slow-motion notice about his insight and ingenuity. He could feel the burst of pride and a new, irrepressible drive to get at his victims.

When the 4:00 o'clock news itself came on, Jackhammer tried hard to reign in his gambling impulse, but he could not suppress it. An inner voice kept whispering: Why go by the book when you still have all the variables totally under your control, when you still overpower all the forces of the enemy? Victory without daring remains hollow.

Jackhammer stood up, swallowed the last gulp of his whiskey, and turned off the TV. Then he picked up his car keys and walked out the door.

"Mr. Carter. How good to hear your voice again."

What?! Carter thought, pounding the FBI timer on the desk in his office. Frantically he shot a glance at his office clock: 5:43 p.m. "Jackhammer. This is a surprise. Or maybe it isn't. What do you want?"

"Well, the shit has finally hit the fan, and I thought you might like to know that I'm the shitter."

How can I keep this guy on the line, Carter asked himself. He did not know any tricks. This was not a troubled loser who might fall for a sympathetic ear. "What do you mean?" Carter asked.

"Oh, Mr. Carter, don't try to act so innocent. You embarrass yourself. I know you're trying to keep me on the line. You have no control over that. But since you asked, I fed the *giardia* into the water system. It was another wake-up call, but only that. Oh, I hadn't planned on the old lady and the young girl dying, but these glitches happen. This *giardia* greeting was not really supposed to be lethal, but only an overture to my next act of public works terrorism, an appetizer to get everyone all riled up."

"I suppose you're not going to tell me what that next act is."

Jackhammer laughed—a wounded hiss in the voice-altering sound box. "No, that would ruin the fun. But you should imagine something far bolder, far more dramatic, and, if I'm in the mood, more lethal. Making people sick has a certain charm, but killing them gets so much more attention."

Carter looked at the FBI's phone-trace timer. The seconds kept ticking. Jackhammer had rarely stayed on this long. "I wouldn't know," said Carter.

"I'd like to meet you sometime, Mr. Carter, have a little chat. Maybe I could even convince you that we have a lot in common. We both tout the power of engineering. If you personally brought my message to the public, we could be an impressive team."

Carter's voice faltered in the excitement that Jackhammer had still not disconnected. Jesus, the FBI had better not screw this one up! "You talk about public works terrorism," Carter said. "Are you implying that your next act has something to do with public infrastructure?"

"That's a stupid question, Mr. Carter. Are you just desperate to say something or do you really expect me to answer?"

"I'm just trying to hear all I can." The time kept moving, and Carter's heart was now pounding hard. "You could give me a hint. That might make it all the more entertaining."

"I suppose I'd better get off. By now, the FBI should've had plenty of time to track down this call. Until next time."

"When's that?" Carter shot back.

"You'll know," Jackhammer said. "No doubt about it. You'll know."

A click knocked in the dial tone, and Carter stared at the timer: one minute and twenty-five seconds. Holy shit, Carter thought and opened his address book to get the FBI tracing contact. Carter dialed, his palm sweaty.

"Mike Pemberton here," a voice answered.

"This is Scott Carter. Jackhammer just called. Did you get a full trace on it?"

"Let me check," Pemberton said. "I wasn't working the monitor." He put Carter on hold for close to a minute, and when he came back, his voice was visibly excited. "I've been told we got the bastard hook, line and sinker. He was at a pay phone, if you can believe it—in Old Town Alexandria."

"Have you called Michelle Taylor?"

"Yeah, and Frank Gentry. We've called the local police on patrol in the area, and we have a whole FBI team going there now. We've asked the police to question anyone leaving the place."

"Where is it in Old Town? Maybe the guy still wants to see me."

"Down by the river, on Prince Street."

"Thanks," Carter said. "I'm heading out."

It was three blocks from where Carter lived.

Carter parked near his house in Old Town, and from the street, he saw the light in his upstairs bedroom go on. So, the automatic timers are doing their job, Carter thought as the last twilight glowed in the west above the roofs of his neighbors. He stood for a moment and did not move. He knew there was nothing he could do for the investigation on site, and suddenly he felt profoundly empty. He did not usually get home this early, and here was the daily, unchanging image of his house—the lights turning on by mechanical contraption, unconnected to anything in the outer world, barren. Every day he unlocked that space and felt powerless to fill it on his own.

Why let it go on, Carter thought. Can't you just approach Michelle again? There's nothing to lose that you haven't already lost.

Carter locked the door to his car and walked east down Prince Street to the river. He could see a police car, its lights flashing, closing off a cul de sac at the edge of a small park on the bank of the Potomac. Carter had often sat in that park on a summer morning reading the newspaper, a thermos of coffee at his side, watching the occasional kid throw rocks and sticks into the cool, brown water, the breeze blowing down the river with reminders of a forest hike in the Shenandoah. He wondered whether Jackhammer had picked this spot for the phone call just to mock him, as if to thumb his nose at the FBI from Carter's own back yard.

Carter looked around. He realized that Jackhammer could be anywhere—that man over there walking up the street, as if pretending he were coming home from work. Carter glanced over his own shoulder and saw his bodyguard walking slowly behind him. Michelle could take over the supposed protection from here, Carter thought, but he now felt exposed walking this last block on his own. He knew that Jackhammer, or his henchmen, could be standing in the next alley with a gun.

No one approached Carter until he reached the police barricade. Frank Gentry, presiding at the fringes, spotted him and offered a stiff hello. "So, you had another conversation," Gentry said. "I've heard the tape. It does not sound good."

"Have you found anything or picked someone up?" Carter asked. His eyes glanced beyond Gentry, but he did not catch Michelle.

"Nothing. We had time to trace the call, but by the time the police got here, Jackhammer was gone. He probably knew exactly what he was doing, perfect timing, having a little fun."

"Do you plan to make public what Jackhammer said?" Carter asked.

"I hadn't thought about that yet. But he didn't tell us anything new. So what's changed?"

"Nothing," Carter said. "And let's not give him that satisfaction. If he wants to announce his terrorism campaign to the press, let him do it, but I don't want to be his mouthpiece. Besides, if he contacts a reporter, that gives you another chance to follow up."

"I have no problem with that. But I'll ask Michelle to contact Board Chairman Duncan and the county manager to give them the latest. Any thoughts on what Jackhammer might hit next?"

"No," Carter said, "It's like a crap shoot. If he follows history, it'll be a new category of public works, but if he's got a way to put *giardia* in the water system, he might have a way to inject something even more dangerous."

"I don't like the sound of it," Gentry said, his jaw tightening to the point that the muscles on his cheeks flexed. "So far he's kept his word with all of his warnings."

Carter looked past Gentry and now saw Michelle approach. She called a last order to one of her people and then hurried over. Was the rush meant for Gentry or for him, Carter wondered.

Taylor did not break from a pure business front, but all Carter could focus on was her beauty. She radiated that mildly ruffled air of rushed activity, as though her suppressed sensuality shimmered just below the surface, ready to break through. "I guess our guy still likes your BWE phone," Taylor said.

"At least it gives us something to go on," Carter said.

"What have you found so far?" Gentry asked Taylor, showing the grim pessimism of a drill sergeant watching his troops fall behind in a timed maneuver.

"Nothing," Taylor said. "We're still dusting for prints, but I don't think this guy is going to be dumb enough to leave something behind. As far as I know, nobody's found a witness who saw someone using the phone. We're also looking for any traces of a car that might have been parked there, or anything someone might have dropped on the sidewalks leading away from here."

Gentry nodded, his jaws still flexing. "Well, keep it up. Pick up gum wrappers if you have to."

"We already have," Taylor said, playing along with what they both knew was probably a hopeless exercise.

"So call Chairman Duncan and let him know," Gentry said. "You might as well get that out of the way."

Taylor walked to a part of the street where passersby could not hear and rang up Duncan on her cell phone. With the crisis, Duncan had stayed late at the county government building, and Taylor quickly explained the new threats and strongly advised that the county set up all the security and patrol measures it could spare. FBI help would follow up.

"When do you expect more definitive results from the water plant and the health commissioner?" Taylor asked.

"Tomorrow," Duncan said. "I can't beat it out of them any faster."

"Call me as soon as you know something."

"I'll do it," he said.

Frustrated, Taylor stabbed the call off, wishing she could read a madman's mind on where he might strike next. She looked around and saw that Gentry had moved to other agents. She returned to Carter.

"It looks like your boss is treating you as an important player," Carter said.

"He's come around," said Taylor. "For a while there, I seemed to be fading out of the picture. Now, with the local engineering connections still the top angle, Gentry authorized people to work for me on research. I'm sticking my neck out and saying Jackhammer lives in the Washington area. So we're looking for any engineer with enough wealth to maybe finance this kind of thing. God knows how long that list'll be."

"Have you contacted the major engineering societies or maybe *ENR*? They've got databases you could start with immediately, at least to get potential names. They probably don't have incomes."

"I've done it," Taylor said, "but we've also got to dig deeper with tax records. The problem there becomes the job titles. Once someone gets into management, the word 'engineer' can disappear. And then on top of that you've got every company in sight calling everybody and their brother an 'engineer,' no matter what their degree's in—even without a degree. Unfortunately it takes some time, and then you still don't know how many holes you might have."

"Hey, some states actually have laws restricting use of the engineer title, but they're never enforced." Carter paused and looked at the FBI team packing up some equipment. "How long until you wrap things up?"

Taylor glanced around. "Maybe half an hour. At least my end of it."

Carter tried to speak as naturally as possible, as though expressing an afterthought. "Have you eaten yet? How about some dinner?"

Taylor was taken by surprise, but on considering the offer, she could not quickly think of an excuse, unsure of whether an excuse was what she wanted. "OK. I guess I *am* hungry."

"Well, *I* am," Carter said. "You finish up your things and I'll wait here."

"All right," Taylor said, questioning what she had gotten herself into. It's just a friendly dinner, she told herself. Nothing more.

Carter began to pace, acting distant and detached, like a commuter waiting for his daily bus, but inside, his nerves were already on a high-speed chase.

Carter suggested the Taos Tavern in Old Town, a southwestern cantina-style restaurant with muraled walls of eggshell white and sun-burnt russet, a glowing, bare-rock butte painted opposite the entrance hall. Carter liked the upscale Tex Mex cuisine and the desert intimacy.

The restaurant was nearly empty that night, and Carter was happy to find the privacy of a corner table. Although tempted, Carter did not help Taylor with her chair. He slid himself into the rough, sturdy wood of the chair opposite. The waiter came soon after to ask about drinks.

"With what we heard from our friend," Carter said, "maybe we ought to hold off on tap water." He said it only half jokingly.

"Beer works for me," Taylor said. She ordered a Dos Equis; Carter, a Sam Adams.

The two wanted to get their minds off work, but Taylor grabbed the chance to ask Carter about all the wealthier civil engineers he knew in the area.

"All I can think of are the ones who made it big by running their own firms," Carter said. "You already know a lot of them." Beyond the familiar lists, Carter offered a few more, and Taylor took notes despite thinking she had already researched most of them.

"So what are you going to do with these guys?" Carter asked. "Talk to all of them?"

"If the number's manageable," Taylor said. "If we get any suspicions, we'll check their bank records to see if we can get a hint of payments to unknown sources."

"Doesn't sound too easy."

"It'll take time," Taylor said, "but let's drop it for now. Haven't we had enough of work?"

They both opened their menus and began scanning the entrées. When they finally ordered, Carter had already finished his first beer, and he immediately ordered a second. He tried to find a topic lighter than the investigation but got only halfway there. "You know, this Jackhammer's got the nerve—a terrorist saying he's promoting the engineering profession. He's basically breaking into my turf."

"I'll hand it to you there. You don't seem to hold back your dedication."

Carter shook his head, suddenly finding the topic discouraging. "I don't really know what dedication I've got anymore. I've had enough jolts to beat down some ideals."

"I'd wager you still have them."

Carter regretted he had steered toward negativity and now tried to turn things around. "That's debatable. You wouldn't believe some of the crazy things I once did. I can't imagine having the nerve now."

"Try me," Taylor said.

Carter took a theatrical deep breath, finding no way to back out, wondering how stupid he would look. "OK, in that case, try this one on for size. Heck, I'm embarrassed to even say it, but I once hired a writer to work up an engineering version of *A Christmas Carol*. Before you laugh, let me tell you that I was really proud of this idea—you know, Scrooge sees what the world would be like without all the work of engineers. According to my wife, the finished product sounded pretty sappy, but I was too involved to believe it. I tried to get ASCE's *Civil Engineering* magazine to publish the thing, but the editor wouldn't do it. He said it didn't fit the so-called editorial profile. What he probably meant was that it sucked."

"I don't know. The idea sounds intriguing."

Carter could not tell whether her half smile represented interest or suppressed ridicule. He continued, head down and charging. "You don't want to get me going on that. I practically memorized the thing for when I talked to school kids about engineering. So here goes. The Scrooge in my story, or the story this writer cooked up, had lived a good and charitable life, gotten rich, and bought all the comforts and conveniences for his home, but like everybody else, he'd lived a life of ignorance—he didn't have any idea who was responsible for creating all the useful and essential stuff around him. In this new *Christmas Carol*, we've got a ghost of engineering, but he doesn't come as an angel or some kind of specter of death, but as a run of the mill middle aged white male." Carter smiled. "Now don't worry, I don't do that 'white male' thing with the kids. That's just a political incorrectness joke for the occasional adult audience." He did not see Taylor laughing, but she was listening. "When I tell little kids this story, I always juice it up and say the antique clock on Scrooge's dresser has just struck 1:00 in the morning and Scrooge wakes from a deep sleep and sees this strange halo of light surrounding a man standing at the foot of his bed. Of course Scrooge is all confused and afraid and looks at the clock on the nightstand, then out the window at the black night, and then rubs his eyes in terror. Did you ever see the Mr. McGoo *Christmas Carol*? That's where I got some of my inspiration, or corruption, for this thing. Anyway, Scrooge yells out, 'Take what you want. My wallet's on the nightstand. There's no other cash in the house.' You see, it being the modern world, Scrooge thinks it's a break-in mugger."

"You tell *that* to school kids?" Taylor asked with a grin.

"No, the mugger part was just for you." Carter was starting to enjoy himself and suddenly felt on a roll, anything to make Taylor offer that marvelous smile. "Anyway, the visitor raises his hand and says, 'Don't be afraid. I am not here to mug you. I am only a spirit who has come to show you a part of the world that you are not aware of but which you see every day.' And the ghost then says, 'Take my hand.'

"Well, Scrooge is all confused and scared by this vision and now feels this irresistible force and puts his bony hand in the firm grip of the guide and feels an incredible lightness take over his body, as if he could skim frictionless across the floor."

"I like that—'frictionless'," Taylor said. "That's a nice engineering touch."

"Man, this whole thing was a syrup of engineering," Carter said. "I had a great time going into classrooms laying it on thick, no matter what the adult critics said."

Taylor took a drink of her beer, smiling despite herself. "So go on. You've got me in suspense."

"Yeah, right," Carter said, "you're too polite. Anyway, the man leads Scrooge straight to the wall of the bedroom, and Scrooge covers his eyes to stop the impact, but they pass through the drywall and the wood just like ghosts, into the twilight stillness of the street."

"You're getting poetical," Taylor said. "Is that you or the ghost writer?"

"The ghost writer, of course. I couldn't come up with these flourishes. Anyway, so Scrooge cries out, 'Where are you taking me?' The ghost stays mum, and they keep going and pass a man on the street. The man doesn't even notice old Scrooge in his pajamas and his engineer guide. 'Just hold my hand,' the ghost says, and Scrooge holds tight as they keep moving and enter an apartment that's been thrown into darkness. There Scrooge sees an old woman still in her nightgown pushing at a light switch, but nothing happens. She gives up and moves to the table and pulls a lamp string, but there's still only darkness. Finally, she lights a candle and touches the cold burners of her electric range and stares at the useless coffee pot."

"Are you sure you didn't tell this story to Jackhammer?" Taylor asked. "Blackouts seem to be a theme for you guys."

"It sounds like it, doesn't it? But there's no coincidence—electric power is a big engineering achievement. Anyway, in the next apartment, a family opens the blinds to get a little light and then opens the kitchen tap and gets only a tiny stream. Before their eyes, the water turns into a brown trickle, until finally, not even gravity can pull down the surface tension of the last dirty drop. And so it goes on—the same in all the apartments and condominiums, and in the meantime, the ghost has pulled Scrooge to the local hospital. There, a young couple, happy with their newborn child, tries to call their folks on a cell phone that suddenly has no bars."

"Jackhammer hasn't attacked the cell phone towers," Taylor said. "We've never really considered that."

"Anything's possible," Carter said. "But you're making this story into something serious."

"Sorry."

"OK. The doctors are shouting because they're on emergency power and are probably going to run out of generator fuel, and they can't scrub down properly without water. Seeing the hospital on the brink, Scrooge and his guide fly back to the streets and move to the edge of town, and there they see a small boy in a car crying because his video game won't perform the commands—the computer hero won't kick somebody's head off like he should. Then up ahead, a car enters a misbanked curve and skids into the grass, and at the river, Scrooge sees cars backed up because the suspension bridge has cracked and is now closed to traffic, while the rising sun reflects on the gossamer cables."

"Another poetical flourish," Taylor said, raising her beer in a playful toast.

"You bet," Carter said. "Now Scrooge, who's obviously horrified, says to the man, 'You have to do something! You can't let this suffering continue!' The ghost does not say a word but now soars across the farmlands and the lakes. Below them, people can't drink the contaminated water and are cold from lack of heat. The victims set off to the cities in their cars, but the motors fuse and the axles break. In the great metropolis, desperate people try to buy fuel and food at inflated prices. They raid the banks for their funds, but the computers and databases no longer function, and the economy comes to a halt. 'Show me no more!' Scrooge shouts."

Carter raised his hands to imitate Scrooge and then, as the waiter arrived with the food, leaned back in embarrassment and shut up. When the plates came down and the waiter left, the two burst out with a laugh.

"They won't let me in here again," Carter said.

"Well, you actually got me to smile about sabotaged infrastructure."

"Don't go there," Carter warned, not wanting the darkness to take over. "So listen, it could get real loud in the classrooms sometimes. I'd shout like an old Scrooge shaking in his pajamas. 'You have to stop it!' Scrooge says. But the ghost is calm despite the calamity and asks, 'Don't you know what has happened?' And Scrooge answers, 'The world has come to an end!' And the spirit says, 'That is one way of saying it.' He then waves his arm at the whole disastrous panorama. 'But I will tell you a secret. You have not seen the real world collapse, but only a terrible dream in which the work of engineers has ceased to exist—nearly everything you touch, nearly everything you depend on, from your everyday life to your extravagant luxuries. And yet you take it all for granted.' And with that, the spirit waves his arm, and Scrooge finds himself back in bed, everything back to normal except that terrifying memory. He sees that everything works, the water and the lights and the telephone, and just like Mr. McGoo, he runs to the window and shouts, 'What a beautiful morning!' Scrooge then sees a man on the sidewalk and yells at the top of his lungs, 'My friend, you don't realize what a good morning it is! You just don't realize!' "

Taylor shook her head with a grin. "I've got to hand it to you, you're a pretty good ham. I can see the kids getting a kick out of that, especially if you go a little crazy."

"I could get pretty rowdy sometimes. But what do you think? Are the adult critics right?"

"Well, the end was a little overdone maybe. It sounded a bit melodramatic and self-serving for engineers. I mean, take away, let's say, garbage collectors or auto mechanics or accountants and you could argue that things would all go to hell too. But it's a great story."

"Garbage collectors. I like that. Bursts my bubble." He toasted her, not quite sure why he had tried to impress Taylor with stories about engineers. That sounded like pure desperation.

"But why do you feel you have to tell tales like this?" she asked slyly. "Do engineers have an inferiority complex?"

"Some do," Carter said. "Plus everybody thinks we're nerds or geeks when we're actually stepping up to the table as leaders in a lot of areas. I mean, just take sustainable communities. You can't plan those without the engineering perspective right there in the mix."

"Well, I've known some engineer nerds," Taylor said.

"So have I," said Carter. "You should hear some of the jokes. Pretty pathetic, really."

"I'm afraid I only know lawyer jokes."

"OK, take this one" Carter said. "What's the difference between an introvert and an extrovert engineer?"

"I don't know."

"The extrovert engineer looks at *your* shoes when he talks to you."

Taylor flashed another of her fabulous smiles. "That's brutal."

"Yeah, I know," Carter said. "It's just one of those generalizations. We civil engineers are actually out there pushing the envelope." Carter sat back. "But there I go again."

"Well," Taylor said lightheartedly, "we could stop to eat our food before it gets cold."

"Sounds smart."

They both dug into their meals, but silence was not that comfortable.

"You know," Taylor said, leaning over her plate, her elbows on the table, her fork dangling in a rakish impropriety. "You've got to be pretty proud of yourself. Most people I knew in college chose their field because it could make them some money. Oh, they preferred this job over that and made their choices on the basis of likes, but they didn't really get that involved, like you do. They got their degree and then they went out to make a living. It's a little sad if you think about it."

"Well, if you're trying to put me on a pedestal, you're a few years too late. I've pretty much sold out."

Taylor looked at him skeptically. "What's that supposed to mean?"

"I went into management and customer relations just for the money. Design is what I love, but in one of the great perversions of modern life, that's lower on the corporate totem pole, no matter how senior you are. To get the big raise they dangled in front of me, I gave in. I took the dough."

"Aren't you exaggerating a little?" she asked. "You've always looked pretty wrapped up in your work."

The waiter interrupted to ask if everything was all right. Carter ordered another beer. "Would you like one, too?" he asked Taylor, expectant about whether she would open up to him more.

"Why not?" Taylor said, cocking her head, intrigued by her own lack of restraint. "I'm not officially on duty anymore."

Carter hesitated until the waiter had left, then went on. "Oh, I'll get wrapped up in my work—you know, in doing a good job—but that's about the extent of it. Somehow I'd always tell myself that this management incarnation was only temporary. When continuing education seminars came around, I'd take the technical classes to keep up. My executive colleagues signed up for all kinds of fad management stuff, and I could feel all superior, but then sometimes I'd tell myself it's all just a game. Whether you do this or that, you get involved and the time passes. Why worry about the details?"

Taylor frowned, inwardly disturbed that he might actually believe it. "The pessimism doesn't fit you," she said. "You don't really think that's true, do you?"

Carter shrugged. Looking at Taylor, he could think only about how, in the end, he would lose her and how such thoughts threatened to turn him bitter. He wondered whether pessimism would embarrass her. "I hadn't really planned on telling you. I'm no complainer. You get punched in the stomach and you grin and bear it, right? So the doctor had some more news. A few days ago he found another one of those melanoma beauty marks."

Taylor straightened slightly in her chair and unconsciously took a deep breath. The news opened a small void that she could not fully control. Carter's resigned face made her feel somewhat helpless—she knew she had nothing useful to offer. "I'm terribly sorry," she said quietly. "What does the doctor say?"

"Not much different than before, supposedly, but in fact, the odds for a bad outcome have gone up. It only makes sense. You start getting these cancers popping up all the time, and they'll do even more repeat performances."

"And there's nothing more the doctors can tell you?"

"Not really," Carter said. "But let's get off this. It's a bore."

Taylor did not know what else she could say, only pat phrases of empathy, but she felt anxious to somehow express her friendship. Without thinking, she reached out and squeezed Carter's hand. She drew back her touch just as quickly.

The surprise contact rushed through Carter's limbs like the shock from a live wire. He did not know what she had intended. "I appreciate it," he said, trying to remain passive.

"Is your work going to be affected?"

"For the sales stuff? Yeah…I don't feel like doing it." He offered a smile, trying to get off this dark side.

The waiter came by with the beers and retrieved the old bottles. For Carter, the drinks had become a swelling stream that pushed his sentiments uncontrollably toward Taylor.

"I can understand that," Taylor said, "it's just that you never seemed to show it."

"I guess I'm a good actor," he said.

Taylor bit her lip, unsure of how much Carter wanted her to dwell on his doubts. "Have you ever thought seriously about going back to design work?"

"Sure," Carter said, "but you get so caught up in the momentum of everyone's expectations, including your own, that you just don't make the move." Carter forced another smile. "But hell, what's the point? If I'm going to keel over, why disrupt things on the way? I always wanted to have kids, and my wife couldn't have them and then she died anyway. Why fight it?"

"I'm not a good source for advice," Taylor said quietly. "I've never had this kind of health scare."

Carter had noticed some emotion in her voice and found it difficult to contain himself. The beer had dismantled his inhibitions and kicked in some fatalism. The soft beauty and charity of Taylor's face overwhelmed what he considered his better judgment. He tried to hold back the tide, but then he just thought "shove it" and pushed aside the games for good. Carter reached out and took Taylor's hand, and as soon as he felt the warmth of her skin, he brought his other hand over.

"I'm sorry," Carter said, determined and talking fast, not wanting to give her a chance to protest. "I know this may not be fair to you, and maybe it's a surprise, but I can't put on any more fronts." He glanced around unconsciously to make sure the waiter was not on his way. "Ever since I met you, all I can think about is you, and whatever happens, having you by my side." Carter looked at her in the mild surprise of his own boldness. "I might as well cut to the chase. I'm in love with you. Hell, more than anyone I've ever loved. There you have it, plain and simple."

Taylor did not pull her hand away, but she realized that not doing it would mislead him unfairly. She wanted to sound kind but could not bring herself to pull any punches. She worked hard not to sound flustered. "I don't know what to say. I'm flattered. I really am. I like you very much, but you've caught me off guard." She squeezed his hand, but then, almost against her will, she found herself putting up defenses. "You don't really know what I've been through lately. I don't know quite how to put this, but you've been so open with me now…" She paused momentarily. "It's not so long ago that I broke up with my boyfriend. It's just too soon for me."

Carter leaned back in his chair, his hands slipping from hers. "So can you translate?" he said.

Taylor opened her mouth in hesitation, and at first nothing came out. Finally she said, "I'm just trying to sort all this out."

Carter had begun to feel a cold, hard resignation flow through him. A weary smile crept into his face. "It'd be better if you were just completely honest. I mean, it would be a pretty sad irony to have the love of your life cut you down with stock excuses."

"Don't talk like that," Taylor said. "I *am* trying to be honest. I'm not telling you I don't want to see you again."

"And you can stand working together when you know how I feel?"

"We'll just have to see how it goes." Taylor was regaining some balance. She did not want to lose Carter as a companion but could not make commitments. "I'm not going to throw you off the investigation just because . . . because . . ."

"Because your partner's constantly checking you out?"

Taylor smiled uneasily. "You wouldn't do that, would you?"

"No, I'll be polite. No grabbing you in the street."

Taylor frowned. "Listen, I'm not going to lie to you. You're a great guy—one of the finest I've met."

"Please, no need for that. It sounds like a compliment I'd get at an awards banquet. From you, a plaque just won't cut it."

Taylor lost her patience. "Will you stop it. Let's just make a truce for right now. OK? Let's just put it all aside. I know how you feel about me, and I'll deal with it. And you're going to have to give me a little space, because we're going to keep working together. OK? You need to promise you're not going to keep talking about it." She did not know if she had made any sense.

Carter offered a bleak chuckle. "Well, I'll sure as hell try, but when my head's spinning, that's not so easy."

"That's fine," Taylor said. "I understand. But you have to realize I can't give any answers right now."

"OK, but can we make a pact so I don't have to feel stupid when I wake up tomorrow? When you want to get rid of me, just do it. No sugar coating. Can you promise me that?"

Taylor smiled in confusion. "Sure. I promise."

Carter leaned back and looked at the food on his plate. He suddenly realized he no longer had to put on a show. He could eat what was left in complete, aching freedom.

Headlights moved across the dark of Taylor's bedroom, starting on the wall and then drifting upwards, fading with unnatural swiftness along the length of the ceiling, and then out of sight. Occasionally, a light would rest on the corner of her room, as though the world had come to a halt and her thoughts had lost their movement. And then, after she had forgotten that anything could change, the light would shift again, building speed and diving to obscurity.

Under the covers, Taylor made no connection between the lights and the realm of traffic on the street outside. She only knew that she could not sleep and that images and doubts and latent thrills drifted in succession across her consciousness. She had gone to bed early, but an hour later she had still not reconciled the shifting conflicts of her dinner with Scott.

The room no longer offered shelter. The neat, simple definitions of her daily life had fallen away and left the space open to the elements—intangible, random spotlights that crawled across her being with a vague, indifferent curiosity. She had thought her relationship to Scott had been neatly compartmentalized. In the previous weeks, he had hinted some attraction, and she had accepted it as a playful compliment, caressing her image of him with a few venturesome daydreams that she had not allowed herself to take seriously. She had always channeled her affection to the natural solidity of his character and the generous reception he gave her ideas and plans. No one had given her more confidence that her work held a certain dignity.

And yet now, Scott seemed bowed by his career and his cancer and had called on her to love him. Simple companionship had dilated into troubling responsibility. Any fun in flirting would be darkened by expectations of commitment. She did not feel prepared for that. She did not know if she ever wanted to be prepared.

As her thoughts played in waves against each other, uncomfortably merging and canceling out, she could not deny a sensual undercurrent. This was no longer fantasy. A mere nod of her head would make it happen. She had become utterly exposed to the slightest weakness in her defenses.

Taylor did not want to tempt herself. She worried that any new affection had its roots in pity, and she could not sacrifice herself on such a one-sided basis. This was not selfishness, she told herself. She could not throw away her own interests when Scott talked about something supposedly permanent. She could not forget the fact that Scott might die in the next few years. Or was that just exaggeration? Melanoma was not a sure killer. It was not liver cancer or lung cancer. People recovered or stayed in remission. But still, how could she even toy with the idea of a life together? He talked about kids and painted himself as a good father, and yet what kind of father could he be if bad luck struck and he wasn't alive to participate? What a terrible shame, she thought. But was it a shame just for him, or also for her? My God, she wondered, what kind of crazy thoughts are you spinning? You're going to have to let this pass. You've just got to tell yourself that he's a friend on the investigation, and that's it. He's responsible for his own life. You can't do anything for him. You can't be expected to take on that kind of burden and not think about your own future first.

Taylor pulled the blanket tight to her chin and tried to make that final resolution snuff out her thoughts. She had important work to do in the morning. She could not afford to go in exhausted.

But when Taylor closed her eyes, the faint, drifting light on the wall filtered through her eyelids and into the turbulence beneath. Soon, she had lifted her lids to see a headlight vanish in the naked darkness. She glanced helplessly to her nightstand. The colon on her digital clock blinked unceasingly in the silence, the eyes of a merciless witness.

18

With her daughter gone, Melissa Campbell could not bear a moment of inactivity, and to cope, she kept her vow to lay her grief on the city. On her lunch hour, she took out a makeshift cardboard sign and began picketing the nearby county government building, calling to the curious, often wary passersby to hold the county accountable until the water was completely safe. She stayed late after work to phone every newspaper and every television and radio station with her story and her plea. Her activism and her personal tragedy—especially her daughter's cute face—played well with reporters, and she started giving interviews and calling victims' families to join her on the streets.

Soon, a small group materialized for her lunchtime demonstrations, chanting peacefully with placards and politely confronting any county official who came through the door. The TV cameras began to show up, using the demonstrations as backdrops for their updates on the Rosslyn water crisis, drawing still more onlookers, until the square became a milling mass of everyday citizens wondering what was going to happen next.

Soon, Campbell was combing the web after work for information on water contamination and cleanup, and monitoring her email for messages from supporters. A young web developer from Campbell's company stayed late to help her set up a website on the company's server. With leaflets and further interviews, Campbell broadcast the URL so victims could post their stories and read updates on demonstration plans. One click, near the bottom of the homepage, offered pictures of her daughter playing in the yard last summer or blowing out the candles on her last birthday cake.

Late in the evening, with everyone in the office gone and the overhead lights above the large room of cubicles off, Campbell would sit in the isolated glow of her head-high partitions, knowing that the fast pace of the day was now over, that she would have to drive home and confront her empty house. She wished she could just work and organize for twenty-four hours a day. As long as she kept pushing, as long as she felt she was doing something to honor her Judy, she could ward off the despair.

James McCracken pored over the interim lab reports and pounded his stubby finger on the last page with a growing thrust of vindication. It was Saturday morning, and he expected the final results by midday, and from all he could see so far, there had been no trace of *giardia* in his water treatment plant. Jackhammer had probably not breached the security of McCracken's own sanctum.

McCracken could not yet be certain—*giardia* was a tough bug to pin down—but the health reports had the smell of a localized contamination, and Jackhammer's admission obviously pointed that way as well. McCracken pulled out a copy of the map where the county's health department had tracked the reported *giardia* cases and saw the clustering in downtown Rosslyn—and then the maddening stray dots all over the place. If the health commissioner would just get him the latest results of the victim interviews, he might be able to nail down the exact location of where Jackhammer had struck. He was guessing that the stray victims had really drunk their water in Rosslyn—and once that was established, he could trace all of them back to the nearest common water main, and then the county and the FBI could start its search there.

All he needed now were the final results from his own lab, but he knew no amount of bellowing would speed things up. The lab procedures took their maddening set time. There was nothing he could do about it.

That morning, Board Chairman Duncan fended off the media and the increasingly vocal demonstrators, giving only a short preliminary statement on the investigative work that still needed to be done. He now stood in his office, looking out the window at the early March sunshine, impatiently waiting for reports from the health commissioner and the water treatment lab.

Duncan had canceled his golf date with a local developer to head up his crisis center and did not know whether to enjoy the tension of the threatening limelight or fear the fallout from a new round of tragedy. Down below, an ever-growing crowd of demonstrators led by Melissa Campbell walked in circles, chanting slogans for the usual collection of passersby. At times, Duncan had grown exasperated with Campbell and her dogged media hype—hell, she wasn't even a resident of Arlington County, he thought—but Duncan had children of his own and knew it was hard to fight her kind of feeling.

The ring of the phone jolted him out of his thoughts and he jumped to answer. "What've you got?" he said.

"I've got the health commissioner on the line," said his assistant.

"Well, put her on!"

"Jim," Connel said, a hint of excitement in her voice. "The interviews have hit pay dirt. So far about fifty percent of all the non-Rosslyn victims have come from a single Rosslyn company, Sylar Integration, Inc. They were all there on a weekend three weeks ago trying to meet a deadline, and they obviously drank the water. As you know, that's where Melissa Campbell works, and her daughter was there that Saturday. Other victims also have a Rosslyn connection. We don't have everyone nailed down, but I'm going to stick my neck out and say they all got the bug in that one small area of Rosslyn."

"Good work!" said Duncan. "That means we can get moving on something. You bring your data to my office right now, and I'll round everybody up and we can figure out where we go from here."

"Will do," Connel said. "I'm on my way."

Duncan immediately rang up his assistant. "Get me Jim McCracken, Special Agent Taylor, Sam Freeport, Nick Handley, Warren Douglas, and Mike O'Connor for a meeting in my office ASAP. Tell them that the health commissioner looks like she's pinned down the boundaries of the *giardia* contamination and that we've got to move on that."

Duncan hung up, dropped into his soft leather desk chair, and wiped his hand across his mouth in a vibrant, optimistic nervousness. He felt that the odds for a breakthrough looked good, and conveniently, he had put himself squarely in the center of it all. The media and the public would notice where everyone had come to hash out their plans.

Taylor phoned Gentry about the news from Duncan, and Gentry announced that he was coming along. Taylor hung up and looked at the floor for a moment. Curiously, she did not mind Gentry's decision. She no longer felt he was butting in—her beat had become the core of the investigation, and if Gentry did not get involved, he would be shirking his duty. She now saw herself as a trusted partner, as open to Gentry's low-keyed bullying as anyone else. What worried her was Scott Carter.

Taylor wanted to bring Scott along, too. He knew Jackhammer best, and he deserved to see where the investigation was heading. He could offer his competent two bits to the usual collection of show-offs. But what would he think if she called him? Would he take it as some kind of sign? No, he couldn't. She had told him point-blank they were going to work together like always. The mess in the background would just have to stay there. The investigation mattered too much to let a swirl of emotions get in the way. But what were those emotions? She no longer trusted herself. Was she just fabricating reasons about why Carter should accompany her? What if he served no practical purpose? What if, in complete good conscience for the investigation, she should *not* call him? Would she still not pick up the phone? Cutting him off would hurt him. He would find out, and he would see she had flatly rejected him. Could she do that? But wait, in what direction was she pushing things—the excuse of the investigation, or not wanting to hurt him? But what about her? Throwing all the other considerations aside, didn't she want him there just for herself. Didn't she?

Taylor dialed Carter, too uneasy to answer her own question.

Carter got the call at his home in Alexandria. Without elaboration, he accepted Taylor's invitation and hung up. He then put his hands in his pockets, wandered to the kitchen door, and looked out. The temperature on the outside thermometer showed 55 degrees, and Carter, taking his right hand out of his pocket, unlatched the storm door and stepped onto the garden path, both hands back in his jeans. The traffic was still quiet on that Saturday morning, and Carter could hear the light breeze pass through the limbs of the old oak high above him. A few green buds showed on the clinging vines of the red brick wall, and the crocuses stood at attention in tight, rigid shoots.

Carter looked at his watch. He was supposed to be in a hurry, but ever since he had opened his soul to Taylor at the restaurant, time seemed to have slipped into the background. Until he received some kind of final declaration, he felt in a perpetual abeyance in which little mattered and little could be done. He fulfilled his responsibilities with outward energy and involvement, but inside he merely waited, letting events flow across his thoughts, his whole life anchored below the surface, dependent for motion on a nod from Michelle that probably would never come.

Carter looked up at the sky and then back at his watch. I guess you had better get dressed and get going, he thought. And you had better keep yourself in line when you see her.

"Well, Mr. Carter, it looks like you've up and joined the FBI," said Freeport with a low-keyed sarcasm. "Good to have you with us again."

"Blame Special Agent Taylor," Carter said. It was Duncan's office, and Carter had arrived on his own. "She's the one who asked me to join you. I might have enjoyed a Saturday off."

"You're always welcome," Freeport said wryly. "Who knows, Nick's running late, so we might need you for the indispensable engineering angle." He tinged the word "indispensable" with sarcasm.

"It's good to feel indispensable," Carter deadpanned.

Carter had made a point of staying away from Taylor. He preferred suffering Freeport's small talk to the stress of facing her, and he let her monopolize Gentry in the corner, where she was briefing her colleague on the latest in the investigation. The few times that Carter glanced in her direction, he could see a maddeningly attractive assurance in her manner, as though she were telling Gentry to listen up if he wanted to get the real low-down. He was happy for her. She was making progress in establishing her stature.

Duncan had gone to the restroom and now returned to find his office full with the crisis team. "Have we got everyone here?" he asked his assistant.

"They're all here except Nick," she said.

The assistant had brought in a pot of coffee and placed it on the conference table alongside a pitcher of water. Each chair had a water glass and a gold-rimmed coffee cup.

"We'll go with that," said Duncan, clapping his hands with a flourish of get-down-to-business determination. "Everyone please sit down."

Carter assumed he should sit with the FBI but made a point of keeping Gentry as a barrier between him and Taylor.

Duncan sat down at the head of the table, introduced everyone present, and put on a face of gravity and concern. Carter wished he could figure out how much in that expression was real and how much was just plain theatrics. He could not tolerate that constant uncertainty.

"Thank you all for coming," Duncan said, "and please help yourselves to coffee. You may need it, because from all appearances we may be up against the clock in trying to stop another attack from Jackhammer. In his last phone call, Jackhammer took responsibility for the *giardia* attack, and he threatened something new. If it's another assault on the water supply, he may already have the means in place right here in Rosslyn."

"Let me get to brass tacks," McCracken said impatiently, clearly troubled by the implications and unable to bear any delay. "How should you be warning the citizens about this?"

"Well, why don't you give me your recommendations," Duncan said, unable to hide his annoyance.

"I'd say we tell everyone in the specific area not to drink their water, boiled or unboiled. Check that; maybe we should tell the people not even to touch it. We don't know what Jackhammer could let loose."

"For how long?"

"Hard to tell," McCracken said, "at least until you check everything out and find the source of the contamination."

"I guess the localized area makes sense," Duncan said, "but I don't think we can shut off the whole city. Jackhammer's done something different every time, so we don't know the new attack will be water. Everyone in greater Rosslyn is boiling their tap water—nobody's drinking it straight." He stared at McCracken. "Are you saying that we actually consider shutting down Rosslyn's water supply?"

"Maybe not," McCracken said grudgingly. "Cutting off everyone completely, for an indefinite period, would not go over too well, to say the least. Especially when it's all just based on speculation. Hell, who says Jackhammer didn't take credit for something that happened through some other fluke?" McCracken looked around the table for an answer. "This Jackhammer wasn't more specific on the phone?"

"He was intentionally vague," Carter said. "He enjoys letting us grope in the dark. And of course, if you turned off the water now and we don't find what he's done, Jackhammer might just wait until you turn it on again. We couldn't keep it off for very long."

"OK," said Duncan, "first things first." He called in his assistant and asked her to contact the emergency announcement outlets. "Have them warn the affected blocks not to even turn on their water, with a notice that water might be cut off altogether, pending developments. Dorothy's written it down for you." He turned back to the group. "OK, let's just track down what we have so far and then get back to the bigger questions later. Dorothy, tell the others what you found so we can move on this."

The health commissioner pulled up a map on a smartboard and pointed to the cluster of red dots in downtown Rosslyn. "I'll make this brief," she said. "If we track the location of where, two or three weeks ago, the non-Rosslyn *giardia* victims came to work or to eat out, and if we combine those points with the Rosslyn residents themselves, the locations all narrow down to this one part of town." She turned to McCracken. "What's the nearest water main that would feed that area and not others?"

McCracken rose to inspect the map from up close. "I'll have to confirm this with the plans I got from the county—and I've got those with me—but we're talking about a main that goes right down this street." His finger swept down the board like a butcher slicing through a side of beef. "Unfortunately, I wouldn't know if these few scattered points up here are real. They could be the first part of the diffusion that got broader as the *giardia* moved down the pipes. If something was planted, it means we've got a fair amount of ground to cover to root it out."

"How could Jackhammer have gotten access?" Gentry asked.

"By digging down to a water main or using man-hole access."

"Which one's more likely?"

"They both look pretty farfetched to me," McCracken said. "Jackhammer would have to have had some pretty interesting equipment to get into a cast-iron pipe and somehow keep the water pressure contained. I've been told you haven't seen any major leaks or pressure loss. But if you want my guess, his men would have more space to maneuver by just digging down through the street."

"So how do we find that point as fast as possible?" Duncan asked. "Nick Handley's not here. Who's going to cover for him?"

"How good are your road maintenance records?" Carter asked Freeport. "If we compare those records for digs to all the breaks in the pavement and sidewalks, we could check if one dig isn't accounted for."

"If you get down to the pot-hole level, we've had our breakdowns in documentation," Freeport admitted. "But we've been putting some improved systems in place to help with that."

Cut the doubletalk, Carter thought. It sounded like the canned pronouncements to some oversight board.

"But these pavement breaks are going to be bigger than pot-holes," McCracken said. "Would the records be accurate on the big stuff?"

"I'd say yes," Freeport said. He did not sound fully convinced but did not appear ready to admit that openly.

"Then we've got something," Gentry said with finality. He was not waiting for anyone else to take charge. "Special Agent Taylor and I will take our cars and start on Clarendon and 15th Street and look for any signs of past roadwork, and I'll call in some extra agents. Mr. Freeport and Mr. McCracken, I'll need help from your people to check out the manholes. Have you got some crews available that can look for something suspicious?"

"We can mobilize them right now," Freeport said.

"All right," Gentry said. "Mr. Freeport, can you get a couple of road and utility crews on immediate standby? We'll use your phone number as the central call in. As soon as somebody finds something suspicious, we'll need a crew to cut through the blacktop. I'll also get my bomb and device experts and put my forensic lab on call. I'll want immediate analysis."

"We'll cooperate in any way possible," Duncan jumped in. He was not going to let Freeport take the credit.

"Absolutely," Freeport said. He passed a small stack of business cards around the table. "There's the number to dial. The calls automatically get forwarded to my cell phone if I've stepped out of my office. I'm on my way to have my people pull out the maintenance records. We'll plot every dig we've done in that area over the past several months. Hell, over the past year."

"Then we're all set," Gentry said, relieved to get out of there. "Mr. McCracken, since we've got to haul ass, could you hit the road in my car and tell me where to look." He turned to Taylor. "Michelle, you told me you'd already picked up a set of county utility plans. You take Scott."

Michelle leaned forward to look past Gentry. "Scott, can you read county piping plans?"

"I assume so."

"Then let's move," Gentry said. "We're gonna have some egg on our face if Jackhammer releases more stuff while we're still sitting around."

"Just tell us what you need," Duncan said. "Call me or Sam."

"Right," said Gentry, showing no patience.

Duncan stood up and nodded an acknowledgment as everyone streamed from the room like a crowd on a sudden gold rush. He then dropped into his chair, frightened but self-satisfied, scanning the empty conference table. No one had touched the coffee or the water. I guess you projected the right sense of urgency, he thought. If you keep that up, you and the city will come out of this fine. Maybe you should schedule a press conference. If one of those guys makes a breakthrough, the public will know you're the one who set them all loose.

Taylor had parked illegally opposite the county office building and now hurried across the street. "I dared them to give me a ticket while we're trying to save the county," Taylor said, unlocking the doors in a hurry. "Now they better lay off while I speed."

In the car, Taylor immediately tossed the county utility plans onto Carter's lap. Her voice shot both anxiousness and determination. "The top one's the one you want, I think. You'll find a street plan with the same coordinates on the bottom of the pile." She handed Carter her notes and started the engine, gunning it and locking into gear. Her tires squealed as she pulled into traffic. "Read off what I wrote down for the health commissioner's easterly points. We're going to assume they're accurate and start from the top. Find me the first fork in the water mains above that area and we'll start there."

"You did your homework," Carter said, feeling awkward with the large sheets piled on his knees.

"I was up bright and early at the Public Works Department getting copies of plans," Taylor said. She swerved sharply to change lanes and noticed Carter steady himself with his arm. "I aim to get there first," she said. "You keep your eyes on the pipes."

"Yes, ma'am," Carter said.

Carter compared the east-west coordinate for the street that McCracken had fingered and then moved to the piping plans. A key told him what a water main looked like, and he followed the prime suspect west until another main branched off. He pointed the way. "I assume you're going to slow down once we start inspecting pavement."

"I'll think about it," Taylor said. "By the way, you got us on the right track bringing up the maintenance records. I appreciate it."

Carter scoffed at the notion. "I was just quick enough to open my mouth with an obvious thing. The others would have had the same idea ten seconds later."

"Maybe," Taylor said, "but I hadn't thought of it yet." She pushed the gas to the floor to get through a yellow light, then braked hard to avoid the car in front of her.

Carter looked ahead. "That light's red," he said. Taylor slammed on the brakes. "I saw," she said, inching her way forward, impatiently scanning the traffic. As soon as she found a gap, she ran the red light. A car behind her honked.

"You don't have one of those portable flashing lights for the roof?" Carter asked

"No. Doesn't come with the territory."

They had reached their destination, and Taylor turned on her emergency flashers and slowed to a crawl. "So what are we looking for?" she asked. "Different-colored pavement and off-color sidewalks?" She was catching her breath.

"That's about it, along with cuts in the asphalt. You watch the left side of the road and I'll take the right."

"You bet," Taylor said.

Carter scanned the terrain, feeling the anticipation of a soldier looking for land mines to protect the battalion coming in from behind.

Suddenly Carter noticed two white segments of concrete in a weathered gray sidewalk. "There!" Carter said, pointing to the right. "Call that one in."

Taylor dialed Freeport and heard him answer personally. "We've got our first candidate," she said with emotion, detailing the location.

"You're pretty quick on your feet," Freeport said. "We're just starting to sort through the database. We'll get back to you as soon as we look up the spot." He confirmed Taylor's phone number and hung up.

Carter had gotten out of the car to inspect the find. "This looks like a simple sidewalk repair," he said, his heart sinking but his thoughts still pushing for a catch. "There's no digging on either side. If a work crew was trying to get underground to a water main, you'd think they'd have needed more area or been more messy about it."

"I can see what you mean," Taylor said. "So let's get a move on. There's gotta be more."

Taylor hurried to the car and hopped in, waiting impatiently for Carter to close his door. She then pushed the car into gear and headed down the one-way street, noticing two large potholes that she dutifully called in without stopping.

Before she had gotten off the phone, Carter pointed, "Look over there!"

They both stared at a long, wide rectangular section of new asphalt adjacent to the curb.

"Tell Sam what we've got," Carter exclaimed. "Don't let him off the phone till he confirms whether the county did this or not." Carter hurriedly straightened the plans on his lap, running his fingers across the grid. "Hell, from the looks of it, this could be right above the water main. The size sure looks big enough."

Taylor relayed the message while she pulled to the side of the road. "They're checking," she told Carter. "Freeport says they should have a record for this kind of thing."

"They'd better!" Carter said, jumping out of the car to inspect the fresh pavement, his excitement building. But he was no expert in roadwork and quickly admitted to himself he did not really know what to look for.

Taylor repeated their location, waited, tapping her fingers on the steering wheel. She waited some more—and then the news shot through. She shouted to Carter. "They don't have this repair on record!" She turned back to her phone and blurted, "Get a road crew over here now to dig this up! We may have something!"

Taylor tossed her phone onto the seat and got out of the car, staring at the rectangular patch. "Do you think this could be it?" she asked in wonder. "Jesus Christ."

"As long as Public Works didn't screw up in their database," Carter said. "It's easy to skimp on the paperwork." The whiff of pessimism hurt.

Taylor shook her head. "I'll bet Sam Freeport never realized some incomplete records could make him look real bad."

"That data's about as glamorous as meter maid tickets," Carter said. "I can feel for him."

Gentry's car squealed to a stop behind Taylor's, and Gentry jumped out. "How did you get here so fast?" Gentry asked.

"I ignored traffic laws," Taylor said.

Gentry grunted, not condoning or praising what she'd done. "What've you got?"

"We've got a big slice of the road that's cut out and no record for it at Public Works."

"Is a road crew on its way?"

"They're supposedly coming."

"OK," Gentry said, "you wait here and don't let anyone do anything until our own people show up. This thing could be booby-trapped. I don't want a county road crew getting the surprise of their lives. For the time being, I'll drive Jim a little farther to see if he doesn't find anything else. I don't want to put all our resources here if the next block has another one not on the county's list. And you give me a call immediately when our people show up."

"Will do," Taylor said.

Gentry nodded stiffly and got into his car.

Taylor wondered whether Gentry would ever manage a thanks or a compliment.

The county road crew arrived twenty minutes later. Gentry and McCracken had already returned without new candidates for digs, and Gentry now tallied the arriving FBI specialists until he had mentally checked off his list. Two police cruisers blocked off the street at each end, and the road crew set up detour signs two blocks away. The passel of FBI, police, and county officials encircled the rectangular plot like a group of mourners at a cemetery awaiting the coffin.

Gentry called over to the road crew foreman. "So, does this look like a repair you guys might have done?"

"Not likely," the foreman said, "unless some crew forgot their steamroller and decided to pack it down by hand."

"All right," Gentry said, "We've done a preliminary check with our sensors, and I'd like you guys to take off the asphalt. My men are then going to pick through this real carefully. I'll want everyone to get way back. We don't know what we have here."

Gentry waived his hand to disperse the onlookers, including the FBI people not involved in the initial phase. Carter had latched on to McCracken, and the two reluctantly backed up down the street. Carter noticed that Taylor had not moved. Get away from there, Carter commanded her in his thoughts. Damn it, do what your boss tells you.

With a roar, the orange Samsung backhoe lurched into place and began breaking up the patch of new pavement, shoving it aside. It took ten minutes, and then the bomb-sniffing dogs came in for their next foray. A team of four FBI bomb squad diggers followed with a slow, hand shovel scrape and probe, testing the ground with detectors as they went.

A colleague pulled McCracken away for a chat, and Carter now stood alone, watching the heads of the bomb squad diggers dip and rise as they worked. As time passed, he felt more and more suspended from the isolated scene. The woman to whom he had bared his heart stood in a distant unreality next to a dig that sought the terrorist who had made Carter his personal target. For the first time that day, Carter looked up at the sky and noticed the bright spring clouds, white and buoyant, moving east in the sunshine. Below, people scraped the dirt for evidence of violence, while Michelle focused on her business, totally separate, perhaps forever removed from him. Nothing could possibly happen until she gave the word, until she told Carter personally that he could go on living. For the moment, Carter had nothing to offer Michelle or the investigation except a powerless patience.

The minutes passed, then an hour, and at each layer of the dig, the electronic sniffers detected just earth and gravel, and the bomb-sniffing dogs, their noses to the ground, gave the go-ahead with a sign of indifference. Carter could hear the men talking in the distance, asking for confirmation on the depth of the water main, or reassurance that no other utility lines stood in their way. Twice Taylor walked the two blocks to tell Carter about progress, but for Carter the long wait had purged the practical sense of purpose he had felt in Taylor's car. Now, any talk of business seemed artificial and insignificant. Carter simply listened, saying little, and inside tried subliminally to keep her nearby, away from any danger. Why was he supposed to stay clear while she exposed herself? But he could not say it out loud. He had no right to interfere. And each time she left him, a part of him seemed to evaporate into the springtime clouds.

At 12:30 p.m., Freeport suddenly appeared on the scene and asked Carter what he knew. Carter shook his head and said, "Not much—except that this has to be Jackhammer's spot. That is, if the county's maintenance records are correct." Freeport's upper lip twitched, but he did not change expression. Carter took no pleasure—he hoped Freeport and his men had hit it right on the money.

Again alone, Carter sat down on the front steps of a two-story home that had now been turned into a dentist's office and stared at the FBI bomb squad sinking deeper into the ground, only the top of their chests visible above the sidewalk. So, was this how the labor of childbirth felt for the father, Carter wondered. You sat uselessly at the side while your partner sweated and groaned and nothing happened for hours, when all you wanted was for the time to finally pass so you could take that squirt in your arms and realize everyone was healthy and everything was going to be fine. Of course, here a birth would mean extracting an instrument of murder.

At 1:30, Carter turned to see Edward Babcock walking slowly up the street in a brown tweed jacket, a tan turtleneck shirt, and brown wool pants, looking like old estate gentry from the 1960s, completely overdressed for this warm day. His eyes rested first on the diggers in the distance, then on Carter. Babcock shook his head with a scowl and closed the final distance to Carter's perch. He sat down on the steps with a groan for stiff limbs. Carter could not believe Babcock had managed to butt in and bother him even here.

"Hello Ed," Carter offered.

"So what have they found?" Babcock asked.

"We think Jackhammer breached the water system, and this may be where he struck. They're digging to find out."

Babcock turned his head to spit off the side of the porch. "This bastard's getting resourceful, isn't he?"

Carter simply nodded, wishing he did not need to keep up the small talk. "So how'd you find out we were digging here? Pay somebody off?"

Babcock chuckled. "You should know by now I've got little volunteer birdies in county government. Somebody was kind enough to give me a call that you'd all had a big emergency meeting and that you'd all headed for the streets."

"So the old boss is still picking up chits," Carter said.

Babcock eyed the crowd of passersby who had gathered at the edge of the police tape to watch. "I wouldn't exactly call this undercover work," he said.

"I suppose not."

"So what's the deal? Did Jackhammer tamper with the water main?"

"It's a definite possibility."

"Well, too bad I haven't heard from you and Miss Taylor lately. I've talked to a few more birdies and there could be some real trouble when it comes to natural gas lines."

"Why, what's up?"

"I understand there are several access areas that would be pretty isolated during darkness. You wouldn't need anything more sophisticated than a bomb with a timing device. Place it, get out, and boom, a pretty big mini-inferno."

"Have you told county government about this?"

Babcock sneered. "I got it from county government. Whether the bastards will do anything with it, I don't know."

"It's a bit hard to station a guard at everything in sight."

"Yeah, but if you gotta be selective, you might as well use a little logic."

Babcock braced his arms on the steps and pushed himself back to his feet. "Well, I'm going to be on my way and get a little exercise. They'll probably be poking around for hours. Let me know what they find."

Carter smirked. "So, am I now one of your birdies?"

"You were supposed to be my eagle," Babcock said with a scowl, "but you never wanted wings."

"We're not all cut out for flying," said Carter.

"Yeah, well, say hello to your little chickadee." He glanced toward the dig. "I can see she feels pretty important."

"She *is* important," Carter said, keeping his jab as polite as he felt possible.

At 1:50, McCracken offered Carter a ham-and-cheese sandwich from a boxful of food he had brought back for the team. Carter had taken several bites when a clamor shot from the hole. Carter saw Taylor and Gentry run to the edge and look in.

Carter broke toward the hole himself, running the two blocks, and pushed his way through the converging road crew, planting himself next to Taylor. Staring down, he saw three dusty men squatting over a dirty metal hump—an oversized barnacle with an antenna rising from the carapace. A few more strokes of the shovels and brooms showed the water main and the flat cross of welded steel flush to the pipe.

"This is no bomb," one of the FBI crew called up to Gentry. "Don't ask me what it is, but I found no trace of explosives or any timing device." The man took some clippers from his back pocket and snipped off the antenna. "That'll cut any long-distance communication for whatever this is supposed to do." He handled the antenna with a handkerchief and gave it to an assistant to place in an evidence bag.

"It's obviously supposed to put *giardia* into the water system," Gentry said with a dry disgust. He turned to his forensic expert. "How do you prefer to work on this?

"I'd like the whole thing back at the lab before I start cracking the device open. I want to make sure of what I've got."

Gentry turned back to his bomb crew. "How long would it take you to get this thing loose?"

"Maybe two hours. We've got our welding equipment in place, but I just hope there aren't any hidden fasteners. Somebody's going to have to turn the water off. We may even have to saw through the pipe."

Gentry snapped his head up and called for McCracken, who had already stepped forward staring at the device.

"It looks like Jackhammer parked some contraption that we've got to pry it loose. Can the city close off the water?"

McCracken looked into the hole with a sense of angry violation. "They can do it," he said, "but give them half an hour. They'll also want to let the people downstream know what's happening."

"Well," Gentry said with impatience, "they'd better not delay us with more public notification. I'm sure people prefer having no water to getting poisoned."

By 5:15, the welders and sawers had pried free the last of the supports and crowbarred the circular caulking. Two men now lifted what looked like the carcass of a giant, stunted spider onto a plank of plywood at the edge of the hole. Scrambling out, the men hoisted the dead weight into a wooden crate, and then into a waiting van.

Taylor followed the work until the door to the van slammed shut. She exchanged words with Gentry, and then turned her head to scan the area. Her eyes came to a rest on Carter. She approached with her fluid walk. "Do you want to come along to the lab?" Taylor asked. "You deserve to hear the results of this as much as anyone."

"Sure," Carter said, somewhat taken aback by her willingness to keep him in tow. "If I didn't come, I'd just be sitting somewhere else waiting for a phone call."

"Good," Taylor said, brushing an amber strand of hair from her forehead. "Give me half an hour and we'll be on our way." She smiled. "And this time I won't run the red lights."

Carter put up his hands in defense. "Don't mind me."

"The hazards of duty?"

"Absolutely," Carter said.

19

On the drive to the FBI lab in Quantico, Virginia, Taylor stuck to business. She told Carter what the FBI team had found in the dirt of the digging—an empty pack of cigarettes and a disposable lighter, among other random scraps. All of them might have been buried when the road was built, but they were worth checking out. Preliminary fingerprint checks showed nothing useful on anything, including the device itself.

"What about inside the thing?" Carter asked. "The machinist who built it might have gotten frustrated by gloves and left a print or two."

"We can only hope," said Taylor. "My main concern is finding out whether Jackhammer had another dose of *giardia* in there—or something else. In his phone call, he referred to another attack. If this was it, we've stopped him."

"Damn sweet, if true," Carter said.

The two spoke little during the rest of the drive, as if they had found an emotional truce where both admitted enough mutual respect to keep questions of affection tightly under wraps.

Taylor soon pulled into the parking lot of a 7-Eleven and suggested Carter pick up a magazine for the wait at the lab.

"You don't keep yours stocked like a doctor's office?" Carter asked.

"No. And I'm going to have all kinds of things to do."

Carter hopped out and grabbed a *Sports Illustrated* and a *Popular Mechanics*. "Hours of reading pleasure," Carter quipped as he got back into the car. "Just hope I don't need it."

"You will," Taylor said.

At the lab, Taylor flashed her ID to the guard at the parking lot gate, hijacked a reserved space, and took Carter inside. Through security, she led him into a small, empty lounge reserved for outsiders. Taylor soon excused herself to make a series of phone calls and to touch base with Gentry.

Carter sat down in a worn, wood-framed easy chair with an imitation black leather seat, one of seven encircling the room as subordinates to a matching black couch. A few framed color photos of various Washington scenes, including the building in which he now sat, strained to break up the emptiness of the plain white walls. If not for the prospect of some good news on Jackhammer, the space would have felt as depressing as a holding pen at the DMV. Carter could not seem to escape such purgatories.

As time passed, Carter expected Taylor to return and explode the silence, but that did not come. Carter opened his *Sports Illustrated* and began to read the latest spring training report, dwelling on a short item about the Washington Nationals, then turning to an article on the closing drive to the NBA playoffs.

Occasionally, Carter would look up and imagine what was happening in the lab. He could picture the painstaking puzzle of dismantling something into its unknown parts, reverse engineering the thing piece by piece so you could figure out how it worked, dusting for prints, looking for clues on where the parts might have been bought or machined. It made him jealous not to be part of that challenge, if only just to escape this limbo. Then he would realize the pointlessness and return to his magazine, trying not to look at his watch and freeze time even more.

Punctuating the hours, Taylor would stop by to offer a few details about progress, but she was basically in the dark herself and showed her excited impatience with a few quiet curses and wry smiles. In the long gaps of her absence, Carter had no choice but to pick up the *Popular Mechanics* and read about the newest diesel engine technologies and a newfangled corkscrew. On one of her visits, Taylor brought Carter a tuna-fish sandwich encased in a triangular, clear-plastic box. When Carter, again alone, opened the machine-processed bread, he could picture the chrome cubicle of a forsaken vending machine.

Carter wondered whether Taylor's constant escapes were not just an excuse to avoid the embarrassment of his presence, and whether, in fact, she was sitting in another room just like this one, letting the time pass in parallel. For Carter, the evening became a colorless, soundless transit, punctuated by the radiance of Taylor's visits. His heart leapt whenever she walked through that door, and sank back into its distant rhythm when she left.

At 9:05 that night, the door burst open and Taylor ran into the room, her eyes aglow and her face flushed. Carter stood up and Taylor raced toward him and did not stop to blurt out some news, but embraced him with a quick, excited hug. "We've done it!" she said, taking a step back from him, too involved in her elation to notice Carter's shock.

Carter had not had the chance to get his arms around her. It had all been too fast and too much of a surprise, and yet now his whole being had the imprint of her body—the firm, inviting pressure, the light touch of her hands on his back, her hair grazing the side of his head, the smell of her perfume. He had to concentrate to understand what she was saying.

"The device had two canisters," Taylor said, the words spilling out. "One was the *giardia*, pretty much empty, the other was a chemical poison, still full and unused, ready to be activated with a walky-talky-like communications device. We're not even going to make the poison's name public, not to give terrorists any ideas."

Carter stared at her, nodding.

"It's incredibly toxic," Taylor said, unable to contain herself. "I'm told that when concentrated, just contact with the skin can give you a fatal poisoning. You develop symptoms after a few months, and you can die within a year."

"No fun," Carter said.

"Jackhammer was going to release that into the Rosslyn water system. The stuff would have been diluted, but over time, long after it had already spread, people would have faced brain damage and lingering complications—god knows, maybe a thousand people—and then you could wait to see if you got any deaths. It's such a sickening crime. It's such—." She was shaking her head.

"But we've stopped him," Carter said.

"Yes," said Taylor, "but my God, it's like when a kid runs into the street and doesn't get run over. Your heart's pounding from what might have happened."

"Did they find anything else—prints, anything?"

"Not yet," she said. "But they're working on it. Right now, just think of it, we've stopped the monster. We blocked his worst attack."

Carter could not take his eyes off her. "So, are you done here?"

When he saw her nod, he had the elated fear that this was his last chance, that somehow the investigation would now change and squeeze him out and that Taylor would then have an excuse to keep her distance. He was determination not to go home. "We've got to celebrate this thing. Right? How about dinner? No excuses."

Taylor looked at him, trying to contain her emotions. Her excitement kept pushing back all the doubts and red flags and warning flashers and made her want to throw it all to hell for the moment. It was the same feeling that had triggered that rash hug and now left her with a subtle shimmer of his presence, as though he had broken through the intellectual image she had always stored of him and implanted himself as a tactile apparition on her bodily imagination. She rose slightly on her toes with pent-up energy. "I'm too wound up to just pack it in. But we already had those god-awful sandwiches."

"Hell, we can just have a drink."

Taylor smiled despite herself. "What about dancing? Latin music. I haven't taken someone to Tío Fuego in months."

Carter grinned back. "What place is that?"

"It's a club. It's Saturday night, and they've got a live Latin band. We can pretend we're dancing on Jackhammer's grave."

"OK, but am I supposed to know how to dance that stuff?"

"You can try like the rest of us."

Carter had not quite synced up with reality, trying to figure out what to do now. Maybe he should just take her hand and lead her out of there. No, she probably wasn't ready for that. She was excited about stopping a terrorist. He happened to be convenient for a celebration. Don't make a big deal of it, because if she then keeps her distance, you can just hang yourself from the rafters.

"You'll have to teach me some steps," Carter said. "I don't know how rock and roll translates into Spanish."

"I've got patience," Taylor said with a smile, "but I'm unforgiving!"

Taylor headed for the door, motioning Carter with her head, then held the door open with playful courtesy. "Can you believe it?" she said, still incredulous at what had happened. "We stopped the son of a bitch. We stopped an incredible agony."

After the long drive to Georgetown, Taylor lucked into a parking space three blocks north of M Street, and the two got out and walked among patrician townhouses and vine-covered gardens and lantern-lit steps. An occasional open curtain showed an upscale, antique decor, reminding Carter of his own house in Alexandria, stoking the exhilaration that he was not home in that emptiness. But the thought became no more than a spark within the flames of walking in the cool, spring-warm night with Michelle.

Carter did not take Taylor's hand, and she did not offer it. They walked like the two business associates they had been since the beginning, except now with a charge passing between them, acknowledged by an occasional glance that could not hide expectancy.

Walking downhill, they crossed the traffic tie-ups of M Street, and then, half a block farther, climbed the steps to the first-floor club, getting in line to pay their cover charge. "My treat," Taylor said, pulling out her wallet.

"I assume you'll let me pick up some drinks?" Carter said.

"I'll think about it," she said.

Inside, the music had not yet started, and the two found a table at the back wall away from the bar, on the top tier of raised tables that cascaded down to the dance floor. Taylor did not see the young bartender, but did not want to take chances and sit close. She took off her pants-suit jacket and hung it over the back of her chair. Carter stayed on his feet to scoot the chair under her.

He looked down at her white silk blouse, smooth and sleek on her shoulders in the dark silver-black half-light of the club. Carter lowered himself into the chair next to her. "They don't exactly start early," Carter said.

"No," said Taylor, "Latin tradition."

The waitress stopped by, and Taylor ordered a frozen margarita; Carter, a margarita on the rocks.

"How about some nachos?" Taylor asked. "I feel like something greasy."

"It'll beat that tuna sandwich," said Carter.

The waitress jotted down the order and left, and the two both dropped momentarily into silence as they looked over the club, watching the people pick their way through the chairs, mostly Hispanics, often in groups who laid claim to adjacent tables and talked in fast Spanish.

"So how'd you get to know this place?" Carter asked.

"I had a Dominican boyfriend who liked to dance."

Carter smiled. "Should I restrain myself, or should I grill you on your dating history?"

"Nothing to hide," Taylor said, glancing at him with amusement. She did not fully understand why she was feeling so brash, only that her spirit had opened up with success.

Eventually the waitress set down the drinks and the band began to move onto stage and take up its instruments, testing the mikes and knocking a few scattered blasts from the trumpets and conga drums.

"So, are you going to give me the first dance?" Taylor asked.

"Let me see what it looks like first," Carter said. "I can't go out there cold."

"So now you're the prudent one?"

Carter laughed. "Oh, I wish."

The two sipped their drinks slowly, but as Carter saw the band get ready to start, he downed his drink and ordered another. You'd better loosen up fast, Carter told himself, or you're going to make a fool of yourself.

"Hey," Taylor said, "don't leave me in the dust." She ordered a second drink for herself. "I'm as thirsty as you are." She hesitated but could not stop the momentum of the next. "And maybe as nervous."

Carter smiled, but was taken off guard. "You don't pull any punches, do you?"

Taylor blushed, but Carter could not see the coloring in the dark. "I guess I can't stand putting up fronts," Taylor said. "I'd like us just to enjoy ourselves and celebrate without all the background I know is piling up on this."

Despite her honesty, Carter noticed that she had only used code in referring to his love. She could not come out and say it.

The bandleader interrupted with a blaring "Good evening" and then launched his group into a pulsing salsa, the amplifiers turned up too loud and the beat electrifying. Carter could see Taylor moving her shoulders just slightly as she watched the first dancers move out onto the floor. They all looked like they had danced this rhythm since birth. Carter was glad to see the second round of drinks head their way, this time with the food.

"Do you really plan to sit this one out?" Taylor asked.

"That was my definite intention."

"So you're learning a lot by watching them?"

"I'm learning that this could be embarrassing."

"Since when are you the one to flinch from a challenge?"

"Good one. Make me feel like a coward."

"Suggest a better technique."

"Threaten to walk out."

"You are hereby threatened."

Carter shook his head and took a deep breath. "OK, you win."

Carter gulped another mouthful of his drink and stood up, letting Taylor lead the way down the steps and onto the dance floor. She took him to the far side, away from the brunt of the tables, and immediately closed her hands into gentle fists and began stepping about unpretentiously, moving her hips to the rhythm, without touching him. Carter stared at the sensuousness of her movements, raising his hands to his sides but not quite knowing what step to try.

Taylor smiled and took his two hands in hers. "No need for anything fancy. You said you've danced. Just flow with a back and forth. We're not going to worry about official steps on a first try."

Carter felt weak at her touch, as though she had offered her whole being and not just the light, playful pressure of her hand. Too many daydreams had condensed into this grazing of skin, and too much hope. Carter could feel the turn of her hips through her steady, guiding grip, and slowly, drawn by her example, his feet began to move, forward and back, his hips dipping slightly to rock through the motion, trying to mirror her movement and lose himself in her smile.

"That's not bad," Taylor said. "I can see the Fox Trot getting a workout!"

"Thanks a lot!" Carter said above the music, finding this banter a strange remnant from another world, with no place in the stream of his excitement.

Carter knew enough about dancing to recognize when he had fouled up the rhythm, and he recovered from stumbles by just stopping to regroup. Slowly, he became more absorbed and managed long strings of reasonable steps, knowing that with Michelle he would love any music, but finding this blare a raucous new escape from so much of his former life.

Taylor let go of his hands and demonstrated a few variations, signaling with her eyes that he should follow her lead.

After two songs, Carter asked for a break. "I need a drink," he said. "How about you?"

"I guess we have those nachos to kill."

Taylor led him back to the table with a playful scolding in her eyes. "I'm not going to give you much of a rest," she said. "Bottoms up, a few bites, and then we're back. You were just getting decent."

"Just don't show me the video tape."

Carter ordered some tequila shots, and the two spent time fishing around the greasy mound of cheese and jalapeños, giving up any pretense of decorum, licking their fingers until they shined. When they got their next round of drinks, the band started playing a number that sent Taylor into a shoulder- and hip-swaying dance in her seat.

"We can't pass this one up," Taylor said. She raised her tequila. "Take a shot. We're wasting time."

"I guess you want me to fall on my face."

Taylor grinned. "Let's ditch your P.E. professional care." She raised her glass to her lips and with a playful glance, popped it down in one quick swallow. Carter followed her lead, the tequila hot to his throat. "Let's go," Taylor said.

Taylor felt a new flush of energy. The drink had lowered her defenses even more, and she felt tempted to take Carter's hand and give him a squeeze of encouragement, but she could not quite bring herself to do it. She knew he had to be holding tremendous expectations. She worried what he might think, but as she stepped onto the dance floor, she did not want to block this spring fever after a long winter of complications. She could feel the rhythm and the drinks take hold of her, making each step more passionate. Despite her subliminal fears, a part of her wanted to captivate Carter, to absorb the power of his adoration and accept his gaze in the seductive movement of her limbs. She felt excited in being viewed as some kind of goddess, and the more she raised the ante, the more pleasure she felt in his company and the more frighteningly attractive he became.

Carter now trafficked in complete confusion. At one moment, Taylor's movements struck him as a lighthearted flirt at an office party; at another, a soulful seduction. Carter became so absorbed in her look that he no longer strained with his dancing—the steps became smooth and free, feeding off the thrill at the sight of her. He could not remember the last time he had felt this kind of abandon. With Linda, it had always been so sedate in comparison, a fresh, stylish breeze instead of this hot wind.

When they again sat down for a break, their clothes patched with sweat, they ordered two beers to beat down their thirst. Struck by this contrast to their daily lives, they drifted to jokes about their jobs and grinned about the bungles of their superiors and the absurd office politics. They found it remarkable how groups of well-intentioned, intelligent people so often disintegrated into pointless backbiting.

The drinks continued to open their talk and blend one dance into the other. They pushed through the relative silence of the band's first break without foundering on the rocks of too much intimacy, then entered the hot breakers of a new sea of music. Only when the band stilled its wind and switched to a slow dance did Carter and Taylor suddenly feel self-conscious. They stood on the dance floor faced with the decision of holding each other close or bolting for the table. Carter had only one answer. He lifted his arms, asking her with his eyes if she would step closer, intentionally feigning lightheartedness to hide the beat of his heart.

Taylor lifted her head and accepted his tentative touch, and they danced cautiously at first, their hands in light pressure on their perspiring backs. Carter could feel the impalpable electricity of Taylor's cheek close to his, and soon he could no longer resist the attraction. Closing his eyes, in a leap of faith, he let his cheek drift closer, until it touched her skin and rested there in limbo. With each passing moment, Carter expected her to pull away, but her cheek remained in place, even reciprocating the pressure, and soon Carter could feel the occasional squeeze of her hand on his back—a mirage-like lightness but unmistakably real.

When the song stopped, Taylor pulled her face away and said thanks with an embarrassed smile, but Carter did not let go of her hand. They walked back to the table, Taylor's hand in his, and when Carter realized they had sat down with their fingers still touching, as though there was nothing else they could do, Carter could no longer contain himself. He could not let the evening stop, and he leaned over and looked Taylor in the eyes and said, "I can't imagine leaving you tonight."

Taylor had known it would come to this, and she had prepared herself, and the profound look in his eyes only endeared him to her more. She knew she was drunk and had lost all logic, and she could think only of taking him in her arms and showing him that the night was not over. She leaned forward and, almost as surprised as he was, kissed him lightly on the lips and then whispered, "Me neither," into his ear.

"Then let's go now," Carter whispered, as though saying anything out loud would break the spell that had come over them.

"Where?" Taylor asked.

"The Four Seasons down the street."

Taylor smiled and shook her head, finding it hard to believe that she had gotten herself into this. She rose and put her arm around his waist, and Carter settled the bill, and they walked outside together, onto the still-busy M Street, then two blocks east past the art galleries and shops to the fringe of Georgetown, where pedestrians disappeared into a more residential quiet. They felt little of their surroundings, only a slight embarrassment when they realized it might look better not to show up arm in arm at the front desk with no luggage. Taylor sat down amid the lush green of tropical plants in the glass-enclosed lobby, and Carter arranged for the room—a double for him and his wife—declining their offer to send the bell-hop for their bags.

Only when the door to the elevator closed behind them and they began to rise, did Carter fully realize that this night was not going to disappear, that it would not explode in his face like so much else in his recent life.

When the elevator opened and he walked down the fifth-floor hall, those thoughts were suddenly driven to the background, and again Carter felt only his hand around Taylor's waist and the brush of her body next to him. At the door, he slid the magnetic key into the slot and looked for the flashing green, and then they were inside, the room in half-light drawing them closer.

The two drifted toward the bed and Carter again looked into Taylor's eyes. He could see she had surrendered to his love, but he did not know if it was just the drinking and the dancing and the chance for adventure. He took her head lightly in his hands and kissed her gently on the lips and tasted the trace of dried perspiration from her upper lip and closed his eyes in a tide of weakness. His lips roamed quietly across her face, kissing her nose, her eyes, her cheeks. She remained passive at first, but then her lips sought him as well, and her hands slipped around his back and finally forward to the buttons on his shirt, pushing them free one by one as their mouths opened and the exploring slipped to a new urgency.

When Carter drew Taylor down to the bed, a strange finality came over him, as though this were somehow a last stand for hope. He ranged across her body with the subconscious skill of a long, barren apprenticeship with Linda. What had become a forced formula in a losing cause now transformed itself into an evocation of Carter's adoration, an overpowering flow to each response of Taylor's achingly fluid body.

After the storm, Carter slipped from Michelle's island into the much broader sea. On his back, his eyes to the ceiling, he felt a sudden disbelief that only now in his life, when a death sentence perhaps waited just outside the door, he had been given this happiness.

Taylor, quietly stunned by her own transport, felt Carter's hand stroke the small of her hip in a trance-like, distant rhythm. She wanted to squeeze him to her heart but could still not face the responsibility of such an admission. She propped her head on her hand and with her finger drew a circle on his chest. Suddenly, she noticed the distant look in his eyes.

"Scott, is something wrong?" she whispered.

Carter turned quickly toward her. "Nothing," he said.

Taylor did not want to push him, but it seemed that his thoughts had still not returned to her. "Scott, do we still need to keep secrets?"

Carter blinked and tried to get a grip on his nostalgia. He looked back at the ceiling, letting her catch his words from there. "It suddenly hit me that it's been more than ten years since I've felt like this. My marriage was good at the beginning, and then bit by bit Linda and I started to drift apart. There was no real conscious decision behind it. It just happened. But even at the beginning, I don't know if I had the fire that I felt with you tonight." He looked back at Taylor. "When I look at you, I get this nasty vision that cancer or Jackhammer may just cut me down, just to spite me, just to get the grinning last word."

Carter squeezed Taylor's hand and laid his head on her shoulder. Taylor wanted to give herself completely, to say they were now one, but it seemed too reckless to give him such hope when she did not know what would become of them. She put her hands on his cheeks and kissed him long and gently on the eyes, and then on the lips. "We've had such a wonderful night," she said. "Don't darken it too much with the future."

"I'll take anything you have to offer," Carter said, smiling to show his willingness.

"So tell me," Taylor whispered, giving him a small, frisky pinch, desperate to lighten their mood. "Where did you learn to make love like that?"

And then the phone rang. Carter went cold at the interruption. "Who the hell's calling at this hour?"

"Are you going to answer it?" Taylor asked. The phone was on his side of the bed.

"I guess so," Carter murmured. He picked it up.

"Well, well," said a hissing voice, "To top everything off, fornication with our little FBI playmate."

Carter jerked up and slapped his hand over the receiver. "It's Jackhammer!" he whispered, swinging his legs out and sitting at the edge of the bed.

"Are you surprised I tracked you down?" Jackhammer asked.

"What do you want?" Carter asked, devastated as he saw Taylor hurriedly gathering her clothes.

"Well, I just couldn't resist the prospect of talking to you on a phone that's not bugged. Oh, eventually your little sex kitten will call her FBI friends and try to get a trace on this call, but it'll take just a little bit longer. We don't have to feel so rushed."

"Why waste time," Carter said. "Let's get to the point. Tell us your new plans, now that we found your poison."

"Well, I knew it wasn't foolproof. I thought it might take the county a little more time than it did, but I'm not worried. It's not the end of the line. I was ready for it."

"How did you find me?"

"What's the big mystery? I had somebody follow you. You act like that's difficult."

"But why waste your energy on me?" Carter asked. "I don't understand that." He turned around and did not see Taylor. Then he heard her in the bathroom making a call on her cell phone.

"You're just irresistible," Jackhammer chuckled. "It's damn charming how you're out to save the world, the do-gooder gone wild. Deflating that bubble gives me a kick. You've been half the fun throughout these glory weeks."

"How can you call killing people fun?" Carter asked, trying hard to prolong the conversation.

"Why do you call screwing that FBI woman fun? You just happen to like it. I happen to like teaching this country a lesson. The killing is just war casualties. It's not central to my mission."

"But now we've stopped you," Carter said. "That probably doesn't feel so good, does it?"

"The best is yet to come," Jackhammer said. "You've just removed one land mine from the battlefield. But my arsenal and my armies don't stop there. You don't realize how little time you all have. Somewhere something truly impressive will take place. No more limitations to Rosslyn. That area's becoming ticklish under everyone's noses. Now you've got to start worrying in every city. Ask yourselves: Where will the great public works terrorist strike next? Will it be Philadelphia? Southeast DC? Richmond? Everyone can now live on the edge. Everyone can start trembling—and right away!"

Taylor hurried out of the bathroom fully dressed and signaled that she was going downstairs. She bent down to the bed and gave him a short kiss on the cheek, then whispered in his ear to keep Jackhammer on the phone. Then she was gone.

Carter put his hand to his forehead and his elbow on his knee, the phone jammed against his ear in a new rage. He trembled in hate that Jackhammer had spoiled his night. Carter had to control himself not to hang up.

"If your stunts are so well hidden," Carter said, "it seems like you could give us a better heads up than that. Your warnings are all too broad. Nobody can really worry about protecting themselves. You'll lose half your fun."

"Don't try to get clever, Mr. Carter. There are times when prudence makes the best offense. In fact, I'm going to have to get off this call before your little piece of tail gets her friends involved. Tell everyone to stay tuned. The grand finale is near!"

"But—" Carter heard the phone go dead. After a moment, he laid down the receiver and stared at the empty room, then at his own nakedness. The hours that had been his deliverance had now been ripped from the world, with only the rough fringes left as a reminder.

Carter stood up to gather his clothes, then slowly became more anxious as he realized he had to go downstairs and find Michelle—to help her with her work, or just to see her, anything but this sudden solitude. He quickly got dressed and pushed his hair into place at the dresser mirror and hurried out the door. He still had Michelle's smell all over him.

Carter found Taylor in the hotel lobby as she was leaving the front desk.

"What have you found?" Carter asked.

"I wanted to know how the front desk would let through a call at 2:00 in the morning. From what they say, a man was pretty frantic, saying that there'd been an emergency in your family. He practically pleaded that they put him through; he even promised to send a tip. It apparently sounded convincing, so they rang us up. It was not a computerized voice at first."

"Can the hotel operator describe it?"

"Sort of, but how do you do that accurately? Besides, how do we know it was Jackhammer who did that part of the talking? Maybe it was one of his henchmen."

"It's never easy, is it?"

Taylor shook her head, looking around as if plotting what to do next. Carter realized she had completely left him for the heat of the investigation.

"I've asked around whether anyone saw us come in and whether they noticed anyone following us," Taylor said. "I also got in touch with my FBI colleagues. Frank's on his way."

"Jackhammer told me we'd been followed. He must have had somebody on our tail since the dig this morning."

"I obviously didn't notice anyone," Taylor said. She smiled weakly. "I must have been distracted."

Carter could feel the world collapsing around him, a whole army of FBI agents ready to invade the hotel and take Michelle away. "I have to see you again," Carter said.

Taylor looked at him mournfully, distraught by her sudden uncertainties. "I can't talk about it now," she said quietly. "I have to regroup. I just don't know what to say at the moment."

Carter implored her with his eyes, fearful of what he might hear. "So that's it, I guess."

She put her hand on Carter's cheek and whispered. "I'm sorry. It's not what I wanted."

Carter took hold of her hand and lowered it in front of him, as though holding a precious object for safekeeping.

"Please, no more right now," Taylor said. "There's too much to do. What else did Jackhammer say? We don't have a tape this time. It's all you."

"He threatened the whole Eastern seaboard, or so it seemed. He said the device we dug up today was not a big loss. He has a 'grand finale' planned, and it's coming soon. He mentioned Philadelphia, DC, and Richmond, throwing out possibilities to show that everybody has to beware."

"Did it sound convincing?"

"How can I tell? But why should we believe the device we found was the only thing he had left?"

"Because that would be awfully convenient."

"It would," Carter said.

Taylor pulled a pad and pen from her bag and handed it to Carter. "Could you write down everything Jackhammer said, as you remember it, while it's still fresh in your mind?"

"Sure," Carter said, thankful to at least hold something Michelle had touched.

"I'm going to stop by Tío Fuego and see if anyone may have seen someone following us. It's a long shot, but I've got to try."

"You be careful," Carter said.

"Sure, and if Frank beats me here, you tell him just to hang on."

"Wait. How are we going to explain this whole business? I suppose we'll now get ourselves splashed in some official report."

Taylor knit her brow. "You've got a point. I'll see if I can get Frank to keep a lid on it." She leaned forward and gave Carter a light kiss on the lips, then turned and left.

Carter stood motionless until she had gone out the door. Finally, he looked around for a chair and took a seat at the side of the lobby where he could still see the front entrance. With the pad on his knee, he began a slow scrawl of the Jackhammer transcript, leaving out mentions of "fornication" and "tail" and "FBI playmate." When he had it all down, he realized that this collection of Jackhammer's words had robbed him of everything.

It took Gentry forty minutes to arrive. Taylor had come back from the club empty-handed and had sat down in the lounge to read Carter's transcript. Gentry entered the hotel with two FBI agents in tow and headed straight for Taylor, signaling the two agents to wait by the door. His hair looked unwashed and his white shirt wrinkled. Taylor and Carter both stood up. Gentry glared at them with the leftover discomfort of being woken in the middle of the night.

"So what the hell happened?" Gentry asked curtly.

"Jackhammer called us," Taylor said.

"Where?"

Taylor looked at the floor and then back at Gentry, her tone firm and unflinching. "In one of the rooms."

Gentry looked from Taylor to Carter with gruff curiosity, only now comprehending. "Well, let's try not to get into *that*.

How did he track you down?"

"He said somebody'd followed us since this morning," Taylor reported, still stoic in her expression.

Gentry squinted. "Aren't you getting a little careless not watching your back?"

"I clearly was," Taylor said.

Impatiently, Gentry ran his hand across his crew-cut hair. "OK, Scott. What did Jackhammer have to say this time?"

Taylor interrupted with the transcript. "I've had Scott write it up."

"Good," Gentry said. He took a moment to skim through the notes, glancing up in midstream. "So now he's threatening every city within two hundred miles?"

"That's what it looks like," Carter said. He lowered his voice. "I need to ask a favor."

"What's that?"

"This is embarrassing for Michelle. How much of the details do you have to report?"

Gentry glared at him with stern, suppressed amusement. "Are you kidding? I don't want to touch this with a ten foot pole. As far as I know, you were having a drink in the bar and got the call from Jackhammer there. Isn't that right?"

"That's right," Carter said.

"Thanks," said Taylor.

Gentry shot back, "You'd better not thank me for anything, or I'll change my mind. I'm not going to be part of any conspiracy. I'm just working for the peace and quiet of this investigation. It has nothing to do with you—or Scott. Is that clear?"

"Sure," Taylor said.

"So what have you covered so far?" Gentry asked.

Michelle recapped her interviews with the front desk, the hotel operator, the doorman, and the staff at Tío Fuego.

"You haven't left much for us, have you?" Gentry said, grudgingly impressed.

"It'd be good for you to take a second run-through," Taylor said. "I was rushed and could have missed something. I also wondered whether we shouldn't check out the pay phones where we were followed. Maybe Jackhammer or his helper wanted to play old school again and call from one of those."

"Did he call right after you arrived?"

"No, about an hour later."

"So if the person who followed you made the call, he had a chance to get anywhere."

"Certainly possible," she said. Taylor did not mention that Jackhammer might have waited just to make the interruption spicier.

"Well, I'll send my two guys to see about witnesses and prints on the pay phones, and to interview the crew at the main entrance. I'll take care of the interviews here."

Taylor realized that with Gentry working the hotel desk, the details of their rendezvous could stay under wraps. "Thanks," Taylor said.

"What the hell's that supposed to mean?"

"Nothing," Taylor said.

Gentry had had enough of these comments and swung around toward the front desk. "Let's go," he said. "Show me who these players are."

Taylor gave Carter a warm glance of good-bye and followed Gentry. Carter watched her as she walked, uncertain about what it had all meant for her, and then headed outside for a cab and the drive to pick up his car from his Rosslyn parking space.

When he arrived, he did not know whether he was fit to drive, so he locked the doors, put the seat back, and did his best to doze for an hour, his thoughts spinning from regret to pleasure and back. By the time he drove home, his bodyguard was back in place outside his house, and Carter realized that napping on the street had probably not been too bright, but safety had been the last thing on Carter's mind. It was 4:30 a.m., and his house stood dark. Carter stepped inside and locked the door behind him. He hung up his jacket in the hall closet, walked upstairs, and sat down on the bed, listening to the silence.

20

Carter woke just after 10:00 a.m., a spring sunshine in the cracks at the edge of the window blind. For a moment, he expected the Four Seasons Hotel, but the surroundings immediately clicked into place, and he sat up on the edge of the bed, then stood up and opened the blinds. He raised the window pane to let in the cool spring air and wondered where he would go today. Nothing had been fixed with the FBI to discuss the new Jackhammer crisis. He would just have to wait for a call, if it ever came.

After a shower, Carter got dressed and went downstairs. He found the thick Sunday *Washington Post* on the front porch with a plastic-wrapped sample of Pasta Primavera promising in loud colors to fill his home with the aroma of Italian herbs. Carter returned to the kitchen to make some instant coffee, and while the bottled water came to a boil (he was not yet ready to use the tap), he cut out the sample spice pack with a pair of scissors and laid it on the counter. Staring at the picture of bright, fresh vegetables, he wondered whether he and Michelle might ever cook that together.

With the coffee crystals tossed in the water and stirred,

Carter took the newspaper and his mug out into the garden and sat down on the iron bench. He felt uncomfortable going through his standard Sunday morning habits without somehow touching base with Michelle, but there was no point in possibly waking her up. God knows when she might have gone to bed.

Page one of *The Post* shouted the news of the injection canister and the new vial of poison. County officials and the FBI speculated on whether Jackhammer had buried other devices, and the commentators dissected the calculated cruelty. Board Chairman Duncan had successfully placed himself in the middle of the discovery effort and took his bows of outrage with the usual platitudes. Carter even found his own name listed as a participant in the Arlington crisis team. At least he was not at the center of this latest episode, Carter thought, or the phone would be ringing with interview requests.

From what he read, Carter saw that the citizens of Rosslyn were showing some signs of panic. They had heard news accounts about the unnamed poison, how it could enter the body even through the skin, and people demanded to know whether they could even risk washing their hands once the water was turned on again, let alone take a shower. In one article, Duncan said that all Arlington water mains were being searched for tampering but that no one had evidence to suggest that Jackhammer had planted more than one of these devices. Carter thought of the total miles of pipe throughout Arlington and how long it might take to inspect the ground and the manholes above every foot of them. And that was assuming Arlington would be the next target. I might even panic, Carter thought.

The news of Jackhammer's call to the hotel about additional cities had not yet hit the papers, but Carter knew that when that came out, the hand wringing and the public outcry of fear would only get worse. Jackhammer was getting what he wanted, Carter thought. The whole region would be hanging on the prospect of what Jackhammer would do next.

At 10:50 that morning, the doorbell rang. Carter looked out the window and saw a no-name delivery van double-parked on the street. He also noticed that the FBI bodyguard had crossed over to question the visitor, and both men now stood on his porch. Carter opened the door. The courier looked to Carter for help. "Hey, I'm just trying to deliver this envelope. What's going on?"

"Don't mind him," Carter said. "They think I'm a marked man"

The agent took down the delivery man's name, company, and license plate number and pulled out a handkerchief to grip the envelope. "Are you expecting anything from Blackstone-Waynewright Engineers?" the agent asked Carter.

"No," Carter said. "A Sunday delivery isn't exactly the most common thing, especially when there's email."

The agent questioned the courier about where he had gotten the envelope, but the courier, a little unnerved by the handkerchief, said it had come from the main office in DC, like any other delivery. He knew nothing else about it. The agent said someone would be in touch with the company.

Carter looked at the envelope. The BWE logo appeared official and the envelope's paper stock was what he would expect. There was no personalized name of a sender. "So what do we do with this?" Carter asked.

"If you're not expecting it, we better take it to the Bureau and have the explosives and bio lab look it over."

"It might just be a CD," Carter said, pointing out the thin square bulge with his eyes.

"You're asking me to make that judgment?" the agent said, putting the envelope in a plastic bag.

Carter smiled grimly. "I guess you don't want that responsibility. Can I come along? The envelope might actually contain business I'm supposed to look at."

"I guess you know the way."

"Unfortunately I do, and it's a hell of a trek."

Carter immediately called Waynewright, then the lead members of his rebuilding team, but no one had sent him a package. Carter considered calling Michelle to mention the incident, but he knew the lab did not need her around to help with their work. He assumed she was busy with other assignments, and besides, she would know he had called just to get back together. She had to make the next move and sort out their relationship. His side needed no more reinforcement.

At the FBI lab, the bodyguard pulled in behind Carter, and they both parked in the visitor spaces. Carter was again banished to a waiting lounge while the agent took the envelope to the weekend explosives team.

Two hours later a lab technician came back with a data CD. "You've gotten another calling card from your friend Jackhammer. No bombs, just some files in .dwg format."

"Sounds like AutoCAD," Carter said.

"We haven't had a chance to read them, but I've made you a copy and scanned for viruses. Maybe you'll want to take a look yourself."

"Definitely. Have you called Frank Gentry and Michelle Taylor?" Carter asked.

"We've called Frank. What I've got to do now is call around and track down a copy of AutoCAD so nothing gets distorted. The full team's not here on Sunday, so we've got to roust somebody out."

"I'll take this back to the office and call in whatever I find out," Carter said.

"Just use your usual contacts," the technician said. "They'll let you know whether someone at the lab has any questions or has something to warn you about."

Carter thanked him, took a deep breath, and left.

On the long drive to Rosslyn, the Jackhammer disk bulldozed Taylor from Carter's thoughts. He dug through the possibilities of what Jackhammer might have sent, infuriated by the non-stop audacity of these contacts, but in the end, he knew that once he pushed through the anger, his mind would emerge to Michelle and their next meeting. He wanted to give her the new evidence personally. He had to, even if it was just to graze the tips of her fingers with his hand.

In Rosslyn, the Sunday morning traffic remained light, and the monotone concrete, asphalt, and glass took on the air of an abandoned high-rise demonstration project. The bodyguard followed Carter into the parking garage of BWE, then up the elevator to the locked door of Carter's floor. The bodyguard then returned downstairs and parked outside to watch the front entrance, making occasional rounds to the back, in cell phone contact in the event Carter needed him.

Carter expected an empty office. The engineers who worked overtime tended to come in on Saturdays, not Sundays, and he was surprised to see light in the hall, and a light through the open door to Waynewright's office. Carter stopped off at his own office, turned on his computer, and then walked down the hall to check what Waynewright was doing. He saw him hunched over his computer in a green flannel hunting shirt, his back to the door. Carter knocked on the door jam and Waynewright jerked around.

"Jesus!" Waynewright blurted. "Are you trying to give me a heart attack!?" He slapped his chest as though trying to slow down his heartbeat, then slumped backwards.

"Sorry," Carter said, "I was just trying to get your attention without scaring you too much."

"Well, you failed. What are you doing here?"

"That's what I was going to ask you."

Waynewright waved his hand in disgust. "Just trying to review an RFP. I could have been out rabbit hunting but I've gotten behind, partly because of you and all your investigative work and your cockeyed demands to be involved in design, and partly because of your Agent Taylor. Do you know that she questioned me again—about my finances! The nerve to drag me into this Jackhammer case, like I'm laundering money to pay for these attacks!"

"She's got a whole list of people," Carter said, trying to calm him down. "Any engineer in the area with enough personal wealth is on her list. Consider yourself flattered. It just means you've been a successful businessman."

"You're always standing up for her," Waynewright said scornfully. "I can smell it a mile away. You better decide where your loyalties are."

Carter had decided but did not bother to broadcast them.

"You still didn't say what you're doing here," Waynewright said.

Something made Carter uneasy, nothing rational, but he did not feel comfortable admitting the truth. "I've just got to catch up on some progress reports for the ANC repairs, and then some odds and ends. My schedule's all out of whack. I'll be happy when this mess finally settles down."

"You're telling me," Waynewright grumbled. "So get going. I've got to finish."

"Sure, so do I."

Carter walked back down the hall to his office and locked the door behind him. He did not want anyone surprising him when he had Jackhammer's files on the screen. He did not know what the FBI might want to make public.

Carter put in his password, and once in the system, inserted the CD and ran another virus scan, just to be sure the FBI lab had not been careless. The disk came up clean, and Carter stared at the file names—read1, read2, read3, and read4, all of them AutoCAD. I guess the order's clear, Carter thought derisively, wondering why Jackhammer messed with four small files instead of just one. Carter clicked on the "read1" icon, and the myriad control buttons appeared around the edge of the screen. Then, on a black background, an array of red 3D I-beams sprung into view, pieced together to form letters:

DEAR FOUR SEASONS STUD:
THE END IS NEAR!
READ ON!

In the lower right-hand corner of the screen was a clip-art picture of a jackhammer. How cute, Carter thought. So what the hell do you have for us now?

Carter called up the next file and watched as a pyloned highway bridge flowed into view, all drawn with the complex 3D layering of a true design file. The heading said: THE TARGET. That got Carter's attention, but then his reaction wilted. Jackhammer would never tell us his plans, Carter told himself. This can't be the real target.

The next file showed the same bridge with bright green boxes placed within the steel rib of the deck, and at the joints between the deck and the pylons. The heading said: EXPLOSIVE PLACEMENTS. Carter rotated the drawing on screen and noticed how the bomb positioning would wipe out key supports and, given enough explosive power, bring the whole road deck down.

The last file came up with the large heading: BYE-BYE! The drawing showed pylon stumps with deck slabs lying in a blue wash at the base—a crude reference to water. A few clip-art cars had been thrown among the electronic ruins, like a child's collage of destruction.

So what bridge was this, Carter asked himself. It was not the Key Bridge or the Memorial Bridge—those had different layouts. Could it be the Roosevelt? But Carter did not recall their exact configuration. Carter flipped to Google and called up a photo of the Roosevelt Bridge, honing in on the deck depth and the proportions of the low-slung arches. He then counted the short support pylons, flipping back to the CAD drawing at every turn, and soon realized that this bridge—which connected Rosslyn to Washington and ran right by the Kennedy Center—looked like a dead ringer for Jackhammer's greeting card.

Carter began to explore the file structure to see if there might be attributes that could identify how Jackhammer had set up his software. If somebody ever got the chance to search a suspect's PC, they could match up configurations. On the primary bridge file, Carter made notes of the layering convention, and wondered if the detail library might hold any clues. He flipped to the first greeting page and was struck by the out-of-place jackhammer clip-art. Carter turned to his own CD clip-art collections and to the art stored on the firm network and searched for "jackhammer." He immediately found candidates and called them up one by one. He had gone through five of them when suddenly a prospect spilled into view. Jesus Christ, Carter thought. He flipped screens between one drawing and the other. Except for the sizing, the images looked identical. So where did this come from? Carter tracked down the network folder and saw that it stored the contents of a promotional CD from a firm hawking a whole library of construction-related art. So what does that give you, Carter asked himself. Well, it's something. It means Jackhammer either bought this clip art or got the same promotional CD. Wouldn't the software company know whom they had targeted in the Washington area? Yeah, Carter murmured to himself—probably every single construction contractor and A/E firm in town. But maybe not. It could narrow things down if the FBI ever got some search warrants to go after a suspect.

Carter felt some hope and realized that an expert—even the computer jocks at BWE—could dig a lot deeper into the CAD file configurations than he could.

Carter decided to send the files to the printer in reduced 8-1/2" by 11" format so he could show them to Taylor and Gentry. Before printing the first file, he temporarily screen-deleted "Dear Four Seasons Stud." He saw no purpose in printing out that part of the evidence.

Then the telephone rang. Carter jumped at the prospect of Michelle.

"Hello, this is Frank," Carter heard when he picked up.

"How's it going?" Carter said. He shifted himself back into sanity gear. "Have you heard what we've got?

"Yeah, my people showed me. A blown-up bridge. What do you make of it?"

"From what I can see, it's the Roosevelt bridge, or something close to it. But I can't imagine Jackhammer telling us in advance what he's planning to blow it up."

"I've got men heading there right now, but it looks like bullshit to me. The bridges have been patrolled for a couple of weeks. He couldn't have planted that many bombs without being noticed."

"So maybe he's just giving us a sample and it's a bridge in another city and it's ready to go right now, before anybody has time to think about it."

"I considered that and put out an alert to every major city with rivers on the east coast," Gentry said. "It turns out there's an awful lot of them."

Carter told him his experts had to go over these CAD files with a fine-tooth comb and check out the configurations and then see what kind of distribution the clip-art library got.

"We're already calling around to bring in the best analysts, and I assume you'll come by the office and give us a complete briefing. But there's another reason I called. Chairman Duncan is at it again, calling the crisis team together. Everybody's real stirred up about the water threat, so I'm going to do my civic duty and attend. I'd like you to come too. I've sent Michelle to track down everybody involved with that courier company—to do some useful work instead of politics."

So maybe there *is* a reason Michelle hasn't called, Carter thought to himself. "Sure I'll come. I've even got some printouts of Jackhammer's message to bring along." Carter paused. "I hope you don't mind that I sliced out that 'stud' reference. It doesn't seem to add much for general consumption."

"I don't know anything," Gentry said.

Carter remembered Gentry's earlier outburst. "So what time's the meeting?"

"In half an hour."

The crisis team could not come to meaningful conclusions. The Roosevelt Bridge threat had simply thrown a distraction in the works. No one, including Carter, believed Jackhammer would give a specific warning, and many suspected he was just trying to shift manpower away from the inspection of water mains and the stepped-up security for county buildings and natural gas lines. Jackhammer's earlier mention of other cities could just be a similar scam.

Drinking water became the focus. More than 600 demonstrators—a much bigger crowd than Melissa Campbell had ever managed to mobilize through her own appeals—had gathered on the plaza in front of the government building demanding safety for themselves and their children. Now it was fear for their own skins that got them to march, not solidarity with one woman's call to put on the pressure.

To keep people away from tap water, the county had already started distribution of free bottled water, but beyond that, the county leadership did not have a comfortable answer. Handley admitted that visual inspections of water main routes would never give one hundred percent security. The mains did not all lie under streets where the digging would be so clearly visible, and the digging could have been on spots that coincided with official, recorded repairs. Digging up every past sidewalk fix and pipe replacement just to be sure was not practical. The best safety solution, a complete cut-off of all water, would bring the whole county to its knees. And for how long? The only time limit would be Jackhammer's actual capture, and that was completely unpredictable, if he was ever caught. Jackhammer had given no indication he could repeat his water-supply attack, so on what grounds could the county take such drastic action? Now restored in Rosslyn, the water would have to stay on.

To give some protection, the county gathered drinking water samples from homes and businesses across Arlington County as often as the county testing lab, and several outside contractors, could keep up with the demand. To test specifically for Jackhammer's poison, the county placed on-site monitors in space donated by several apartment complexes and businesses. Every half hour, a technician put a sample of tap water through its paces.

Duncan did not like all the potential holes in all the scenarios but did not have anything better to offer. "God help us if this Jackhammer beats us to the punch," Duncan said.

21

That afternoon, Taylor hung up the phone in her Washington office and stared at the floor. Tuvia Goldblat, the Israeli international terrorist expert, was again passing through town and had asked to hear how the investigation was going, and whether the international connection was truly dead. Taylor knew better, and before the call ended, he had proved her right and asked her to dinner.

Taylor turned him down politely and hung up in good time, and after lifting her head, she tried to understand the feeling that had come over her. Being blatantly pursued by men while the investigation heated up irritated her, but she realized the only exception had become Scott. He had stayed in her thoughts all that Sunday with surprising intensity, and she found it difficult to resist the idea of running back to him. But that would be dangerous. He would probably take that as a "yes" to his declaration of love. She could not do that unless she was absolutely sure of herself. But how could she know? All her past relationships now looked so distant and strangely incomplete. For some of them, she could blame only herself. She had often felt some superiority to the men, a subsurface sense that within her love, she was using them merely for romantic and social pleasure. And now Scott felt different, and that scared her, because she also thought of the cancer and that future threat to his life, and it shocked her to think she was actually thinking that far ahead.

Taylor tried to get back to her work but found little left on her immediate agenda. The morning pursuit of the courier company had not yet produced anything useful. She had tracked down the company's owner in Silver Spring and convinced him to take her to his DC office and go over their package receipt data. It turned out Jackhammer's envelope had been dropped in a night delivery slot with a fifty-dollar bill attached, along with a wordprocessed note, printed on BWE stationary, stating that the envelope should be delivered to Scott Carter in Alexandria. The weekend clerk had considered the cash payment and healthy tip somewhat unusual, but not enough to refuse delivery, let alone to contact the authorities. Businesses always paid through the nose to get things sent before deadlines, even on Sunday. Everyone got behind schedule, and everyone had become spoiled that they could always make up for poor planning.

So far, Taylor had found no witnesses who had noticed a person stop at the after-hours drop-off slot. She was not surprised. It had happened in a nonresidential area, probably in the dark of the early morning, and if Jackhammer himself had done it, he would have known how to keep his identity hidden. Nevertheless, she had produced flyers to ask the few neighborhood residents for tips and called the local TV and radio stations to run the story with a tips-hot-line phone number.

It was now 4:20 p.m., and Taylor decided to wrap things up and head for home. She could no longer concentrate, and she did not want her thoughts to veer off to Scott. She hoped she could find some distraction with TV and dinner, but on the drive to her condominium, Taylor's resolution collapsed. The question of what to do about Scott had turned into a worrisome pleasure. Emotions knocked against logic as she unlocked her apartment door, and once inside, the rooms felt empty of all answers. After several vacant walks from kitchen to living room, Taylor decided to call a close friend. Mary had moved to San Diego six months ago after getting married, and on leaving, she had challenged Taylor to find a man and stop hopping around. Taylor had considered her friend's tone too traditional and confining, but she wondered what Mary would say now. Maybe Mary would give her the courage to listen to what her heart seemed to be telling her.

The phone in San Diego rang for a long time, then kicked to the answering machine. Taylor could feel the abandonment grow, and she was ready to hang up after leaving a message when a woman finally cut in.

"Is that you Mary?" Taylor asked.

"Michelle?"

"Yes. It's me!"

"How great to hear from you!" Mary said. Her voice sounded bright and free, as though a winter in the California sun had already rubbed off on her. "I was out in the garden and had to rush in. It's been so long since we talked."

"It must have been before the Jackhammer case broke. I've been pretty tied up and distracted."

"I won't hold it against you," Mary said. "Oh my god, I even saw you on TV! You were standing at one of the press conferences. It's a terrible thing, this business, but I felt like I knew a celebrity."

"Sure, dream on. So how's life been?"

"Everything's been great. Bill's career is really taking off with the film production group. He made the right move.

And we've got a great house near the coast. I was just outside in our garden. Can you believe it, I've gotten to like the smell of manure."

"Are you kidding me? California must be getting to you."

"Oh, don't be so square. It feels great digging around with vegetables. You should try it."

"Sure, Mary. So are you working?"

"Well, I was going to. Then something got in the way." She hesitated. "My god, I haven't even told my mother yet. Should I tell you?"

"Give me a break. I'll come out and arrest you if you don't."

"All right. Can you believe it. I'm pregnant!"

"Get outta here!"

"What more can I say?"

"That's wonderful! How long?"

"I'm in the second month. It wasn't exactly planned, but Bill's excited. We thought: What's the difference having a baby now instead of a year from now like we'd thought?"

"I'm so happy for you!" Taylor said. She laughed. "Do you remember all the times we'd talk about the jerks we'd known. We sometimes wondered whether this would ever happen."

"Sure, but it did. Oh, I wish Bill could be at home more—he's got a lot of pressure at work—but I can't ask for everything. So what about you?"

Taylor hesitated. "Well, that's partly why I called. You see, I've met this guy . . ."

"Go on."

"Well, apparently the guy's crazy about me."

"Get to the point. Guys have always been crazy about you. Where do *you* stand?"

"Oh Mary, I think I'm actually starting to fall in love with the guy, but I'm afraid."

"About what?"

"He's had a bout with cancer."

"Oh, no." Mary's voice dropped off. "Do you mean he has something terminal?"

"You can't really say that. It's malignant melanoma, the worst kind of skin cancer. They've been able to remove it the two times it's cropped up, but you never know when it's going to come back or spread to an organ. It's like living with a sword strung over your head."

A doubt had entered Mary's voice. "Oh, Michelle. I don't know. Have you already told this guy that you love him?"

"Not directly, but he must feel a little hope."

"You mean you slept with him?"

"Yes, once. In fact, last night."

"Who is he? What does he do?"

"He's the engineer who's been working on the investigation with me. You may have seen him on the news. He saved a group of people from the elevator when Jackhammer blew up the ANC building."

"Oh, I'm sure he's a wonderful guy," Mary said, "but Michelle, you have to think about this. Are you sure you're not just feeling sorry for him, wanting to please him because he loves you so much?"

"I'd thought about that, but no, I don't think so."

"Everybody wants to be generous to good people, but, Michelle, you have to put yourself first when it comes to love. Think about it, just because a guy's crazy about you doesn't mean you have to reciprocate, no matter how much you break his heart. A person would be a fool to do that. You'd have to agree."

"I would," Taylor said somewhat plaintively, "but I can't say that's the case."

"But you haven't moved ahead with this relationship. Am I right? So it's all up to you, and think of what you'll have to go through. You'll be committing yourself to someone . . . if I understand you correctly . . . to someone who, in a worst case, might not be alive in a few years."

"But he could also live a full life," Michelle protested quietly. "The odds are good for that too."

"But you're so beautiful and smart," Mary said. "You could have any man you wanted. You're not getting any younger."

"I know, but I can't see myself being so rational in all this. Did you ever read about Richard Feynman, the famous physicist, you know, on the Manhattan Project? I always found it touching how this guy married a woman who had tuberculosis. He did it against the protests of his parents, and Feynman moved out to the lab in Los Alamos and she stayed in Albuquerque and they were together until she died."

"You're sounding dangerously romantic," Mary said. "Feelings can change. You have to look hard before you commit yourself to something like this. You can't sacrifice your life just because it feels noble. A few months from now it's not going to feel the same. The Camelot feeling wears off. Trust me."

"I *am* looking hard," Michelle said in a quiet frustration, "and that's why it's so difficult. My feelings just don't jibe with all these reasonable arguments."

"Isn't that always the case? And that's why you have friends. Somebody on the outside can take a more balanced look at all this. I'm just thinking of your own good."

"Oh, I know you're right," Taylor said, trying to convince herself, but she was inwardly distressed at the unexpected tack of her friend's advice. Hadn't Mary always been such a booster for romanticism and marriage? "It *would* seem crazy to latch on to someone who might not live. When I think about it, after all the men who've come on to me, it's hard to believe it would then come to this. It does seem absurd."

"I don't want to sound harsh," Mary said, "but you've got it right. You've got to put this behind you."

Taylor nodded to herself, finding it hard to speak. "I suppose I do," she said finally. But her own words felt like a punch in the gut.

Late that afternoon, Carter sat in the den with the TV turned to the Spurs and Lakers, but he was thinking of Michelle and making excuses for why she had not called him. Gentry had sent her on an assignment, he told himself, and that could take a whole day. She was not going to interrupt for a courtesy call. Besides, she had to be a little confused about the situation, probably embarrassed because Gentry had caught them. That's natural, Carter thought. She's just got to sort things out and then she'll get back to you. Give her time.

In the fourth quarter, the phone suddenly rang, but when he picked up, Carter's heart immediately sank. It was not Michelle; it was Edward Babcock.

"Scott, sorry to bother you," Babcock said, charging ahead as though calling Carter at home were completely natural. "Meeting you yesterday wetted my appetite. I'd like to discuss some of the dangers the county faces, get your perspective since you're up to your ears in this mess. Hell, despite our differences, I can probably trust your judgment as much as anybody's. I've got my doubts about those jokers at Public Works. They're sitting on their hands. If you take away the few friends I still have over there, they all look at me like some rough-neck outsider they can just push aside."

And I don't blame them, Carter thought. "What did you have in mind?" he asked, almost welcoming the distraction.

"How about this evening at my place, in about an hour, or a little later if you need more time. I've invited over Melissa Campbell as well.

"Melissa Campbell?"

"Sounds crazy, I'll admit," Babcock said. "I thought I could maybe use her to get the county's attention. They won't listen to an over-the-hill engineer, but they may listen to this woman, even if she is a crackpot. If I feed her the information, she could take it and have an impact."

"I'm not going to commit to any kind of publicity plot to embarrass Public Works," Carter said. "I'm working with them, you know."

"Plot? Give me a break," Babcock said. "I'm just out to protect people, no different from you. Besides, you wouldn't be part of it. I'd just get your input. You don't have to tell Ms. Campbell anything. You could keep us on the straight and narrow, be the honest broker."

"Should Michelle Taylor come along?"

"Aw, now you're getting too official. She's part of the insiders. That's the last thing I want."

"Let me think about it," Carter said. "I don't know yet if I'll have another commitment. Meetings come up all the time."

"Don't accept one," Babcock said. "I know you want to stop this public works terrorism just like the rest of us. You call me as soon as you can."

"All right," Carter said. "I'll let you know."

Carter hung up the phone and began to walk toward the kitchen to get a new beer, when a breeze of uncertainty suddenly grazed his thoughts, like a shadow passing over a lake at sunset, chilling him. He did not really know what it was until he opened the refrigerator and the light inside startled him. When he thought a moment longer, he went cold. "Public works terrorism," he said to himself, closing the refrigerator door.

Carter found it difficult to believe the possible import of those words. He stood motionless for a moment, searching his memory, then began walking to his study, first slowly, then faster and faster, until finally he had dashed through the door and brought out the box of newspaper clippings related to the Jackhammer case. He had collected them since the beginning, thinking he might have a use for them some day—he did not know for whom, maybe some future family—and now he rifled through the box, skimming through every article to see whether someone had used the expression "public works terrorism." He could not recall that they had, and as he went through the now yellowing newspapers and the dog-eared sheets from the national news magazines, he could not find those exact words anywhere. He then ran to his computer and Googled the phrase and found it only in some government reports and what for him were a few obscure blogs.

Carter knew where he had heard the words. Jackhammer had called himself 'the great public works terrorist' in his last phone call, and before that? Carter did not have to look far. It was the call just before that, when Jackhammer had used the phone booth near Carter's house. Carter remembered asking Gentry not to make that Jackhammer tape public. Gentry had obliged and the phrase had not gotten into the regular news feeds.

But that could all be a coincidence, Carter told himself. The expression was not some special code. It was regular English. He had probably used it himself. He was surprised that so few in the media had used it. Babcock could have come up with it on his own, like the writers in those blogs. That was certainly the explanation, but Carter could not put aside the troubling connections, how Babcock had appeared on Taylor's list of wealthy local engineers, how he had worked at the Arlington Public Works Department. Jesus Christ, Carter thought, was it possible?

No, Carter said to himself. Why would Babcock be campaigning against Public Works to find Jackhammer if he was the guy himself? That made no sense. What did make sense, Carter now realized, was to accept Babcock's invitation just to see what might come out of it. Talking to Babcock was no fun, but why not take the opportunity to keep his ears open. Besides, maybe he could save Melissa Campbell from being used by this man.

Carter searched his computer directories to get a jump on where Babcock lived, calling up an old ASCE committee roster and then cross-referencing it on the web. He found a home address in Rosslyn. OK, Carter thought, wondering if that should mean anything. He jotted down the street number, wondering if the address was still valid, and called Taylor. She did not pick up.

Carter decided to leave a message. He told her about where he was headed and a short recap of his speculations. He emphasized that any suspicions were incredibly far-fetched but that he thought she should know.

Carter stepped out the back door into the shadowed spring breeze of the garden, the last sun just catching the highest leaves of the oak. He was still trying to come to grips with his thoughts. OK, what if you wanted to find out if Babcock was the man, as crazy as it seems, what would you need to know? One thing immediately jumped out—get a look at Babcock's computer and see if Jackhammer's greeting card

CAD files were still there, if Babcock were careless enough to leave them hanging around. So what are you going to do, ask to play solitaire on Babcock's PC? Not exactly feasible.

Carter walked back inside and called Todd Kirkland. Kirkland had a habit of screening his calls, and the answering machine had kicked in for Carter's message when Kirkland finally picked up.

"I thought you were some charity guy," Kirkland said. "They can bleed off your whole salary with their sob stories."

"Well, that's not the point of my call," Carter said. "I actually want your technical advice. It's related to this whole Jackhammer case."

"I'm all ears," Kirkland said, apparently still chewing on dinner.

"If you wanted to find out the contents of somebody's hard drive, what would you need to know to hack into his computer?"

"Why, have you got a suspect?"

"That's beside the point at the moment."

"Oh, I get it. Hush-hush."

"Call it what you want," Carter said impatiently. "We're just talking theory here. What would you want to know?"

"I'd want to know the guy's IP address, and to help get that, his operating system, his Internet provider, and the browser he's using. Hell, while you're at it, get me his password too, but I assume you're not talking about making this too easy."

"The person's email address could give you the provider, and someone might be able to get the operating system and browser he's using. If you had that, do you think you could get into the guy's PC?"

"That's not a lot to go on. I'd still want his IP address."

"So how would you do that?"

"The easiest might be sending him an email that he's likely to open. I could make it look like it's from a friendly source. Who might be such a source?"

"Let's say it was me."

"I could imitate you any day. If he opens a link I give him, that could pull his IP address. Then when he's online, I should be able to get into his computer—and get arrested for it."

"What if his online security is top notch?"

"Better than BWE's?"

"You've got a point."

"Who says this suspect hasn't obliterated the files you're looking for?"

"Maybe he has," Carter said.

"Of course, the guy could be good at making bombs but be totally unsophisticated when it comes to computers. Face it, I've seen old-timers, respected engineers, who didn't even know there's a wastebasket!"

"Well, we have no idea, do we. But the first step would be finding the basic information. Hacking would be a later decision."

"Are you asking me to hack into somebody's computer?"

"I'm not asking anything, right now," Carter said. "The FBI may want to take the lead on this. I just want to know the options."

"I'm a respectable white hat hacker," Kirkland said, "but I'll have to admit, this sounds like fun—Scott Carter asking me to break the law to stop a terrorist. That's something for one of those engineering ethics columns."

"Don't suck me into ethics," Carter said. "One step at a time."

Half an hour later, Carter called Babcock to confirm their meeting and to get Babcock's address. It matched what he had found earlier. Carter then grabbed his wallet off the kitchen counter and headed outside. He walked across the street to where his FBI bodyguard had parked. The bodyguard got out of his car when he saw Carter coming.

"What's up?" the man said. His name was Richard Sanchez and served as Carter's weekend protection.

Carter looked around to make sure no pedestrians were passing. "Listen, this is all going to seem a little crazy, but there's this engineer I know, Ed Babcock, and I'm wondering whether he might somehow be involved in this Jackhammer thing. I've got no proof. It's totally crazy, but he's invited me over to talk shop, so I've accepted just to feel the guy out."

"You're not going to confront him with it, I suppose?"

"No, not even close. Ed's just trying to get Arlington Public Works to pay attention to him more and wants to pass some ideas by me. That's going to be the extent of it."

"Don't you want to call the Bureau?"

"No, this isn't anything official. But for good measure, I've left Michelle Taylor a message. I also figured you'd be following me. When I get there, you can wait out front."

"Are you putting yourself in any danger? It's my job to prevent that."

"Not a chance. I know the guy. It's just a simple meeting like all the others I've already had with him."

"So how do you expect to get anything out of it?"

"I'm just playing it by ear, seeing if there might be a way to find out something about his computer."

"I can't physically stop you," Sanchez said, "but I don't exactly like the idea of you doing this alone."

"It wouldn't be natural if I dragged somebody else along."

"All right. How long do you think this meeting will last?"

"Maybe an hour."

"OK, if I don't hear from you after an hour, I'll come upstairs and say hello."

Carter thought about it for a moment. "I guess that can't hurt," he said. "There's no secret about me having a bodyguard."

22

Carter wondered how many times he had been forced to drive up the George Washington Parkway with a storm of uncertainty in his head, but he could not remember racing through this much expectation. Maybe he had the chance to put this whole Babcock speculation to rest if he could just fish for some information. It shouldn't be hard to steer Babcock's conversation to computer use, to talk about getting in touch via email and mention something about security glitches with web browsers and Outlook, to see if he bites, but Carter just had to keep things natural. Don't push it. Wait till it flows your way, and then you can serve it to Michelle on a silver platter. Todd Kirkland wouldn't need to be the hacker. The FBI could do that. Hell, if this works out and one suspect is crossed off the list or you actually get an arrest, you can let Michelle take all the credit. Of course, the jackpot rests on the flimsy premise that Jackhammer's turn of a common phrase is frighteningly rare. That seemed like creative paranoia. He did not know whether, in the end, the FBI would even want to follow up.

Carter turned northwest off the parkway, past the Iwo Jima Memorial, and pulled into Rosslyn, the high-rises blocking the last western twilight. Babcock's condominium was the first in the row of buildings, and Carter drove farther up the road and found a parking space after circling the block once. His bodyguard pulled up next to him.

"I'll just stand in the entrance driveway and stay in the car," Sanchez said. "If they give me any flack, I'll wait across the street."

"Since when are they going to kick out the FBI?"

"Because I hadn't intended to tell them who I am."

"So what time have you got?" Carter asked.

"7:08."

"OK, I guess we've synchronized our watches. Kind of like Boy Scouts."

"Those were the days," Sanchez said.

"Wish me luck," said Carter, not hinting how seriously he meant it.

Carter walked down the sidewalk, quickening his pace to ease the sudden new tension, and entered the luxury foyer and its bank of intercoms. He scanned the list for Babcock and entered the code.

"Yes?" a gruff voice answered.

"Ed, it's Scott Carter."

"Come on up," Babcock said. "I'll buzz you in."

Carter heard the shrill grate of the door lock, like a misfiring dentist's drill, and pushed the glass door open. He looked around to see whether his bodyguard was still there, but the agent was parked to the side, out of view. An elevator stood open, and Carter stepped in and punched the tenth floor. The elevator began to rise.

Carter kept reviewing his conversation options, playing the parts in his head, and as he thought, he suddenly looked forward to meeting Melissa Campbell. He had not seen her since she had barged into the board chairman's office and disrupted their emergency meeting. He had been both impressed and shaken by the look in her eyes. He thought it might be interesting to learn more about what made her tick. She had garnered quite a following with her tenacity.

When the elevator opened, Carter checked the numbers on the wall sign and followed the arrow toward Babcock's condominium. Before Carter got there, Babcock stepped into the hall. He wore a blue blazer, a white polo shirt, and gray slacks, looking ruggedly handsome, like an aging golfer who could still put his weight into a 250-yard drive. He had the smile and the handshake of a hustler.

"For a while, I'd pretty much written you off," Babcock said. "I didn't think you really had much taste for my opinions."

"Generally too busy," Carter lied, retrieving his hand from Babcock's.

"Well, you ought to be interested," Babcock said. "You remember when I came to your office? Didn't I tell you this Jackhammer had plans to raise all kinds of hell? And look what he did with the water system! You guys need to listen to an old bull like me!"

"Well, that's why I'm here," Carter said, letting Babcock show him inside.

Babcock led Carter through a small foyer into a dimly lit living room—dark walnut furniture and smoke-gray carpet. A high bookshelf covered a wall, and various bronze Remingtons—each with a straining horse—stood on the credenzas and tables. On the walls, Carter could make out framed portraits of Rough Rider Theodore Roosevelt and General George Patton. The whole showed the unnatural neatness of a single man who could afford a maid to clean well and often.

"Make yourself at home," Babcock said, motioning toward the couch.

Carter stopped at the shelves and admired all the engineering books, from mechanical to electrical to civil. These were not just leftovers from college, but more recent editions. "That's quite a collection," Carter said. "Do you still keep up?"

"I dabble," Babcock said, stepping toward the shelves himself. "But there's never enough time."

Carter walked to the end of the bookshelf, scanning the titles as if to compliment Babcock's taste, and noticed an open door to a study. A computer on the desk had a standard Windows screen saver shifting its logo across the black. Carter turned his attention back to the books. He wondered how unsophisticated Babcock might be. People who knew the minimum of how things worked would probably have loaded their own screen saver. On the other hand, maybe Ed just didn't care about graphics.

"Hey, I used this finite element analysis textbook in college," Carter said, shifting Babcock's attention. Carter still had his mind on the PC.

"I got it as some joke door prize when I served on this engineering school advisory board," Babcock said. "Way back when, we outside practitioners helped give input to the old fogy academics. That was a pointless piece of garbage. The professors did what the hell they wanted in the end anyway. We were just put there for show so they could act like they were letting the real world into civil engineering education. There were even articles in the engineering press about it, making it look like some great new movement. What a joke."

"Can't really comment on that one," Carter said, "but I do know that everyone hated that course when I was in college. In fact, the professor knew it was so notorious that he gave extra credit for the best summer vacation picture that featured the book. Heck, in the fall you'd come into the class and see the book impaled on the spear of a scuba diver or have a bunch of beautiful babes in bikinis surrounding some guy reading the book on the beach. I'll have to hand it to the professor. He made us put the book to good use!"

"Sounds like my kind of guy," Babcock said with a grin. "So why don't you sit down? What'll you drink? Is scotch on the rocks OK?"

"Sure," Carter said.

Carter stayed on his feet and got one quick glance toward the computer before Babcock reappeared. "Hey, are you going to sit down or not?" Babcock asked.

Carter lowered himself onto the couch and accepted the drink, wondering where his suspicions had come from. This was the same old bastard he had always known.

With a grunt, Babcock dropped into the chair opposite. He took a big swallow and eyed his glass. "Who knows how many more of these I'll still get to enjoy. The way the doctors are these days, they want to cut you off completely from everything worthwhile." Babcock sneered. "I suppose scotch doesn't hurt your melanoma."

The reference surprised Carter, but he let it slide. "The doctors never mentioned it."

"They probably will," Babcock said, already downing the last swallow of what Carter had noticed was a double. "But now's the time to no longer care." Babcock grinned with a biting, yet far-away indifference.

Carter did not know how to react and changed the subject. "I was actually looking forward to meeting Melissa Campbell. I'll have to say, you two are about the oddest couple I could imagine. When do you expect her?"

"I don't know why you'd want to see her. She's a crazed raving lunatic."

Carter hesitated. "What happened to Ms. Campbell being your partner to warn the city?"

"That was all bullshit," Babcock said. "She's not coming."

"OK," said Carter, "I can't say I understand."

A weary, offended grin stole across Babcock's face, as though he could finally throw off conformity. "I'm sure you don't," he said, staring at Carter. "Maybe you don't realize *you* disgust me too."

That was enough for Carter. He set down his drink and began to stand up. "I don't have to take this."

Babcock laughed and pulled a 9 millimeter Beretta from his inside blazer pocket and pointed it at Carter, motioning him to sit down. "Oh yes you do," Babcock said, quickly pulling a four-inch silencer from his outside pocket and screwing it to the end of the pistol, keeping aim the whole time.

Carter stared at the weapon and lowered himself to the couch.

"Cat got your tongue?" Babcock said.

Carter took a deep breath, his heart pounding. His disbelief had not yet processed the connections. "What the hell are you doing, Ed?"

Babcock laughed, the guffaw of someone who enjoys the pleasure of seeing a victim squirm. "Why call me Ed? Maybe there's another name that would be more impressive."

OK, Carter thought frantically, if this is Jackhammer, how did he suddenly get suspicious? I didn't hint at anything.

"You're always so cooperative and generous," Babcock said. "It makes a trap so much easier. And now it's got you dead."

"I don't know what you're talking about," Carter said, trying to steal time. The simplicity of his original plan now looked like the foolishness of a child.

"Oh, yes you do," Babcock said. "Or your FBI broad would have told you soon enough. You see, Special Agent Taylor was snooping through everybody's financial records and I realized that pretty soon she was going to stumble on a little indiscretion of mine. One of my contacts blew it and left a connection to me. I could have wrung his neck, but now it doesn't matter anymore. I'm just about done, and I couldn't resist bringing you in for the grand finale. I was telling myself: Now wouldn't it be fitting to have Scott Carter take part in Jackhammer's final act, to rub his nose in it, like you do with a dog in its own shit for potty training? But you know, there's always that side that wants to be prudent." Babcock chuckled. "But the prudent thing just doesn't pack the same punch!"

"So this invitation was a set-up from the start."

"It worked, didn't it? And now I can play it however I like. I can kill you right here after I tell you what's up, or if the coast is clear, I can take you along."

Carter swallowed. Why hadn't he told Sanchez to come up after just half an hour? What was he trying to prove with this caper? Impress Michelle? Carter tried to regroup and show some self-control. Maybe that would keep Babcock talking. "You know, I'd actually grown suspicious. That's why I accepted your invitation."

"How could you possibly have been suspicious?" Babcock asked, a growl of offense in his voice.

"You said 'public works terrorism' on the phone. Those were Jackhammer's words."

Babcock scowled in disbelief. "So, a trivial carelessness . . . I guess it had to be. For most of the important stuff, I'd covered my tracks." Babcock let out a resigned chuckle. "But how convenient. You get suspicious just as I set my curtain call. I guess the fates are watching over me. Greater forces have thrown in their support." Babcock returned to a snide, focused stare at Carter.

Carter tried to push any tremor from his voice. "So what do you have planned?"

"Not so fast," Babcock said. "Let's just hang out for a bit, chat a little, sort everything out. No need to rush things and make mistakes."

Carter did not see an opening to jump Babcock, even if he had taken the self-defense course that, like so many other things, he had put off because he was always too busy. Any lunge would have put a bullet in his chest.

Babcock waved his gun and ordered Carter to lie face down on the couch, then pulled a pair of handcuffs from his left jacket pocket. "Hands behind your back," Babcock ordered with the same off-hand dominance of telling a secretary to type a letter. "Any funny business and I blow your head off. No sweat off my back. What's one more murder?"

Carter felt the gun barrel cold on the base of his skull and the metal handcuffs closing cool around his wrists. He was quite sure Babcock would kill him, either now or later. With everything in the open, Babcock could not afford to let him live. So, Carter thought, when it all came down to it, he had wanted to be the hero for Michelle, but this was not what he had had in mind.

Babcock sat back down in the chair opposite the couch. "Sit up," Babcock ordered. He again motioned with his gun barrel.

Carter rolled to his side and struggled to right himself. He cursed himself for not looking at his watch before getting handcuffed. Within less than an hour Sanchez would be checking in. But what could Sanchez do? As soon as Babcock sensed trouble, he could still get his kicks by bumping off his prisoner. You've got to keep Babcock talking, Carter thought. Babcock seemed ready to oblige.

"So did you ever get suspicious before this?" Babcock asked. "My front held up pretty well, didn't it?"

"I've got to hand it to you. Before today, I couldn't point to anything."

"Good. I don't like sloppiness."

"Are you going to explain why you're doing all this?" Carter asked. "We may have had our differences in the past, but I always had respect for what you'd accomplished. How did killing people suddenly become one of your ideals? When it comes down to it, you've written off your country."

Babcock's eyes gleamed in fierce amusement. "You're just so goddamn naive, Scott. You're looking at the fringes instead of the core, the rotten core. Look at our degenerate society. Everybody's become weak-willed. Everybody just turns off logic and says the scum of society deserves to have the upper hand." Babcock's voice began to tremble, and his eyes suddenly grew cold. "Nobody stands up for what's right because they're afraid some whining liberals are going to raise their cry-baby ruckus! Since when did the goddamn complainers' vision suddenly become the standard? When did they ever feel the power of a smoking bulldozer piling up earth? The rock becomes part of your own body. You're building the foundation for prosperity. You're lifting up the country and carrying it on your back to the mountaintop. You've worked out all the variables and made all the calculations and you've blasted your own personal stamp on this new backbone of reality. Have you ever seen the sunrise come up on a construction site? Have you? You get the shadows cutting across the concrete molds and you see we've raised monoliths greater than any Stonehenge, because these are going to power our society. I had that all in my hands, and then they took it away!"

Babcock grew quieter, more icily bitter, his eyes practically punching Carter with their anger. "I had all that and then these blasted bastards told me—*me*—I can no longer build with my own two hands and my own brain. Do you realize the power I packed? Do you realize that even as I was running my business I'd get down into all the complex design issues? I don't think anyone knew the brains I brought to the table. I could design everyone into the ground, *while* I kept the business going. Do you realize the energy that takes, the sheer will? And what did they do? They took away my P.E. license! They told me I couldn't put my stamp on anything. These sick little people with their shriveled little souls thought they were superior and could call me out for plan stamping. They were just out to get me because the weak can't stand the strong. They have to beat down the heroes so the mice can rule. I could have reapplied for the license later, but I was never going to come crawling back to them. I'd never give them that pleasure!"

"When was this?" Carter asked. "I never heard about it."

"About six years ago. I worked the system to keep it quiet. I could still lead my own business if I played it right, but they thought I'd just rolled over with the rest. It didn't enter their heads that I didn't need a license to destroy. I could still show them what I pack without their chicken-shit consent. I could still show them. Everyone! The whole stinking society!"

"Is that where my plan stamping run-in came from?"

"Yeah, just to give you a taste," Babcock said with a morbid sneer. "From the beginning you fit the bill so perfectly to keep in the limelight—both for good and bad. What better high-profile speechmaker to let people know about the tough, leadership side of engineering? Once you were thrown in the spotlight—pure chance, mind you—I couldn't resist milking you as the poster child. But you also have your rotten, creeping liberal ideas that make me want to puke. That's why it was so much fun making you squirm, because I started to see you as a symbol of everything gone to hell, of putting poison in the heads of Congress and the state legislatures. Now, to build the foundation for what makes our country great, we spend years filing environmental impact statements. Years! We have to sit down at these public hearings and hear a bunch of psycho snivelers talk like they wanted to go back and live in teepees. They want to shovel under all our progress! They want to stop the great works of mankind to save a snail darter! When I see that, I want to take a knife and skin them alive, skin *you* alive, hang you up in the forest so you can let the animals of your sweet environment eat your flesh. That'll serve everybody right, the wolves and the lions crushing the snail darter. We're supposed to be the wolves and the lions, Scott. We need to stand up for power and progress and control over chaos. I never would have believed I'd say something good about those commie Chinese, but hell, they don't cut off their own balls like we do. If they've got a vision of what needs to be built to raise their country to the next level, they goddamn build it! They push all the whiners out of the way. They bury them so mankind can climb to a new zenith. I'll give them credit for that, even though it makes me choke to think they're the ones moving forward and not us. And here, in the country that was supposed to be the model of prosperity and force for the earth, where are the heroes like me? We're made invisible! They try to emasculate us. They'll say an architect built that bridge and not me, an engineer. They'll lump my name with any goddamn scum of a repairman. I'm at a hotel and my doorknob doesn't work and they say they'll send up the 'building engineer.' I'm ready to go down and strangle that receptionist. Wring her neck! But oh, they like to shovel all that money to the doctors and lawyers and put them up as the only career any smart person would ever want to go after. Lawyers! Liars and cheats and bloodsuckers, and society puts them out there as the beacon for their children, the sign of success!" Jackhammer's chest heaved as he pulled in some air, unable to let up. "I won't take it! I won't take being mocked by crackpots at public hearings, like I'm some kind of criminal, when those naggers are the criminals. We're approaching the sewer as a country. Even engineering, where you'd think logic would make its last stand, has started to sink into the gutter. I hear engineer leaders kowtowing to intelligent growth and livable communities, these sickening buzzwords of slime and surrender, as though our whole purpose was supposed to make people feel good and become stinking spoiled brats. Hell, even on the technical side the young engineer upstarts are all becoming a bunch of slackers who don't know what it means to design something. They just plug their numbers into the design software and get their drawings. They have no feel for their solutions, no idea of what works and what doesn't. When I was young we slugged it out with the real calculations. We had the mud and steel in our hands and in our guts. We knew in our bones what things should look like and could depend on ourselves to see if the results fit the hard reality. Now every corner of society has this rot, and it needs a shock to reverse it. It needs a bolt of lightning to blow out the mold and start fresh. I'm one who can start the process. Others can then follow, and the few people who die on the way are no worse off than in the death they're already living."

Carter was breathing hard from this verbal attack, frightened by how everything had become so twisted and false. He worked to keep his voice even, still just trying to stretch things and survive. "But it doesn't make sense, Ed. By hounding me, you just put yourself at risk. You just gave yourself more chances to screw up, more clues for the FBI to check out."

"Hell, yes!" Babcock exclaimed. "Just like right now! For all I know you've got an FBI battalion waiting outside, just itching to come in. But it's like going to the big ball game.

Sure, the game's the main thing, but who can resist the hot dogs and the beer? You just gotta have those sidelights when there's a break in the action." His eyes turned steely. "And what the hell. In the end, it doesn't matter. I happen to have a death sentence on my head. The doctors say I shouldn't even be alive. But I guess destiny had something else in mind and wanted me to fulfill my mission, to take something great to my grave. I don't give a horse's ass what happens after this. They could put me in jail for life and I'd only be able to serve a few months! Hell, if they condemned me to death, the fucking bastards wouldn't have a chance to give me the injection in time! The bureaucracy would have me sitting on death row for years, eating up taxpayer money. And then some pinko lawyer would try to stay the execution." Babcock was nearly trembling in anger. "Don't you see where this country is headed? We can't even kill the child rapists and the drug dealers! We act like they're worth keeping around! Man oh man, I'd rather die in an FBI shoot-out than even see that sickness firsthand." A faint smile returned to Jackhammer's face. "That means I don't fear what might happen, or what tricks you might pull. I'll just blow your head off and not give it a second thought. Maybe you ought to keep that in mind as you witness my final masterwork."

Carter simply nodded, but he had to buy more time. He guessed Babcock would be proud of his technical toys. "How'd you manage the voice synthesizer on the phone calls? Is that something you built?"

"Absolutely," Babcock said. "Pieced it together from components I bought from an online electronics catalog. All these years I've been studying electronics and mechanical design just for these opportunities. It's your corny Engineers Week theme taken to the hilt: Turning Ideas Into Reality!"

"I won't knock the feeling."

"Well, you're no slouch of a designer. I'll give you credit for that. But you lack depth. You don't have the range from mechanical to electrical to civil. I'd like to know how many engineers out there could accomplish what I've done. How many?"

"I certainly haven't met them," Carter said.

"Are you trying to be cute?"

Carter shook his head. "Not at all."

"Just watch yourself," Babcock said, waving the gun barrel up and down.

"What about our ASCE Section meeting?" Carter asked, trying desperately to come up with topics in this sham of a conversation. "You were there with me. How'd you also phone the place at the same time?"

"You can't figure that out for yourself?" Babcock asked derisively.

"I could take a stab. You rigged up some kind of recording."

"Well, that was difficult, wasn't it? Of course, for the phone call that the restaurant personnel got, I needed a real person to interact. But you see, when you got on the call, you wouldn't know that the first voice had been different."

"Makes sense," Carter said.

A knock on the door startled them both. Carter did not know what time it was, but he knew one hour had not passed.

"Since when is security letting people up without my OK?" Babcock grumbled. He now whispered to Carter, his voice hard. "Get in the other chair where I can still see you." Babcock pointed his gun at a recliner in the corner. It would put Carter out of sight from anyone standing outside. Carter stood up and moved. "One sound and you're dead," Babcock whispered. Carter nodded.

Babcock walked to the door, keeping his eyes on Carter, then looked through the peephole. A smile spread across his face, and he winked at Scott.

Babcock put the gun behind his back, kept his hand on the trigger, and opened the door's dead-bolt lock. He then swung the door halfway open.

"How nice to see you Miss. Taylor," Babcock said, his voice ingratiating but projecting surprise. "What brings you here?"

"I wanted to review a few findings. I thought you might have some insights."

"Hell, are you here to ask the same questions Scott already did?"

"Was he here?" Taylor asked.

"He came and went. We discussed a few of my concerns. I guess you'll want to hear the whole thing yourself, so you might as well come in."

Carter tensed. He saw what would happen. Michelle would come in and get cuffed and executed just like him. "It's Jackhammer!" Carter cried. "He's got a gun!"

Babcock ducked sideways and rammed the door closed, knocking the dead-bolt in place. Carter heard a shot, but he immediately realized Michelle had not hit her mark.

Carter stood up, ready to run to the other room, but found himself staring down a gun barrel aimed at his chest.

"Good-bye, Mr. Carter," Babcock said, his lips shaking from rage, his fingers poised to pull the trigger. "You did not behave."

Carter threw himself to the floor behind the couch. He heard Babcock's footsteps approach, like the slow-motion tick of a clock, deepened by the eerie, other-worldly pace. At each tick, Carter tensed for the expected shot, wave-like bursts in which he faced death and then took a quick breath of life before dying again.

"This is very disappointing," Babcock said from above. "I'd so much wanted to kill you for pulling a stunt like that.

But now it looks like I have to use you just a little bit longer. A damn shame."

Carter listened but did not quite know whether the words were meant for him or for a character in a play he had already left. A kick in the ribs set Carter straight.

"Get up!" Babcock ordered. "We're going for a little drive. Your body should give me adequate protection. Consider yourself honored."

Carter worked his way to his feet, realizing how difficult such a simple maneuver became without the push or balance of his arms. By the time he had made it, he was sweating, not from exertion, but from fear.

Babcock grabbed him by the arm. "OK," he said, pushing the gun in the back of Carter's head. "We're going out that door before your broad calls in reinforcements. One false move and I shoot her, and then I shoot you. It's all very simple."

Carter did not answer but let himself be shoved to the door. "Your lover-boy's coming out!" Babcock shouted. He undid the lock and pushed Carter through. Carter saw Taylor at the end of the short hall. She had ducked partially behind the corner, her gun pointed right at him, and everything telescoped to just one goal—to be with Michelle one more time.

"All right, Miss. Taylor," Babcock said. He was now out in the hall, holding Carter as a screen. "Call off any back-up right now or I blow your lover-boy's head off. This is the end of the line for me, so I don't care who I take with me. If I notice just one other agent or cop snooping around or following us in his car, Scott's gone. Let's go lady, let me see you make that call."

Taylor did not hesitate. She pulled out her cell phone and told Sanchez to stay put and to have Gentry's team stay clear. She told him that any failure to follow her orders could result in a hostage, Scott Carter, being killed. She repeated that twice, loud, to make sure both Sanchez and Babcock understood—and to impress on herself what had become her only priority.

In front of her, the elevator opened, and Taylor shouted for anyone to stay back, but a man heard too late, already a step outside, and Babcock fired and dropped him. The silencer gave off no more than a muffled puff, but Carter saw the pool of blood spread steadily, fed from a small, neat hole in the side of the man's skull.

"That's just to show you I'm serious, Miss. Taylor. No funny business. If I even see you behind me, I'll do the same to Scott."

"All right," Taylor said, her voice faltering. She did not have much experience with deadly force. Only two other times had she confronted a loaded gun, and that at a much greater distance. Those times she had managed to keep her decisions reasonably impersonal, to assess the situation as she had been trained to do. But this time, she was not succeeding. Surgeons were not supposed to operate on their own family, and she knew why. Her mind had thrown out the guidelines, the statistics on most-favorable outcomes. She could concentrate only on keeping Scott safe at that instant, and every instant, no matter how that might affect his fate later.

Slowly, Babcock pulled Carter to the other end of the hall, keeping him as a shield, and then pushed the button for the service elevator. Stunned by the sight of the dead man, Carter could not tell how long it took for the elevator to arrive, but it seemed like a very long time. The door opened and Babcock pulled Carter in, slamming him against the side of the compartment. When the door closed, Carter thought that this would be the end of him. Babcock had made his getaway and would no longer need protection. But that was just the faulty logic of fear, Carter realized. Babcock would want a hostage until he had accomplished his mission.

In the basement parking garage, the elevator opened to a short, Mexican cleaning lady. She held a mop in a wheeled bucket and stared in surprise at the sight in front of her. Babcock shifted his gun for a moment, pulled the trigger, and dropped the woman before she had a chance to gasp. He then pushed the gun back into Carter's neck. Jesus Christ! Carter thought, sucking deep breaths.

The parking garage looked deserted. Babcock slipped the gun into his jacket pocket and kept it aimed at Carter's back, then pushed Carter toward his black Mercedes. He swung the back door open, lowered Carter's head, and shoved him onto the floor, then unfolded a blanket and threw it across Carter's body. Carter lifted his head briefly and caught the edge of the blanket on his nose and then settled back, realizing he had managed to keep his eyes from under the cover. He was now lying on his side facing the front, his bent knees rammed between the seats, his side aching where he had hit the drive shaft.

Babcock jumped behind the wheel and pulled another pair of handcuffs from the glove compartment. He slipped one ring around the passenger seat-belt base and the other around Carter's belt. To make it reach, he pulled Carter's stomach flush to the gap between the two front seats. Carter could smell the leather of the seat back pressed tight against his face as Babcock clicked the seat-belt closed.

"That should keep you," Babcock said, putting the gun to Carter's belly. "Now let's see if your broad follows instructions better than you do. If I happen to notice her, or anybody else, I can just pop you right in the stomach. That way you'll have a little time to think and a little more time for pain before you die."

Babcock squealed his tires as he pulled out of the parking space, and squealed them again around two sharp corners, then hit the brakes at the garage exit. Carter could hear the automatic garage door grinding and could feel the gun barrel hard in his stomach. Babcock seemed nervously animated on having an audience for his thoughts.

"Well, this'll be the first test," Babcock said. "They've got me as a sitting duck right here. Your broad could be waiting right out front, ready to shoot me down if I don't duck fast enough. But even if they hit me, I'll still have enough strength to pull this trigger, as long as they don't hit me right in the head. I'm no doctor, so I'm not sure how that would work. Of course, your Miss. Taylor also doesn't know where you'll be sitting and whether she's got a good, clean shot at me. Somehow I have the feeling your little chickadee won't want to risk that." Babcock laughed. "Why do I have that feeling?"

The grind of the garage door stopped. Babcock accelerated up the steep incline of the exit, ducking his head. Carter's weight shifted backwards and the cuffs pulled tight at Carter's belt. His breath quickened as the car leveled out, but he did not hear a shot. The car bounced at the side of the road as Babcock careened left, and then left again.

"Nice and easy," Babcock said, letting off the accelerator. "No need to get a ticket when I've got more important things to do." He checked in the rearview mirror and to both sides and did not see anything suspicious. "So far it looks like we could be free and clear. Everyone seems to be behaving."

Carter strained his neck to see upward out the back window, but all he could see was Babcock's high rise condominium receding behind him, then the lights of the next Rosslyn building coming into view. Carter suddenly locked on the thought that his life might depend on tracking the car's movements, and he shifted more to his back and moved his neck toward the window and began counting the blocks from the gaps in the buildings. He had gotten to two blocks when Babcock turned left. He had counted to one when Babcock turned right. Carter realized that at this rate he had no chance of remembering an exact location—Babcock must be driving a maze to lose a possible tail. Carter stopped counting and just started mouthing the directions—west, south, then west again—and he could only hope Rosslyn kept to a ninety degree grid or his attempt at anything useful would be shot to hell.

Babcock kept up the zigzag, then gunned it through an intersection and made a sharp, squealing turn to the north. When he then turned sharply east, Babcock suddenly let out a scream and pulled into what Carter thought must be the parking lot to a low-rise apartment house. Babcock slammed on the breaks and continued to scream, then moved his car behind a utility van off in the corner. He was hissing and spitting and clutching his stomach, and he jammed the gear shift into park and reached into his pocket for a box of pills. His torso doubled over as he dumped two pills into his palm, then tipped up to chew them down.

Carter could not see what was happening. He wondered if a sniper had shot Babcock, but he had not heard a blast, and from what he could tell, the windows were still intact.

Babcock's screams had shifted to curses and groans. "Goddamn this shit. Damn!" He was still clutching his gut, hyperventilating. "Oh, Mr. Carter, you are witnessing the Armageddon. My body is about to blow itself up, but not on schedule." He sucked in some air. "I'll get through this one. This one I'll beat. But the next one may kill me. That's OK. Just one more destination." He grabbed his stomach and groaned. "Just one more."

He lifted his torso and looked around grimacing. The van hid his car from the road, and he saw nothing in his rearview mirror. "I wonder if that bitch of yours was following me. I don't really know, but it looks like we lost her."

Babcock jammed the gun barrel back into Carter's stomach, glancing off Carter's rib. Carter let out a grunt at the pain but did not shout. He did not want to give Babcock that pleasure. The gun barrel kept punching him in the stomach while Babcock railed. "That's what I'd like to do," he growled, gaining some more composure as the pain dropped below the threshold of agony. "I'd love to just blast a hole in your gut. Rip those insides with a bore-hole tunnel. You deserve some of this! Not me! You should share it a little! But I think I still need a hostage just to be sure."

Babcock looked into the rearview mirror with the anger of a cornered bull scraping to get his revenge, but the silence kept beating him back. No one had pulled in behind him. He had no one to charge, and then, slowly, the ongoing silence shifted his rage to some satisfaction that he was still free. With a little luck, he could still give them the slip for good.

Babcock opened the door to his car and ducked as he got out, inching his way to the front of the van to look out. A quick glance showed the side street was empty—just a stray pedestrian who apparently lived there.

Hearing steps, Carter lowered his head back under the blanket. For a moment he hoped a policeman would look in, but as soon as the door slammed shut, the gun barrel was back in his stomach. Babcock groaned in pleasure. "We're on our way my boy. You're going to the promised land!"

The sight of Scott with a gun to his head had hit Taylor hard. In her thoughts she saw Scott merged with the man who had stepped from the elevator to catch a quick bullet. She saw Scott down on the floor bleeding from his head.

When the service elevator had closed over Babcock, Taylor had punched at her own elevator and frantically cursed it to move faster. When she finally reached the ground floor, she had run to the security desk.

"How many exits out of your parking garage?!"

"Just one on the south side."

Taylor ran out the main door and down the block to Sanchez. He stepped out onto the sidewalk when he saw her coming.

"Give me your keys!" she said, tossing him her own. "You can have my car if you need it. It's parked around the corner, a red Eclipse. Edward Babcock is Jackhammer and he probably knows what I drive. He's got Scott Carter hostage. He's going to shoot him if he even thinks I'm following, or if he thinks anybody else is on his tail."

"I warned Mr. Carter, but he insisted!"

"Listen!" Taylor said. "As soon as Babcock comes out, I need you to go in and see what kind of trail he's left. He's already killed a man."

Taylor turned and saw the garage door begin to open. "This could be him!" Taylor ducked into the car, lying flat on the front seat. "Get away from the car and tell me what you see."

"The garage door's almost open. It's a black Mercedes. Now it's coming out pretty fast. The driver's down low. Now he's up. An older guy in the front. Nobody else. He's coming up Fairfax Drive and turning left onto North Lynn."

"Is it Babcock?"

"I don't know Babcock."

"Shit!" Taylor said, inching her eyes up over the edge of the door. She immediately saw it was him and ducked down. "OK, go inside and see if he left Scott behind. I assume he's got Scott in the car. If not, he's thrown away his only protection. Can I get up now?"

"You better hurry or you're going to lose him."

"I can't get too close or he'll kill the hostage." She had intentionally not used Scott's name, but that game did not seem to help.

Sanchez ran into Babcock's high-rise, and Taylor started the car, a white, unmarked Chevy Impala, which she did not think would be conspicuous. Slowly, she pulled onto the street and strained to keep her car out of sight but still close enough to follow Babcock's movements. When she realized how difficult that would be, she began to second-guess herself. She should have been standing by the garage door waiting for Babcock to drive out. Yes, it would have been risky. She might have lost Scott right there, but she might have had a clean shot at Babcock's head. She could have stood on the driver's side and had that split second to assess the situation and drill him. But she had not even considered it. She had been intimidated by Babcock's threat against Scott. Maybe she was not the person to be handling this case right now. But what did that matter? She was the only one on Babcock's tail, and there were no substitutes ready to take her place. She also knew she would not have allowed a replacement. She still wanted sole control over the risks Scott had to face.

Taylor put her phone on speaker and called FBI headquarters. "This is Special Agent Michelle Taylor. I'm trailing Edward Babcock, a.k.a. Jackhammer. He's in a large black Mercedes sedan, I think an S series, with Virginia plates—can't see the number—just the driver visible, a man in his sixties, no beard, silver hair. Have Frank Gentry and his team been mobilized? I called that in earlier."

"They're almost set. They'll just need your instructions on where to go."

Taylor saw Babcock turn left, and she sped up not to miss the hole in the traffic. "I don't know where he'll end up, but they can't get close to him. Do you understand? Scott Carter's a hostage, and Babcock has threatened to kill him if he so much as sees one of us, so I'm staying way back myself. Babcock's armed and dangerous. He's already killed a man. Frank's team or the police can't do anything except stay in the general area that I designate and be available to move in when I give the word. Do you understand that?"

"Understood."

Babcock had turned again and was now out of sight. Taylor pushed on the gas but not enough to lean her car around the corner. Babcock would wise up in a minute if he saw that.

The drive then became a maze of turns, a stop and go of Taylor keeping her distance and then gunning it to the next corner, until finally, when she veered through a sudden red light, Babcock was gone.

Taylor was not willing to accept it. The guy must be going in circles, she thought. She frantically looked into all the driveways to see if Babcock had slipped into one of those. Seeing nothing, she came to a two-way cross street. She did not see the Mercedes in either direction. She made an immediate random choice but then saw nothing ahead and nothing in the driveways and curbside parking spaces. She strained to get to the next corner to see if Babcock might still be in sight, but he wasn't. The sick, aching feeling that she had lost everything plowed through her. She started racing, hoping to outpace her despair, but it did no good. Each corner turned up another blank of anonymous cars.

Sanchez ran to the condominium security desk, flashed his FBI badge, got the man's phone number in case he had questions, and headed to the bottom of the building's parking garage. He found nothing on the bottom floor, checking between and behind every car for Carter but doing it fast, knowing Babcock would not have had time to make a complicated dump of a body. As he trotted up the ramp to the next floor, he saw the cleaning lady by the elevator prone in the twisted heap of the dead. He immediately called that in to headquarters and realized Babcock might have gotten out at this floor. He called the front desk to see whether Babcock had a reserved parking space. Babcock did.

Sanchez started scanning the numbers painted on the blacktop and realized he was in the right place. When he reached Babcock's space, it was empty, but no Scott Carter. Sanchez took more time to search the whole level, looking behind all the cars, but he turned up nothing. He realized Babcock could have stopped at any floor and dumped Carter's body, so he ran up the next ramp and made a full round, and then the next, and then up the elevator, stopping at every residential floor. When he came to Babcock's level, the door opened to the dead man, the pool of blood dark but still not dry. Sanchez swallowed and pulled out his phone.

Taylor came to a stop at the northeast corner of Rosslyn, where she could watch the bridge exists to Georgetown and downtown DC, realizing Babcock could be heading west away from her. She parked at the side of the road with the dead weight of having lost the hostage, someone who seemed closer to her than she could imagine. She knew her chances were slim of still catching Babcock and maybe saving Scott, and the odds only got worse with every scenario she passed through her head.

Taylor had already called in her status and asked for backup, hoping that some police cruiser might spot the Mercedes approaching some location where they might get a shot. And that was the problem. They could not turn on their sirens and chase Babcock down. If they did that, Scott would be dead. She had no doubt. And even an unmarked car could easily give itself away if Babcock kept up his weave and then saw the same headlights always coming in from behind.

She could not figure out what she was feeling. She had clenched into standard law enforcement procedures and done what she thought was right, but now as she sat—the lights of the cars one stab after another—she carried the brutal ache in her chest at the thought of losing Scott. It threatened to turn her focus into desperation, to the point that she felt she was choking, then forcing herself back into a copy of self-control. Since no one was looking, she let the wetness rise into her eyes, wiping it away every so often to keep her sight to the passing cars clear.

Taylor had just pulled a tissue from her pocket when her hand stopped short. She saw the black Mercedes enter the intersection from the west and accelerate toward the Roosevelt Bridge. Her heart skipped as she checked her rear view mirror for traffic and then pushed on the gas, unable to believe her luck. The street led to I-66, which brought Northern Virginia traffic across the river to the mall of Washington, D.C. As soon as she pulled into the freeway, she caught sight of the Mercedes and could blend in with the other cars breaking the speed limit.

She was ready to call headquarters when her phone rang. She did not recognize the number. "Hello?"

"This is Richard Sanchez."

"What have you got?"

"No sign of Scott. I searched everywhere in the parking garage but didn't find him. I know Babcock was there. He left a dead cleaning lady by the elevator door, shot in the chest, and the other guy you already know about."

"OK, thanks. You finish up there. I'm actually tailing the guy."

"Really? That's good. Be careful."

"I'll try."

The windows had turned black with nothing but night sky, and Carter realized they must have left Rosslyn. He had tracked their directions until the end, holding on to his thoughts even when they had stopped in the parking lot, and from what he could guess, they were now heading east. With no buildings around, that either meant heading past the Iwo Jima Memorial or entering the tail end of I-66. Carter still tried to sense a change of direction, but he knew that any gradual turns would be impossible to add up. If they were actually crossing the river, he would soon get the right-angled grid of DC.

"Comfortable back there?" Babcock asked. "Do you even realize where you're going? It's damn stupid for me to tell you, but you know, I have a good feeling I'll be able to do everything as planned. The way things have shaped up, this could be my last day on this degenerate earth. I was never going to screw around with the law if they ever started breathing down my neck. Too disgusting with those Miranda rights; too sick how they handle criminals with kid gloves. No, if it ever comes to that, I'll just finish my business, go out to my cabin in the mountains and bump myself off. Now I'll have the pleasure of bumping you off as well with a last glass of whiskey. Are you going to join me in that?"

"You didn't tell me what your plans are in town," Carter said, in constant pain from the strain of his position. "Shouldn't I know that if we're going to be suicide partners?"

"I didn't tell you, did I?" Babcock chuckled. "Well shit, I'm sitting here telling myself that that would be a dumb thing to do, but then again, what would it matter? If you get out of this fix, that means they've knocked me off—and dead, why should I care? I'm no romantic. In my casket, I won't have any more pleasure. So let's focus on now. How about it? The idea of you participating in my final act looks so damn delicious. While everybody's waiting to be maimed or die, they can have you spouting a silly prayer for them. You can be their representative in fear, feeling the poison approach while they don't know what's going to hit them, like blind babes. How does it feel to be their representative in suffering?"

"So you've planted another device on a water main?"

Babcock guffawed with relish. "In fact, I have. That's the beauty of it. You found that other one in Rosslyn and like kiddies got all excited, like you'd stopped me, but you'd just downed one of my fighter planes. There's another one right on your tail with the radar locked on."

"Where?" Carter asked.

"You've got a one-track mind, Scott. Don't be so goddamn square. I'm not ready to tell you that."

Carter saw only the blackness out the window and imagined the Kennedy Center and Georgetown to the north in the distance. He then gained new bearings when the car sloped down to a stop and Carter saw the tops of trees from what must have been the start of Constitution Avenue.

"Still no sign of your woman," Babcock said with satisfaction. "That's good. That's real good. Your little lady seems concerned about your safety. How sweet."

Carter tried to block out Babcock's quips. He knew anger would only cloud his judgment. A part of Carter wanted to face his death head on, in peace. For months now he had tried to prepare himself for the ultimate threat of his cancer, or a Jackhammer sniper. He wanted to muster a little courage and dignity and, when the time came, go out feeling in control. But now the situation would not cooperate. With his face pressed to the front seat, his arms wrenched behind his back, his knees twisted, Carter found it difficult to clear his mind of the physical constraints. When he was not craning his neck to see out the window and plot the car's course, his senses were filled by the smell of the dusty carpet and the expensive leather, the bumps from the suspension, the hum of the motor, and the ache of his hip and ribs. His mind rarely moved beyond that imposing material presence, as though his brain cast off all higher needs as a price for survival. What Carter feared most was being shot in this position, naked of preparation, overcome by pointless sensations, unable to say good-bye to anyone. Even that last drink of whiskey in Babcock's cabin now looked like a deliverance.

As Taylor laid down her phone, she focused on Babcock in the distance and agonized over which way to play it. Maybe she should risk getting closer. In the dark, Babcock would probably not see her face. She could then pull up next to him and shoot him point blank. But what if he saw her first? He could pull the trigger on Scott. Or if she nailed him, the car could flip out of control into the river. If only she could call in some snipers for when Babcock slowed down. But where would she place them? She had no idea where Babcock was headed. And what if Babcock had somehow booby trapped Scott? But Babcock would have said something about that, right? For that to be a deterrent, wouldn't the pursuers have to know? Unless the man doesn't care and just wants to kill, no matter what. Stop it, Taylor told herself. You're letting fear get the best of you. Keep your cool, damn it. You'd better.

Babcock turned left onto 18th Street, and Taylor slowed down to keep her distance. Traffic was light on that Sunday evening, and Taylor again worried about Babcock spotting her. She could only see the shape of Babcock's head, so maybe Babcock could see no more of her. It did not look like Babcock was trying to lose her. He drove steadily, as though not wanting to attract attention.

Frank Gentry suddenly called. "Michelle, where have you got him?"

"I'm heading up 18th from Constitution. Now that he's in the city, can we set up some kind of net that would pick him up wherever he goes? It'll have to be unmarked cars. We can't spook him. I can't see Scott, but he's got to be in the car."

"I'll work on it. How close can we get?"

"I don't want anyone close!" Taylor blurted, immediately regretting her emotion. "Babcock's already killed two people in cold blood at his condo. He'll kill the hostage at the drop of a hat."

"Then what do you recommend?" Gentry asked, not hiding his irritation at Taylor's tone.

"Get some snipers on call and wait for my instructions. I'm the only one with a bead on Jackhammer right now. So for the moment you have to depend on me."

"Don't get cute with me, Michelle. I know you've got an emotional stake in this thing. You let me make the decisions, do you understand?"

"I understand," said Taylor. To herself she said: They had better be the right ones.

Babcock turned east on K Street, still moving steadily, like an old traveling salesman making his worn-out rounds. At 16th, Babcock turned into the curbside service lane. It was blocked from the rest of the street by a narrow concrete median. He drove two blocks on the side lane, then, at the next intersection, pulled back into the through-lanes, drove four more blocks, and then made a calm U-turn and began heading west.

"Shit!" Taylor thought. Babcock was now heading straight toward her. He was approaching fast, his shape through the windshield growing steadily larger. She realized that ducking would only attract his attention. Terrified, she faced straight ahead, gripping the steering wheel.

Babcock was now clearly in view, nearly next to her. He would see her, she thought desperately. He would shoot Scott.

Taylor let her eyes slip sideways to watch Babcock pass. He had only one hand on the wheel. He was talking with someone. He was not looking her way! Taylor pushed on the gas just a little—and then she was past him, her heart ready to burst. OK, she told herself, no U-turns or you could blow everything. Taylor turned left at the next corner and then made a U-turn where Babcock could not see her. Now don't turn off K Street, Taylor pleaded to Babcock.

Taylor pulled back onto K. She had seen Babcock talking. He had held the wheel with only one hand. Did it mean he had a gun pointed at Scott? Taylor looked into the distance and saw Babcock two blocks ahead. He was moving faster than before and Taylor stepped on the gas. What's he doing? Taylor wondered. He can't know I'm behind him or he would have looked my way. But if he didn't think he was being followed, why would he make a U-turn? Has he finished what he needed to do? Maybe he's completed his mission. Maybe it's all over and he's heading to some hide-out. Does that mean he doesn't need Scott anymore?

Taylor called Gentry. "Babcock has changed direction. He's now heading west on K street at 20th. He doesn't seem to have picked up my scent—when he turned, he drove right past me—but now I'm sure he's got Scott. He was talking to someone. I don't know what he did, but he may have activated some kind of bomb or another water main device, because he pulled into the service lane in the sixteen hundred block on the south side, for no real reason, and then, four blocks later, turned all the way around. Send somebody in to check it out."

"OK," Gentry said. "We're going to stake out the routes west across the Key Bridge and up Canal Road. I can also get men in place for all the bridges. We've got the main routes east staked out. I hope to hell he doesn't turn back that way. It'll just make things more complicated."

"What do you plan to do?" Taylor asked.

"I need to get some more visual reports. What's your assessment of where Scott is?"

"I didn't see anything, so I'd say he's on the floor in the back."

"It gives us a clear shot at Babcock, if we want to take it. Unfortunately, there might be bystanders."

"Such as Scott," Taylor said. "Babcock probably has a gun on him. Anything less than a perfect shot and we could lose our hostage. We can't risk that. That's not me talking, that's just by the book."

"I'm not ready to shoot," Gentry said. "Hell, my snipers aren't even in place. But we've also got to realize that if Babcock gets Scott out of town, we've got less of a chance to blend in and surprise him. The odds for Scott go way down. We've got to weigh that."

"I know," Taylor said. "I know."

When Babcock made his U-turn, he began to laugh with the sonorous chortle of an executioner. "It's all over, my friend!" he said. "I've done it. Right under the city's nose! Oh, now you have to be my witness. You've got to know what's coming—not just your own death but the reign of terror descending on this degenerate capital. Lord, this was my biggest feat yet. The revelation of the angel of Armageddon." He snorted in happy contempt. "Three months ago, on a Sunday night, right here in this city, we did a dig on a water main. Right here, and not one city official or cop even guessed what was going on. And now they get their payback. Right now I've got a huge dose of delectable stuff going into the water system. And on this drive I turned it on—with a garage-door opener from Home Depot! I just added a few enhancements so the thing gives a return signal to confirm I've made a connection. Great, simple, resourceful engineering, and right now, under our feet, slowly pluming out with each flush of a toilet, with each faucet flow, is a bumper load of my calling card. When people start coming to work tomorrow morning, the real show will begin. Sodom and Gomorra getting their due! The vengeance of the righteous over the sinners! And everything's just blind fate! Can you imagine the drama of that? Whoever happens to be thirsty, whoever happens to mix that cup of coffee at the office or in their condo, will die. The statistical diffusion of that chemical in the water, the random interaction of molecules, the chance actions of animal beings, will all add up in a statistical interplay that is incalculable, and yet will nevertheless happen! The chemical will enter some people; some people it won't. Some live; some die. And I was the one who set it all into motion, the watchmaker God who has wound up the city and now sits back to await its destruction."

Carter did not say anything. He feared Babcock's heightened exuberance. He did not think he could count on Babcock acting with any leftover reason. The things Babcock was admitting made no sense if he was hell-bent on success. The man apparently craved an immediate audience and flourish, and Carter realized that could mean anything from a grandstanding suicide to the pleasure of a theatrical execution of Carter himself.

Carter thought he knew where he was. When they had first entered the long slope heading north from the Mall, Carter had counted the level beds of the intersections and then sensed a downward slope and had judged he was somewhere around M. For the count east, he had not been so sure, but if somebody searched for Babcock's dig, they should be able to find it, if Carter could only tell them.

Carter did not feel good about his chances, and he only hoped that Michelle or someone could find the water main without him. A part of him withdrew from Babcock's ravings and settled into the shocks of the road on his body—an unnatural, random heartbeat that mirrored how his life had finally and fully slipped from his control. The only constant above the physical pain of his position—soon overtaking everything—was the image of Michelle. She was all he could picture, and almost against his will he thought of a new life with her and a new job, just starting over. He didn't know why he had stayed at BWE so long, shunting himself into sales for a boss with the rough edges of Waynewright. Any shift to work under Blackstone would just become too complicated, basically slapping Waynewright in the face, and it would not get him back into design. He would have to find a new firm and marry Michelle and make everything new, but as the car hit a pothole, he snapped out of his thoughts and knew he was just spinning fantasies before he got plugged.

"Now nothing matters!" Babcock roared in delight. "They can put up a roadblock and shoot their guns. Hell, I'll just barrel right through them and take my chances. What do I care! I've done it! All my plans designed, built, and completed. All of them! What a track record! Hell, this is what life's all about, isn't it Scott, my boy?! Isn't it?!" He thrust the gun barrel harder into Carter's stomach. "What, are you asleep back there?! When was the last time you knew you'd changed the world, that you'd completed everything you'd put your sweat to, that you'd outsmarted everyone?! The same ones who said you had no right to do any more engineering! Damnation, what a feeling to die with!"

Taylor saw Babcock stop at a red light. She slowed down to keep her distance, worried that Babcock might notice her change in speed. The signal stayed red for a long time, and Taylor had to slow down even more.

Suddenly, before the light had turned green, Babcock shot forward, veering to the next street.

"I think Babcock's spotted me!" Taylor shouted into Gentry's open line. "He's heading west on Pennsylvania toward Georgetown. He'll hit M Street any second. Have you got snipers in place on the other side?"

"We're working on it," Gentry said. "Just a few more minutes. Won't he get tied up in traffic? That'll buy us some time."

"There's the usual. Maybe he thinks the crowds will protect him."

Taylor saw the Four Seasons Hotel on her left and felt the life go out of her. Scott could already be dead, and if he wasn't, more delay just brought that closer. The snipers would somehow have to deal with the traffic and the passersby. Things might look suspicious. Babcock might notice. And realizing that, something snapped inside of her.

"I'm looping around to cut him off," Taylor said. "Have someone watch in case Babcock turns north into Wisconsin. I'm assuming he keeps going west. And don't anyone come this side of the Key Bridge to distract him. Do you understand?! I don't want anyone spooking him!"

"What're you up to?!" Gentry shouted. "Don't play the Lone Ranger!"

"I've got to drive."

Taylor turned right, slowly, just in case Babcock was watching. Maybe that will put him at ease, she thought. Then she floored it, heading uphill, her heartbeat racing like the RPMs of the motor.

Taylor debated frantically where to turn west, trying to remember which street would take her clear across Georgetown and not dead end at Wisconsin. She picked one and squealed her tires. Someone honked, and Taylor pushed hard on the gas, holding back just enough not to hit anyone.

The narrow two-way street passed between fashionable old townhomes and parked cars on both sides of the street. They left barely enough room for two cars to pass. Taylor saw no oncoming traffic and pushed her car to forty miles per hour. She knew it was crazy, but she had to beat Babcock to the Key Bridge stoplight.

At the first four-way stop, Taylor slowed down and laid on the horn, then barreled through, bouncing in a pot hole that she had seen too late. "Damn!" she cursed, stepping on the gas again, hoping she had not busted a tire.

Half a block later a car began to pull from of a curbside parking space. Taylor braked and swung left, but too much and glanced off a parked car. She felt the jolt and the sickening scrape of metal. "Damn!" she shouted again, but managed to steady her course and keep going. The car behind honked in outrage. Taylor now knew there was no turning back.

One block before Wisconsin, Taylor had to slow down, honking her horn to warn the pedestrians. At the intersection, she pulled to the left to pass three cars that were stacked up at the red light, forcing the oncoming cars to the side. A taxi pulled into the intersection just as Taylor was coming through. He hit the breaks, and Taylor cut the wheel to avoid him, then straightened herself and floored it as soon as everyone had scattered. My God, what are you doing, she thought to herself. But she was not capable of letting up.

After three more blocks she had gone far enough, but she saw no place to park. She swerved left and barreled onto the sidewalk, screeching to a stop, and jumped out of her car. She ran down the steep hill toward M Street.

He's going to recognize me, Taylor thought desperately. How am I going to do this? She reached to the back of her head, pulled the pin from her French braid, and shook the hair free to her shoulders. Then she saw a young couple on the opposite side of the street. The woman was wearing a blue Georgetown windbreaker. Taylor dashed across the street and pulled out her FBI badge. "Gimme the jacket," Taylor shouted. "It's an emergency!" The couple, too startled to read the badge in the dark, stepped back against the wall of the building. "Give me the jacket!" Taylor screamed, exposing the gun in her holster and reaching for it dramatically. The woman lifted her hands and then took off the jacket. Taylor ripped the windbreaker away.

"You'll get it back!" Taylor shouted as she continued down the hill, holstering her gun and pulling her arms into the sleeves.

At M Street, Taylor raised the hood over her head and peeked around the corner, her heart beating so hard she found it difficult to think more than five minutes ahead. She did not see Babcock's Mercedes. She despaired that he had already passed, or had turned off to elude her, but she stayed her ground. After twenty seconds, she suddenly saw Babcock's car in the left-hand west-bound lane, his speed held in check by the traffic.

In the end, he must think he's not being followed, Taylor thought hopefully. She looked at the traffic light, and her plans began to race in a clockwork of anxiousness. The light was still green. Babcock would probably make it through, even if it turned yellow in the next moment. Taylor checked the oncoming traffic. It was steady but still left gaps that might allow her to miss a shot and not hit a bystander. She did not see any pedestrians crossing the street. But she couldn't miss, she told herself. Missing meant killing Scott, if he wasn't dead already.

From behind the corner, Taylor watched Babcock's Mercedes approach. She adjusted her hood, pulled her gun from her holster, and stepped onto the M Street sidewalk, her gun resting out of sight on her thigh, the jacket covering her blouse and hair. She then entered the street and turned west, pretending like she was headed for the driver's side of a parked car near the intersection. She took out her keys and pretended to press the remote. She scratched her cheek to clear the hood from her peripheral vision and in that split second, she saw the Mercedes pull up next to her. When it was even, she swung sideways, planted both feet, and fired through the passenger window.

She did not know whether Babcock had seen her. The glass shattered, and she thought she had hit him, but she did not wait to find out. She kept his body in her sights and fired a second time, then a third. Babcock slumped against the driver's side door from the force of the shots, but his car continued to move forward like a lumbering, wounded animal, slamming into the next car stopped by the backup. Pedestrians screamed and dove for cover. Taylor circled the car, her gun trained on Babcock's head, inching to the front. She could now see the blanket and a body on the floor of the back seat motionless. Terrified, Taylor pulled open the front door and planted her feet, prepared to fill Babcock with lead, but she realized there was no more need. Babcock's body slumped sideways onto the pavement, his head and chest bloody, his trigger finger caught in his gun. That turned Taylor cold. She grabbed the weapon but could not tell whether it had been used.

Please help me God, she thought to herself and leapt to the back door, ripping it open and pulling off the blanket. "Scott!" she shouted.

"Michelle," Carter groaned, convinced one of the gun shots must have been Babcock's, but he could not feel where it had hit him. All he could feel was his heart pounding as he strained his neck to see Michelle leaning over him.

"Are you all right?" Michelle cried.

"I don't know. I think so," Carter said, the shock slowly giving way to relief and then to joy. "Man oh man, am I glad to see you! How about undoing these handcuffs."

Taylor just wanted to touch him to confirm that he was fine, but she got out of the car and slipped to Babcock's body. She did not even see the crowd that had gathered to watch her nor hear the sirens in the distance. She leaned over, keeping her fingers clear of the blood, and searched Babcock's pockets. In the side jacket pocket she found a key chain, grabbed it, and came around to sit in the back seat above Carter. She fumbled through a few keys before she found one that fit, then unlocked the handcuffs from Carter's belt, then from his wrists. Finally, she put her hand under his arm and helped pull him onto the seat next to her. When he was sitting, she wrapped her arms around his neck and hugged him tightly. "I thought I'd lost you," she said.

Carter pulled back, held her face in his hands, and kissed her, hardly able to believe what he was doing. He then forced himself to regroup. "Babcock set off another device on a water main," he said. "He told me that while we were driving, after we turned around. It's apparently the same chemical we found unused in Rosslyn. It's spreading right now." He gave her his best guess of a location.

"I'll bet it's near 14th and K," Taylor said. She was all business again. "I was following when he made a U-turn. Have you got a number to call?" Suddenly she was jumping out of the back seat. "Have you got a phone?"

"Yes," Carter said. "I've got McCracken's number. He must know his DC colleagues."

"OK, do it. I left my phone in my car. I'll be right back."

Taylor began running uphill to Sanchez's dented Impala and soon heard a shout from the stunned young woman who had lost her jacket. Without breaking stride, Taylor took off the windbreaker and tossed it in her direction. "Thanks!" she called.

Carter stepped out onto the street, the crowd staring at him, and pulled out his wallet, searching for the contact slip from the county emergency meeting. The sight of Babcock's bloody body and the thought of the poison undermined his relief. Carter found the number and laid the slip down on the roof of the car, his hands shaking, and dialed.

OK, McCracken, I hope you're working late!

McCracken picked up after the first ring. Carter shot out the details about the possible water main breech. "Do you know who to contact in DC?" Carter asked. "Tell them to turn off the pumps for the whole city if that's what it takes. There's no time to dig the thing up. And get a hold of the TV and radio stations and tell them to warn everybody not to even touch the water. The stuff can get into your body by contact."

"Right," McCracken said, "but what about Jackhammer?"

"We got him," Carter said. "The bastard's dead."

Before McCracken had hung up, he had already pulled up his address book and scrolled for the DC Water and Sewer Authority. He had toured their treatment plant just a year ago and knew some of the operators, and recently he had spoken to the leadership on security issues after the Jackhammer scare. The District did not have huge changes in elevation, but even with that, to keep water pressure constant across altitudes, the District was divided into seven separate service zones. With that, McCracken figured they had a chance to shut off just a localized part of the city, if they could find the exact location of Jackhammer's dig.

Dialing fast, McCracken had to try two numbers before he got a hold of someone. The man did not recognize McCracken's name, so McCracken practically shouted at him that they had to shut down the service area around 14th and K, and maybe a much larger perimeter.

"I can't shut down the city's water because I get an anonymous phone call," the man said, flustered but scared.

"Anonymous?! Google me if you don't believe who I am!" McCracken blurted, ready to burst, but then immediately realizing that the man was not off base. "All right," McCracken said, taking a breath. "Give me the number of Shirley Bradford." She was the head of the DC water authority. "I'll have her call you back. I want her home phone and her cell, and if you don't give me that, you can answer for the dead you'll have on your hands. And while you're waiting, use another line to call the FBI. Mention the name Frank Gentry. He heads the Jackhammer investigation. Maybe you'll get the confirmation about the Jackhammer poison before Shirley calls you."

It took the man two minutes to get the information, and McCracken waited as though sitting on hot coals. McCracken barked a thanks and then got Bradford on her cell—apparently she was at home eating a late dinner. She recognized McCracken and said she would get right on it, but McCracken knew that behind her no-nonsense front she was squirming just like he was. "Are your folks going to call the TV and radio stations to get out the warnings?" he asked, ready to do that himself if that's what it took. She told him she'd take care of that personally and get the mayor's office involved. She hung up.

McCracken leaned back in his office chair, feeling the same outrage as he had felt when Jackhammer had violated his own water system, but now at least with the satisfaction that Jackhammer had been taken out. He wondered how difficult it would be for DC to keep this poison in check. If they couldn't be certain of the breach location, then there were more than a thousand miles of pipe to deal with. If they were shooting in the dark, they would have to shut down the whole city. Jesus, he thought, had that ever been done before? And even if just one service area did it, there were still slopes and elevation changes to the pipes, so even when you closed off the main valves, just the weight of the water could push something into the lower floor of a building. And ultimately how the hell were they going to blow off the water from the breached section of pipe if contact with the skin could already maim you? They couldn't just flush it down into the storm sewer. They'd have to rig some kind of flexible piping to bleed it off into tanker trucks. Jesus, McCracken thought, they'd have their work cut out for them.

Carter pocketed his phone and rubbed his hand across his eyes, closing them hard. When he opened them again, he saw Gentry and some plainclothes FBI agents running towards him, some DC police closing in from the other side.

"Are you all right?" Gentry asked, motioning for his men to secure the area.

"As good as it gets under the circumstances," Carter said.

"Where's Michelle?"

"She left her phone in the car. She went up the hill to call in Jackhammer's attack." Carter filled him in about the water main.

"You're not hit?" Gentry asked, turning to an aide and telling him to call in the breach as well.

"No. Michelle took the guy out." Carter looked over at Babcock. Each time the crime scene photographer set off a flash, the skin of the body turned skeletal-white. Babcock looked remarkably peaceful amid all the commotion. You don't deserve it, Carter thought. You should have suffered.

Carter turned back to Gentry. "Hell, Michelle ought to get a medal. She saved my life."

Gentry scanned the scene, police cars now flashing their lights on all sides. "Maybe she should," he said grudgingly. He turned around to see Taylor approach. "Did you get hold of the DC waterworks?" he asked.

"Headquarters patched me through. They're going to shut off that whole part of town and narrow it down after that. I think we've got a good idea of which water main we're talking about." She was breathing hard, trying not to smile too much for Gentry.

Gentry passed his hand over his crew-cut head and then squeezed the back of his neck. "How the hell'd you find out Babcock was Jackhammer?" he asked Taylor. "Your bank lead was just circumstantial."

"Scott got a hint on his own and like some crazy idiot went over to Babcock's place. I don't even know the details. All I know is that that's where the shooting started."

"Maybe Scott deserves a medal too."

"Why, who else does?" Taylor asked, the tension slowly beginning to wash free.

Gentry eyed her. "Who authorized you to break off on your own?"

"I made a judgment call and acted on it."

"Well, it was damn risky."

"Everything was risky," Taylor said.

Gentry looked at the ground. "All right," he grunted, "nice work." He just managed to look at her with a rough smile before blasting some orders at his forensics team and stepping away to rein in the DC cops pouring into the area.

Taylor put her arm around Carter's waist and gave him a squeeze.

And then, after all the debriefings, they were walking fast, driven by something unspoken between them to move away from the commotion, arm in arm down M Street and onto the height of the Key Bridge and the dark of the river, the lights of Rosslyn in the distance. The night breeze drifted down the Potomac with the damp smell of spring, and Carter felt that inexpressible sense that he had moved back in time to a moment of great promise, like the summer nights when he was young, with a girl at his side and the wind blowing high through the trees of a Virginia campground, where everything felt possible.

The violent lights of the police cars and emergency vehicles had disappeared into another consciousness. The only thing left was the view—the reflected light of the shore restaurants and the Watergate and the Kennedy Center, all of it a mirror to Carter's own elation.

Holding Michelle at his side, her hair on his shoulder, he suddenly felt a desperateness in the hard thought of dying, postponed that night but still out there, maybe just around the corner. He spoke quietly but quickly, still staring across the water. "I have to change my life, I don't know, get a new job, but I don't think I can do it without you. I don't know if it's fair to you. I'm damaged goods, so how can I ask you to take on that kind of future? But if you don't, I can't say I really care much about anything."

Taylor straightened and turned to face Carter. She took his head in her hands and pulled it toward her and kissed him.

As she came up for air, she wiped a tear from her cheek. "Scott, I was ready to give you up. I lied to myself, but when Babcock had that gun to your head . . ." Her eyes fell.

"So what does that mean?" Carter asked, not yet sure what he was hearing.

"Just die a little later," Taylor said, tears running down her face across her smile.

"I'll try," Carter said, aware of how pointless that promise was.

Taylor still had her hands on his cheeks and her eyes on his, and when she pulled him close and kissed him again, Carter could tell she was going to give him that chance.

About The Author

Stefan Jaeger was born in 1952 in Bloomington, Indiana, and received a bachelor's degree in physics and astronomy from the University of Michigan in Ann Arbor. After graduation, he pursued an interest in writing fiction and spent numerous years living abroad, including Europe, South America, and the Middle East, teaching English as a second language and in the interim receiving a master's degree in applied linguistics from Indiana University. In 1984 he settled in the Washington, D.C., area and there began his ongoing work for engineering associations, with an initial focus in the editorial arena. His most recent position is managing director with the American Society of Civil Engineers in Reston, Virginia.

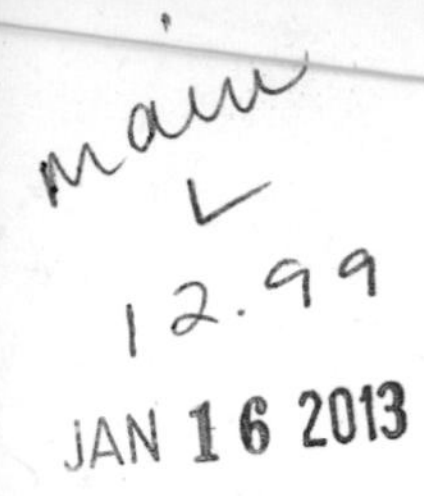

Made in the USA
Lexington, KY
28 December 2012